WHAT THE COWBOY WANTS FOR CHRISTMAS

MAISEY YATES

Santa's on His Way

Published by Kensington Publishing Corporation

Santa's on His Way

Lisa Jackson
Maisey Yates
Stacy Finz
Nicole Helm

ZEBRA BOOKS
Kensington Publishing Corp.
www.kensingtonbooks.com

CONTENTS

CHAPTER 1

There was something borderline sadistic about Christmas music playing in comforting, melodic strains when your eyes were still burning from your daylong crying jag, and your whole body was nearly numb from the ten hour cross-country trip that had included five hours on one plane, a mind-numbing wait in the small terminal in Salt Lake City, and a short, but bumpy, flight in a prop plane that felt more like a toy than an actual vehicle.

She needed the cheer to stop. She turned the car radio off and focused on the sounds of her tires moving over the snow-covered gravel road, weariness overtaking her completely.

Meg O'Neill felt like a boomerang.

She had flung herself across the country yesterday, only to be sent right back. Okay, so she was the one who had flung herself back. All the while calling herself every evil name she knew.

What kind of idiot was she? What kind of idiot was she to think that surprising Charlie in New York for Christmas was a good idea? What kind of idiot was she to take him seriously when he said it was for real this time?

Over and over again she did this. Over and over again she trusted him.

By now, she should be well aware that Charlie said things and then those things fell through. He was always ready for more, and then something happened.

In this case, the something seemed to be that he had tripped and fallen directly between some woman's thighs. That was most certainly an impediment to the much alluded to marriage proposal that Meg was beginning to realize was never going to come.

Unlike Charlie's bedmate. Who seemed to have the *coming* under control.

Do you still want to marry him?

She wiped a tear off her cheek and sniffed loudly as she pulled her car into her best friend's driveway. It was snowing fiercely outside, the weather in the mountains above Bend, Oregon, looking good for anyone with plans to ski Mount Bachelor over the holiday but looking pretty crappy for anyone who actually had to try to get around.

She tightened her hold on the steering wheel and took a deep, shaking breath. Did she still want Charlie to propose to her? Their relationship was complicated, and it had never been traditional in any sense.

But she had loved Charlie for thirteen years. Since she was a teenager. She had always seen . . . Had always seen a future with him. And he had always acted like there would be one. Once he got to a certain place. Once he had built his life up to where he wanted it to be. Security, that was what he had said.

And with any other guy, maybe Meg would have thought it was an excuse. But she knew Charlie. She knew his background, and why this kind of thing was difficult for him. It was just one of the many reasons she had accepted their strange arrangement.

But over the years it had come with its fair share of heartache. And this was the worst.

She could only hope that Noah was home. And honest to God, if she walked in and Noah was with someone, too, she was going to have a meltdown.

She sighed heavily and turned the engine off, listening to it continue to pop and hiss in the cold weather for a moment. Then she took a deep breath and got out of the car, shuffling through the dry snow on the ground, the powdery flakes sluicing over her boots.

She made sure to walk noisily up the front steps, just as a warning. Just in case. She really couldn't take surprising somebody else in a compromising situation this weekend

She lifted her hand and knocked, then stood there, bouncing up and down, freezing while she waited. Her cheeks were cold, because they were wet. Because she was still crying. Off and on. The flight from New York to the West Coast was long enough, but she'd had a layover and then she'd had to drive from the airport to Noah's place up out of Bend.

It wasn't like she had cried the whole time. Just off and on with alarming frequency, occasionally making the people next to her deeply uncomfortable.

She heard heavy footsteps and nearly sagged with relief. He was here. He was here, and he was going to make everything better, because that was what Noah Carter always did.

The door jerked open, and she was greeted by Noah, looking . . . Well, different somehow, mostly because he looked grumpy. He was sporting a fuller beard than she was used to seeing on him, but it had been a couple of weeks since she had seen him last, and his dark brows were locked together in an expression of irritation.

Something tightened, low and deep inside of her, a strange restlessness that had been intensifying around Noah lately. She didn't like it. So she did what she'd been doing for months now. She ignored it. There was no room inside of her for any more feelings right now.

It only took a moment for Noah's cranky expression to shift, his brown eyes to soften, fill with concern. "Meg? I thought you were going to be in New York for Christmas."

"Well," she said, sniffing loudly. "Surprise. To me, too."

"Are you okay?" he asked.

Her lip wobbled. "Yes."

"You're not. Come inside."

She complied, walking into Noah's small, comforting living room. She loved his old ranch house. She was so proud of him, of what he had built for himself here. This little place to call his own. She was proud of all of them, really.

She, Noah, and Charlie had been in foster care together when they were teenagers, and at that point each of them had been through so much crap it was amazing they were still standing, much less functional.

But that home—their last home—had been one that was full of support, and they had gotten the exact right kind of guidance to get a good start on adulthood. And once they had aged out of the system, they still had each other.

Charlie had gone on to make a successful career for himself in finance, Meg had her brewery in downtown Bend, and Noah had the ranch. Which, objectively, she had to admit she liked better than the insane bustle of the city. But Charlie had made it sound like he was ready to come back. Charlie had made it sound like he was finally ready to get married.

You know it's you, he had said to her, so long ago, but more than once since. *It always has been. And it always will be. The time just has to be right.*

She was really sick of waiting for the time to be right. She was starting to suspect that it never would be.

She plopped down on Noah's couch, sinking into the brown leather cushions, pulling a red pillow into her lap. "I was going to New York to surprise Charlie."

Noah suddenly looked pained, and it made her wonder what he thought about her. About this. Suddenly, she was starting to look at the situation with a strange kind of detached clarity.

She looked up. "Noah, am I pathetic?"

Noah shook his head. "No."

"I'm serious." She flung the pillow to the side, slamming it down onto the couch. "Am I pathetic? Do you think I am? Does he think I am?"

"Meg," Noah said, keeping his tone as measured as possible. "Charlie does whatever Charlie wants to do. No one has ever been able to tell him anything else. You know that. Charlie also says a lot of things."

"Apparently, he wants to do other women." She frowned. "But that's how it's always been."

Charlie had been the only one for Meg since she was fifteen years old. And while she'd never thought he'd lived like a monk, she had believed he'd had . . . well, that his feelings were all for her. Now she wondered.

"Meg," Noah said, sounding placating, and it made her want to punch him in the stomach.

"I'm not stupid," she said, shaking her head. "I started my own business. My own really *successful* business. And I'm not gullible. I've been consistently let down by the people in my life from childhood, so I kind of expect it. But I trusted him. And he told me . . ."

Noah knew almost everything about her. He was her best friend. But they had never really talked about *this*. If only because the stuff between her and Charlie always seemed to rub him the wrong way. And maybe she had never told anybody about this aspect of her relationship with Charlie because part of her had always suspected that they might give her the dose of reality she was desperate to avoid.

"He told me he was going to marry me," she said, the word sounding hollow and so ridiculous in Noah's warm living room. "And he made it really clear that . . . that he really wanted it to be soon. We've been talking a lot lately. He said he was going to come back here. In the next year. And that when he did he would be ready to settle down. And I'm so . . . I thought that meant a certain thing. And now . . . I don't even think he meant it. Or maybe he did. Maybe part of him meant it. But I don't think he's ever going to do it. If I had my way, I would have married Charlie eight years ago. Well, I probably would have married him thirteen years ago— let's be real. But fifteen-year-olds can't get married here." She tried to force a laugh. "But he's just been . . . He's been putting me on hold, and I've been letting him, haven't I?"

"That son of a bitch."

Her eyes widened. She had never seen Noah look as furious as he did now, and certainly not when referencing Charlie, who as far as Meg knew was like a brother to Noah.

"Well," she said slowly.

"Don't defend him, Meg. His Peter Pan ass doesn't want to grow up, and that's not your problem."

But she did want to defend him. In spite of everything that had happened in the past twenty-four hours, part of her still reflexively wanted to defend Charlie. And what was that? She supposed it was down to more than a decade of loving him, and less than a day of wanting to throw him through a window.

She was just more practiced at the former than the latter.

"He's had it hard," she said, knowing she sounded defensive.

"And you haven't? Why should he get to run around doing whatever he wants while you stand on vigilant watch like some heroine in a Greek tragedy?"

"That's love," she said, feeling defensive.

"No, that's bullshit."

"I'm going to go," she said, standing up, her chest feeling so achy that she thought it might cave in.

"The weather is crazy out there. You probably shouldn't try to drive back down."

"I just . . . I thought I needed to talk to you, but you're not telling me—"

"What you want to hear? Well, that should be a good thing, Meg, considering that I think Charlie has spent a long time telling you what you want to hear whether or not it's true."

Those words burned.

Meg stood up, flinging aside the throw pillow, even though it already was to the side, but she felt the need to make some kind of dramatic gesture and started toward the door.

"Meg," Noah said, his voice hard. But she ignored him, and she went back out into the blizzard.

CHAPTER 2

Noah wanted to fly to New York and kill Charlie himself. It didn't matter that the man was like a brother to him, or maybe that was why he wanted to kill him, actually. Noah expected better from him. And he damn well expected better for Meg.

Well, that was the real issue. If he was honest.

He couldn't be neutral on the subject of Megan and Charlie, no matter how hard he tried to be. It had been clear early on that Meg only had eyes for Charlie and it didn't mean anything that she had tied Noah up in knots since he was seventeen. It wasn't how the dice had fallen, and he wasn't one to beat his head against a brick wall.

More than that, Meg was too important to him to go messing it up. And so, over the years as he had watched her make herself sick over Charlie, he hadn't done a thing. Even while he had wanted her. Every time she smiled. Every time he caught that light feminine scent of hers—the peony-scented soap she used mixed with something that was just her—his whole body tightened.

But he was practiced at pretending it wasn't happening. He did not stand around waiting. Because he could never put that on her. Could never put it on their friendship. It didn't matter that he wanted Meg; he had known all this time that it could never be.

But seeing her like that . . .

Well, it made him want to either punch Charlie or kiss Meg.

But then he always wanted to kiss Meg. He had ever since he had first met her, back when he had been an angry seventeen-year-old boy and had known exactly what the feelings coursing through his body were when he looked at the sweet, beautiful girl who had been brought to live with his foster family.

She'd had it hard, her parents unable to care for her because of their addictions. But there had been some innocence left in her, and that had been apparent. Noah's had been long gone. In every sense of the word. And he had known that touching her, taking advantage of her in any way, would be an unforgivable sin.

All of those thoughts had only mattered for a few moments, anyway. Because it wasn't long after that—just a few minutes, really—that Meg had met Charlie. And it had been immediately clear that Charlie had her affection from moment one.

It wasn't really a mystery to Noah as to why. Charlie was blond, had that kind of All-American football player handsomeness that people prized so much. And along with that, he had an easy smile, a kind of relaxed demeanor. Something Noah had certainly never possessed. But then in Noah's experience if you relaxed that was when someone could get a shot in. Physically or emotionally, and by the time Noah had been sent to that last foster home he had been well past the point of letting anyone land a blow.

They had become friends, all three of them. Quickly, easily.

Meg had always loved Charlie, while Charlie mostly loved himself. And Noah burned.

When a few moments ticked by and Meg did not reappear, he realized that her stubborn ass was actually going to try to drive back down the mountain in this weather. He put a coat on, grabbed his cowboy hat off the peg by the door, and walked outside into the bitter cold. He had worked outside all day, balls deep in a snowbank, so heading back outside now was low on his list. But letting anything happen to Meg was unthinkable.

He shoved his hands in his pockets and walked toward the dirt road that led back down to the main highway, following the fresh tracks left by Meg's car.

He only had to walk around one bend before he found her, stuck.

He rolled his eyes, making his way over to the vehicle. Then he knocked on the window. She jumped, brushed a cinnamon curl away from her face, and treated him to a dark glare.

"I'm sorry, Meg, were you going to stay here all night?"

Her sherry-colored eyes flashed with annoyance. "No," she said, her voice muffled by the window.

"Dealing with wounded pride, were you?"

She growled and pushed the car door open, nearly pushing it into Noah's gut. "I feel like my pride has taken quite enough hits for one day." Her shoulders sagged. "Can I stay here tonight, Noah?"

Snowflakes were falling, landing in her curls, sprinkling across her nose, joining the freckles that were there already. His stomach tightened and he told his body to calm the hell down. Meg had to stay here tonight, because she couldn't get back down the mountain. She was his friend, and they had spent the night under the same roof countless times when they were kids.

But also, Charlie had finally wounded her to the point where she was ready to at least *show* Noah that she was upset with him. Usually she protected Charlie at all costs. Even when his behavior was beyond forgiveness.

It made Noah feel like finally, for the first time, the door was wedged open.

A door for what? You're going to offer Meg marriage? As if you'd ever lie about it like Charlie does?

Hell no. Noah's life had been too . . .

All he knew was violence. All he knew was pain. Neglect. Growing up in a drug house made you a cynic very early on. Taking care of your mother when she was passed out from yet another overdose, putting a wadded-up sweatshirt underneath her head so that she could lie more comfortably on the bathroom floor when you were only six years old, took all of the light and hope out of life pretty damn quickly.

He didn't harbor dreams about setting up his life. About having a family. He was content with his ranch. Content with his friends.

He looked back at Meg. At her fresh-faced beauty. At that beautiful body he had always wanted to touch. All right, maybe he wasn't completely satisfied. But there was nothing that a man in his position could offer a woman like her. Meg wanted that family she had never had. She and Charlie always had to some degree.

It was why Meg was so sweet and loyal to those around her. Why Charlie collected people.

Noah had held on to his two closest friends, and them alone.

Charlie wanted more. Meg wanted more.

Noah just wanted to survive.

"Of course you can stay here, Meg. But you should have listened to me, because now your car is stuck."

"You're my eternal big brother," she groused, opening up the car door again, reaching inside, and taking out a duffel bag. "At least I have supplies."

He let the big-brother shot hit him square on. That was how she saw him. Like a brother.

Dammit to hell.

"Thank heaven for small miracles, huh?" He reached out, taking the bag from her hands and hefting it over his shoulder.

Meg didn't say anything. She simply trailed behind him, following him back to the house.

"I feel so stupid," she said softly as they walked inside, and he closed the door behind them.

"Don't feel stupid, Meg. Charlie deals in charming people. And I think he has good intentions. I think he does care about you. But he's . . ."

"Broken," she said, her tone fractured. "Like the rest of us."

Pain shafted through Noah. Not at the reminder that he was broken—he knew that. But over the fact that Meg seemed to think that she was. Not in his mind. She could never be broken to him.

"I don't know, but I'm kind of tired of defending him," Noah said. "It's a reflex. I've been doing it half my life. But Charlie is his own damn man, and he can make his own decisions. So he ought to make better ones. He certainly shouldn't have kept stringing you along for the past decade if he never meant to do anything."

Meg sighed sadly, then sank onto the couch, folding her hands into her lap. Her chin-length curls fell forward as she lowered her head. "This is going to sound really stupid, Noah. Can you handle more of my stupid?"

"Sure," he said. "But for the record, I've never thought you were stupid."

"Never?" She lifted her head, narrowing her eyes.

"A lost cause where he's concerned, maybe," he said. "But never stupid."

She laughed. "Okay, I guess that's a small compensation."

"Tell me," he said, sitting on the couch next to her. He fought the urge to reach out and take her hand in his. Because there was no reason for him to touch her. No reason at all. "Tell me what happened."

"He made it sound like it was time for the two of us to make things more official. You know . . ." She cleared her throat. "You know Charlie has always told me that he loves me, right?"

Noah felt like he'd been punched in the chest. At the thought that Charlie shared such words easily with Meg when Noah himself hadn't spoken those words out loud since he was a little boy, trying to wake up his passed-out mother, tears rolling down his cheeks. He wasn't sure he would ever be able to say them again. Not even to Meg.

But apparently, Charlie was able to let it all go freely. It didn't seem fair.

"No," Noah said.

"Well, he has. And I . . . I fell in love with him the minute I saw him. I was so lonely, and then I went to live with Jim and Nancy, and you were both there. And he . . . It was just . . ."

"It was always him," Noah finished for her. He knew that, because the same had been true for him. Except, in his case, always Meg.

And they were one doomed, messed-up triangle.

"He made me think it was real. He made me think it was possible. And I wanted to go to New York for Christmas to surprise him. Because I wanted to finally be with him."

"Right, of course you did. You wanted to be with the man you loved for Christmas."

"No," Meg said, shaking her head. "I wanted to finally *be with him*. Like . . . I was going to New York to sleep with him."

Noah did his best to process that statement, and all of the implications buried in it. "Okay."

"Because I never have," she added.

All of the air rushed out of Noah's lungs. That was something that had never occurred to him. Not even for a moment. He had done his damnedest over the years to never think about Meg and Charlie together like that. But of course, he had assumed that the two of them had slept together. He'd assumed that every time Charlie came around they did. And he always did his best to look the other way. Apparently, he had been looking so far the other way he had missed the fact that it had never happened at all.

He had tried to connect the dots, all of the blank spots, and he had come up with the absolute wrong idea about what was going on between the two of them.

"Never?" Noah asked.

Meg shook her head. "I felt like it was my only power in the situation. And I know that what Charlie and I have isn't healthy. It's not . . ." She balled her hands into fists and shoved them up against her eyes. "It's not even real. And I wanted it to be so badly. I needed it to be. He was my only comfort after my parents lost me to the state. Feeling the way that I did about him, hoping the way that I did . . . It was what kept me going somehow, and even though I've had other things in my life as an adult, it was always there. This one constant."

"You've never had sex with Charlie," Noah said, processing the words even as he spoke them.

"That's what I said," she responded.

And that made him wonder. It made him wonder things he shouldn't. It made him feel things he shouldn't. Meg had come to live with Jim and Nancy when she was fifteen. And unless there had been other men while she was holding a torch for Charlie . . .

"I'm just sad and pathetic," she moaned. "And I was not supposed to be a virgin *still* this Christmas. That was supposed to be my gift to myself." Her cheeks turned bright red. "I shouldn't have said that."

No, she sure as hell shouldn't. Because that put things in Noah's mind that he had absolutely no business thinking. He had done his damnedest not to think of Meg as anything more than a friend for so long, and he had done a pretty piss-poor job of it—that was true enough.

And now he was being confronted with the fact that no one had had Meg in the way that he wanted to have her. Not Charlie. Not *anyone*.

All of those fantasies that he had about Meg had not been fulfilled by another man. And he had been convinced that they had been; of course he had. He had thought that long ago Charlie had been given everything that *he* wanted. Examining a different truth, coming to grips with the fact that he hadn't . . .

Noah wanted her. He wanted her in a thousand different ways, in every different position. He wanted her whether she had been with one hundred men or none. None of it mattered to him. Because she was Meg, and nothing could ever change that.

But knowing that she was untouched did something to him. Knowing that no other man had had her the way that he fantasized about having her. About the way he had always wanted . . . It was a helluva thing.

And he was a man; he wasn't a stone.

"I—"

She held up a hand. "I know. You don't know what to say to that. Because I am ridiculous and you're trying to say anything but that. Because you're a good man and you don't want me to feel stupid. But I do."

"Charlie is one hell of a dumb jerk," he said.

"Excuse me?"

"I just . . . I assumed . . ."

"You thought we were sleeping together."

"Of course I did. The way you feel about him is an open secret."

She looked shocked by that, and then sad. "Can I ask you something? Has . . . has the way he feels about me also been an open secret?"

Noah didn't know how to answer that. Because there were too many different ways he could take that question. It would be easy to deliberately misunderstand, or to give an ambiguous answer.

"I'll say this," he said finally. "If Charlie loved you the way you deserve to be loved, then he would have made it official a long time ago. He would never have left you untouched. And he would certainly never have touched another woman. I don't know what else to say but that."

"I guess . . . I guess maybe it's me." Her small shoulders folded inward, her face tragically sad. "You know . . . No one else has ever really wanted me, so I suppose that it has something to do with me."

Fire burned inside of him. A dull roar sounding in his ears. "It's not you," he said. "A man would have to be blind or a fool not to want you, Meg O'Neill."

CHAPTER 3

Meg looked at Noah, at his eyes, blazing with intensity, and she felt her entire being tighten up. She didn't know how she had ended up in this conversation with him. She didn't know why she had admitted to him that she was still a virgin. It was just that she was all out of sorts and distressed, and the way he was looking at her right now was making her feel something else entirely. But even more intense than that was the shock of the words he had just spoken.

Suddenly, she felt like her heart was going to escape through the front of her chest, just beat its way through her body, and flop out on the floor. The way he was looking at her . . . No man had ever looked at her that way.

It was strange. Like seeing him for the first time. Like looking at a stranger.

It was as if all those strange, unsettled feelings she'd had for him over the past few months had suddenly been distilled. Intensified as she looked at him.

His dark gaze was tortured, his lips pressed into a grim line. And she really noticed those lips. The fact that they looked firm, and certain, and she wondered what it would be like to kiss him.

She was a virgin, but she had most certainly kissed Charlie. She wasn't a stranger to a few of the bases in the game, either, so to speak. But Charlie was smooth, clean-shaven, with a much softer mouth.

For the first time, she wondered what it might feel like to kiss a man who had facial hair. To press her fingertips against the rough skin on his face.

For the first time, she wondered what it might be like to touch a man who wasn't Charlie. A man who was so different. Dark where Charlie was fair.

And the man she was wondering about was her best friend.

She had a problem. She had several problems, but right now this was the most pressing, the most distressing. "I . . . I need a drink," she said, standing up, shaking her hands out.

"You need a drink?" he echoed.

"Just tea. Tea would be good."

"I don't exactly have a robust stash of tea," Noah responded, clearly a little bit shell-shocked by the abrupt conversation change.

"I don't need a robust selection. I just need a warm beverage. I could pretty happily drown my feelings in alcohol, but I feel like that would be setting a bad precedent. Probably I should just try to ease my frozen heart with something comforting."

"Whiskey could do that," he said.

"No doubt. But just the tea."

Noah stood up, pushing up the sleeves on those muscular forearms she had a hard time taking her eyes off. Then he made his way into the kitchen, grabbed a teakettle out of one of the cupboards, and filled it with water before setting it on the burner.

She was filled, yet again, with an intense, full feeling. Satisfaction. And that at least was welcome.

It cheered her, watching her friend move around his kitchen, operate in this life that he had created for himself. He had come such a long way from when they were children. And that forced her to think about the other ways he had changed since they were children. He had always been attractive, and she had always felt a strange sense of pride about that. That this man she cared for so much, who was her friend, was so good-looking. The way women tripped over themselves when they talked to him, and the fact that he was invariably with her and not them, often made her feel smug, even though what they shared was friendship and nothing more.

But she was looking at him now. Really looking at him. He was . . . He was handsome. He had that kind of classic masculinity about him. Strength. A hardness that stood in bright contrast to Charlie's learned sophistication.

She had always been so impressed with the way that Charlie had fashioned a new identity for himself. The way he had built such a sophisticated persona. One that allowed him to move in circles with people who had grown up with more money than any of them could ever dream of. It impressed her. The way he had stepped outside of himself, stepped outside of their experiences.

But there were other things that she had overlooked. Other changes that had happened in Charlie that she had purposely left unexamined so that she didn't have to grapple with the negative connotations.

The way he faked a smile to put people in the room at ease, even when it was dishonest, even when something untoward was happening. The way he flirted with women, as though it were easy, as though sexual connections were cheap.

And then there was Noah. Noah, who didn't treat anything like it was easy. Whose face seemed carved in stone, and for whom smiles were treated like gold dust. Noah, who had carved a life for himself here. Who had grown into himself rather than changing who he was.

He was Noah. Still Noah. Wearing battered jeans and an old shirt. That same handsome face he'd always had, with a few more lines around his eyes, and a heavier beard.

It had been so easy to be caught up in the glory of Charlie's transformation. From a poor foster kid to a successful businessman. But there was a quiet triumph in the way that Noah had transitioned from an angry teenager to this man who now ran his own ranch. This man who didn't seem to get outside adulation from anybody. Who seemed to find his own satisfaction within himself.

And somehow conveyed that while he was doing something as mundane as making tea.

Or maybe Meg had officially lost her mind.

That possibility could not be overlooked.

She blinked, shaking her head and pacing around the living room.

"Are you going to see Jim and Nancy for Christmas this year?" she asked.

"I was planning on going over for dinner," he responded. "Assuming I can get down my damn driveway."

"Yes. Always assuming that."

"Of course, my truck is going to be better equipped than that little thing you were trying to drive down the mountain."

"Right. Well. No need to rub my face in it."

"I don't want to rub your face in anything," he said. "I'm sorry that today was terrible."

"Yeah," she said softly, "you and me both."

They only looked at each other for a moment, and the strange looming tension stretched between them.

But this was Noah, her friend, and there was no reason to be feeling tension. So she had told him that she was a virgin. What did that matter? She knew him well enough to know that he wasn't one. Actually, she had always gotten the feeling that Noah was quietly expert at sex. At least, that was the impression she had gotten from the various women in town who had been with him and from his general nonchalance regarding the subject.

Why did thinking that all of a sudden make her feel hot?

Without thinking, she pressed a hand to her cheek. Yes, she was definitely a little bit warm.

"Is everything all right, Meg?"

"Yeah," she responded. "I mean, as all right as it can be, considering."

"Right." Noah took a deep breath and leaned against the island in the kitchen, staring over at her, his dark eyes serious. "What do you love about Charlie? I mean, God knows I like the guy; he's the closest thing I have to a brother. But why do you *love* him? I'm not blind, Meg. I know you've always loved him. I knew it from that first moment. But what I don't understand is why?"

"He's . . ." She struggled to find words. And suddenly, the reality of everything tumbled in on her, and she wanted to cry even more than she had earlier. Because she couldn't list a reason that wasn't superficial. Like the fact that they had met each other when they were going through a hard time. Like the fact that he had been there for a lot of different turning points in her life. But the same could be said for Noah or a few of her other friends.

Charlie had actually been there *least* of all. Focusing on building his own company while she was starting her brewery. Missing out on her grand opening because he had been doing some kind of deal in San Francisco.

Standing there, facing down Noah, she was forced to admit—at least to herself—that she loved Charlie because it was a habit. Because she had told herself at fifteen that she did, and because he had told her that someday he would marry her and, in the very deepest part of her, she didn't believe that anyone else would.

Habit. Desperation. Fear.

There were three of the worst reasons she could possibly think of to love somebody, and yet those were the only reasons she had left for loving Charlie.

Hell, she had even held on to her virginity all this time in spite of the fact that she had made out with him on couches late at night more than once. Holding back had always seemed an easy thing. And obviously, Charlie had been having sex with whomever he wanted, so it didn't matter to him that she was withholding.

Now, standing in the desolate ruin of her years-long attachment to the man, she could see it all clearly.

She looked up at Noah. "Not a single good reason. And I'm not just saying that because I'm mad. I loved him from the moment I saw him and I never wanted that to change because there was something safe in loving him forever. Something so secure in having settled on that so long ago. And I . . . I would have married him, Noah."

"Well," he responded, clearly unsure of what to say.

And then he was saved by the kettle whistle.

He turned and pulled the thing off the burner, pouring her a mug of hot water and placing a tea bag inside.

Something built in her chest, and she couldn't explain quite what. Anger at Charlie, mixed with anger at herself. A strange sense that there was some kind of timer ticking down in her life. On all those wasted years, months, days, *moments,* with Charlie. All those firsts. Her first kiss. Her first love. Her first heartbreak.

She could only be thankful that she hadn't made him her first lover.

It had been her intention to have sex last night. And there was something hungry inside of her that was all but growling every time she looked at Noah.

She didn't know what it was, and she didn't know why. But she had felt the impact of him harder than she ever had when he'd opened the door to her earlier today.

And there had been all those things over the past months that she had ignored. Those strange little flutters when he had looked at her a certain way, when his hand had brushed against hers. Because she had loved Charlie and no one else. She had married herself to that notion with a myopic view.

She felt . . . free now. Released.

And it made her want to do something with that freedom.

She crossed the kitchen, moving to pick up the mug. Her heart was pounding wildly, her pulse throbbing in her temple. She turned to face Noah, who was appraising her closely, something intense on his face, the lines by his eyes deeper now, and . . . sexy.

That realization slammed into her like a freight train. Noah was *sexy*.

She had felt it, had *known* it, somewhere inside of herself for a while, but she had done her damnedest to ignore it.

The planes and angles of his face were well-defined, hard, and suddenly, her fingertips itched to learn the shape of it. To know what it was like to touch his beard. And maybe it wasn't about him. Maybe it was about any beard, any new face. But she didn't think so.

Because that sharp, insistent tightening that had become more and more persistent in Noah's presence over the past few months was suddenly burning inside her, bright and intense.

She had pushed it down, and she had ignored it, because surely it couldn't be attraction. She was in love with another man, their best friend, in fact, so feeling anything for Noah had to be an impossibility.

But as she stood there, looking at him, she realized that she did feel something. It didn't center in her heart the way her feelings for Charlie did. No, these feelings originated from a much lower place.

Not that she didn't care for Noah; she did. But this was something else entirely. Something completely separate from anything she had felt before.

"Noah," she said, her voice unsteady.

"What?" he asked, but she didn't miss the edge to the word.

"Can I . . . can I see something?" She swallowed hard and walked forward on unsteady feet, lifting her hand slowly and pressing her fingertips against his cheek.

A strange sensation shivered inside of her, low and deep, radiating through her in a way a simple touch never had.

Touching Charlie was always electric. A spark wrapped in insecurity. The emotional drama that was always rife in their connection, and the deep uncertainty that she always felt about what would happen next.

Would he say that he loved her? Would he say that right now there wasn't anything standing between them?

When he came into town, would he rush right to her place? Or would he manufacture some excuse about being too busy to see her at all?

This was . . . It was something else entirely. And of course it was, because Noah was her friend and she'd had more than a decade of that friendship. But this current between them now was unlike anything she had ever experienced before. Unlike the feelings she associated with love, with attraction, and very unlike the feelings she associated with their friendship.

"Be very careful," Noah said, his voice suddenly rougher. Unfamiliar. He didn't sound like Noah anymore. Or, maybe scarier still, he did. But Noah in a way she'd never experienced him.

"Be careful of what?" she asked, her voice soft, almost a whisper. "It's just me."

She let her fingertips drift down toward his mouth, and she found her arm being caught in his iron grip. He stopped her exploration, his blunt fingers digging into her skin. Touching him was like standing in front of a furnace.

She looked up at him, her eyes wide.

"I don't know what you think this is," he nearly growled. "I don't know what you think I am. If you talked yourself into believing that I'm part of some King Arthur bullshit, or if you just think I really am your brother."

Her throat was dry, and she tried to swallow, and she didn't know what to say, except for the most absurd thing. "That's the second reference you've made to literature since I came over."

He released his hold on her and dropped his hand back to his side. "What the hell does that have to do with anything?"

"Well, I was the one who was always reading about Camelot, and Odysseus, and I used to make you listen to me talk about it. You always told me it was boring. But you must have listened."

He looked at her like she had grown another head. "Of course I listened to you. You're my friend, Meg. If you talk to me, I listen. Even if it's literary bullshit I couldn't care less about."

She felt as if someone had wrapped their hand around her heart and squeezed it tight. There was just something about that, that simple statement—crass and so very Noah as it was—that did something to her.

Because he said it so simply. That she was his friend and because she was his friend, he had listened to her. Listened to her talk about things that didn't actually interest him. More than that, he remembered.

He remembered, and his skin had felt so good beneath her fingertips, and she had wanted to explore him more thoroughly. But he was her friend. He was right. So the impulse was messed up, putting it mildly.

Still, right now, her entire life felt messed up. It was Christmas Eve, and she had been determined to make herself a new woman this holiday.

Plus, Noah was her friend. More than that, she trusted him. More than anyone else on earth. She felt that with a deep certainty she didn't even question.

And the way she had felt when she had touched him . . .

It hadn't been that dramatic version of love she had always associated with Charlie. It had been something richer. Something more. And she wanted to figure it all out. To explore that possibility.

"What if I told you I didn't want you to be a knight in shining armor right now?" she asked, the words slow and trembling.

"I'm not going to play a guessing game with you," he said, his voice rough.

"I don't mean to make you guess. It's just that . . . I don't . . . I don't really know what I'm doing. I don't really know what I'm feeling."

She reached up again, putting her hand back on his face, sliding her thumb over his cheek. She had never touched him like this. They had hugged, more times than she could count, and there had been casual brushes of her hand against his, but she had never touched his face. It was such a strange, intimate thing. One of the few things that had always been off-limits with Noah. Touching.

"I can tell you what I'm feeling," he said, sounding angry. "I'm feeling like if you keep doing this, if you keep testing me, teasing me, then I'm going to do something. . . . Meg, I'm sure as hell about to ruin our friendship. And, if you keep going, I can guarantee that you're not going to spend another Christmas as a virgin."

She wondered if he had said those words to scare her, because he certainly hadn't said them to comfort her. But they didn't do either, not really. No, those words hit her square in the stomach, the impact taking her breath away. Those words made her feel like a woman on the edge, trembling, dying for what might come next.

She had been ready. Ready to finally have the experience, and maybe it seemed nonsensical to transfer that desire from Charlie to somebody else so easily, but it only underscored the fact that actually her desire hadn't been for Charlie in a very long time. She'd just been following those plans she had made so long ago when she was a girl and not a woman.

But she was a woman now. A woman who was experiencing desire, real, adult desire, in a way that she hadn't ever before.

That was the difference. The difference between a fluttery, teenage girl's infatuation and a woman's sexual need. It had nothing to do with love, emotion, or the desire for marriage. Nothing to do with holding her body back, or giving it out to get a man to do what she wanted him to do.

She didn't want anything from Noah. Nothing more than she already got from him, anyway. Because he was her rock. Steady and sure, and so much everything to her that she couldn't even quite put it into words.

She didn't need more from their relationship. And that was okay. But right now, she wanted him.

Right now, when she closed her eyes and thought of the word

"sex," it was Noah that she thought of. Noah's body pressed against hers. She wanted to see it, touch it, learn it. Wanted to know if he had hair on his chest, to see if there was yet even more contrast between himself and Charlie.

She felt a stab of guilt over that. Charlie shouldn't have anything to do with this. But her emotions were a little bit raw, even if she was sure she didn't want him anymore. And it was less about Charlie and more about the fact that she had spent so many years fixated on one guy. So many years mired in an ideal she'd created as a teenager.

This was her moment to kick-start a new life, the moment to make a clean break. And who better to do it with than with a man she trusted so implicitly?

After she did this with Noah, there would be no going back. And part of her wondered if she needed that. If she needed to take this moment to slam the door completely on Charlie, and her decade's worth of feelings.

"I don't want to leave your house a virgin," she said, the words choked.

He grabbed hold of her face, gripping her chin between his thumb and forefinger. "Why? You've never acted like you wanted me, Meg. We've been friends since we were teenagers, and you have never looked at me that way."

"That's not true," she said, shaking her head. "Recently . . . I've been . . . It's been so confusing, Noah, because I've been feeling things for you. . . . And I didn't want to call it attraction, because I thought I was in love with Charlie and it didn't seem right to feel something for you. You're my friend. . . . I didn't want to do anything to ruin that. But I don't think anything could ruin us, could it?"

Her question might be more hopeful than anything else, but Noah was one of the few constants in her life. And if anyone could help her with this, if anyone could fix this, it would be Noah. He had been doing things like that ever since she was fifteen years old. Easing her fears, making her feel cared for when nobody else had.

Abandoned by her parents, who had loved drugs and alcohol more than they had ever loved their daughter, she'd found in Noah the most wonderful, blessed security.

Maybe now, maybe tonight, he could be that for her again. But they weren't teenagers anymore. And what she needed from him was not the kind of comfort a girl needed. She needed him to comfort her the way a man comforted a woman.

"Noah," she whispered, "I want you to kiss me."

He didn't release his hold on her. "If I kiss you," he said, his tone full of warning, "we're not going back."

"Kiss me."

CHAPTER 4

Even though Noah knew that Meg was responding to Charlie more than she was responding to him in this moment, he was a man, and he didn't possess the self-control or the pride to care.

Because she was looking at him just the way he had always fantasized, standing there with her face tilted upward, golden eyes glittering, her full lips looking so lush and tempting that he felt he deserved a damned medal—or maybe canonization—for having never touched them with his own before.

Either way, he wasn't going to refuse the demand now.

He walked toward her, and she took a step back, until she butted up against the cabinets. He placed his hands on either side of her, flat over the countertop, bracketing her in. And then he paused. He looked at her, giving her just a moment. Just a breath. Just enough space to decide if she really wanted this, or if she was going to run screaming from the room.

Because he knew the moment his lips touched hers he would be lost. So the chance had to be given now; otherwise it wouldn't be given at all.

She didn't protest. Instead, she just stood there, staring him down. And in that moment, he was reminded of Meg as she had been at fifteen. Wary, but hopeful in a way that he doubted he ever could be.

She had been like a feral cat that needed to be coaxed out from under the bed that first day. But there had been something about her that had made him want to do just that. Coax her. Befriend her. His own life had been marked by his mother's addiction and her boyfriend's violence toward them both. He hadn't known any tenderness. Not shown toward him. And he hadn't felt much inclined to show any to anyone else.

Until Meg.

He'd taken some of the money he'd earned working as a hand at a local ranch and bought her a package of cookies. She'd opened her bedroom door and looked at him with large eyes, saying nothing before grabbing the package and closing the door on him again.

But after that, they became friends.

Part of him would always see her that way, as that creature she'd been.

But layered over that memory was the reality of Meg as a woman. Beautiful. Mature. Lush. Everything he had ever wanted, everything he had ever fantasized about, and more.

She was demanding that he kiss her, and as much as he wanted to be noble . . . as much as he wanted her to do it because she wanted him, and not simply because she was angry with Charlie, a large part of him simply didn't care.

The large part of him below his belt, currently growing larger and harder.

Yeah, that was the easiest way to think of it.

That his dick was all in.

But he knew it was more than that. It was evident. Completely and utterly obvious in the way that it was impossible for him to breathe. In the way each and every heartbeat felt like it was splintering something in his chest.

He had kissed a lot of women. But since he was seventeen there had never been a single moment spent kissing when he hadn't wished, at least in part, he were kissing Megan instead.

This would be the first time since he had met her that he would actually be pressing his lips against the woman he really wanted.

So he took a moment. A moment just to appreciate that. To revel in it.

Then he leaned in, and her breasts rose on an indrawn breath, and he thought for a moment she might protest. But then she didn't have the chance. It was too late. He caught whatever words she had been about to speak with his mouth as he claimed her. Utterly. Completely.

He kept his palms pressed flat against the counter at first, and then he angled his head, deepening the kiss, sliding his tongue against the seam of her lips, and dipping it into hers.

She tasted like desire fulfilled. Hope. Meg. Like everything he had ever wanted, and a whole hell of a lot of things he hadn't known to want.

An erotic daydream come to blinding, screeching light, and all he could do was his best not to set her up on the counter and start tearing her clothes off as he settled between her legs.

She was a virgin. No matter how difficult that was to believe, Meg, his Meg, had never had a man inside of her before. And she wanted him to be the first.

The very idea made his knees buckle.

And dimly, in the back of his mind, he knew that he was just her second choice. Hell, worse than that, he might just be her revenge choice. But he couldn't care. He just couldn't.

Not when he was made entirely of need. And need like that didn't have room for pride.

She was his fantasy. Had been since he was seventeen years old.

That was bigger than he was. Bigger than Charlie. Bigger than whatever had happened to her today.

He lifted his hands from the counter and cupped her face, tasting her even deeper, his heart about to rage through his chest.

He knew this wasn't Meg's fantasy. He knew *he* wasn't.

She had gone to New York to be with the man she had longed for since she was a teenager, and had instead found herself flung into the arms of the man who had wanted her for half of his life.

He supposed if she couldn't get everything she wanted, he might as well get what he wanted. What he needed.

She made a small distressed sound, and even though he had made the determination that he wasn't going to stop once he had started, he couldn't continue if Meg was in distress.

He lifted his face from hers, staring down at her. "What?"

"I don't understand," she mumbled.

"Is my kissing confusing?"

"No." She was breathless, and she looked dazed. She lifted her hand and brushed her fingertips over his lips. "I didn't know kissing could feel like that."

Pure masculine triumph rioted through him.

"How much experience do you have with it?"

Her cheeks colored. "Enough."

"Charlie?" She nodded. "What else did you do?" It was important to know.

The color in her cheeks darkened. "Do we really want to talk about this?"

"Yeah," he said. "Because you're going to compare the two of us. So I want to know exactly what I'm up against."

She cleared her throat. "I don't . . . I don't know how to talk about this."

"Did you ever get him off?"

She looked down. "Yes."

"How?"

Meg bit her lip. "With my . . . my hand."

He slid his thumb along her lower lip. "Never with your mouth?"

She shook her head. "No."

"Did he ever get you off?"

She shook her head again, and this time he wasn't quite sure what to feel. Angry or triumphant in some way. He couldn't pick.

"He's an idiot."

He kissed her again, pressing the length of his body against hers, pushing her back against the counter as he consumed her, as he gave in to the beast that was roaring inside of him. Then he picked her up, cradling her against his chest as he walked them both back to his bedroom.

He knew it was nothing compared to Charlie's penthouse in Manhattan. But there was also no other woman in his bed, so he supposed that put him ahead of the game.

He set Meg down in the center of his bed, and she looked up at him, her curls tumbled into her face, her eyes wide. She was . . . she was more beautiful than he could possibly imagine, now that she was his. Now that he had held her in his arms, conquered her mouth with his.

"I have . . ." Meg cleared her throat. "I have condoms in my overnight bag."

He huffed out a laugh. "Meg, I have condoms."

She blinked, then looked away from him. "Of course you do."

"I'm not a monk and I've never pretended to be. But I also never made any promises that I didn't keep."

Meg drew her knees up to her chest. "That's true. You haven't."

He moved over to the bed, pressing his knee down onto the mattress, leaning in toward her. "I'm going to promise you something right now," he said. "For every orgasm I have, you're going to have at least three. I'm going to make you feel good. I'm going to make this all about you. You're going to have your first time tonight, Meg O'Neill, and I am going to make it the best damn sex on earth." He kissed her lips. "I'm going to give you your first time, your second time, your third time. And when all this is over, you're going to be glad you waited."

You're going to be glad you waited for me.

He didn't say that last part. Because there was no point wrenching his chest open and showing her the contents of it. Not when he knew there was nothing he could do with those feelings.

"And you can trust me," he said, straightening and grabbing the hem of his T-shirt, pulling it up over his head. "I promise you that."

She was staring at him, her expression somewhat owlish. She blinked.

He frowned. "What?"

"I didn't . . . Noah, I didn't know."

"You didn't know what?"

She propped herself up, getting onto her knees and moving to the edge of the bed. "I didn't know you looked like that." She reached out, pressing her palm flat against his stomach. Then she walked her fingers up his abs, like they were climbing a ladder. "I just didn't. . . ."

"I've been in front of you the whole time," he said. "I think you didn't look."

She frowned, tilting her head to the side. "I guess not. I mean, checking out your friend's abs is not exactly appropriate."

"Is this appropriate?" He took a step toward her, forcing her to press her hand more firmly against him.

The breath rushed out of her. "No. Not appropriate at all."

"Do you want me to tell you something else that isn't appropriate?"

"Well, I guess you might as well. . . ."

"I'm not going to be surprised when you take your shirt off. Not about the size of your breasts, not about the contour of your waist. Not about the shape of your hips. And when you take off your bra, all you're going to be doing is answering a few questions that I've had for a long time. And you know why that is?"

"Why?" The word was a whisper.

"Because I have wanted you for so long I've forgotten what it's like to live without that feeling inside of me. I've forgotten what it means to be satisfied. I feel like I've been hungry for thirteen years. Constantly."

Meg drew away from him then, leaning back on the mattress, her face going a little bit pale. "You said that you hadn't been a monk."

"Oh, I haven't been. We all eat a salad when we want steak sometimes; that's a fact." He moved onto the bed, leaned over her, his hands on either side of her shoulders. "I am so fucking sick of salad."

"Noah." She whispered his name like it was a foreign word, one she had never spoken before. That should appall him; it should make him question everything he had just said to her. Instead, he found it only turned him on more.

That she was the one who felt overwhelmed, that she was the one who felt breathless, shaky and like it was all out of her control. Because that was how he felt. Every day. Sure, he had learned to push it down deep; there was no other option. But it was always there. Living inside of him. That need for her had gone unsatisfied, unanswered, for so long.

"Does that scare you?" He slid his thumb along her cheekbone. "I don't want to scare you."

"It doesn't scare me," she said, swallowing hard. "But I wonder how I didn't see it."

She looked up, her eyes meeting his. "It's because you were looking at him," he responded.

Meg's face crumpled for a moment, and then she took a deep breath, regaining her composure. Then she reached out, her hand pressed over his chest, over his heart. He grabbed hold of it, held it there, let her feel the effect she was having on his body. Let her feel just how hard and fast his heart was beating.

Then he lifted her hand to his lips, kissing each fingertip softly, glorying in the feel of her trembling beneath his touch. Finally, finally he was doing to her just a fraction of what she had done to him for so long.

But this small moment, this calm before the storm, wasn't going to last. Because he was going to get caught up in the hurricane the moment it hit. But before then, he wanted to enjoy it. Wanted to look at her and memorize the contours of her face. Commit to his soul the longing that he could see in her eyes.

Longing for him. *Finally* for him.

"I might have been looking at him before," she said softly. "But I'm looking at you right now, Noah."

Her words were filled with wonder, filled with awe, as though she couldn't believe it any more than he could. But that didn't matter. It didn't matter whether or not this made sense to her; he didn't need it to. He just needed her to be here. Just needed her to be willing.

"And I'm looking at you," he said, not taking his eyes off of her for a moment. "Take your clothes off, Meg. Show me. I've waited a long damn time for this."

She blinked, rapidly, her eyes glittering in the soft light. "I spent so long waiting for someone else, it didn't occur to me that someone might have been waiting for me."

"Believe me. I've been waiting for you. But I didn't ever think I would have you."

With trembling fingers she lifted the hem of her sweater up, revealing a pale wedge of skin, peeling it up over her head, uncovering a red lace bra. That bra was for another man. He knew that. But that other man was an idiot, and he hadn't gotten to see it.

But Noah did. Noah was here. And he wanted her.

He didn't care who the bra was for. She was never going to look at it again without thinking of him.

He reached out, sliding his finger just beneath the edge of the lace, finally touching the soft curves of her breast as he had fantasized about doing so many times before.

He had to grit his teeth to keep a growl from escaping, something completely uncontrolled and uncivilized. But he felt like both of those things.

And then, suddenly, he couldn't wait. Not for one more moment. He reached around behind her, unhooking the bra and tugging it free from her body. He cast it onto the floor; he didn't care where it went. Because he couldn't look away from her. Not now.

Her breasts were perfect. Just the perfect size for his hands. His mouth. Of course, that would have been true no matter what. Because it was Meg. And if he'd believed he had a soul, and he believed souls had mates, he would have believed she was his.

She looked up at him, her expression worried. "Are they okay?"

He laughed, but it didn't sound like anything but a strangled, tortured sound. He couldn't speak. So he didn't. Instead, he leaned forward, pressing a kiss to the plumpest part of one breast. Then he nuzzled the tightened bud at the tip with his nose before taking hold of it between his lips and sucking her in deep.

She gasped, her head falling back, her body arching more firmly against him. He pressed one palm flat between her shoulder blades, holding her to his mouth as he continued to pleasure her. Her fingers laced through his hair, and he transferred his attentions to her other breast.

"Noah!" She gasped his name like a prayer, and he reveled in it. That it was his name on her lips. That he was the one making her feel like this. Charlie, *idiot* Charlie, had never even gotten her off. It was a waste.

Her body was made for pleasure. And yes, he was looking forward to it giving him some, too. But mostly, he just wanted to look at her, pleasure her, taste her.

Yeah, he really needed to taste her.

He grabbed hold of the waistband on her leggings—and said a small prayer of thanks that she was wearing stretchy traveling clothes—and wrenched them down her thighs in one smooth motion, along with her panties. That left her completely naked.

Meg O'Neill was finally naked in his bed.

He rocked back so that he was sitting on his knees, so that he could get a better look at her. She was breathing hard, her breasts rising and falling with the motion, her soft stomach pitching in the same rhythm.

She was soft all over. He could tell just by looking at her. And he loved it.

"Still doing okay?"

"Don't stop touching me," she said, the words breathless.

And even as those words cut into him like a knife, he grinned. Because it hurt. All of this hurt. It was too sharp, too clear, too much. But he would gladly exist in it forever.

"I think I can handle that," he said. He leaned forward, pressing a kiss to her rib cage, beneath the lower curve of her breast.

She gasped. He would remember the sounds forever. Meg, his Meg, making sounds of pleasure for him. Only for him.

"You know what's funny," he said, trailing kisses down the center of her stomach.

"I don't really find anything funny right now, Noah," she said.

"It's funny," he continued, "that I've known you for so long, and never seen you naked. That I've known you for so long, that I know so much about you, but I don't know what you sound like when you come. Does any man know that?"

He looked up, his eyes meeting hers. Her cheeks were pink, her embarrassment apparent. It only made her hotter to him.

"No," she whispered.

This time, he could not hold back the growl of satisfaction that rose up in his throat. Yes, part of him was offended that Charlie had never given her an orgasm. But a good portion of him was smug that he would be the first one to do it.

He pressed a kiss lower on her midsection, then lower still, curling his hand around her leg and parting her thighs.

She tensed, attempting to close her legs, to hide herself. He denied her, pressing a kiss high on her thigh, loving that he made her tremble from his touch.

"No one's ever done this for you before, have they?"

He didn't wait for a response. Instead, he pressed his mouth directly over her center, taking a long, slow taste of her, sliding his tongue through her slick folds. Sucking her until she made a short, sharp sound.

He lost himself in that. In the sweet sounds of pleasure she made, in the flavor of her desire on his tongue. He gripped her hips hard, pulling her up against his mouth, tasting her deeper, before adding his hands to his efforts. He pressed one finger deep inside of her, then a second as he continued his sensual assault.

"Yes," he said against her skin. "Come on, Meg; come for me."

"Noah." The word was shaky, but she grabbed hold of his head, holding him to her as she subconsciously moved her hips in time with the thrusts of his fingers.

"That's right," he growled. "Come for me. For me."

She made a small, strangled sound but didn't say any actual words. And suddenly, he needed them. Because there was no other woman as far as he was concerned. And he needed—desperately needed—for her to be thinking of no other man.

"Who's making you feel like this, Meg?"

"You," she said, the word sounding weak and wrung out.

"Not good enough. My name. Give me my name."

"Noah," she gasped as she convulsed around him, her orgasm coming hard and intense. He could feel it, in the way she grabbed hold of his hair, pulling hard, the way she squeezed her thighs shut, pressing against his ears.

"Noah," she said his name again, and he thought right about now he could die happy.

Almost.

He still needed to be inside her.

CHAPTER 5

Meg could hardly breathe. Her orgasm had rocked her completely, but no more than experiencing it with Noah had.

She had never heard her friend use words like that before. Had never imagined him doing these things to her. Had never imagined him making her feel these things. But now that he had, she couldn't imagine how she had looked at him before.

Twenty minutes to wipe out thirteen years.

She wasn't quite sure how that worked. How that was possible.

Except it had been a pretty damned fabulous orgasm.

Noah stood up, making his way to his nightstand and opening the top drawer.

He took out a box of condoms and set it on the surface, then worked his belt free of the buckle, pushing his jeans and underwear down to the floor.

Her throat dried. He was ... He was the most beautiful man. His chest was broad, covered with dark hair, his abs well defined, his muscles a result of the hard labor that he did on the ranch every day, rather than hours in the gym. She supposed, all in all, it didn't matter, since muscles were muscles.

But imagining him chopping wood was hotter than imagining any exercise that took place on a weight machine.

And then there was the rest of him. The very masculine rest of him.

"Noah . . . You're . . . Bigger than I—" She clapped her hand over her mouth. Feeling like a complete idiot.

He arched one eyebrow. The expression was so very him that it made all her breath rush out of her lungs. That was the thing; the last twenty minutes had not erased the last thirteen years. She was still so very aware that this was her friend. That this was the man who had brought her cookies and comforted her when she had first come to Jim and Nancy's house. That he was the man who had stood by her through so many different stages in her life.

Graduation. Opening her own business.

It was fitting in so many ways that he was the one to do this now.

In ways she hadn't even imagined.

"Go ahead," he said. "Finish that sentence, Meg. I'm very interested."

"I'm going to sound like bad porn."

"What do you know about bad porn?"

"I'm a twenty-eight-year-old virgin, Noah. I know quite a bit about porn, bad, good, and in-between."

He chuckled, but it wasn't an easy sound. "Fair enough. Still. I want to hear what you were going to say."

"Just that . . ." She cleared her throat. "You're bigger than he is."

"I'm caught between feeling like I really didn't need to know that about my friend and feeling pretty damn pleased."

Her face was so hot she thought it might be on fire. "Well, *I'm* pleased."

He treated her to a cocky smile and tore open a packet, rolling the latex down over his hard length, his grip on his shaft firm. And much more arousing than she would have imagined it could be.

He made his way back to the bed, grabbed hold of her face, and kissed her, deep and fierce, and she forgot what they had been talking about. She forgot that there had ever been another man to compare him to. Noah was the first and only man to give her an orgasm. And he was going to be the first one to be inside of her.

She forgot to be nervous, because she was so hot for him she couldn't feel anything but desire. Slick want between her thighs, and a building sense of restlessness that she had thought would have been taken care of by her orgasm.

But no, she was ready again.

Her heart slammed against her breastbone, her nipples tight, her breasts feeling heavy, aching. And he seemed to sense that, because one large, rough hand came up to cup her sensitized skin. He slid a callused thumb over one tightened bud and then swallowed the sound of pleasure that she made as he licked deep into her mouth.

He moved his hands down her body, grabbed hold of her hips, and settled between her legs, the thick, blunt head of his arousal pressing against the entrance to her body. She gritted her teeth as he began to press inside of her, stretching her, filling her.

It hurt. She had known that it would.

What she hadn't anticipated was that it would make her chest feel full, too. That having Noah inside of her would suddenly make the world feel like it had turned on its head.

She looked up into his dark eyes as he held tightly to her hips, thrusting forward hard and seating himself fully inside of her. His mouth was set into a grim line, his jaw held tight. She could see just how much self-control it was taking him to remain still for a moment, the cords in his neck standing out, his breathing hard and uneven.

She gripped his shoulders, sliding her fingertips down his back, along the line of his spine, all the way to his tight ass. She had definitely looked at Noah's ass before. Because she was a woman, flesh and blood, and not made of stone.

And it was a nice one.

Even nicer naked. Even nicer with her hands on it.

Much nicer when he was inside of her. So big, thick, and intense.

She kept waiting for him to move, but he didn't. Instead, he grabbed hold of her chin with his thumb and forefinger, holding her face steady as he looked down at her, his dark eyes like fire.

Her own eyes stung, her throat getting tight, hard rock settling in the center of it.

He kissed her. Tender. Sweet. Completely at odds with every delicious, dirty thing that had come before it.

Then he began to move.

And the world shifted.

Because even as the pleasure built, all-consuming and intense, she couldn't forget that it was Noah inside of her. Noah above her. *Noah.*

She clung to him, wrapped her legs around him as he thrust into her, hard and intense, his expression that of a stranger, even while his face remained familiar.

She lifted her hand, traced the lines on his face, touched his lips. Then he closed the distance between them, kissing her while he continued to move inside of her. She was lost.

Meg held his face between her hands, kissing him intently. The only sounds in the room were her fractured breathing, his skin slapping against hers.

And her heart, pounding in her head. Seeming to speak his name each and every time.

Noah. Noah. Noah.

And it was his name on her lips when she climaxed again, pleasure ripping through her, seeming to tear her in two.

He lowered his head, burying his face in her neck as his whole muscular body shuddered against her, as he froze, pulsing inside of her as he found his release.

He moved away from her, rolling to the side, his chest pitching with each breath. She looked up at the ceiling, at the wooden beams that crossed over the simple plaster. Then she looked at the wall, the paneling barren of any kind of art.

The plaid blanket was scratchy beneath her skin, definitely not the kind of bedding that would have been on that big bed in that penthouse in New York.

She looked to the side, at the man beside her. At the lines next to his eyes, that dark beard. His heavily muscled arms and chiseled stomach.

So very different from the man she had imagined going to bed with.

And she knew, in this moment, that she wouldn't trade the way things had happened for anything.

CHAPTER 6

When Noah woke up, the room was cold. He'd let the fire die overnight, and he'd clearly forgotten to turn on the space heater in the small room. Mostly because he'd been distracted. By Meg.

Meg, whose bare bottom was nestled up against his hardness. Meg, who was breathing steadily and deeply as she slept up against him. In his bed.

Meg. Finally.

He moved his hand over her curves, down to her hip, and she stirred beneath his touch.

"Noah?" she asked sleepily.

And the fact that it was his name she had said, that she wasn't confused even for a moment about who she was with, did something to him. Pride was the least of his concerns, really. But even he didn't want to believe she was thinking about being with Charlie while she was here with him.

Second choice was one thing. The only available guy to use while she fantasized about someone else was another.

"Yeah," he said, dropping a kiss onto her lips.

"I guess I fell asleep," she said.

"Yeah," he responded. "Me too."

She turned over so that she was facing him, and he could barely make out her glittering eyes in the darkness. "Was I okay?"

He huffed out a laugh. "It's a miracle the top of my head didn't blow off."

"Is that a compliment?"

"Yes, it was a very crass compliment, which unfortunately is all I'm capable of."

She laughed, then snuggled more deeply against him. "That's not true."

"Sure it is. You were supposed to lose your virginity in some high-rise apartment. Not in this place."

"I'm not sorry," she said. "I'm not sorry that I'm here. I'm not sorry that it's you. You talk yourself down, Noah, but you're the one who brought me cookies."

He wasn't even going to pretend he didn't remember that, even though he probably should. Even though discretion was the better part of making sure you didn't get your guts ripped out. He didn't have much discretion with Meg. At least, not anymore. He had spent so many years keeping it all locked up; now that he had set it free, it was all but impossible to put it back in the cage.

"They were just cookies," he said.

"Noah, I was the little girl that no one paid attention to. And once I was taken from my parents, I was the little girl that bounced from place to place. And even though there were good homes in between those times when I went back to my mom and dad, it was all very temporary. And there didn't ever seem to be a point in anyone getting to know me, because they were only going to have to give me away. And I know that some of that came from me. Some of it was me holding myself back because I knew I was going to lose the nice people who had taken me in, that I was going to go back to that house where no one looked in my direction, so why should I try? Why should I try to connect with anyone?"

"You never acted hard because of it," he said. "I remember seeing you for the first time and thinking that you were still soft. And I couldn't fathom how."

"I wished I weren't. I wished that I were more like you."

"Why?" he asked.

"Because you seemed bulletproof. Like nothing could hurt you."

He shifted, suddenly feeling uncomfortable. "And how did Charlie seem?"

She lowered her head, pressing her face to the center of his chest and taking a deep breath. "Safe."

"I didn't seem safe?" He posed the question gently.

"No, it's just... No. 'Safe' is not the word I would use to describe you. And ironically, it's not exactly the word I would use to describe Charlie now. Except... I don't know, maybe 'nonthreatening' is a better word. But it was funny tonight, you telling me that you were my friend, so of course you remembered me talking about books. And you remembering the cookies. I don't think he would remember any of that. And I'm not trying to compare the two of you."

"Meg, we've been friends for thirteen years. The three of us. And during most of that time you and Charlie had the relationship that you had. I think comparison is somewhat inescapable." Even if it did gall him a little bit, he had to be fair. Or he had to try to be.

"I spent a long time being ignored," Meg said. "And when I first came to Jim and Nancy's, I was ready to fly under the radar there, too. To just hide away until I got moved on. But you didn't let me. You drew me out, and you brought me cookies. And you made me feel like it was worth knowing somebody. Charlie made me laugh—I think he makes us both laugh. And that's one reason it's easy to forgive all of the crap he does. The fact that he isn't dependable. The fact that he doesn't show up when he says he will, and he..."

"Offers to marry you while he's sleeping with someone else?"

Meg sighed heavily. "Did he do that to you, too? Because that is surprising."

Noah laughed. "No. But I would have punched him in the face. You know, instead of flying all the way back here."

Meg shook her head. "I didn't even yell at him. I *apologized*. I apologized for showing up unannounced. I wish I hadn't done that. I was embarrassed, and I was upset. And the more I think about it, the more I think *he* should have been the one who was embarrassed and upset."

"Hell yes, he should be," Noah said. "And if he knew what was good for him, he should have chased you to the airport. He should be calling you every few minutes, begging you to take him back."

"No one has ever done that for me," she said, the words matter-of-fact rather than self-pitying in any way. "I've always thought my parents were relieved when I got taken from them. Every time it happened. When Child Services showed up, and they knew that they didn't have to deal with me anymore. That they didn't have to carry the burden that was me." She sighed. "I imagine Charlie feels the same way."

Noah locked his teeth together, clenching them tight, and he wrapped his arms around Meg, pulling her up against his body. "Do you know why they felt that way?"

"Because I'm high maintenance?"

"Because they've never loved anything in their lives more than they love themselves. That's sad. For them more than it is for you. And with Charlie . . . It's the same. He's broken, and he doesn't know how to make himself uncomfortable for someone else."

"You make me sound like a rock in someone's shoe."

"That's just life, Meg. It's not you being a problem. It's that anything in life that has value costs a little something of yourself. What about your brewery? Is it always fun?"

"Is your ranch always fun?"

"No. And you know it isn't. But it means everything to me. I was a kid who had nothing, and I started working at this place when I was in high school. I never imagined when I started that I would have the chance to buy it. That old John Anderson would offer to carry the loan for me so that I could buy the place when he retired. Sure, it costs. It costs in sweat, and in blood. In time. But I have something to show for it. Something I can hold with both hands. I can go outside and dig through the snow, kneel down, and get a handful of dirt that belongs to me. For a kid who never owned anything, let me tell you, that's a hell of a thing."

He let his hands drift down her back, skimming over her curves, coming to rest on her ass. "And let me tell you something else. It would have been easier sometimes not to try. We were never shown an example about why trying mattered. Mostly, we saw what giving in to failure looked like. What I know is that sometimes not wanting anything feels a lot easier. But this . . . trying . . . You get more in the end."

"You got more than you bargained for," she said, lifting her face and nipping his chin.

Electric arousal shot through him. "Not nearly enough," he growled, pushing her onto her back and looking down at her. "I'd like a little more, actually."

She smiled up at him, reached out, and touched his face. She kept doing that. Touching him like she was trying to orient herself to the fact that she could. Touching him like she was trying to make sure this was real. He liked it. He liked it a little bit too much.

"Please," she said, the word simple and beautiful.

He kissed her, reaching over and grabbing another condom off the nightstand, trying to keep on kissing her while he tore the thing open and rolled it onto himself with one hand.

He didn't have the patience for foreplay, not this time, and when he pushed inside of her for a moment he was afraid that he had hurt her. The way she gasped, the way she stiffened for a moment. But then she rolled her hips up against him, taking him in even deeper, and she sighed, a deep, satisfied sound that he had never even fantasized about hearing from her lips.

He kissed her again, gathering her wrists and pulling them up over her head, holding them fast while he teased her breasts with his other hand, as he moved inside of her, driving them both crazy.

He had never thought something like this was possible. When he had fantasized about being with Meg, he had only ever let it be sexual. When he had imagined getting her naked, she had become some kind of porn bot in his mind. He had to admit it, even if he hated to. He certainly hadn't imagined talking about cookies, and the past. About hard work and sacrifice. The kinds of things he would normally talk about with Meg, and with no one else, even while they were naked together.

This was something he hadn't anticipated. Something he hadn't even wanted. And now that he had it, it was breaking his chest apart, making him feel things he hadn't imagined were possible for him to feel.

The room had been cold when they'd woken up, but it was warm now, their bodies creating heat together. Or maybe the heat was just inside of him. He had always burned for her, but now it was blazing out of control. And now it was something more than sex.

In his fantasies, sweet, beautiful Meg was his friend during the day and his lover at night. But during the last few hours those things had all melted together, and he wasn't sure he could ever separate them out again.

He didn't know what that meant. He didn't know if he wanted to know what it meant.

She grabbed hold of his shoulders, her fingernails digging into his skin. She raked them down his back as she panted his name in his ear, as she wrapped her legs around his hips and took him in deeper, her internal muscles pulsing around him as she found her pleasure.

And he wasn't far behind, his self-control unraveling completely, the fire inside of him burning out of control.

When it was over, she lay against him, her hand pressed to his chest, right over his heart.

"Noah?"

"What?" he asked, looking up at the ceiling.

"It's Christmas Eve," she said.

"Yeah" He tightened his hold on her. "It is."

She wrapped her arms around him, her breath hot against his skin. "Merry Christmas Eve, Noah."

And for some reason, his throat was so tight, he couldn't answer.

CHAPTER 7

It was almost noon by the time Meg and Noah committed to getting out of bed. Noah had gone into the kitchen earlier in search of food, and coffee, and they had both indulged before indulging in each other again.

Then they had napped, and when they'd woken up Noah had told her to get on her knees and hang on to the headboard while he showed her a brand-new position that only made her curious about what else the two of them might explore.

But it was Jim and Nancy's Christmas party tonight. They had a big one every year, inviting all of the foster children who had ever passed through their house. And people gathered from all over the state, sometimes all over the country, to come back to see them.

Suddenly, she felt slightly shamefaced that she had planned on missing it so that she could go hook up with Charlie, who would also be missing it.

"Do you always go to Jim and Nancy's party?" she asked, swinging her legs over the side of the bed and hunting around for her clothes.

"Yeah," he said. "Every year."

She had missed a few years here and there. Because of the brewery or because Charlie had needed a date to something.

She looked over at Noah and battled with a little bit of internal disappointment as he covered his extremely gorgeous ass with his jeans and then pulled a tight T-shirt over his head, followed by a sweater.

"It's late," he said. "I have to go out and do some overdue work. You're welcome to . . . stay here."

She finished putting on her own sweater and tugged idly at a loose thread on the sleeve. "Could I . . . Can I go with you? It would be interesting to see the place. I haven't actually gone on the grand tour in a while."

"You're going to freeze your pretty backside off," he said, making no effort to hide the fact that he was definitely checking her out.

It made her feel giddy. Seeing him like this. Really seeing him as a man. Not just her friend. He was both. Because all of those feelings she'd always had for him were still there. There were just other feelings, too.

"I'm sure my backside will be fine," she said.

"Do you need to go down to the brewery before the party?"

She shook her head, following him out of the bedroom and back into the living room. "Everything was all set for me to be on vacation for the next week. So I'm actually the least busy that I've been for a very long time."

"Well, I guess Charlie isn't completely useless then."

She frowned. "How do you figure that?"

Noah reached out, wrapped his arm around her waist, and pulled her close. "Because of him, I have the next week with you."

Then he kissed her, and her knees went weak, and for a few minutes she couldn't even remember who Charlie was.

They spent the day working outside—well, more accurately, Meg followed Noah around while he did the work. And she rode shotgun in his truck, watching him lift heavy things and in general be manly and sexy in ways she couldn't believe she had never noticed before.

Well, she had noticed. It was just that she hadn't allowed herself to put the appropriate label to it. But now, suddenly, all those feelings that she'd had for him for quite a while made a lot more sense.

That kind of light giddiness she felt when he looked at her, that tightening in her stomach when he got close and she smelled the soap he used, layered over the top of his skin.

She was attracted to him. And she had pushed it down deep for a very long time.

She sighed and looked in the mirror, reasonably happy with what she had managed to accomplish in Noah's small, Spartan bathroom. She had brought makeup and a dress with her to New York, so she had it in her bag at his house, and she figured it was as good an outfit as any to wear to the Christmas party.

The dark green material clung to her curves, and it was a little bit sexier than she would normally wear to something local. She had bought the dress with New York in mind. With no one she knew but Charlie in mind.

It was another thing entirely to show up in something so figure hugging at a party where she would know 90 percent of the attendees. With the man she was currently sleeping with. A man people would be pretty shocked to find out she was sleeping with.

But everyone had known about her attachment to Charlie, so she supposed that she and Noah weren't exactly a weirder pairing. And there was really no reason to keep it a secret.

She frowned. Unless there was. Unless Noah wouldn't want people to know. Because it wasn't as if they had made plans for the future.

Did she even want to make plans for the future? She had been married to a very specific future for a long time. Maybe she needed to have none for a while.

Her stomach churning, she walked out of the bathroom, to see Noah standing there wearing a button-up flannel shirt, the sleeves pushed to his elbows, revealing those muscular forearms that she knew were as solid and strong as they looked.

His dark hair was a little bit tousled, and it made her think of running her fingers through it, which she had done more times than she could count over the last twenty-four hours.

And for some reason, she had a strange sense of déjà vu. A flashback to that time she had opened her bedroom door when she was fifteen years old, to see seventeen-year-old Noah standing there with a package of cookies.

She had taken them and gone back into her room. Overwhelmed

by the emotion evoked by such a small gesture. Because there had been a shortage of small, thoughtful gestures in her life.

Not from him, though. He had started their relationship with one. And he had spent every moment since adding to it. There was a whole mountain of wonderful inside of her, built up by Noah. It wasn't the same as Charlie, who dazzled with a smile. Who had held her and kissed her, and made giant promises that he could never live up to.

Noah had never made a promise. He had never done a single flashy thing in his life. He had just shown her that she mattered. In small ways that had become big. That had shaped her.

And suddenly, it didn't matter what they called it. It didn't matter what they planned for the future. Because beneath all of it was the deep, underlying trust she had felt for him from the moment he had handed her that package of cookies.

Things had always been okay between them. She had to believe that they always would be. That this was another brick added to her personal structure. Added by him. Which was fitting. Because whatever he might say about how he had been hard and she had been soft when she had first come to live with Jim and Nancy, the fact of the matter was she had been more like a wounded animal.

Vulnerable. Needy. But in no position to trust anyone.

And he had reached out. In spite of all the things he'd been through. Noah continually reached out. He continually gave. Whatever he thought about himself, however he might describe himself, his actions spoke loud and clear.

It was so much easier to give weight to money, flash, and dramatic transformations. And somehow so easy to miss the simple, deeply meaningful actions of a good man.

"I'm ready to go," she said, clearing her throat. "Do you think the driveway is going to be passable?"

If worse came to worst, they would be snowed in at Noah's place, and honestly, that wasn't so bad as worst-case scenarios went. She could take off her dress, and he could take off his shirt, and they could keep each other warm.

"Everything looks good. You okay?"

"I'm great."

He smiled, and it made her stomach curl in on itself. "You look great."

"So do you." She took the two steps toward him to close the distance between them and cupped his cheek, kissing him lightly. "I'm proud to have you be my date."

Her words and her kiss burned into him the whole way down to town and only intensified when he pulled into Jim and Nancy's driveway. Meg was happy to be his date, apparently. Not concerned at all by the potential complications.

And he had no idea why he had a problem with it.

Here he was, attending this party with his fantasy woman, and he felt cold down in his gut.

But when they got out of the truck and he opened her door for her, she stepped right into his arms and rested her head on his chest for a moment, and he decided not to listen to any of those concerns. Instead, he grabbed hold of her hand, lacing his fingers through hers as they walked up to the front door.

The entire porch was lit up with white lights and bedecked with garlands. Greenery laced with cranberry-colored velvet bows. The same decorations that Jim and Nancy had put up for years. And the big wreath on the door, though it had fresh greenery as it always did, looked the same, too. White lights, dark red bow. There was a familiarity to all of this that Noah found comforting. Always had. For a kid like him, who had spent so many years bouncing around the system—preferable to being kicked around in his own house—familiarity and consistency were comforting on a bone-deep level.

But this year it was different. Because while he was going with Meg, which was common enough, this year she was holding his hand. This year, he knew what she looked like naked.

This year, she was his.

They didn't even have to knock before the door opened and Nancy was there, wearing a bright red Christmas sweater and a necklace made of flashing Christmas lights. Her dark brown eyes went to their hands first and then up to their faces.

If the new development surprised her, she didn't let it show. But then he imagined that a woman who had taken some fifty foster children in over the past few years wasn't surprised by much.

"Noah! Meg." She leaned forward, pulling them both in for a hug. "So glad that you're here. Meg, I thought you were going to be out of town this year?"

"My plans changed," she said, tightening her hold on his hand and leaning a little bit closer to him.

Nancy smiled. "Change is good."

And that, he had a feeling, was the only thing Nancy was going to say on the subject. The room was already packed with people from the community and with the now familiar faces of the grown children Nancy and Jim had had a hand in raising.

A lot of those kids had kids of their own, partners. Every year, the party got bigger. A testament to the good work that Jim and Nancy had done.

Jim was manning the drink station, wearing the world's ugliest Christmas sweater and a pair of reindeer antlers covering his bald head. He waved a pair of ice tongs in their direction, flashing them both a smile.

The most amusing thing about the entire event was the fact that nobody really reacted to him and Meg showing up as a couple. They mingled with their friends and acquaintances, and Meg frequently touched him in a way that signified their change in relationship status.

Noah was starting to feel almost relaxed, which was unusual for him in any circumstance.

Then the front door opened again, and he looked up as the cold air rushed in.

And there he was.

Blond hair pushed back off of his forehead, white snowflakes clearly visible on the shoulders of his expensive-looking wool coat.

Charlie had come home for Christmas.

CHAPTER 8

Meg's mouth went dry, her entire body trembling inside when she saw Charlie standing there on the front step. Reflexively, she took a small step away from Noah, and she could see instantly that it had been a mistake. She inched back toward him, but he stepped to the side, clearly not interested in her attempt at making amends for that initial response.

Charlie was not supposed to be here. Charlie was supposed to be in New York in bed with a supermodel. He wasn't supposed to be here. Wasn't supposed to be back here testing the newly formed bond between her and Noah. Wasn't supposed to be here . . .

Bringing back the reality of the situation.

What is the reality? Did you really need him to show up to confirm what you already know? That he isn't what you want anymore?

She looked over at Noah, who was looking grim faced and taciturn, and she knew that even though they were in for a fight later, she wanted him. She wanted to have the fight. Well, she didn't want to have the fight, but if it was the only way to move forward she was willing to have it.

Whatever work it took.

Charlie greeted Nancy, pulling her in for a hug, and then he walked across the room to do the same for Jim. They both looked happy to see Charlie; nobody was ever anything but happy to see Charlie. It was impossible to be angry with him. Meg wasn't even angry with him. Not really.

Because you don't want him.

Well, that was the thing.

Then, like a homing beacon, Charlie's gaze found hers across the room, and he started to walk toward her and Noah.

"Hey," he said to Noah, pulling him in for a quick hug that, to Noah's credit, did not immediately result in Charlie being punched in the face.

"Hi, Charlie," Noah said, shoving his hands in his pockets. "I didn't think you were coming back to the West Coast for Christmas."

"I wasn't," Charlie said. "But I need to talk to Meg."

That *did* make Noah bristle. And Meg stepped slightly between them. "It's okay," she said to Noah.

Charlie frowned. "Of course it is," Charlie said, putting his hand on her lower back and beginning to guide her away from Noah.

Suddenly, Charlie's arm was removed from its place and Meg found herself walking forward by herself. She looked back and saw that Noah had taken hold of Charlie's wrist. "It is if *she* says it is," he said, squaring his shoulders, his dark eyes dangerous.

Meg had a sudden vision of Noah throwing Charlie into the punch bowl.

"It's fine," she said, reaching out and putting her hand on Noah's arm. "It's fine."

Charlie looked between them, his expression one of confusion and irritation. Well, he wasn't going to get any less irritated in the next few minutes.

"Come on," she said. "Let's go out back."

They walked through the party, and Meg was dimly aware that they were being watched. Most closely by Jim, whose expression of concern was especially comical in contrast with the reindeer antlers. But then she supposed that even though no one was saying anything, everyone was aware of the drama inherent in her coming and holding hands with Noah, only to have Charlie show up.

As Noah had told her yesterday, her feelings for Charlie had been something of an open secret.

They walked out onto the back deck, which was illuminated with the same sort of Christmas lights that were hung out front, casting glitter down onto the snow.

Meg wrapped her arms around her body, more for security than for warmth. "You came."

"I did. I'm sorry about what happened. And I probably should have just called you, or texted you or something, but it seemed like something we need to talk about in person."

She shook her head. "The thing is, Charlie, I don't really know if you needed to do any of that. You have never pretended that it was only me."

"That's the thing," he said. "For me, it is, Meg. And other women... It's got nothing to do with us. It's just physical. That's all."

Meg bristled, because if there was one thing she *did* know, it was that if he found out she had slept with Noah he would not brush it off similarly.

"I can't do it anymore," she said. "I don't want to. I don't want to wait for you to decide suddenly that you're ready to be with me. I was ready to be with you thirteen years ago. And... I'm not now."

"What?" Poor Charlie. He looked genuinely confused and completely shocked.

"I cared for you back then, Charlie. And mostly, I've carried on doing it because I didn't know what else to do with myself. But I do now."

"Meg—"

"I slept with Noah," she said, stepping over his words. "I am sleeping with Noah."

Snowflakes fell into Charlie's blond hair, onto his pale eyelashes, and if it weren't for the enraged expression in his blue eyes he might have looked a like a Christmas angel. "Noah?"

"Charlie, I literally caught you naked with somebody else two days ago. And I know there have been a lot of someone elses over the years. I do not need your anger and indignation."

"Look, Meg, if you had blown off steam with a stranger at any point over the last thirteen years, I wouldn't have said a damn thing. But my best friend?"

Anger tore through her, thirteen years' worth of it. "He's *my* best friend," she said. "And he's been a friend to me from the moment I met him. He remembers that I like *The Odyssey*."

"What?"

"Exactly." She flung her arms out wide. "You don't remember. He remembers. And we . . . The three of us . . . We are a little bit messed up, and there's no denying that. I don't claim to know exactly what love is. I don't know. I thought that maybe it was commitment, over anything else. That it was butterflies in my stomach and a feeling of excitement and uncertainty. But I look around here, at this party, at all these children whose lives were changed by Nancy and Jim, and I think that maybe that's love. The being there. Always. Through everything."

She cleared her throat. "And I look at Noah, and his ranch. And I remember all the little things he did for me—that I was so convinced were little—and I think maybe that's love. Not big promises that can't be kept." She swallowed hard, shaking her head, a tear falling down her cheek. "He never made me a single promise, Charlie. He was just there. And I think . . . I think that might be what love is."

"You're dropping all this on me now, Meg? Because suddenly you decide to change the rules of what's going on between us and I'm the bad guy?"

"Charlie . . ."

"Let me get this straight. You're mad because I was with someone else when you were ready to make a commitment, but you didn't actually talk to me or tell me that you were coming to visit. And then I come back here and find out that you're basically doing the same thing."

Everything felt twisted around in her head, and her feelings were twisted around in her heart. She knew that she shouldn't feel guilty. But she'd spent so long justifying Charlie's behavior that it was hard not to feel something when he stood there, looking like she had just punched him in the stomach.

It wasn't love. No, it wasn't that. She was never going to convince herself it was that again. But she didn't hate him. Even if she wished that she could.

Actually, the real reason she couldn't hate him was probably because it had never been love. What was the point of being angry over the fact that she had been spared a lifetime with him when she realized she didn't actually want one?

"Stop it," she said. "You hurt me, Charlie. And this isn't the first time. I buried it. I buried the hurt as best I could, because I felt so desperate for some kind of security. I didn't want to abandon my feelings for you, because . . . Well, I felt sorry for both of us. We both had it hard enough. I know that your parents really screwed you up. Mine screwed me up, too. And Noah's. None of it's fair. Everything that happened to us before . . . It isn't fair. But I can't keep submitting myself to this. I can't."

"Are you comparing me to our parents? Meg, I'm a millionaire." Charlie's eyes were as cold as the air around them. "I'm successful. I am not my parents."

"That's a really convenient shield for you, isn't it? You don't know how to love anyone more than you love yourself. You might have money, Charlie, but you haven't fixed everything about who you are."

"And he has? He's gonna move you into that little cabin of his? Give you a bunch of babies? What kind of life is that? You want to talk about going right back to where we came from . . . Well, go ahead, Meg. It's your life. We could have had a life. But not now."

Charlie stormed back into the house and Meg took a deep breath of the dry, frigid air, trying to get hold of her temper. She wasn't second-guessing anything. If anything, she just saw it all more clearly.

She looked back through the window and saw Charlie, headed for Noah.

"Dammit, Charlie," she said under her breath as she tore back into the house.

"This is how you expect me to find out that you're fucking my girlfriend?" Charlie asked, loud enough for the entire room to hear.

And then he took a wild swing at Noah, who dodged it neatly. "Come on, Charlie," Noah said. "You and I both know that I've been dodging hits like that from bigger men than you since I was a lot smaller than I am now."

Charlie's face turned red, and he took another swing at Noah, who moved to the side, sending Charlie and his very expensive wool coat straight into the punch bowl.

Noah's hands were clenched into fists, and Meg knew that it was taking every ounce of his self-control not give Charlie the punch in the face he deserved.

Meg, for her part, felt only appalled. Because this was the man she had spent thirteen years pining after. And once she had dropped all of the excuses for him, once she had admitted to herself that she didn't want that future she'd been planning for so long . . . well, she'd discovered it just wasn't worth it. Not that Charlie wasn't worth it as a human, just that he wasn't worth her heartbreak.

"Boys, come on," Nancy said, putting her hand on Noah's shoulder and drawing him back slightly. Then she looked down at Charlie, who was still on the floor, covered in punch. "Charlie, I didn't think I was going to have to break up a fight between the two of you. I didn't even have to do it when you were teenagers."

The entire party was staring at the spectacle they'd made, and if Meg could have sneaked out and burrowed into a snowbank for cover she would have.

"Sorry," Charlie said, getting up, not able to look at Nancy.

And that just made Meg feel sad. Because all of their history, the history among the three of them, and Jim and Nancy, was definitely still there. And however Charlie was acting now, he did care. He did hold all those old feelings in. And it still mattered to him—millionaire or not—if he disappointed Nancy.

Those feelings that she was having now—that pity—still wasn't love.

But what she felt for Noah, standing there strong, not moving in on his friend, even though said friend had just tried to attack him, that was.

"I think you should go," Meg said to Charlie. "Maybe we'll talk another time."

Charlie shook his head. "I don't know about that." Then he got up and walked out of the room, out of the house, and onto the street. She heard a car engine start, and it wasn't until then that conversation started in the room again.

Meg looked helplessly at Nancy. "I'm so sorry."

Jim came over and put his hand on his wife's shoulder. "This is not the first fight our house has played host to."

Nancy waved a hand. "We've seen it all."

"Well, you shouldn't have had to."

Nancy reached over and pulled Megan in for a hug. "It was never a have to, Meg. We only ever *wanted* to." She patted Meg's cheek. "I'm happy for you. Charlie is a good boy underneath everything. But Noah is a good man."

She released her hold on Meg, and Meg stood back, looking over at Noah, who was still standing there as if he were waiting for a blow.

"Come on," Meg said, grabbing hold of his arm. "Let's talk."

They went down the hall, heading toward what was Noah's old bedroom. Once they were inside, the door closed behind them, Noah pushed his hand through his dark hair. "What did you tell him?"

"I told him we're together."

"I see. And did his jealousy spur him to profess his undying love? Are you going back to him?"

Meg felt as if she had been punched in the stomach. "No. Why would you think that? I don't . . . I've been doing a lot of thinking over the past couple of days, Noah. And the conclusion I've come to is probably the easiest one ever. I don't love Charlie. Charlie was a habit. And Charlie was security. And you know how I feel about that. People like you and me . . . It's so hard. Change. Because all through my childhood change wasn't necessarily good. Change was hard, and sometimes change was bad. Jim and Nancy's house, being with them, that was the happiest I ever was."

She took a deep breath. "And I made a decision about you and Charlie, found a way to keep you both in my life. And I didn't want to change it. Not for anything. Because I couldn't bear the idea of changing our dynamic. I wanted Charlie when I was fifteen. And I didn't understand what the hell it meant. To love someone. I didn't understand anything. Not then. How could I? He was handsome, and he smiled easily, and back then that felt a lot like love."

She looked down at her hands. "But you know what? Fifteen-year-old girls are stupid. They gravitate toward shiny, insubstantial things, and that's exactly what I did with him. And I missed the real thing even when he handed me a package of cookies." She took a deep, shuddering breath. "Noah, I love you. And I don't even think that's a brand-new revelation. I think it's been inside of me for a long time. I just didn't understand what it was. But dealing with all of this, all of this Charlie stuff, made me ask myself why I thought I loved him. And then it made me ask myself what I think love is. It's you. It's always been you."

CHAPTER 9

Noah looked down at the woman standing in front of him, her eyes blazing with her earnestness. He knew that she meant it. At least, she thought she did. Because Meg would never lie to him, not about this. He trusted that. In many ways he trusted her more than he trusted anyone else. The problem was, he didn't really trust anyone else. What he had said to Charlie was true. He had been dodging blows his whole damned life.

And somehow he hadn't seen this one coming. He also hadn't realized that it would strike him with more impact than any physical beating ever could have.

Meg. The woman he had always wanted, looking up at him and telling him that she loved him.

Love. He had never for one moment allowed himself to think the words. Not when it came to her. Not when it came to anybody. Because what good was it? What would it benefit either of them?

Love carried such a host of things, a wealth of deep meaning that he didn't think he could live up to.

"What does that mean?"

"That's what I've been working out," she said. "I thought that it was butterflies and drama. But I think it's a lot closer to cookies and dependability—"

"Okay. So I'm the stability you're looking for. That's what you're saying."

"No. That's not what I said."

"Yes, Meg, you just said it. Charlie is not giving you the security you want, and you want someone who will. Because you're afraid of change. Hell, all of us are. Nobody gets it better than I do."

"Noah," she said, reaching out and grabbing hold of his arm. "That isn't what I meant. And you know me better than that. I would *never* use you."

"You would never use me on purpose. But you came back from New York with a broken heart and the first thing you did was come to me. You wanted to lose your virginity with Charlie, but it didn't happen, so you used me instead. And now you've decided that he's not a good prospect so you want me. Because you're so damned desperate for stability."

"That's not fair," she protested.

"Who gives a damn about fair, Meg? Have we ever had it fair? Was it fair that my mother dated a parade of increasingly abusive douchebags my entire life? I never expected life to be fair. The fact that you seem to think it should be after all this time is pretty surprising."

"No," she started again. "I'm sorry about all that happened to you. I am. I always have been. I'm sorry about what happened to me. I'm sorry that my parents loved drugs more than they loved me. I'm sorry that it contributed to me making poor decisions. I'm sorry that a lack of examples of love in my life made me accept bad things for a while. But I'm done with that. I know what I want now. I've gone through a whole lot of crap to get here, but now I'm here. And I get it. I understand who I'm supposed to be. And who I'm supposed to be with. I was blind. But I'm not now."

"Great. Well, your come to Noah moment has been pretty great, but I think you have a lot of shit to work out, and you probably need to do it without me."

Meg wobbled, then sat down on the bed. "What?"

"You heard me."

"I did, but it doesn't make any sense. You're the one who said you've always wanted me. You're the one . . . and now you're saying we have to wait?"

"Yes. You're the one who made it clear you always wanted Charlie, and only when it became very obvious he wasn't going to give you what you wanted did you decide that you wanted me."

"That's not fair," she insisted. "I just didn't understand. I do now. I do, because you showed me. I couldn't have possibly understood it before this. But that's like criticizing me for being blind and not realizing the sky was blue until I was able to see. This isn't just me taking the easy way out. This is me realizing that I want more. That I deserve more."

"I always wanted you," he said, firming up his jaw. "I wanted to take you to bed, Meg, and that's why I never did anything about it. Because I knew that you wanted marriage. I knew that you wanted a family. I'm not a coward. Nothing scares me. I held back because you deserved better. Then you came to me, and I figured Charlie had done enough damage that I might as well just go ahead and take what you were offering."

"You're a liar," she said, standing up and flinging her petite frame at him. "You are afraid. You're afraid to take this. And I get it. We've had these discussions over and over again. It doesn't matter how much Jim and Nancy cared for us for those years we lived with them. It doesn't matter that we have good friends, good jobs. In our hearts we still feel like foster kids. We still feel like kids who were given away. You don't have to tell me about your past—I already know. You don't have to tell me how it feels, because I know that, too. But we have to . . . Dammit, Noah, we have to move past this. We have to. We have to want what's better for ourselves, because nobody's going to hand it to us. At this point, we're the ones who are choosing to let what our parents did to us decide who we are. We're almost thirty. Everything that's happening to us now, good and bad, is because of what we decided to do with our lives."

"We can't do this," he said.

The words felt torn from him, cutting into him like jagged glass. He wanted . . . He wanted to reach out and take what she was offering. He wanted to pretend that what she wanted was actually possible. For just a moment. He wanted to imagine that future. Meg, in that little house with him. Meg forever. His wife. Maybe they would even have some kids.

But what would happen if it all broke? Where would that leave him? Where would it leave *them*?

By the time he was ten, he had watched love turn sour more times than most people saw in a lifetime.

He would be damned if he would be part of that with Meg.

All he knew now was that he had to leave. He had to stop this. Had to stop this impossible madness before he reached out and took hold of it. Before his weakness overcame him and he gave in and damn the consequences.

He had his life. And Meg had never figured into it as anything more than a friend. He had accepted that, even when it hurt. He had made his peace with it, and now she was acting like . . . like they could have something real.

He didn't need that. He had his ranch. That piece of ground was all his. The evidence of how far he had come.

But he had gone as far as he could go. Anything more was just asking too much.

"No," he said, his voice rough, the words fractured.

"Noah," she said, her voice trembling. "Please."

"I can't."

Then he turned and walked out of the room, leaving her sitting on the bed. He tried to ignore the sound of her tears. Tried to ignore the fact that everything in him wanted to turn back around and fix this.

Never once in his entire life had he wished that he could go back in time. He had never wanted to be that helpless, downtrodden kid he'd once been. But right now he'd go back in a heartbeat. At least then fixing things with Meg would be simpler. Feelings would be simpler. There was nothing simple about anything to do with this. Not now. It was all just broken and shattered and complicated as hell. Impossible to fix.

He walked out without saying good-bye to Jim and Nancy, because he certainly didn't deserve any kindness from them. Not after what had happened. No, he didn't deserve a damn thing.

And that was the problem. Meg was offering him everything. And he knew that he just wasn't a man who could take it.

CHAPTER 10

Maybe it was a little bit of a cowardly thing to do, but Meg spent the rest of the night hiding in that old bedroom. One of the children Nancy and Jim had been caring for had left for college in September and it hadn't been filled yet, which worked out nicely for Meg, since she needed a place to burrow.

She cried for a while, lying across the bed, and then she got up, rifling through the collection of books that were still in the bedroom, finding one of her old favorites and settling down with it. She read "The Lady of Shalott" about four times, but mostly, she just overrelated to the feeling of being "a pale, pale corpse" floating down the river.

And then the door to the bedroom opened and she sat up to see Nancy coming on through.

"Well, that was more excitement than we've had in a while," she said, settling down on the edge of the bed next to Meg.

"I was so well behaved when I lived here, I thought maybe it was my time to make a splash?"

Nancy laughed softly. "Yes, you were always very well behaved, Meg. Sometimes a little bit too well behaved. It made me wonder if they had stolen the spark from you."

Meg frowned. "I don't think so. Or at least, not permanently."

"It's hard," Nancy said, her brown eyes earnest. "It's hard to move on from a childhood like that. I know it is. I've watched so many of you try. And a lot of you have succeeded. But not all. It's just not simple. Whatever it is, it's not simple or easy."

"I wish it was," Meg said. "I wish it was as easy as deciding not to feel something anymore. I don't want to. I don't want to have problems. I don't want . . . I don't want Noah to have them."

"But it's not that simple, is it?"

"He doesn't believe that I want him. Or, that's what he says. I think he's actually just scared. But it didn't go over well when I told him that."

Nancy's dark eyebrows shot up. "What? A man didn't like being told that he was scared?"

Meg laughed reluctantly, her heart feeling a little bit tender. "I know, right?"

"Noah has always been special. Serious. Hardworking. I've never met a boy so bound and determined to do the right thing. He wanted to be responsible. With everything that he had. He took a job right when he started living with us, and he worked faithfully at that job. I've never seen someone work so hard. And now he owns the ranch. I don't think there's a thing in the world that he takes lightly, least of all your affection."

Meg frowned. "You think he's afraid of hurting me?"

"I think so. I also think he's afraid of you hurting him, because he's human. And because you can only hit someone so many times before they start believing that everything is an attack. Before they don't trust a single thing."

Meg leaned forward, a tear sliding miserably down her cheek. "He can trust me."

"You ran after Charlie for all those years. In that whole time Noah looked at you as if the ground you walked on was pure gold. He's loved you since the beginning. And I think that his rejecting you now has nothing to do with not trusting you. It has everything to do with the fact that he doesn't know what to do with a good thing now that he has it." Nancy took Meg's hand. "How many good things has he had?"

"I want to be a good thing for him." Meg shook her head. "I love him. I really do. And I think I have for a long time. I just . . ."

She swallowed hard. "Do you think I was protecting myself? With Charlie?" She laughed. "I know that sounds ridiculous. I know it sounds really silly. But I was so upset when I came back from New York. When I caught Charlie . . . Well, he was with someone else. And I went straight to Noah. It didn't take long for . . ." She looked up at Nancy meaningfully.

Nancy lifted a hand. "I don't need details. I can figure it out."

"Anyway. It's just that I was hurt Charlie did that to me. But I wasn't devastated. I thought maybe I was. And I actually think I worked really hard at convincing myself I was. But ending up in Noah's arms was about the easiest thing I've ever done. And I don't think it would have been if what I felt for Charlie was really love. I think I took the substitute because I knew it would be easier to lose. Noah and I have only been together for a night, and already losing him is worse than anything I ever went through with my parents. I feel like part of myself got ripped out. I don't know what I'm supposed to do about that. What if . . . What if we can't work it out? What if we can't actually move past where we came from?"

"That's possible, Meg. I can't lie to you. Because the scars that both of you have go deep, and it's not the simplest thing in the world to erase all of that, I know. But look at you. You own a business; you're successful. You're strong. And even though I think you might be right, and you might have been protecting yourself to a degree, you also gave your affection easily. That's not a bad thing. For Noah, for Charlie . . . I always saw you as the glue that held all of you together. You were soft, and sweet, and you still smiled, and I think both of those boys were drawn to that. Noah . . . He's hard. He's a tough nut. But he comes here, every year. He's the truest, most faithful person. And he has proven it time and again. I think when push comes to shove, in the end, he'll be true to you. Like he always has been. He might have to go off and be scared for a while, and I can't say as I blame him. But you know his heart, Meg. You've watched him for years. You know who he is. He's not the kind of man who runs. At least, not forever."

Misery swamped Meg's chest as all of her old doubts, all of her own insecurities, rose up inside her like little monsters. "What if I'm the first thing he really runs from? What if I'm not important enough?"

"That's not the issue, Meg. You're too important. That's what scares him. Never worry that you aren't enough. You are now, and you always have been." Nancy leaned forward and pressed a kiss to Meg's forehead. "Take your time," Nancy said, standing up and getting ready to leave.

"Nancy," Meg asked, "would you mind if I stayed here tonight?"

Nancy smiled, the lines around her eyes growing deeper. "Of course you can stay. Have Christmas morning with all of us. Eat cinnamon rolls."

"I don't want to put you out."

"You never have. We love you. Be confident in that. Always."

Then Nancy turned and walked out the door, and Meg was left with a jumble of emotions rioting through her chest.

But the biggest one, the one that burned the brightest, was love. Even though Noah had left her hurt. Even though he had left her in many ways, she still loved him. She loved Nancy, and Jim, and the fact that even though fate had done its best to make sure she didn't have a family, she had ended up with one anyway. One that was better than blood. One that was all about choice. Choosing to have one another. To stick with one another. To love one another.

She lay back on the bed, and she was keenly aware of how empty it was. How funny, that she had only spent one night with Noah and yet it felt like it had been forever. It felt like it had been the only right thing, and it was gone.

"Merry Christmas Eve," she said to the ceiling.

Noah woke up on Christmas morning and decided that if he were in fact a grinch he would most definitely go around town and steal Christmas today. He wasn't feeling very festive. He wasn't feeling much of anything except grief that hit low and horrible every time he took a breath.

But it didn't really matter that it was Christmas. He had chores to do. That was one thing he liked about ranch life. The work never changed. Cows didn't care if it was a holiday. No. They just wanted to be fed.

He went outside and took a deep breath, watching as the cloud rose from his lips and disappeared into the snowy white morning.

He had Meg. For one night, he had held her in his arms. And then he had blown it all to hell.

No real surprise there.

She said that she loved him. And he knew that she thought she did. But it felt impossible. That she could finally want him. After all this time. That he could be anything to her but a consolation prize.

Does it matter if you are?

Part of him said no. It absolutely did not matter. As long as he had Meg, what the hell did he care? Except he did. That was the problem.

And why can't you accept the fact that you might be her choice?

Because it didn't fit together in his mind. It didn't fit with anything he knew about himself, didn't fit with everything he had been raised to believe.

He hadn't been the first choice for his own mother. Why would he be for Meg?

He gritted his teeth against the bitter cold and all of the emotions rising in his chest and walked down the porch, shuffling through the snow and heading out toward the barn.

He wasn't the kind of man who engendered deep emotions in other people. Not lasting ones. But he had this place. It was constant. It was his. Blood, sweat, and tears in this dirt. It was what made him a man. This piece of property that he had spent his entire adult life working toward.

What the hell did he need anything else for?

He kept on walking, and his foot hit a rock, making him stumble, his toe digging deep into the soft mud, scraping away the snow and revealing a deep trench of dirt. His dirt. His damned dirt.

He just stood there for a moment, staring at it. He had built his entire life here. On this place. On this ground. And he had convinced himself that it was everything. That it was all he needed.

He bent down, dropping his knee to the cold, frozen ground, the chill seeping through the denim of his pants. He picked up a handful of the mud in his gloved hand, squeezed it tight.

And he felt nothing. Absolutely nothing.

It was dirt. Just dirt. It didn't know that he owned it. And it didn't care.

He couldn't figure out why that made him feel dizzy. Why that made it hard to breathe.

Except the sudden realization that everything he had spent all this time working on might not matter so much was a pain that surpassed most things. Except losing Meg. That still hurt worse.

He had a pile of dirt and no woman. And just a week ago, he would have said that was how he liked it. That he was fine with it. With friendship between himself and Meg, and hookups on the side.

He wondered then if he brought her back here to stay, to live, if he made her his wife . . . Could that breathe life into this place? Could it breathe life into him?

He doubted it. He didn't think anything could.

He had spent too many years being batted around. Too many years having it proven to him, over and over again, that he was nothing. That he didn't matter.

And he was afraid. Damn it all, she was right. He was afraid. And he always had been. It was the real reason he had never gone after her. Because if he made her the center of his world any more than she already was, and he lost her, he had known that there would be no coming back from that.

He had allowed her feelings for Charlie to win. He had sat back and resented them all the while telling himself there was nothing he could do. He hadn't fought for the woman that . . . that he *loved*. Hadn't even spoken the words out loud to anybody because he couldn't say them to *her*. Because he was too scared of being rejected.

Because he had said them too many times to an unresponsive mother while she lay passed out on the bathroom floor. Had said them to her too many times while his face still throbbed from the beating delivered by one of her boyfriends.

And he had been afraid of what those words could mean, of the ways in which Meg could hurt him if he ever gave them to her.

So he had sat back like a coward and let another man hear them from her lips. Had nearly let that other man marry her.

But it had to stop. It just did. Because there was no point in protecting himself now. He was screwed. He hurt so badly every time he breathed, was so lonely he could scarcely stand himself. And he had just had the worst moment of clarity ever concerning the ranch and the fact that it was just unfeeling dirt. So there was not even any comfort to be found in that.

He had nothing to lose. And everything to gain.

The possibility of *everything* scared the living hell out of him.

Sitting here like this on his knees, in the snow, by himself scared him even more. And he supposed that was the thing.

He had to be more scared of life without her so that he could finally make the move. Could finally say the words.

And that really did underscore all the things she had said to him earlier. That sometimes things changed just enough for you to reevaluate everything you thought you knew.

He wasn't second to Charlie, any more than she was second to the ranch. He wasn't worthless any more than she wasn't worth the sacrifice.

He stood up, determined to finish his chores as quickly as possible. He had to get down into town. He had to find Meg.

Maybe it wasn't too late for the two of them to have a Merry Christmas after all.

CHAPTER 11

Meg was having the worst Christmas morning ever.

Well, the cinnamon rolls that Nancy had made were a decent enough bright spot, but still, as Christmas mornings went, it was pretty awful.

She had watched Nancy and Jim's current foster kids open their presents and had tried her very best to smile. And then she had gone back to Noah's old bedroom like a pathetic mole trying to hide beneath a pile of blankets.

She should go home. It was just that she had arranged for everything to be taken care of for her to be gone for this couple of days, so she didn't really feel any urgency. Same with the brewery. There really was no point in going in. Plus, it was closed today anyway.

Consequently, there was no good distraction for her heartbreak.

She was marinating in it. Which was somewhat therapeutic in a way. And if it didn't hurt quite so bad maybe she would even be interested in the contrast between losing Noah and losing Charlie.

She felt as if a rock had settled in her stomach. In the past couple of days she had lost both of her friends. But more than that, she had learned exactly what she wanted from a romantic relationship, taken a chance on it, and gotten it thrown back in her face.

Which was not fun. Not even a little bit.

There was a knock on the door and Meg groaned. She wasn't really in the mood to be social. Which, she supposed, meant she probably should have gone back home to her apartment, where she lived alone. Except she hadn't done that, she had stayed here, because she wanted to feel not so alone while she was being alone.

She didn't really see why that should be so difficult.

Meg got up slowly and went across the room, opening the door a crack. Only to see a package of cookies being shoved through the small opening.

Her heart clenched tight, her chest feeling like it might break. "If all you brought is cookies, then you can take them and shove them up your . . . Well."

"I'm leading with the cookies. I thought they might be a good peace offering." Noah's voice made her light-headed. She was so easy. Even when she was angry at him. It was strange. The veil had been ripped from before her eyes, forcing her to see Charlie as he really was. And she just couldn't go back to seeing him the way she used to. She didn't want to, either.

This was different. Noah hadn't betrayed her. He had hurt her, but she knew that he had hurt himself in the process. He hadn't done it because he was thoughtless. No. He was anything but thoughtless.

"I thought the cookies were a nice gesture, all things considered," he said.

She still didn't let him in.

"No. Cookies *were* a nice gesture when you didn't know me and you had nothing to be sorry for."

"I *am* sorry," he said, his voice rough.

"Sorry for what you said to me? Sorry for what you did to us? Or are you just sorry and you want to be friends?" She opened the door a crack, frowning deeply. "Or are you sorry and you think that I should sleep with you? Was that your plan? You thought that we could sleep together and be friends or something?"

"Can I come in instead of talking about sex in the hallway with impressionable youth potentially within earshot?"

She sighed and opened the door, letting him in. Then she closed it behind him. "Okay. Go ahead. Give me the cookies." She extended her hand.

"I thought the cookies were insufficient?"

"They are. But I want them and whatever else you have."

He handed her the package and she sniffed. "Chewy. Chewy chocolate chip cookies. Just like you like."

"Because they are the best."

"We all make choices, Meg."

"I'm sorry. Is there another choice to make?"

"Crunchy."

She let out an exasperated, "The wrong choice."

"The correct choice, I think you mean."

"You're already in danger of never being forgiven, so if I were you, I would tread very carefully on the subject of chocolate chip cookies."

Noah sighed heavily and pushed his hand through his dark hair, then ran it back down his face. "I don't actually care about cookies. I care about *you*." He took a step forward, wrapping his arm around her waist and drawing her up against his body. "I love you, Meg."

Her throat went dry, her eyes filling. "I figured you probably did," she said, feeling a little bit weak in the knees.

She reached up and touched his cheek, and it was hard to remember that before yesterday she hadn't ever done that. That these intimacies were new. Because they felt right. Because they felt essential.

These feelings for Noah weren't new. They were just uncovered.

And she was ready for them now. Was ready to embrace them and not hide from them. Not bury them beneath excuses and decisions that her fifteen-year-old self had made in all of her limited wisdom.

"I love you, too," she said.

She knew that he had more to say. That he had a grand speech all built up inside of him. At least, she assumed he did. But she didn't need to hear it to know that she loved him. To know that, in the end, that would be how she felt.

He didn't need to be perfect. He didn't need to say all the right things. He just needed to be here.

If there was one thing she knew about Noah, it was that he excelled at being there. At listening.

"I went back to my ranch expecting to feel...I don't know. Like I was complete. Because I had convinced myself that I was. Usually, I go out there and the ground feels alive. It didn't. This morning, it felt like a frozen block. And underneath that was dirt. Nothing but dirt. It didn't love me back. I've had a lot of years of not being loved back, Meg, so I thought that maybe I could handle it. But you...You made me hope."

She laughed, shaky, unsteady. "I'm sorry about that."

"Hope is a pretty damned amazing thing for a kid who can't remember what it's like. I feel like I was born old sometimes. Watching my mother suffer from drugs the way she did. Being a slave to all of her addictions—from heroin to men—I didn't know what hope looked like. But gradually, I began to see glimpses of it. And, in the end, I put all my hope in hard work. In dependability. In the land. And the great thing about the ranch is that you can pour yourself into it endlessly and it never goes away. There's always work to be done. It's that stability we keep talking about. Yeah, sometimes the weather fights back. Sometimes things don't go as planned. But in the end, it's not over unless you say it is."

He shook his head. "Caring about another person doesn't work that way," he said. "You can't control what they do. If you really love them, you shouldn't even want to. You should want them to be themselves. You should want their happiness above anything else. And I do. I do. But I also want you with me. I want it so bad it scares the hell out of me. It's not like anything else I've ever felt. It's been there, all this time. I knew I wanted you, but I didn't know it would be like this. I didn't know anything could be like this."

He angled his head and bent down, capturing her lips with his. Warmth flooded her. Warmth and hope. Love. She dropped the package of cookies and wrapped her arms around his neck, held on to him tightly, and kissed him. With everything she had.

"Noah," she whispered when they parted. "You were always there for me. You showed me what lasting friendship could be.

What faithfulness looks like. Our parents didn't give us a solid foundation, but I know that together we're going to build one. Something real."

"I believe it," he said, his voice rough. "The reason that I... that I couldn't... Meg, I was comfortable with the fact that I couldn't have you. It was a great place for me to be in. One where I had convinced myself there was nothing I could do. But hell, if I had been brave enough to fight for you, I sure as hell could have fought. If I had been ready for it, I would have. But I wasn't. I was hiding. Because I knew that what we would have together would be more than friendship. And it would be more than sex. I knew it would be everything, and I knew it would mean opening myself up. Really. And that..."

"I understand," she said. "I think I was doing the same. I set my sights on something impossible. On something that wouldn't break me. I convinced myself that I wanted Charlie for thirteen years, and when all of those plans went to hell I was wounded, but all I did was cry. When you rejected me after I had built up thoughts of a future with you for a full twenty-four hours—I felt like everything was broken inside of me. And that was what I had been avoiding."

He huffed out a laugh. "Me too. I guess I did a pretty bad job protecting us both."

"It doesn't matter," she said softly, going up on her tiptoes and brushing another kiss over his mouth. "We're strong enough to stand a little bit of pain. And anything worth having is certainly worth a fight. I'm just glad we both realized it before it was too late."

"I love you. I always have."

She held on to his face, stroked his beard with her thumbs. "Same."

"So what now?"

"You have to marry me," she said. "And have my babies and the whole nine yards. I don't want halfway. Not with you. Not ever. I want it all. And I don't want to wait."

She waited for him to turn tail and run. Or at least look nervous. But instead, he smiled. "I want that, too. Meg O'Neill, will you move out to my ranch with me and live in modest accommodations that will become increasingly crowded as we add to our family, and will probably be messy and loud for as long as we both shall live?"

She smiled. "I will."

"I love you," he said again. She would never get tired of hearing it.

"I love you, too," she said. "Forever."

"Merry Christmas, Meg."

"Merry Christmas, Noah."

EPILOGUE

Noah never missed Jim and Nancy's Christmas party. Not one year since he'd first come to live at their house all those years ago.

But tonight it was looking like he wasn't going to make it.

"Noah," Meg scolded. "You're going to have to slow down, because if you drift off the road, and I end up giving birth in a snowbank, I'm going to have to kick your ass. You know, once I recover."

"Well, I really don't want you kicking my ass," Noah said dryly, not making any effort to slow down. His wife was about to have a baby, on Christmas Eve, and calm wasn't on his list this year.

"Why do I get the feeling you aren't scared of me?" Meg said, sounding pouty.

"Because you're a marshmallow on a good day. And today you're an extremely round marshmallow having contractions."

"I am not a—owwwww."

Tension crept up Noah's spine, and he kept on driving until they got to St. Charles and pulled into the birthing center.

They got checked in pretty quickly, and what followed were the roughest few hours of Noah's life. Though he imagined if he said that to his wife he'd get punched.

Considering she was doing all the work.

But seeing Meg in pain hurt him; watching her struggle in any way hurt.

It all melted away when their daughter came into the world at midnight on a white Christmas, with the snow glittering outside.

Holly Carter was the prettiest baby he'd ever seen. One of the two miracles he'd experienced in his life.

The other miracle was that Meg loved him. And that was the miracle that had changed everything.

A nurse poked her head in after a soft courtesy knock, and Noah and Meg looked toward the door.

"You have visitors," the nurse said. "Should I send them away?"

Meg shook her head. "No. Let them come in."

It was Nancy and Jim, and a whole tray of cinnamon rolls. And, most surprising of all, they'd brought a bouquet of flowers from Charlie.

Noah and Meg's relationship with him wasn't quite what it had been, but . . . he was family. There was no way around it. And even with things strained as they'd been, the three of them cared for one another.

It struck Noah then, surrounded by these people, by his family, with his wife and daughter in the hospital bed, that he had more now than he'd ever thought possible when he was a child.

Young Noah had become a cynic far too soon. It had taken him years to unlearn his cynicism, to break down the walls. But it had been worth every risk.

He had spent so many years craving stability, craving control, but that had required him to close off his heart. His throat tightened, a wave of emotion overwhelming him.

He had lost all his control. But what he'd gained was so much better.

Love.

Meg looked down at their baby and kissed her fuzzy head. Then Meg looked back up at him. "It's Christmas, Noah," she murmured.

His heart expanded, and he thought his chest would burst.

"Yes, it is." He looked around the room, at all of the people. Living, breathing. So much more than that dirt he'd claimed as sacred ground so long ago. "Yes, it is."

Snowed In

Stacy Finz

CHAPTER 1

"At least he has jowls now," Rachel Johnson said to an empty kitchen as she stared at her phone, scanning a *California Lawyer* article about her ex. She was killing time before the oven bell rang on her signature sweet buns.

This had become her routine. Up before dawn so she could get into Tart Me Up and begin baking before her doors opened at seven o'clock sharp. That's when a line started forming, sometimes wrapping around the block, with anxious customers waiting for Rachel's made-from-scratch pastries and specialty sandwiches. And with Hanukkah behind them and Christmas just around the corner, she was swamped with special orders. Too busy to be reading about asshat Jeremy Banks. "Trial Lawyer of the Year," she harrumphed. "More like thieving scumbag of the year."

Her phone chimed with a text from Marcia, her former legal assistant who'd tipped her off to the story in the first place. "Well, did you read it yet?"

"Yep," she wrote back. "He's a troll."

"You don't know the half of it."

Unfortunately, she did. "Try to avoid working with him." A smart woman like Marcia was exactly the type Jeremy stole ideas from, then passed off as his own. Rachel knew how that worked firsthand. "Got to get back to my baking. Talk to you later."

"You made the right choice," Marcia texted, and signed off.

In her heart Rachel knew Marcia was right, but some days were a struggle. A few years ago, Rachel had left a major corporate law job with a six-figure salary to move to Glory Junction and open her own bakery. While she loved baking and the fulfillment of watching people's faces light up when they bit into one of her buttery buns or flaky croissants, she was working harder than ever and making a lot less money. It was an economy of scale thing. Even though she did a gangbuster business, there were only so many pastries she could make in her tiny kitchen. By the time she paid the rent, the utilities, and her employees, there wasn't a lot left over.

She needed to sell more and branch out into a full-service restaurant, but her small shop wouldn't accommodate the kind of production she had in mind. Not much in Glory Junction would, except the Old Watermill House. If things went as planned—fingers crossed—she'd turn the historic flour mill into a huge industrial kitchen where she could do all her baking, and still have room for a large restaurant specializing in rustic country cooking.

The oven dinged and she took out sheets of puffy cinnamon buns and slid new pans in with Danish. Around six-thirty, Samantha arrived and together they stocked the glass cases at the counter. Sam started the coffee and Rachel took the chairs off the tops of the tables in preparation for the rush. It was the same every morning and she'd found the ritual to be soothing, almost spiritual.

Feeding people felt good. A lot better than fighting with them in court. And the Sierra Nevada was breathtaking, especially this time of year when the snowy mountains were as white as her coconut frosting and the icicles on the tall pines shimmered like rock candy. Every winter, the Glory Junction Chamber of Commerce went all out with decorations. Ribbons, garland, wreaths, an enormous menorah, and a twenty-foot noble pine, decked out in colored balls and candy canes. Horse-drawn carriages, carrying tourists and skiers, clip-clopped up and down Main Street, like something out of an old-time movie.

Rachel loved it. The first time she'd come to Glory Junction was during the holidays to ski with her family, and even as a little girl she was awed by the majestic snowcapped mountains. So much so that it had been the first place she'd looked when scouting out a location for her bakery—and new life.

"We good to go?" she asked Samantha as the first customers began cuing up outside the door.

"Everything is in readiness."

Rachel didn't know what she'd do without her young assistant, though lately she'd been riding her to go to college. Sam had taken a gap year after graduating from Glory Junction High School, but the break appeared to be turning into a permanent situation. And Sam had too much potential. . . . Ah, jeez, Rachel told herself to stop acting like one of her parents. Leave the girl be. Sam had to find her own way in the world. Rachel, after all, had gone to college and law school and had spent five dog-eat-dog years in the corporate world only to realize it wasn't the life for her.

She unlocked the door and turned the sign to "Open." A few seconds later, the bakery filled with customers. Last year, she'd installed a ticket machine to keep people from fighting over who was next.

Boden Farmer tracked in snow with those stupid biker boots of his, took a number, and leaned against the wall. He'd just gotten an Italian coffee machine delivered to his bar, Old Glory, which Rachel fervently hoped didn't cut into her business. Why a place that served chicken wings, burgers, and fries needed an industrial espresso machine was beyond her.

He bobbed his chin at her in greeting, then folded his arms over his massive chest. She waved back just to be polite. It was no secret they didn't like each other. She'd tried, she really had, but the man was difficult. Bossy and way too sure of himself. They did a lot of catering around town and he was such a control freak. He also thought he was the sexiest man alive, which he most assuredly wasn't. Not even close.

"Hey, Rach. How's life treating you?" Colt Garner stepped up to the case and pointed to the ham and cheese croissants. "I'll take two of those."

"Sure." Unlike Boden, the police chief was the sexiest man alive. Unfortunately, he was also taken, married to Glory Junction's resident celebrity fashion designer. "Let me heat those for you."

"Thanks. And a cup of coffee, too, please."

"Coming right up."

The chief joined Boden at the wall while he waited. The two men were friends, both craft-beer connoisseurs. Rachel heated the sandwiches, poured Colt his cup of coffee, and got him out the door in record time. Having a town to keep safe, the chief was usually in a hurry.

Boden not so much.

Rachel noted he had his usual gaggle of groupies around him. She supposed in a town this small it didn't take much to be The Bachelor.

"Hot barkeep at ten o'clock," Sam whispered as she perfected an angel on the top of Benjamin Schuster's latte.

"Not you too?"

Samantha made a growling noise and Rachel rolled her eyes. "He's way too old for you."

"I've got daddy issues."

Rachel shook her head. "We're both going to have financial issues if he uses that new Illy to start serving breakfast."

"Old Glory's a gastro pub, Rach. I don't think breakfast is Boden's jam, but even if it is, you have him hands down in the baked goods department. Besides, you've got Oprah's endorsement and that's freaking gold, girl."

Somehow Tart Me Up had made Oprah Winfrey's list of Favorite Things. The day the list came out, people from all over California trekked up the mountain for a taste of Rachel's pastries. Many were still coming, which made her even more anxious to open a second location with a full restaurant. She wanted to strike while the iron was hot.

Boden sauntered up to the counter when his number was called and perused the glass case. "What's good today?"

"Everything," Rachel said, trying to sound congenial. "What are you in the mood for?"

He lifted his eyes from the case, met her gaze, and broke into a slow grin. "Something sweet."

Not sure if he was taking a swipe at her, she pretended to contemplate a recommendation. "Then I'd go with a cinnamon bun."

"Cinnamon bun it is, then. And a cup of that fine Colombian." She arched a brow. "Your new coffee machine on the fritz?"

"It's working." Apparently, he wasn't going to give her any insight into his future coffee plans. Coffee was good business. Thanks to Starbucks, customers were used to paying upwards of three bucks a cup. The profit margin on that was phenomenal, much better than that on baked goods.

"I heard you got the Canadell wedding," he said.

"Yep. Are you doing the bar?"

"Uh-huh."

Great, Christmas Eve with Boden Farmer. Good times. "Nice couple," she said, trying to speed things along. There was a backlog of customers on the street and it was cold outside. The forecast said snow. But the usually aloof Boden was in a chatty mood.

"Real nice and that house they have . . ." He let out a low whistle.

It was indeed pretty amazing and the kitchen was a caterer's dream. The house was secluded, though, and the road was rough, not ideal for getting all her equipment up there. But for what the Canadells were paying she'd rent a snowcat if she had to.

"It should be a lovely affair." She slid the bag with Boden's cinnamon roll at him and handed him his coffee.

"You think you could stop by Old Glory after you close up so we could go over a few things?"

What was there to go over? She was in charge of the food; he was in charge of the booze. But that was Boden, always trying to take charge. It wasn't as if she didn't know what she was doing. She'd gotten her start in the hospitality industry, catering—much to her parents' chagrin.

"Three years at Stanford Law and you're ladling soup for a living," her father would say when she left the law for culinary school. "If you don't like working on the legal team for Dole, then work somewhere else. But for God's sake, Rachel, food service?" Dole was one of the largest produce companies in the world. But her father, a Ninth Circuit appellate court judge, didn't get the irony.

Boden stood there, tapping his toe. Because she didn't have time to argue with him she agreed and observed as every female head turned to watch him walk out the door.

"That's some prime USDA beef right there," Rita Tucker said, and broke into a three-pack-a-day cough.

"Good morning, Mayor. What can I get you?"

"I'll have one of those sweet buns you're so famous for and a cup of joe."

"You got it." Rachel threw a complimentary oatmeal cookie in the bag. It didn't hurt to butter up the mayor, who along with the city council held Rachel's future in their collective hands.

Glory Junction owned the Old Watermill House and the city got to choose which business to award the lease to. With its prime location—downtown, right on the Glory Junction River—and abundance of charm and space, Rachel wouldn't be the only one vying for the property.

Breakfast faded into lunch and when Rachel finally came up for air it was closing time. She and Sam cleaned, took out the trash, and wrapped up what little was left over in the cases to donate to a local church that fed the homeless.

"I'll lock up if you'll drop these off." Rachel nudged her head at the church offerings. "Then you can go get your Christmas shopping done."

"You're sure?"

"Of course. You're the best employee I have; I don't want you quitting on me."

"Even if I go to school?"

"That's a different story." Rachel studied Samantha for a second. "SF State in the fall?"

Sam shrugged. "I was thinking CalArts."

What a peculiar choice, Rachel thought. In the year Sam had been working at the bakery, she'd never mentioned an interest in the arts. Then Rachel remembered the drawings. On the rare occasions when things got slow, Sam would sketch. On a napkin, a coffee cup, the kitchen chalkboard, her iPhone, pretty much any blank surface she could find.

"That's fantastic," Rachel said, and kissed the top of Samantha's head, which happened to be fuchsia today. The kid changed hair color as often as Rachel changed socks. "Good for you. Have you already applied?"

Sam shook her head.

"Should we work on that?"

"Maybe." Sam's expression lost some of its earlier enthusiasm and Rachel wondered if she feared she wouldn't get in. Rachel knew it was a competitive school. "Not tonight, though."

"Not tonight but maybe tomorrow, yes?" She didn't want to push, but the spark in Sam at the mere mention of CalArts was inspiring. Rachel wished someone had fostered her interests when she was a girl. Rachel's parents—her mother was also a lawyer—had always operated on the assumption that she'd follow in their footsteps. And then it became the expectation.

"We'll see," Sam said, and grabbed her backpack. "See you tomorrow."

Before she left, Rachel lined her bowls of bread dough on the kitchen counter to rise, locked the cash drawer in the safe, and turned on the alarm. It was even colder than when she'd arrived at four in the morning. She could feel it in her bones that more snow was on the way. And though it was barely six it was already dark. Despite the frigid temperature, she walked to Old Glory. It was only a block away and she wanted to take in the decorations along Main Street. The Christmas lights flickered on, illuminating downtown in a magical glow. She huddled deeper into her down coat and tried to avoid the berms of snow that had been plowed against the curbs by the street cleaners.

For mid-week, there was still plenty of people milling around the storefronts. She supposed they were down from Glory Junction's five ski resorts to eat or shop. Even this late in the day, she could see the gondolas and lifts going up and down the mountainsides.

Felix, the owner of the Morning Glory diner, was clearing his walkway and she made her way across the road to say hello.

"How's business?"

"So good I need more help." Felix was notorious for losing employees. He had a reputation as being surly, but Rachel thought it was a lot of bluster. Underneath the surface, he was a sweetheart. "How 'bout you?"

"Crazy busy and bursting at the seams." As soon as the words left her mouth, Rachel wished she hadn't said them. While she didn't think Felix was competing for the Old Watermill House, she didn't know for sure. His diner was wildly popular, and he might be looking to expand.

"You need a bigger space."

She wondered if he was fishing for information. The mill house had been a major topic of conversation lately, a lot of it focused on who would take it over. For more than a decade the dilapidated building had sat empty. But as Glory Junction's economy had begun to rebound from the recession, the city, realizing it had a gold mine on its hands, had rehabbed the historical structure. They were taking business proposals in two days.

She studied him for a second and quickly dismissed the idea. Felix was a straight shooter. If he was interested in the Old Watermill House, he would say so.

"I do indeed," she said, and left it at that.

Besides Samantha, no one knew she was making a pitch for the place. She had learned from Jeremy that loose lips sink career ships and she wanted the venue so badly she could taste it, even if it took every dime she had to cover new equipment, tables, chairs, and a staff. That's why she took on catering jobs. "See you around, Felix."

She headed to Old Glory and grabbed a seat at the bar. Boden was at the other end, flirting with two female patrons Rachel had never seen before. Tourists, she assumed. She took the opportunity to check him out and see what all the female hoopla was about. He wasn't what she would call classically handsome, though objectively speaking she could see his appeal if you liked bad-boy types. He was rugged and a little rough around the edges, with a slightly crooked nose that looked as if it might have been broken a time or two. Dark piratical eyes made him seem a little shady or dangerous and he had uneven facial features. "Raw" was the best way to describe him.

With him leaning over the bar she got a good look at his backside. Nothing to complain about there. The mayor's words rang in her ears. "Prime USDA beef." She mentally slapped herself for objectifying someone like that. It was awful, but the man did have a very nice body. Tall, at least six-two, broad, and extremely toned, like he could handle himself in a bar fight. The very notion made Rachel shudder with distaste.

"Hey, Rach. What can I get you?" Ingrid, one of Boden's bartenders, asked.

Rachel wasn't much of a drinker and glanced behind the bar to consider her options. Old Glory was known for its vast selection of craft beers and when in Rome . . . "How about an IPA?"

Ingrid laughed. "We've got a lot of them, but since the boss is buying, you should go with a Pliny the Younger."

Rachel slid a sideways glance at Boden. She hadn't realized he knew she was here. The man must have eyes in the back of his head. She flinched at the possibility that he'd caught her checking out his ass. "Why?"

"First and foremost, it's really good. But it's also hard to get. The bulk of it is only sold through the brewery in Santa Rosa. Boden has an in with the owners."

"Oh, well, in that case I'll try it." Because she'd taken a pastry path in culinary school she wasn't as up on craft beer or even wine as she should be, but she liked to keep informed. "Thanks, Ingrid."

Ingrid returned with a pint glass a few minutes later, and just as Rachel was taking a taste Boden sauntered over.

"You like it?"

"It's nice . . . hoppy," which, duh, weren't all beers hoppy? It's just that this one seemed particularly so.

"Good palate." He leaned over the bar like he'd done with the other women. "That's because there's triple the hops as a standard IPA."

"It's lovely." She lifted the glass in a salute.

"Yes, it is." He grinned, and she noted that he had very white, straight teeth, which somehow seemed incongruous with the rest of him. "It's loud in here. Why don't we go back to my office?"

"All right."

He picked up her beer, held the end of the bar door up for her, and ushered her through the kitchen. She'd never seen it before and took her time to have a look around. It was laid out efficiently with the range, oven, fryer, and griddle neatly arranged in stations. There was a prep area and a small section for expediting.

His office, like the rest of the bar, was covered in American flags. An old leather love seat sat kitty-corner to an oak desk, cluttered with paperwork. Behind it hung a portrait of an older man in a military uniform.

"Your father?" she asked.

"Nope." He turned to stare at the photograph. "But he should've been."

Rachel waited for him to elaborate, but he didn't, her cue to mind her own business. He motioned for her to take the chair facing the desk and he sat behind it, placing her beer down.

"I just wanted to talk about the setup Saturday." He leaned back and she mentally prepared herself for a mansplaining session. "In addition to a host bar, the couple wants us to pass out glasses of Champagne throughout the evening. I don't have staff for that and was wondering if I could borrow a few of your servers. Of course, I'd compensate them . . . or you . . . however you want to work it."

She thought about it. What he was proposing was perfectly reasonable. But because the wedding was Christmas Eve, she was short staffed. Most of her servers were locals who moonlighted to make a few extra bucks but wanted to stay home with their families for the holiday. "Honestly, I don't know if I can spare anyone. It's a skeleton crew to begin with. You can't hire a couple of your bartenders?"

"We're open that night and I need whoever is willing to work, here."

"Is there any chance you could talk the couple into setting up a Champagne station? That way we'd only need one pourer, two at most."

He let out a breath. "I sort of promised."

She knew how that went. The last thing you wanted to do was tell a nervous bride that the caterer was changing her vision of the perfect wedding. "Maybe Foster knows a few people who can do it."

The florist had grown up in Glory Junction, knew everyone in town, and was tapped in at the ski resorts. There was bound to be someone at one of the hotels looking for holiday work.

"Already asked," Boden said.

She contemplated how she could help, even though a part of her brain whispered, *This isn't my problem.* Because the last time she'd been collegial and helped a "friend" he ran off with her job.

And now, wouldn't you know it, he was Lawyer of the freaking Year.

CHAPTER 2

Rachel Johnson was a difficult woman to read. Everyone knew she was a former blue-chip lawyer from San Francisco and that her parents were hotshot legal eagles. Other than that, Boden knew very little about her. Maybe because she rarely gave him the time of day and when they worked catering gigs together she spent most of the night trying to call the shots: telling him where to set up his bar, when to prepare for the toast, and generally dictating how he should do his job.

It annoyed the crap out of him. He'd been bartending since he was twenty-one, fourteen years. He didn't need anyone giving him pointers. But it was a small town and a tight-knit community, so it didn't pay to alienate anyone, especially the town sweetheart. Oddly enough, no one besides him thought Rachel was a first-class snob. The whole town loved her and her sticky buns, which he thought were just okay. A little too sweet.

Now her real buns . . . well, they were better than just okay. But that was territory he didn't want to get into. The truth was he found her very attractive. Kind of a soap commercial model with that peaches and cream skin of hers. Jennifer Aniston with brown eyes. He'd always had a thing for the actress. But even a big Hollywood star seemed more accessible than Rachel Johnson.

"Look, don't worry about it," he said. "I'll figure something out."

She was already getting out of her chair. "Worse comes to worst, you can always resort to the pouring station. Everything will be so hectic the bride and groom probably won't notice."

"Yep." Except he liked to keep his promises.

"Thanks for the beer."

"Don't mention it." He walked her through the kitchen back to the bar, which was quickly filling up. On Wednesdays, he did a hump-day happy hour with cheap drinks and snacks. It was mostly for the locals, who were starting to get priced out of the restaurants in town with all the ski resort business. He didn't want to see that happen.

He noticed a couple of guys standing in the corner, giving Rachel the once-over. They looked like they were up from San Francisco or Los Angeles. Expensive haircuts, shiny North Face jackets, and he could smell their cologne over the spilled beer and fried food.

"Where is it?"

He looked at her. "Where is what?"

"The new Illy?"

He laughed. "You covet my coffee machine, don't you?"

She shrugged. "A little bit, yeah."

He laughed again, then flipped up his brows. "You want to touch it?"

She rolled her eyes. "Seriously, why do you need an industrial coffeemaker?"

Good question. His specialty was craft beer. There were nearly forty on tap now. But the après-ski crowd, like the dudes in the corner, wanted their hot drinks. Irish coffees, espresso martinis, morning roosters. They were a pain in the ass to make, but the markup was good.

Just to play with her he said, "I'm thinking of opening the place for breakfast. I do a killer Hangtown Fry."

For a minute her face fell; then she realized he was messing with her. "What do you really plan to do with it?"

"Drinks." He nudged his head at the city dudes. "They like the girly stuff."

"That's sexist," she said with that imperial way of hers that never failed to annoy him. But she also seemed relieved.

"I was kidding, Rachel. It was a joke." The woman really was a cold fish.

She scanned the back of the bar. "Why don't you have it out?"

Jeez, what did she think, he was selling black-market coffee in the back? Humorless and distrustful. What a combo. The truth was he hadn't even taken it out of the box yet. "I've got to figure out where to put it." Old Glory was getting a little cramped, but not for long. When he got his brewery up and running he'd have extra space for equipment and to store the surplus booze he used for catering gigs.

Boden looked up as two young women pressed against the bar, trying to get Ingrid's attention. If they were twenty-one he was eighty. "Hang on a sec." He grabbed Rachel a stool at the bar and went to check the girls' IDs.

When he came back, one of the city guys had cozied up to Rachel and was talking to her. Boden figured he'd be her type. He had Ivy League tattooed on his forehead. Boden had never made it past high school, unless he included the business and craft-beer courses he'd taken at a community college when he'd lived in Oceanside.

She broke her conversation with frat boy and turned to Boden. "Is everything okay?"

"Yeah. Kids up on their winter break to ski and think we don't card here in the boondocks."

She followed his gaze toward the girls, who he'd comped a couple of Cokes and were now engaged in a game of darts with a few local guys. Since he served food, Old Glory was open to all ages, which sometimes made it difficult to determine who was legal to drink and who wasn't. Over the years, Boden had acquired a knack for it. Besides the fact that it was a hefty fine if the ABC caught you, he was dead set against serving alcohol to minors.

"I better get going." She slung the strap of her handbag over her shoulder and frat boy's face fell.

"See you Saturday night." Boden would probably see her as soon as tomorrow when he went into the bakery to get his morning fix. But he said it just to get a rise out of her buddy. "I'll walk you out."

A gust of wind slapped him as he opened the door. "Looks like a storm's moving in. Take it easy driving." He knew she lived in a town house not far from one of the resorts. That's the kind of town it was; everyone knew everyone else's address.

She looked up at the moonless sky and said, "You too," and smiled because he lived on top of the bar, another thing he was going to change when he opened the brewery.

And then he just stood there, coatless, with his hands jammed in the pockets of his jeans, basking in Rachel Johnson's smile, a smile that was a little like sunshine, even though everything else about her was dead of winter.

He watched her walk away, then forced himself to go inside to work on his proposal for the Old Watermill House. It still needed a few tweaks before the Friday deadline. He was pretty sure he had the advantage, though he didn't know who his competition was yet. But the mayor and council members were basing their decision on revenue for the city. Seemed like a brewery would be a slam dunk. Besides making beer, he planned to have a taproom with a full-service restaurant. The Old Watermill House was big enough for all that and then some. With incredible views of the river and plans for an exhibition brewing area, the place would appeal to locals and tourists alike.

Boden looked up at the picture of Gunny that hung over his desk. If it hadn't been for him, Old Glory never would've been possible. But it wasn't the full dream and Boden owed it to the man, his mentor and the only one who'd ever given a shit about him, to see it realized, even if Gunny couldn't.

Screw cancer!

"This is for you, old man. We're gonna do it."

Twenty-two years ago, Jake Hornsby, aka Gunny, came into Boden's life through the revolving door his mother had for boyfriends. True to form, Desiree Farmer quickly tired of Gunny. But Gunny lived just down the block and kept an eye on Boden. The marine gunnery sergeant had a knack for keeping young men in line and Lord knew Boden needed a firm hand. At fourteen he'd already heisted his first car and by fifteen he faced time in juvenile hall. Gunny swooped in, vouched for Boden in court, and for the most part, took over raising him.

In Gunny's garage, Boden learned how to brew beer. He wasn't yet old enough to drink it, but brewing was something they did together, a way for Gunny to keep him off the street. And Gunny was the quintessential beer hobbyist. He read articles about how to perfect his home brew, bought every gadget and every piece of amateur beer-making equipment known to mankind, and spent hours playing with recipes. They were like chemists in a laboratory. Gunny would blast classic rock on a boom box and tell stories about Desert Storm.

When Gunny retired from the military he opened a small pub near Camp Pendleton where his marine buddies could hang out. Boden used to help the pub's short-order cook on the weekends and after graduating from high school worked there full-time. But Gunny's real dream was to open a small brewery. The plan was for Boden to get an associate's degree in business, then partner with Gunny. But then Gunny got prostate cancer and their only plan was to get him well. After two years of fighting, the big "C" won. Gunny left the pub and all his worldly possessions to Boden with the caveat that he sell the place, get an education, and launch his life somewhere else. Boden did sell the bar, took the money, went north, and opened Old Glory in homage to Gunny.

He covered it in American flags and served the best local craft brews he could find to memorialize the best man he ever knew. The US of A and good beer were the two things Gunny loved most in this world. All that was missing was the brewery component, and Boden planned to move heaven and earth to make it happen.

"Hey." Ingrid poked her head inside his office. "I'm taking my break. Cassie's covering me."

Boden got to his feet. "I'll back her up."

The place was busier than before, with a crowd standing shoulder to shoulder at the bar. The hump-night specials lured 'em in. All four Garner brothers were at their usual table and Boden waved. Colt Garner, the eldest, had voiced interest in being a silent investor in the brewery. Like Boden, he was a craft-beer nut. There were a few others who'd also said they'd like to sign on to the project. The extra capital would come in handy to make all the improvements Boden had in mind for the mill house, including a killer apartment on-site. In the meantime, he'd been taking catering gigs to add to the kitty.

TJ Garner managed to squeeze in at the end of the bar. "It's crowded tonight," he shouted over the noise and jukebox. "I need a refill on whatever Colt got."

Boden filled a pitcher. Most craft-beer joints only did pints, but the locals would riot if he got that high-assed about it. So he kept a few inexpensive brews on tap that he could serve in pitchers.

"How you guys doing? I'm guessing business is good." The Garners owned an adventure company, and with all the snow they'd been getting, their ski tours must've been booked solid.

"We've been busy, that's for sure. You coming to the open house Christmas Eve?" Every year, Garner Adventure threw a big party at their office building down the street.

"I'm doing the bar for the Canadells' wedding."

"It's the niece, right?" There were a bunch of Canadells in Glory Junction. The bride's aunt and uncle were the only full-timers, though. They ran an insurance company in town. "I hear her parents own quite the vacation home up in the mountains."

"Yep. I went up there a few weeks ago to scope it out. The place is off the hook. Where do people get that kind of money?"

TJ laughed. "Sorry you'll miss the GA party. One of us will be over in the afternoon to pick up the kegs. That work?"

"Hey, this is a full-service operation. I'll deliver them before I head up the mountain."

"Thanks, Boden." TJ took his pitcher. "Catch you later."

Boden finished out the night behind the bar. Despite the crowd, everyone was fairly low-key. No fights, no broken barware, no drama. Someone kept feeding quarters into the jukebox, playing Christmas songs. Without Gunny, the holidays were tough on Boden. A loner by nature, he wasn't big on most celebrations. But Christmas . . . well, it had a way of bringing out the lonely.

More than likely Desiree was snugged up with one of her biker boyfriends somewhere. Boden had lost count of her men and had frankly stopped caring a long time ago. It was her life to spend it any way she wanted, so long as it wasn't with him.

At two, he hollered last call to the handful of stragglers and began mopping up. Then he returned to his office to work on the proposal but fell asleep at his desk. By the time he dragged his ass upstairs to his apartment, he was dead on his feet.

The next morning, he was up by eight, ready to do it all over again. He thought about having breakfast at the Morning Glory but nixed the idea for Tart Me Up instead. He told himself he liked the coffee better, but the truth was he wanted his Rachel fix. His napalm in the morning. She was definitely too toxic for a steady diet, but it didn't mean a guy didn't like to play with fire every now and again.

He waited five minutes for the water to get hot—pipes that probably dated back to the Gold Rush—before jumping into the shower and taking a quick one. He wanted to get the paperwork for the Old Watermill House in order before he opened for lunch.

As usual the bakery was packed. Rachel worked the front counter with Sam and another kid Boden didn't know. He rested his hip against the wall, waiting for his number to be called. By the time they got to him, the crowd had thinned and it looked as if the rush was waning.

"Morning," he said to Rachel, noticing her curves even through the white apron. "I'll have an egg croissant and some caffeine." She started to pour his coffee into a to-go cup and he stopped her. "For here." May as well, now that there were tables available. If he took it to go everything would be cold when he got to Old Glory. It was snowing. Nothing heavy but enough that he'd bundled up.

He picked a table near the counter and Rachel brought him his breakfast sandwich and coffee. She had flour in her hair and a little on her chin.

"Take a load off." He motioned to the chair across from him at the bistro table.

"I've got rolls in the oven I have to check on." She made small talk with all the other customers but never with him. Maybe he looked like the Big Bad Wolf.

"What's that?" Poking out of her apron pocket was the top of a form that looked suspiciously like the front page of the application for the Old Watermill House. "You bidding on the mill house?"

Her face turned red and Boden had his answer. He'd known he'd have competition, but the space seemed too large for a bakery, unless she wanted to start selling to supermarkets and restaurants and needed a commissary kitchen.

"Why? Are you?"

He'd only told Ingrid and the group of possible investors, not wanting to advertise his future plans until the place was his. But he didn't want to lie, either. "Yup. For a brewery and taproom with a restaurant. What's your proposal?"

Her face had instantly gone from sunny to dark. "I'm still up in the air with exactly what I want to do." Which Boden knew was a polite way of saying, "It's none of your damn business."

"Right," he said, wondering why she was being so secretive. By tomorrow all the applicants would be going before the council, and although the pitches were being made in private, in a town like Glory Junction it would take, oh, about five seconds for word to spread.

"I've got to get back to the kitchen." She turned and walked away.

He watched that very fine ass of hers disappear behind the counter and remembered why he disliked her so much.

CHAPTER 3

Rachel thought her presentation before the council went well. Better than well. She'd nailed it. All those years as a litigator had trained her to make an eloquent and compelling case, though she preferred the tranquility of her kitchen to the combativeness of a courtroom.

As she'd laid out her proposal, she saw Rita Tucker, the mayor, and a couple of the council members nodding their heads. They particularly liked the fact that Rachel would be keeping her Main Street bakery in addition to the full-service restaurant.

But where she really had them was with her revenue projections. If everything went as planned, the project would be quite lucrative. More so than a knitting store, which she knew firsthand was Hattie Taylor's proposal. Hattie already owned the Yarn Barn in the Starbucks strip mall and wanted to expand to a larger space where she could give classes and open a small store with locally made sweaters, afghans, and other knitted items. It was a great idea and Hattie was a doll, but half the time her sweet little shop was empty.

Boden was Rachel's fiercest opponent. Not only was Old Glory wildly popular—and she was guessing just as profitable—but also the entire town fawned over him. Her biggest hope was that the city council didn't want another bar in Glory Junction. It was a distinct possibility. Between Old Glory and the resort hotels there were a number of places for people to get their drink on and then drive on the windy, mountainous roads. A potentially deadly mixture and with any luck a major justification for the city to choose her over him.

Her thoughts must've conjured him, because on the way out of city hall she nearly collided with Boden.

"Sorry, I was looking at my phone." He nudged his head at the council chambers. "You make your pitch?"

"As a matter of fact, I did," she said, noticing that he'd worn a tie. She'd never seen him in anything other than jeans, a flannel shirt, and biker boots. In the summer he wore T-shirts that stretched across his wide chest, showed off a pair of bulging biceps and a tattoo of a beer-filled stein. The knot was a little crooked and she itched to straighten it.

"How'd it go?"

"Great," she said with confidence.

"What did they ask you?"

The last thing she wanted to do was give anything away. She and Boden were competitors after all. She was always on her guard for the snake in the grass, posing as a charming suitor. Fool me once, shame on you. Fool me twice . . . "You haven't gone yet?"

"Nope, I'm up in ten minutes." He held up a folder, which must've been his presentation.

She'd used a PowerPoint. More professional.

"I've never seen you dress like that." He waved his hand over her suit, a leftover from her lawyer days. "Sharp." His mouth curled up when he said it, leading her to believe that he thought just the opposite.

Not that she cared.

"You too. Nice tie." A little fatter than what was in style. And crooked.

"Thanks. It's my good-luck tie." He flashed a cocky grin. "Want to have a drink tonight to celebrate?"

Was he trying to get her goat because he thought he had this in the bag? "Seems premature, don't you think? They're not announcing the winning bid until after Christmas."

"I just meant celebrating that it's over. I don't know about you, but my proposal took a lot of effort and planning."

"Mine too," she said, and even to her own ears it sounded defensive. Even bitchy. At the same time, she didn't want to be a pushover. Not with Boden, who was starting to raise her hackles. Too friendly. Too agreeable. Asking her out for drinks. What was next? Sleeping with her, then stealing her job, or in this case her real estate? "Maybe another time. I've got a long night ahead of me, prepping for the wedding. And I'm leaving first thing Christmas morning to go to my folks'."

"Roger that. I just figured at some point you'd take a break and we could toast each other. No worries. I'll see you tomorrow, then." He started to walk away.

"Did you get anyone to help pass the Champagne?"

"Yep, I'm good." He tapped on his watch. "I better get going."

"Uh-huh. Good luck," she said because it seemed rude not to.

Rachel took Main Street back to the bakery, where Sam was running the store while she was away. She had three other employees, including two high school kids who helped on the weekends. But for the most part, she did all the baking herself. When she got the Old Watermill House she planned to hire a few full-time bakers so she could focus more on running the two businesses. Not that she would ever give up being in the kitchen entirely. She loved it too much to quit. And in a warped sort of way she had Jeremy to thank for that.

When he got the chief counsel job at Dole—the one that was supposed to be hers—it forced her to reevaluate her life. That's when she decided it was time to *follow her bliss*. And here she was, taking the next step. It was a huge investment, but her heart told her it was worth it.

Rachel pulled her coat tighter, dodging patches of snow on the sidewalk in her high heels. The wind howled and the sky had turned dark, even though it wasn't even noon yet. The idea of lugging food and all her catering equipment to the Canadell house in this weather was daunting. But the gig paid well and would help toward her mill house project.

Boden had sure come on confident that he'd won the bid. Wasn't that just like him? Always so self-assured. She did have to admit that he looked good in a necktie, even if he couldn't pull off a Windsor knot to save his life. He'd also shaved. She didn't think she'd ever seen him before without a layer of scruff or at least a shadow. Either way, he had an arresting face; Rachel would give him that.

She wondered what his drink invitation was about. He'd never shown a romantic interest in her before. In fact, he'd always been cordial but standoffish where she was concerned. This sudden desire to have drinks seemed more like an opportunity for him to gather intel since they were competing for the same space. Or maybe Jeremy had her overanalyzing every exchange with a man because the decision was now up to the council.

It didn't really matter, because there would be no drinks. Boden wasn't for her, nor was she for him. The next time she got involved with a man, they would be on totally different career tracks. A doctor, a plumber, a certified public accountant, anything but a lawyer or someone in the restaurant industry.

By the time she got inside the bakery, her toes were frozen. She quickly popped into her tiny office and exchanged her high heels for a pair of warm socks and clogs. Sam had turned on the Christmas playlist Rachel had compiled, and the music sent a rush of warmth through her. She loved the holidays. The food, the cheer, the decorations, just everything about it.

Sam stuck her head inside. "We've already run out of pumpkin spice muffins."

"I'll bake another batch."

"How did it go?"

"Good . . . I think. Boden was going in as I was coming out."

"You'll get it over him," Sam said, and cocked a brow. "I'd be happy to console him when the city makes the announcement. We can get a room somewhere and I'll—"

"Stop it. Find yourself a nice young man." What was everyone's obsession with Boden Farmer? "What makes you so sure?"

"You've got Oprah on your side. No one would dare go up against Oprah."

Rachel laughed. She'd gotten a lot of mileage out of that silly list but doubted it held weight as far as the city was concerned. She'd done the best she could do; now it was out of her hands. "We'll see. I just have to be patient and wait," which wouldn't be easy. She'd never been good at relinquishing control.

"Besides the muffins, anything else I should know about?"

Sam shook her head. "Not that I can think of . . . oh, your bride called. She's freaking out about the weather. Says the forecast is predicting a storm."

"That was the chance she took by scheduling her wedding this time of year. I'll call her . . . calm her down. We'll probably get a good dump of snow, but the county will clear the roads." It was a ski resort town. Life went on regardless of stormy weather.

"I'll go ahead and start preparing for the lunch onslaught," Samantha said. "And FYI: There's also been a run on gingerbread scones. You may want to make more of those, too."

Customers were buying them by the dozen to take home.

"I'm on it." Rachel headed to the kitchen, planning to call her nervous bride as soon as she got the muffins in the oven and her scone batter started.

Outside, she could see a flurry of white. Small flakes had started falling and with the streetlights draped in garland it felt like she was looking into a snow globe. She took a second to take it all in and sighed with delight. Glory Junction was prettier than a Christmas card.

Ten minutes later the rush started, and by the time Rachel stopped to take a breather it was four o'clock. Pretty soon, a new crop of people would flood the bakery before closing to pick up special orders and take advantage of Rachel's nearly day-old half-off sale. There wasn't a whole lot left in the cases.

She had just enough time to call back her bride and then start the prep for tomorrow's big wedding. It was going to be a long night. Boden's drink offer floated through her head and she realized she hadn't eaten since breakfast. Rachael grabbed the last of her freshly baked pumpkin spice muffins and a cup of coffee and took them with her to her office. Nibbling, she dialed the phone.

"Hey, Tara, it's Rachel Johnson calling you back."

"It's snowing. I got to my aunt's house about an hour ago and since then I swear we've gotten two feet."

Rachel didn't think so. "It'll be fine. We knew there was a strong chance of snow. Think of how beautiful it'll look. A fairytale white wedding. Are most of your guests here?"

Tara took a deep breath over the phone. "Many of them. They're staying at the Four Seasons."

"When are you headed to your parents'?" The house was a good ten miles out of town, up in the mountains. Luckily, it was a county-maintained road.

"Not until tomorrow. My wedding planner wants to give the decorators plenty of space." Rachel knew that was code for the wedding planner didn't want an antsy bride second-guessing their work. "Foster is going tonight with the flowers. The stylist is coming to my aunt's first thing to do my hair and makeup. Then I'm riding up with my dad. My mom's going earlier to make sure everything looks good."

"Is the groom here?"

"At the Four Seasons."

"Then it sounds like you're all set," Rachel said. "A little snow won't get in the way."

"I guess not. You're good, right? You won't have any trouble getting the food up the mountain?"

"Nope." Other than the hassle of maneuvering in the cold and wet, Rachel had catered events in worse conditions than these. "I'll be there first thing in the morning."

"I e-mailed you the code to get inside."

Rachel hung up and for the next five hours she prepped, making the dough for her yeast rolls, preparing twelve dozen tiny quiches, and brining two twenty-pound turkeys. A giant pot of butternut squash soup simmered on the stove. Tomorrow she'd reheat it and serve the soup in minimugs. The rest she'd prepare the morning of the reception. The only thing left to do tonight was put the finishing touches on Tara and Dan's wedding cake.

Instead of going fussy, the bride and groom had opted for a traditional *bûche de noël* in white chocolate and planned to supplement dessert with apple pie. Rachel thought it was a delightful nod to the holidays.

Before leaving, she wrapped everything in plastic, packed boxes with her ingredients, and lined up a row of ice chests. In the morning, Sam and Leslie would help her load everything into the bakery truck. Tara's parents' kitchen boasted multiple ovens, prep sinks, and a Sub-Zero fridge the size of a restaurant's. It would be a pleasure to finish the wedding meal there in the quiet hours, before the rest of the crew showed up and the festivities started.

On her way home, she drove slowly on the slick roads. It had stopped snowing, but the streets hadn't yet been cleared and the two-mile trip was a bear. The minute she got inside, she flipped on the lights and turned on the heat. Her town house was a cozy two-bedroom with an open floor plan, a large stone fireplace, a good-size kitchen, and views of the mountains to die for. Rachel loved it, even if it meant sharing a wall with her neighbors. It was new construction and most of the residents were part-timers who came on the weekends to ski. On the weekdays, it was quiet and a nice respite from the bakery.

Her answering machine flashed. The only ones who insisted on calling her on a landline were her parents, who were self-proclaimed Luddites. She pressed the button.

"Rachel, it's your mother." Rachel's mouth ticked up. As if she didn't know her mother's voice. "Just checking to see what time you're coming. Your sister, Jack, and the girls are staying over Christmas Eve. The girls will be anxious to open their gifts in the morning." There was a long pause as if she was waiting for Rachel to respond. "Call me."

Rachel glanced at the mantle clock. It was too late to call. She'd touch base with her mother first thing in the morning. It was a four-hour drive to Atherton, where her parents lived. If she left early enough she could be there in time for Christmas brunch. But first she had a wedding to get through.

It was still dark outside when her alarm went off. Rachel showered and dressed in layers, packing a pair of black pants and a crisp white tuxedo blouse that she'd change into for the reception. She loaded her car and headed to the bakery, but the wind and snow made seeing difficult. Rachel hoped the weather died down by the time she drove up the mountain.

Sam and Leslie were waiting when she got there. They had already filled the ice chests and were busy packing up her equipment. She'd delivered the dinnerware and serving pieces days ago so the decorators could set up the buffet tables and Foster could place the flowers. It was one less thing she'd have to carry, thank goodness. They loaded the van and Rachel did a quick walk through the kitchen to make sure she hadn't forgotten anything.

"You sure you don't want one of us to come with you?" Sam asked.

"Yes, but I'll need you both at around three, so leave yourself plenty of time to get there." In this weather, traffic moved at a snail's pace. Folks up from the city who weren't used to driving in the snow.

"We will. You're sure you're okay to unload on your own?"

"I'll be fine. Just hold down the fort, here." The bakery was closing early and she expected a morning rush with customers picking up their special orders.

She hopped in the driver's seat and took it slow. The snow hadn't let up and the plows weren't out yet. All she had to do was make it ten miles. By noon, city and county workers would clear the streets. She crawled along the windy road, her windshield wipers struggling to keep up with the flurry of flakes sticking to the windows. Soon, she'd have zero visibility.

At one point, she found a turnout, pulled over, and cleaned the glass with a scraper. It was time for new blades on her wipers. She started off again, climbing higher into the pines as the wind lashed the van, making it rock back and forth. The snow kept coming, but she could see the sun slipping through the clouds and figured by midday the worst of it would be over. Tara and her wedding planner had studied the weather patterns for Christmas Eve in the Sierra, going back ten years. Snow and wind, but nothing epic. Nothing that would prevent prepared guests from getting to the venue.

By the time she pulled up to the big circular driveway, she had to steady her nerves. The drive had been hairier than she'd expected. There was a familiar-looking pickup parked by the service door. It took her a few seconds to process that it was Boden's. Why he was here this early was a mystery. She got down from the cab and opened the tail lift to start unloading. Halfway to the house, he came down the driveway and greeted her, shielding his eyes with his hands.

"I'll move my truck so you can back in and get closer to the door." He took the ice chest from her and started back to the house.

She waited for him to move and turned her truck around, trying to get it as close as she could to the service entrance. It was difficult to see with the snow obscuring her back windshield. Boden jogged up the hill from where he'd parked his pickup and guided her.

He had on a down jacket and a ski cap and still looked like he was freezing his tail off. In her rearview mirror she saw him blowing on his gloveless hands a few times. She did the best she could to straighten the van and pressed the parking brake. Boden immediately started pulling out boxes from the back and lugging them to the kitchen.

She'd been looking forward to having the place to herself for a couple of hours to work before the rest of the workers descended, but she was thankful to have Boden's help. It was nice of him to pitch in the way he was.

"Is anyone else here?" She began arranging her perishables in the huge refrigerator.

"Foster just left and the bride's mother and wedding planner are here, checking off their lists." He eyed the row of boxes he'd helped to bring in. "You wouldn't by chance be hiding a cup of coffee in one of those, would you?"

"No, but I have this." She rummaged through the packages and held up a bag of beans. "I'll start a pot."

"You're a goddess."

She glanced over at him. There'd been a flirtatious hitch in his voice, which she suspected was the way he communicated with women. All women.

She found the coffeemaker, a built-in stainless-steel number that looked almost as fancy as Boden's Illy. The kitchen didn't lack for high-end appliances, that's for sure.

"The bride's folks must be loaded," Boden whispered.

She nodded. "It's a gorgeous place. How come you're here so early?"

"I wanted to get the bar set up in case the weather gets worse. Now all I have to do is get myself here."

Smart. "Don't you think it'll clear up?"

"Not according to AccuWeather. It's predicting ten inches of snow."

"That's this morning's forecast?" Last night, the weather said two inches. This wasn't good.

"Yup. The bride's wedding planner checked with the county. They'll keep the road plowed and they've got a shuttle at the Four Seasons to get folks here. They even have a backup generator in case the power goes out. It should be fine, but I didn't want the hassle of dragging the bar and liquor through piles of snow."

She let out a breath. "I just hope my servers will be able to get in."

"They're all local, right?" he asked, and she nodded. "They know the drill."

She poured the coffee beans into the grinder and flicked the switch. Boden gave her a quick once-over. She was still bundled up in her jacket and snow boots, but a silly part of her wished she'd worn something better than yoga pants and an old sweater.

"Aren't you warm in that?" he asked, motioning at her heavy scarf and woolen hat. "It has to be seventy degrees in here."

She noted he'd taken off his jacket and hung it over one of the chairs in the breakfast room. He had on a pair of faded jeans and one of his signature flannel shirts with a black thermal peeking out from under his collar. The pages of an L.L.Bean catalog flashed through her head.

The whir of the grinder stopped and the smell of coffee began to fill the room. She took off the scarf and hat and tucked them inside a tote bag. He stood idly against the counter waiting for the coffee to finish brewing and watched as she unzipped her jacket, then helped tug it off and hung it neatly over the chair next to his.

Impatient, she poured them each a cup before the pot was full and brushed against him as she handed him the warm mug. His fingers touched hers and she could've sworn she felt a current of electricity. That's when the lights flickered and everything went dark.

CHAPTER 4

"Shit," Boden said, and felt for Rachel as his eyes adjusted to the dark. "You okay?"

She'd let out a little yelp when the power went off and he worried she might've spilled coffee on herself.

"The lights . . . it just startled me is all. You said they have a generator?"

"Yeah. I'm gonna go look for Mrs. Canadell and see if I can help her get it going."

He started to find his way in the dark, but the lights switched on as fast as they'd gone off. "I guess we're back in business. It was probably just the wind."

Rachel peered out the window and grimaced. "It's really blowing."

"Yoo-hoo." Mrs. Canadell swept into the kitchen with the wedding planner. Kristi, Boden thought she'd said earlier. He was usually pretty good with names, but he'd been carrying in boxes of liquor and trying not to slip on the ice at the time of the introductions.

"That about gave me a heart attack." Mrs. Canadell put her hand to her chest.

Boden glanced at the clock flashing on the double wall ovens and leaned over to reset it. "You want to show me where the generator is in case it happens again?"

"Oh, you're a doll." She patted his arm and Boden watched as Rachel bit back a smile. What could he say? Middle-aged women dug him? Hell, all women dug him with the exception of one brown-eyed pastry chef.

"We have to leave soon," Kristi said. "Mrs. Canadell has a hair appointment and I have to help Tara get ready. But I'll be back in a couple of hours."

"I'm fine," Rachel said, and looked at Boden.

"As soon as you show Rach and me how to work the generator I'm gonna take off, too." He still had to open Old Glory, oversee the lunch service, change into something more presentable for a wedding, and get back to the Canadell house in time to tend bar.

"Charles stores it in the shed outside." She led Boden and Rachel across the yard to a small outbuilding where a portable gas generator sat. The unit appeared high-powered enough to at least keep the lights, heat, and refrigerator going in the event of an outage.

"There are the extension cords." Mrs. Canadell pointed. "Charles says the gasoline is on the top shelf in a red can."

"Okay." He turned to Rachel. "Do you know how to work it?"

"I think so. I have one for the bakery but have only had to use it twice."

"You have some flashlights?" he asked Mrs. Canadell, and she opened a drawer in a work bench where there was at least a dozen. He'd give the Canadells credit; they came equipped for an emergency. "Let's take a few of these into the house; that way one of us can make it back to the garage in the dark."

He and Rachel scooped up a few and they returned to the kitchen. Kristi and Mrs. Canadell said their good-byes and took off.

"You gonna be okay without me?" he asked Rachel, who pulled a chef coat from her giant tote bag and began setting out ingredients.

"Of course."

"You want me to give you a refresher on how to use the generator?"

"Boden, I run an entire business on my own. Before that I was second in command of legal for a multinational corporation."

He cocked a brow. "Only second?"

The comment had been meant as a joke, but she didn't take it too well, shooting daggers at him. "Take off. Do what you need to do."

"All right." He tested the coffeepot with his hand to see if it was still hot. "One more cup and I'm outta here."

He watched her move around the kitchen as he mainlined caffeine. No makeup, her hair twisted up in a barrette, a pair of reading glasses perched on the tip of her nose, and he felt blood rush straight to his groin. She was something else. And, as far as he knew, single. There was a rumor that before Colt Garner got married she'd had a thing for him. But in a small town rumors weren't too reliable. In any event, he'd never seen her with a guy at Old Glory or anywhere else for that matter.

Whatever her status was, she wasn't interested in him. She'd made that perfectly clear when she'd rebuffed his innocent drink invitation. He could've sworn she recoiled when he'd asked. It wasn't like it was a date or anything. It was just a way to keep things friendly between them when the city made a decision on the mill house. By Boden's estimation she was his only competition. No one else bidding was a real contender. A knitting store, an antiques mall, an artist collective were all nice ideas, but at the end of the day, did they make money? Boden sincerely doubted it. Judging by the lines around the block, Tart Me Up was a successful business with room to grow. And Old Glory . . . yeah, he was killing it. He just didn't want any hard feelings when the city deemed him the winner.

"Thanks for the coffee." He washed out his cup and grabbed his jacket. "See ya this afternoon."

She glanced up from chopping vegetables. "Drive safely."

"Keep this with you." He stuck a flashlight in the pocket of her smock and walked out the back door.

The snow made it difficult to see as he inched down the driveway. He was three-quarters of the way down when he slammed on his brakes.

"Ah, crap!" he said out loud.

CHAPTER 5

Just as Rachel fell into a groove, the sound of an engine pulled her from her preparations. She shoved a lock of hair out of her eyes with her forearm and looked outside to see Boden's pickup coming up the hill. What was he doing back?

The wind ripped through the trees so violently they looked ready to snap and flurries of white swirled in the air. She rushed across the kitchen and opened the door.

"What happened?"

He came inside, his face chapped from the cold. "A big oak came down and is covering the driveway. It's too big to move and needs to be cut. Do you have a number for Kristi or Mrs. Canadell? They need to get someone out here, because no shuttle bus is getting around it."

"Let me get my phone." Rachel crossed the kitchen and searched through her tote bag. "I'm not getting a signal; how about you?"

"I've got one. What's the number?"

She read it off and he told Kristi about the tree. "She's on it." He slipped his phone back into his pocket. "But I'm stuck here until it's moved."

Oddly enough, she was happy he was staying and told herself it was because it was spooky in an empty house in the middle of nowhere, alone. "Want something to eat? I can make you a few eggs."

He appeared surprised by the offer. "Sure. Thanks, that's really nice of you."

"Occasionally, I can be nice. But don't get too used to it," she teased. "Are you freaking out about not getting to the bar?"

"Nah, I shot Ingrid a text. She's got the keys and knows what to do."

"Thank goodness I have Samantha. She'll be running Tart Me Up, today. Luckily, we close early . . . we're mostly staying open so people can pick up their Christmas orders." Jeez, she was babbling. She never babbled.

Boden nodded and she busied herself making eggs, heating one of the yeast rolls, and pouring him a third cup of coffee. He sat at the center island watching her cook.

"Are we not talking about the elephant in the room?"

Oh boy, did he think she was attracted to him? Because she wasn't. "I don't know what you're talking about."

"The Old Watermill House. Don't you want to know how my presentation went?"

Oh, that. "How did it go?" Honestly, she could live without knowing. It would only work her up. Her parents' blatant disapproval would give her enough indigestion over the weekend. Lying awake at night wondering if Boden had beat her out on the mill house was only going to add another layer of stress.

But before he could answer, the lights flickered off and on.

She held her breath, waiting for it to happen again. "The wind doesn't seem to be letting up."

He stared out the window. "Nope."

She reached for a plate in the cupboard and served him the eggs and the roll, which had browned to perfection. Good ovens.

"Why don't you take half of this?"

"I ate before I came," she said, and stood back while he dug in.

"Good," he said around a bite of food.

People thought scrambled eggs were easy, but she knew better. To make them perfectly golden and soft enough to be custardy was an art form. "I'm glad you like them."

He looked up and held her gaze. "How come you're being so nice? You usually act like you don't like me."

Well, that had been blunt. "I like you just fine, but I view you as a competitor for something I want. Very badly."

"The mill house?" He continued to lock eyes and consider her. "Yeah, I can see that. I want it, too. But even before that you didn't like me."

That wasn't exactly true, but she had gone out of her way to avoid him, even when they were working the same parties. On those occasions, they usually butted heads. Neither of them wanted to relinquish control, she supposed. "Since we're being honest here, you always seem a little full of yourself."

He threw his head back and laughed. "Where do you get that? I'm just a mild-mannered bartender."

"Right." She stifled an eye roll. Nothing about him was mild mannered. He walked into a room and people took notice. Not because he was the most handsome man alive but because he had a presence about him. A vibe that was all alpha.

A vibe that reminded her of Jeremy. There, she'd said it.

The lights flickered off again and she held her breath, hoping they would come back on. Staring out the window to gauge the winds, she felt him come up behind her.

"This time, I think it's out for a while." He reached inside her apron pocket and plucked out the flashlight. "I'll give it a few minutes. If they don't come back on, I'll start the generator."

She turned, realizing her mistake when she came up against his chest. He'd inadvertently boxed her in. They stood like that for a few seconds and then he quickly backed away.

"I can't do much without electricity," she said for the sake of breaking the awkward silence. It meant she'd get behind schedule.

"I'll help you when we get the lights back on."

"Do you think you should check with Kristi to see if they got someone to clear the tree away?"

"I'll give them another twenty minutes or so. With the snow coming down the way it is, it won't be easy finding someone."

He pressed his hand into the small of her back and guided her to the breakfast room, where they sat around the table.

"You ever see a place like this?" In the dim room, she could see him examining the open-beam ceilings and hand-hewn logs.

"My parents'," she said. "It's not rustic like this, but it's roughly the same size."

He let out a whistle. "So, you're a rich girl, huh?"

She chuckled. "No, I'm the daughter of well-to-do parents. How about you?"

"Not even close. At least not my mother. She worked for a mechanic, answering his phones and filing his paperwork. Never knew my father. The guy who for the most part raised me had a little money. He left it to me when he died and I used it to buy Old Glory."

His openness surprised her. Boden had always seemed like the private type. "I'm sorry . . . was he the man in the picture above your desk?"

"Yep. Marine Gunnery Sergeant Jake Hornsby. One of a kind."

"It sounds like you admired him."

"I loved him." The words were said with such poignancy they made her ache. That kind of raw emotion was another thing she hadn't expected from Boden. Then again, she hardly knew him, but he seemed to be one of those guys who played it cool. Tough.

"I'm sorry you lost him."

"Yeah, me too." He glanced at his phone. "Five more minutes."

"Five more minutes." She nodded, hoping the power would come on by itself. "Good thing I did a lot of the prep work last night."

"Not much to do as far as the bar."

A tree branch scraped the window and she jumped. "Jeez, it's blowing out there."

"Hopefully this is the worst of it."

"The bride must be freaking out," she said. "Has it been twenty minutes yet? I'll go down with you."

"No need." He got up and shrugged into his jacket. "If the lights aren't on by the time I come back I'll fire up the generator."

"I could do that while you're gone."

"Nah, why should we both freeze our asses off?"

"I just figured if the tree had been moved you could go back to town, to Old Glory."

"I'd like to make sure everything is up and running first." He reached into his jacket pocket and pulled a ski cap over his head.

A part of her was relieved because she wasn't sure she would know how to work the damn generator, but another part of her didn't want to be reliant, especially not on Boden. "I should come, too, then."

He cocked an eyebrow. "You afraid of the dark?"

"No, but it's a little eerie here alone."

"Suit yourself, but you better bundle up."

One look outside the window and she could see a layer of ice covering an ornate birdbath near the garage. The branches, heavy with snow, looked ready to snap. He helped her on with her jacket and she waited in the cab of his truck while he swept the snow off his windshield.

"I may have to shovel us out." He got in the driver's seat and after a few attempts managed to get traction.

They nosed their way down and he huffed out a curse. "No one's here yet." He stopped short and they got out to take a look.

"Whoa! It's a good thing this didn't fall on anything." The tree was huge, maybe ten feet long and maybe five feet thick.

"No one is getting around it, that's for sure." Boden whipped out his phone. "No bars."

She checked hers. "Me neither. Do you think anyone is even coming out?"

He shrugged. "Either Kristi couldn't find anyone or they couldn't get up the driveway. I suppose I could see if there's a chainsaw in the garage and cut the tree up myself."

"That would take hours, don't you think?"

"Probably. But I could cut enough so a vehicle could at least get through, that is, if the road is even passable."

She was beginning to suspect that it was a lost cause. At the rate the snow was coming down they were looking at a full-blown blizzard. "I don't think you should be out in this." Especially with a chainsaw.

"Let's go back to the house and see if cell reception is better there," he said.

It took them twice as long to return, the visibility was so bad. They slogged through the snow to the shed and Boden wheeled the generator outside, moved it under the roof's overhang, plugged it into the transfer switch, and flicked the circuit breakers. It was clear he knew what he was doing, but when he pulled the cord the generator wouldn't start.

"Dirty fuel," he muttered to himself, and looked up at Rachel. "People always forget to clean the engine when the lights come back on."

He messed with it for a while but couldn't get so much as a hum from the motor. "You should go in the house. No need for us both to freeze our tails off."

She didn't know that the house would be any warmer than the garage with the heat off, but she felt silly standing there, looking over his shoulder with nothing to do. "I'll try to call Kristi and let her know what's going on here."

Boden gave a slight nod, distracted while he fidgeted with the generator. She watched him for a few seconds, admiring the way his jeans molded to his fine backside as he hunkered over the machine, deep in concentration. A few sexy thoughts flitted through her head and she quickly willed them away. She and Boden were stuck in a snowstorm for goodness' sake. There were more pressing things to think about than visualizing what Boden would look like naked.

She really needed to start dating again. Between the bakery and catering, she'd let her social life fall by the wayside. And when she got the Old Watermill House, her workload would double. But she was thirty-six and would like to have a man in her life while there was still time to have children. Just not Boden Farmer. He was enticing to be sure, but completely wrong for her, starting with the fact that they were both vying for the same dream.

And only one of them could win.

She passed through the mudroom and, despite the power outage, could still see well enough to find her way to the kitchen. Unfortunately, there still weren't any bars on her cell. Even so, she tried several times to call out, to no avail, and pondered the wisdom of turning it off to preserve the battery. In the end, she decided to leave it on in case Kristi called and managed to get through. For the next thirty minutes, she busied herself cleaning up from their coffee break. It was still warm enough to take off her outerwear, but without heat it wouldn't take long before a house this size got drafty.

"I can't get it to work." Boden came in, frustration written all over his face. "Any luck getting a call out?"

"Nope. I've got zero reception."

"What about a text?"

"If I can't make a call, I can't text, Boden." There he went second-guessing her. It reminded her of their other catering assignments where he was always offering his unsolicited opinions about everything, including how she should do the cake service to coincide with the toasts, which of course was his purview.

"Sometimes you can," he said, ignoring her peevishness and trying on his own phone. "See." He held up his cell to show her that a text to Kristi had indeed been sent.

"Let's wait to see if it actually gets delivered."

He shook his head. "Did they teach you negativity in law school?"

It was ridiculous to fight with him at a time like this, but she couldn't help it and fired back, "Nope, just plain old common sense."

He let out a huff of breath and shrugged out of his jacket. "Is there any prep we can do in the dark?"

She'd give him credit for taking the high road and offering to help. Though that's how it had started with Jeremy.

"Not really." She'd already organized her serving pieces. Everything else required the stove, the mixer, the food processor, electricity. "You think this wedding is even going to happen?"

"There you go being negative again." He grinned and glanced out the window. "But, yeah, this time I think there's cause to worry."

Boden checked his phone and held it up. "See. Delivered."

"No response from Kristi, though." She probably couldn't get through, which meant they were screwed.

"Nope." He looked outside again. "It's really coming down. At this point I wouldn't drive in this unless I had to."

"I guess we're stuck."

He sank into one of the breakfast room chairs. "Until someone deals with the tree we are." He gazed around the room. "I can think of worse places to be stuck."

"I bet you can think of better people to be stuck with, though," she said, going for a little levity.

"Not really." He gave her a slow once-over that should've been too brazen, bordering on predatory, but it wasn't. She felt perfectly safe with Boden. "When that stick comes out, you're not half-bad. You made me eggs, after all."

She did not have a stick up her ass but refused to take the bait.

"I'm sure lots of women have made you breakfast." The words were out of her mouth before she realized how they sounded. She'd meant women like his mother.

He didn't respond, just continued looking at her. "What's your deal, anyway? How come you're not seeing anyone?"

She took one of the other chairs, tired of standing. "What makes you think I'm not?"

"Just a hunch." Again, with the grin. It was meant either to be teasing or to get under her skin. Rachel hadn't decided yet. "Anyone I know?"

"No." She wanted to make up something—a fictional Prince Charming, even though she knew damned well they didn't exist—but had never been good at lying. "I don't have time to date."

He surprised her by nodding, instead of flashing another one of those smug smiles. "Yep, same here."

The rumors were that he dated his female staff, another reason he was completely unsuitable. She had strong feelings about bosses who dated their subordinates, having dealt with plenty of those kinds of cases as an attorney. The story was often the same. Someone in a position of authority taking advantage of someone who was just trying to hold on to a job.

"A good reason not to open a second bar and brewery, right?" Her lips curved up. She could give as good as she got. Oftentimes, even better.

"Same could be said for a second bakery. Why do you need all that space, anyway?"

There was no sense in keeping it a secret any longer. They'd both made their pitches to the city. Now it was up to the council. "Restaurant."

He leaned his chair back on two legs, a move that had always annoyed her.

"A restaurant, huh? You mean like Tart Me Up?"

He was digging for information, but the holidays had put her in a generous mood. "Nope. Full service. Breakfast, lunch, and dinner."

The look on his face was like a gift that kept on giving. First, surprise. Then, *oh shit*. "Good for you. We could use more full-service restaurants in Glory Junction. You planning to serve alcohol?"

"What would a restaurant be without drinks?" She threw up her hands. What she wasn't planning to do was make alcohol her primary focus, which she was hoping would give her an edge over Boden in the city's eyes.

"You have a liquor license?"

"Not yet, but I will." He knew as well as she did that she needed the space first. Boden already had one because he owned a bar.

"They're not easy to get, you know?"

"I'm not too worried about it," she said with obnoxious nonchalance. It was fun poking at him.

"I suppose you'll use your bad-ass lawyer skills to get one." He smirked. Her being a lawyer seemed to touch a nerve with him. How many times had he brought it up in the last couple of days?

"It sure won't hurt." It wouldn't help, either, but why not rub it in?

"What did the city think of your restaurant proposal?" he asked.

"They loved it. What about your brewery?"

"Who doesn't like scads of money—and the good it'll do for this town?" He gave her a challenging look, like he'd already won.

"Money is good. Drunken driving, not so much." From the way he avoided eye contact, Rachel knew she'd one-upped him. Her proposal probably wouldn't generate as much revenue for the city as his, but bars and liquor stores were sticking points in small towns.

"I thought you were serving alcohol at your restaurant?"

She'd give him credit for being pugnacious. "A glass of wine with a nice dinner isn't the same thing as a bar."

"I serve food."

She started to argue, but he stopped her. "Enough. We'll see what the city decides. May the best ma—person win."

It killed her that he was getting the last word, but she didn't want to appear petty or *lawyerish*. "Anything from Kristi?"

He glanced down at his phone and shook his head. "It's nearly noon. I'd like to hear the news and see if the roads are passable. What do you say we get in my truck and turn on the radio?"

"I think it's a good idea." She put on her jacket and zipped it to her chin.

But even that wasn't enough to keep out the cold. It lashed through her clothes like a whip, stinging her skin. Boden opened his truck doors and they scooted in. It took two tries to get the engine started, and a few minutes later they had heat. Boden played with the radio dial until he found a local news station out of Sacramento. They listened while the newscaster read a story about Christmas festivities in the state's capital.

"They do weather every fifteen minutes," Boden said.

"My parents said it was sunny where they are." Unlike the rest of the state, the Sierra Nevada had some of the snowiest weather in the country. In Southern California, people were probably going to the beach. "How about where your mom lives?"

"Dunno, since I don't know where she lives."

For a beat she was stunned silent. "The two of you don't keep in touch?"

"Nope. Desiree's got her own thing going."

"Oh . . . I'm sorry."

"Don't be; there's nothing to be sorry about."

Before she could respond the forecaster announced that Donner Pass and a number of other roads had been closed due to the storm and that most of Nevada County was experiencing a power outage and downed phone lines. The utility companies were hoping to have everything up and running by nightfall. The newscaster signed off with an inane remark about Santa not getting lost in the dark.

"Doesn't sound too promising for the bride and groom." Boden shut off the engine. "With all those roads shut down, no one will show to get rid of the tree. Regardless, I don't see a hundred guests getting up the mountain."

She had to agree with him. "What do we do?"

"Nothing we can do but hang tight until the weather dies down. I'll find where they keep the firewood. Go back in the house and try to stay warm."

"I'll help." With the two of them, they could haul in a good load twice as fast. Even with their ski jackets, neither of them was dressed to endure this weather for too long.

He started to argue but seemed to think better of it. Between the wind and the snow, they could barely see where they were going. Boden grabbed her hand and led her around the side of the house, using the brown shingle siding as a guide. Sure enough they found a woodshed a few yards away. Boden grabbed a pair of woolen gloves from his pockets and loaded them both with logs. With them encumbered by the wind and snow, the simple chore took twice as long. Together, they trudged through the snow to the back door through which they carried the wood to the living room.

"Holy hell, it's cold out there."

Rachel was too busy shivering to comment.

"I'll get a fire going. In the meantime, why don't you find a blanket or something that'll keep us warm until we have a nice blaze?"

She went in search of a couple of quilts, feeling a little weird about helping herself to the Canadells' things. It was silly, she knew. No one would want them to freeze. In a linen closet in the south wing of the house, she found a down comforter and a wool afghan. If the power came back on, she'd fold them up and put them away.

By the time she got to the great room, Boden had already started the fire. It wasn't much yet, so she stood as close as she could to the hearth, trying to get dry.

"I bet you could find a robe or something to change into,"

Boden said as he removed his jacket and laid it on the floor near the fireplace.

"I'm okay." No way was she getting naked with Boden in the house.

He took her in from head to toe. "It's up to you. But you're gonna get sick in those wet clothes."

She wanted to point out that his were just as wet but refrained. Knowing Boden, he'd drop trou right in front of her to prove a point. Or to embarrass her. Admittedly, she was curious whether he was a boxers or briefs guy. The thought of him going commando under his Levis flashed in her head and she immediately shut it down.

"You already look a little flushed," he said.

If you only knew. "It's the fire." She wrapped herself in one of the blankets and moved to the couch, a leather sectional with piles of Navajo pillows that must've cost a fortune. The Canadells had planned to close the room off for the wedding reception, using an enormous screened porch on the side of the house, instead. That room also had a fireplace and views of a pond and the surrounding Sierra mountains. It would've been the most romantic party setting she'd ever catered, but with less than five hours until show time there was little hope of pulling it off. Not as long as the storm persisted, and even then, she didn't know whether the roads could be cleared in time.

"Poor Tara. Her perfect wedding, ruined by Mother Nature."

Boden shrugged. "It'll be a story they can tell their grandkids. Besides, people focus too much on the pomp and not enough on the marriage."

"That's awfully cynical, don't you think? The ceremony . . . the party . . . it's a celebration of a new life together. It's about sharing that new beginning with loved ones."

"You work for Hallmark now?"

"Wow, someone must've done a number on you."

He laughed. "Nope, I'm just a realist. You know how many brawls start in Old Glory because one half of a couple finds out the other one is stepping out on him or her? Too many to count."

"Does that mean you don't believe in love?"

"I'm not saying that. All I'm saying is I don't believe in all the bullshit that goes with it." He sank into the seat next to her. "Give me some of that blanket."

Before she could toss him the afghan, he moved closer and tugged half of her comforter across his lap. With the fire crackling it was a cozy tableau. That was until an ear-piercing chirp rent the stillness.

CHAPTER 6

"What the hell is that?" Boden jumped to his feet.

The noise continued to sound on and off like a drill and it took him until the initial shock wore off to realize it was a smoke alarm. "Can you tell where it's coming from?"

"Somewhere up there." Rachel pointed at the rafters.

The ceilings were at least twenty feet high. No way was he getting up there without a very tall ladder.

"Should we worry that it's a fire?" she asked.

"I think it's from the smoke." The Canadells probably hadn't cleaned their flue in a while.

Because it was a vacation home, he was guessing the fireplace rarely got used. "Let's crack a couple of windows."

It wasn't the best way to conserve heat, but it was better than listening to the alarm. He opened one of the French doors while Rachel waved her hands in the air, trying to diffuse the smoke. He started to laugh because she looked like a bird flapping its wings.

She shot him a death glare. "You have a better idea?"

Not really. "Open more windows, and a fan would be good. Did you see one while hunting up the blankets?"

"No, but it wasn't as if I was keeping my eye out for one. And it's not like it would work, anyway."

Right, no electricity. "Let me see what I can find." He grabbed his jacket off the floor and searched the pocket for one of the flashlights they'd gotten from the shed. "In the meantime, open some of these windows."

"We're going to freeze."

"We could go upstairs and get under the covers in one of the bedrooms." The idea appealed to him more than he wanted to admit. It also made him think of every cheesy snowed-in movie he'd ever seen.

Rachel rolled her eyes and covered her ears. "Go find something to make it stop."

"Anyone ever tell you you're bossy?" Instead of waiting for her comeback, he took off in search of anything that would help scatter the smoke.

He finally found a telescoping rod to manually open the skylights. The alarm chirped incessantly, despite their efforts to air out the place. But perhaps opening the transoms would help dissipate the smoke faster. It was worth trying.

"Whoa, it's cold." And it was about to get colder.

"Could you hear the alarm upstairs?"

"Why? You reconsidering my idea to get in bed together?"

She shook her head dismissively. Rachel Johnson didn't have much of a sense of humor.

"You can probably hear the goddamn alarm in China." He used the rod to open two of the skylights just enough to let some of the smoke out. "This is one hell of a storm. From upstairs, you can see all the way to the main road, except you can't because it's covered in snow. No one is getting in or out of here for a while."

"I'm supposed to go to my folks' tomorrow." She pulled the blanket around herself. "They'll worry when I don't show up."

"You try your phone again?"

She let out a breath. "Nothing."

"I tried mine upstairs," he said. "And, yeah, nothing." He squeezed her shoulder. "All they have to do is turn on the news and they'll know you're snowed in. Most everyone in town is aware that we were catering this wedding; they'll figure it out."

"I hope so." She looked so dejected that it got to him. Christmas was a time for family, at least if you had one.

He guided her back to the sectional, tugged off his boots, and propped his feet on the coffee table. "You were looking forward to it, huh?"

"Not really."

"No?" He tilted his head in surprise.

"I love my family, but they're stressful. Very judgy."

"Of you? Why? You're a lawyer, a successful business owner, beloved by your community." Hell, she was the poster child for high achiever. "Your personality, on the other hand, could use some work. Is that why they judge you?"

She poked him in the arm. "My personality is just fine. They don't understand why I'm no longer practicing law and they definitely don't get the bakery."

"Do they know about Oprah?" He tried to suppress a grin. That Oprah shit had gotten her more mileage than Gunny's old GMC pickup truck.

She hitched her shoulders. "Yes, but it's not Trial Lawyer of the Year." She pointed at the fire. "You hear that?"

"What?"

"Exactly. No smoke alarm anymore."

Well, I'll be damned. He'd been so caught up with this new revelation about Miss Perfect Rachel Johnson that he hadn't even noticed. "What does Trial Lawyer of the Year have to do with anything?"

"It's nothing." She waved him off. "Are you hungry? We have enough food to feed an army and it's all going to spoil if the power doesn't come on soon."

"I doubt it, not in this cold. But yeah, I could eat."

They made their way to the kitchen, where Rachel opened the fridge and began lining up various dishes on the counter.

"I wish I had a way to heat some of this stuff, but there are cheeses and veggies and . . . wedding cake." She turned to him and grimaced. "Do we dare eat it?"

"Let me see." He came up behind her and took a peek over her shoulder. "What the hell kind of wedding cake is that? It looks like it came off that tree in the driveway."

She twisted around, her face level to his chest, and he had an urge to dip down and sample those pretty red lips of hers. He'd bet they were better than cake.

"It's a *bûche de noël*." When he stared at her blankly, she said, "You know, a Yule log."

"Never heard of it. Is it a wedding-holiday thing?"

"It's a French Christmas cake."

"Well, there you go. I'm American."

She shoved his chest. "They sell 'em at Safeway, you jackass."

"Is that where you got this one?" For some stupid reason, he loved seeing her riled up. Maybe it was the way her breasts heaved, giving him a nice view of her cleavage.

"Just for that, you're not getting any." She licked a speck of chocolate off her finger and he felt his groin tighten. Then she thrust a bag of baby carrots at him. "You can have those."

"You know what these"—he held up the bag—"go good with?"

"Feel free to enlighten me."

"Beer." He pushed away from the fridge, wandered onto the porch where his bar was set up, and returned a few minutes later with two pints of pale ale.

"Should we eat here or by the fire?"

"Fire," he said. The kitchen had turned as cold as an icebox.

She made quick work of arranging cold cuts and cheeses on a big wooden board, filling a basket with crackers, and putting together a crudité platter. Together, they carried everything into the great room. Boden put another log on the fire.

"Should we risk shutting the door?"

"Sure, let's live dangerously." He winked and met her on the couch.

"Dig in." She handed him a plate and a napkin and made sure to put his beer on a coaster before wrapping herself in the blanket again.

"You cold?"

"Aren't you?"

"Nah, you heat me up, Rachel."

"You're an idiot, but since you're good at building fires, I'll let you stay." She swiped a cherry tomato from the veggie assortment and popped it into her mouth.

He filled a plate and took a slug of beer. "Where were we? Oh yeah, you were telling me about why your parents disapprove of you."

"I believe we were done talking about that and had moved on to why you don't keep in touch with your mother, the woman who gave you life."

That's what he got for dueling with an attorney. But the truth was he was enjoying himself. "That's about all she did for me. But if you must know, she's the one who moved and didn't leave a forwarding address."

She put her beer down, a stunned expression on her face. "Your mother doesn't want you to know where she is?"

"I doubt it was that deliberate, since she never gave me much thought at all. She was what you would call an absentee parent."

Rachel turned to face him. "Was she a druggie?"

He laughed, because how did someone automatically jump to that conclusion? "She wasn't an addict if that's what you mean, but she liked to party." And men. She liked them better than caring for her son. "It's not a big deal. I had Gunny and he was all I needed."

She didn't say anything, which made Boden uncomfortable. "You're not feeling sorry for me, are you? Because I turned out just fine. A successful businessman, pillar of the community, champion fire builder, and I'm Mr. January."

"Don't get carried away. That calendar is a joke. I know Rita Tucker means well, but let's face it, half the time the pictures are out of focus and the costumes she has you wear . . . uh, there are no words."

He laughed. "We raised twenty grand for the volunteer fire department with that pervy calendar of the mayor's, so zip it."

"That's because all the women buy it to look at Win Garner."

"Win?" He pretended to choke. "I don't like to brag but . . ." He stared down at his crotch. "I'm sure Win's got other assets, though."

"That's your problem, Boden; you're a little too high on yourself." She patted his leg and again he felt his groin tighten.

"Nothing wrong with a healthy self-esteem." He got up and closed the skylights. "Looks like we're okay with the smoke for now."

"I think the wind from up there was actually blowing hot air." She cracked a smile. "Or maybe that was you."

"Hey, you're the lawyer." He came back, plucked a cracker off her plate, and took a bite. "Why don't your parents like the bakery?"

"It's not the bakery they don't like; it's the fact that I ditched being an attorney to open it."

"Ah." He leaned his head back on the couch. "Why did you take down your shingle?" He'd always wondered. She'd probably banked six figures a year as a lawyer for half the work of running a bakery. He knew she got to Tart Me Up before the sun rose every day and spent her nights catering.

"It wasn't making me happy; it's as simple as that."

He held her gaze. "And Tart Me Up does?"

Her expression turned serene and her face glowed. "Yes," she said, and for a second her countenance blinded him. She really was quite beautiful.

"That's good. Same with me and Old Glory."

"And the brewery?" She took off her snow boots and propped her feet next to his. With the fire blazing, the stockings hanging off the mantel, and the big Christmas tree in the corner it felt cozy. Too cozy.

"A dream and my homage to Gunny."

"Is that supposed to make me feel guilty?" She watched him over the rim of her beer glass.

He tapped his against hers until it made a clinking sound. "As I said before, may the best person win."

"What will you do if it's me?"

She knew damned well there weren't any other available buildings in Glory Junction big enough for a brewery. The fact was there was a shortage of commercial space, period. Named one of the best ski resort towns in California by nearly every major publication, the town had outgrown itself. That's why timing was crucial. If he waited too long one of the big dogs would come in and he'd be forced out by the competition.

"I'll cross that bridge when I get there," he said. "How about you?"

"I don't plan to lose."

She began stacking their empty plates. Her hands were delicate, not what he would've expected from someone who kneaded dough all day. Then again, they probably had machines for that. Her fingers were long and slender and for a beat he let himself think about what they'd be like on his skin, in his hair.

"What?" She caught him staring.

"You're a very attractive woman, Rachel Johnson."

She snorted. "Seriously? Does that work for you at Old Glory?"

"Pretty much." He laced his hands behind his head. "But I never say anything I don't mean."

She looked at him as if she was gauging whether he was telling the truth, then said, "Help me with the dishes." She grabbed the cold cut board and headed for the kitchen.

The light from the fire illuminated the room, but it was getting difficult to see in the rest of the house. He followed her with a pile of dishes in one hand and a flashlight in the other. "You don't believe you're attractive?"

"The question isn't whether I'm attractive; it's whether you're trying to get inside my pants."

"Oh, I'm definitely trying to do that."

She surprised him by laughing. "You're more honest than most; I'll give you that."

He helped her load the dishwasher, even though they couldn't turn it on. They were close enough that he could smell her perfume, something feminine and arousing. "So, what do you think?"

She turned so they were face-to-face, a smile playing on her lips. "About sleeping with the enemy?"

His lips twitched and he gazed around the dark room. "We've got nothing else to do, right?" He'd had sex for dumber reasons. But his nonchalance with her was a bit of an act. Maybe he liked the challenge she posed. Or maybe he just liked her, even if she was out of his league. "Think of it as a Christmas present to ourselves."

In a surprise move, she went up on tiptoes, brushed a soft kiss against his lips, and winked. "I don't think you need me to while away the hours. From the looks of things, you've got this all on your own."

"Huh?" he asked, and followed her gaze south of his belt.

"Something in your pants is vibrating."

CHAPTER 7

Rachel watched Boden fish his phone out of his pocket.

"Looks like we've got cell reception," he said while reading a text. "Kristi says she couldn't get anyone to come about the tree, that all of Glory Junction is without power, roads are closed... blah, blah, blah."

"What does she say about the wedding?"

He gave her a look. "Are you kidding? No wedding, at least not today. She says we should stay safe and warm."

"Can you text her back and ask about the generator?"

"I can try. But what can she do about it from there?"

Good point, and they'd managed without it thus far. Rachel figured they could go a little longer.

She pulled her phone from her tote bag to see if she, too, had reception. No bars. "You must have a different carrier than I do," she said as she tried to send a text to her parents, but it wouldn't go through. "May I use yours?"

"Sure." He tossed it to her and she dashed off a quick message to tell them that she likely wouldn't be able to make it tomorrow.

"Did it go through?" Boden asked.

"It says 'sent.'" She showed him the screen.

He quickly tapped out his own text, which Rachel presumed

was to someone at Old Glory. The thought that he didn't talk to his mother made her sad. As far as she knew, he didn't have anyone else. The phone vibrated again.

"Your parents say to call them as soon as you can. In the meantime, they don't want you to drive." He cracked a smile. "Now I know where you get your bossiness from."

She ignored the comment. "I'm glad they got the text. One less thing to worry about. How 'bout you?"

"Ingrid said they closed the bar and everyone made it home okay."

"That's good, though I guess you were counting on the income."

He shrugged. "It is what it is."

"Oh, I should send a text to Sam, make sure everything is okay at the bakery."

He handed her his phone again. "See if you can get a call out this time."

She dialed, but nothing happened. "Nope. I hope I can still text." She sent a short message to Samantha but didn't receive anything back. "Looks like reception is dead again."

"We can try later."

She nodded, wondering if he was going to return to their earlier conversation. The man was certainly sure of himself. As if she'd actually agree to a brief affair with him. First off, she didn't do casual hookups. And second, if she did, he'd be the last man with whom she'd get involved. Sleeping with the enemy, indeed.

She finished cleaning up the best she could, which wasn't easy in the dark. They'd lost whatever daylight they'd had from the storm.

"I should probably get more firewood," Boden said as she rubbed her arms from the cold. "There's no telling when the heat will come back on, and if it gets any worse it won't be a good idea to go outside."

"Let's do it," she said, thankful that she wasn't here alone. Under normal circumstances, she was pretty self-sufficient, but in a situation like this, two heads were better than one.

They both bundled up and ventured outside, unprepared for how much worse it had gotten since the last time they fetched wood.

Fighting the wind, alone, was a struggle. And with the whiteout situation, finding their way to the woodshed seemed like an exercise in futility. But Boden must've been an Eagle Scout or something, because he was undaunted by the extreme conditions and pushed forward. She held on to the tail of his jacket, fearful they'd get separated and she wouldn't be able to find her way back to the house.

"You should go back," he hollered over the howling wind.

"No way. I'll never find it. I can barely see a foot in front of me. I think this was a really bad idea."

"Better than running out of fuel for the fire. Just hang on to me."

He pressed ahead, using his sheer size against the elements. She was sure that having to drag her along behind him wasn't helping matters. But they were stuck now. The flashlight at least helped them see directly in front of them. Little by little they inched their way through the snow, which was thigh deep for Rachel in some places.

"Almost there," he shouted.

She couldn't tell how he knew that. Everything looked like a white blur to her. She could barely make out the trees. Her arms, fingers, and toes were numb. This was surely how people got hypothermia and died, she thought to herself. Even her lips felt frozen.

By the time they reached the wooden outbuilding, she was breathing hard. Regrettably, the shed didn't provide much shelter. It was basically a three-sided pole barn.

"Stay here." Boden maneuvered her between a stack of wood and one of the walls.

"Where are you going?" The idea of him leaving her didn't sit well. They should stick together.

"To get that wheelbarrow." He flashed the light at the side of the building, but she couldn't make out anything that looked remotely like a wheelbarrow. Just a lot of white. "I saw it there earlier."

Good thing, because she didn't think she could carry wood and hang on to him at the same time. She'd never been a Brownie, let alone an Eagle Scout. But Boden seemed to have thought all this out ahead of time.

She shoved her hands in her pockets and clenched her teeth, so they wouldn't chatter while she waited for Boden to return. It felt like an hour had passed before she heard him approach.

"Okay, let's load her up."

She tried to gather up a few logs, but her limbs didn't want to work. The truth was she could barely feel them anymore.

"Come here." Boden tugged her closer and began briskly rubbing her arms up and down. "Better."

"N-o-o-o-o. S-o-o-o c-o-o-o-l-d."

"We'll be back soon; then you can sit by the fire."

How come he could string a full sentence together when she could barely speak? He wrapped her in a bear hug and held her for a few seconds. The heat it generated made her feel better and she hung on probably a little longer than she should've.

"I'm gonna load the wood now," he whispered next to her ear, and slowly broke away.

Together, they piled the wheelbarrow as high as they could with logs and started their return trek. It was only about thirty feet to the house, but it felt like a mile up a mountain. Boden did the heavy lifting, pushing the wheelbarrow through the snow. No easy feat. She hung on to his jacket for dear life.

"You okay?"

"I think I've lost a couple of toes."

"Nah, it's just the wind. It makes everything feel colder." He forced the wheelbarrow the rest of the way, parking it right outside the mudroom door. "Go on in. Sit by the fire. I'm going to stack the wood up right here in the hallway."

He must've been freezing, too; otherwise he would've placed the logs in the wood holder in the great room. She supposed the Canadells didn't use the house often enough in wintertime to have stacked logs there already.

As soon as she got warm, she'd figure out how to boil water for tea in the fireplace. She stripped off her layers and set them in front of the fire to dry and stood with her legs pressed against the hearth and her hands stretched out as close to the flames as she could get them.

"Warmer?" Boden came in and immediately removed his jacket. His jeans were soaking wet, as were her yoga pants. "This time, we really need to get out of these wet clothes." He nudged his head at the comforter lying on the couch. "Wrap yourself in that. I'll take the other one."

He was right. Even the tops of her socks were soaked. She grabbed the blanket and started to walk out.

"Where you going?"

"To find a bathroom to take off my clothes."

"Suit yourself, but why leave the warmth of the fire? I'll turn my back for God's sake."

"Maybe I have to go. You ever think of that?"

"You always have to win, don't you?" He handed her the flashlight. "I think there's one right down the hallway."

She made a detour to the kitchen and grabbed her tote bag with her change of clothes. It was a bit formal for sitting around a fire in a blizzard, but it would be warmer than just the blanket. And, frankly, Boden and his proposition were a little too tempting. Better to keep a couple of layers of fabric between them.

The last man she'd been with was Jeremy, nearly three years ago. Since then, it had been quite a dry spell. And if she had to guess, Boden was well practiced when it came to women.

By the time she returned to the great room, Boden was wrapped in the afghan. His pants, sweatshirt, jacket, and socks had been draped over the hearth to dry. She tried hard not to visualize his body parts under the blanket.

He eyed her up and down, amused. "Your catering uniform, huh?"

"Yep." She looked down at her black pants and white tuxedo top and realized how ridiculous she must look. "It's warm." It really wasn't, but it was dry. And it covered her from her neck to ankles. Her feet, now bare, were freezing.

She lined her wet clothes up next to Boden's. As soon as her socks were dry she planned to put them back on.

"I spotted a basket of slippers in the mudroom." Boden got up. "I'll get you a pair."

He took the flashlight and disappeared. She glanced around the room, letting her eyes adjust to the firelight. It really was a beautiful space. Mammoth rough-hewn beams. Polished wide-plank floors. A fireplace mantel carved from an ancient pine log. And the holiday decorations looked like something from a magazine.

There were worse places to be held hostage by the weather. And worse men to be stuck with, she supposed. If she wanted to be honest, Boden had not only been resourceful; he'd also been a perfect gentleman. Okay, maybe not so much if she considered him propositioning her. But there'd been no pressure, and not once had she felt unsafe with him. Just the opposite in fact.

"I didn't know what size, so I brought a couple of pairs." He tossed her two different pairs of shearling slippers and she tucked her feet into the larger pair.

She hummed with appreciation. "I'm getting a pair of these when I get home. Thank you, Boden." She glanced down at his still bare feet. "You didn't find a pair for yourself?"

"I wear an extra-large." He winked and she rolled her eyes. "You want some brandy? I've got a few good bottles in the bar. It'll warm us up."

"I was thinking of making tea."

"Nah, brandy is better."

She fixed him with a look and had to laugh at how absurd he looked in the blanket, which he wore poncho-style. It was red, white, and green and looked as if it had been hand crocheted. "You trying to liquor me up?"

"I'm trying to liquor myself up. You're free to have tea, though."

She followed him onto the porch. Without the heat lamps on, it was like the frozen tundra. He ducked behind the bar and found a bottle of Courvoisier, poured it into a snifter, and swirled the glass. Somehow the refinement of it all seemed at odds with Boden's blue-collar biker image. Then again, the huge Christmas doily he had wrapped around him didn't exactly fit in with that persona, either. She supposed that even if Boden tried, he couldn't escape the art of being manly.

Honest to goodness, she couldn't think of a more manly man.

"You sure you don't want one?" he asked.

"Okay, you talked me into it."

His mouth curved up. "It's good stuff." He poured another balloon glass, handed it to her, and raised his drink in a toast. "As the great Tom Waits says, 'You can learn a lot about a woman by getting smashed with her.'"

"You get a lot of women smashed, huh?"

"I'm a bartender, Rachel."

She held his gaze over the rim of her glass, then took a slow sip, letting the warm liquid wash down her throat.

"Let's go drink by the fire." He grabbed the bottle by the neck, came out from behind the bar, and led the way with the flashlight.

She wondered how he managed to keep the blanket from slipping off and kind of hoped she could get a peek at that fine backside of his. No such luck. He spread out on the sectional and she took the seat next to him.

"How long you think this will last?" She stared out the French doors where the snow continued to come down in sheets.

"Who can say? In the meantime, we've got food and heat and good company."

She studied him to see if he was being facetious. Nope, he seemed to mean it, which surprised her. She'd always gotten the impression that he disliked her as much as she distrusted him.

"What plans did you have for Christmas?" she asked, curious. Perhaps one of the Garner brothers had invited him for dinner. He was friendly with all of them and without family . . . well, she hoped someone had thought to include him.

"Work on my books." He propped his heels up on the coffee table and she couldn't help note that he really did have big feet.

"For Old Glory?" That was no way to spend the holiday.

"Yep. I don't know about you, but there never seems to be enough time in the day for bookkeeping."

"Don't I know it. But on Christmas?" She mentally kicked herself once the words left her mouth. It was an insensitive thing to say.

"Why not? The bar's closed."

This time she held her tongue and just nodded. "It looks like there's a good chance we'll be here."

"Yep." He got up, walked to the hearth, and felt his clothing. "Still not dry."

"I wouldn't worry about it. The blanket's a really good look for you."

He bobbed his head at her. "I'm only wearing it to protect your delicate sensibilities. Otherwise, I'd sit here in the buff, drinking my cognac."

"Don't let me stop you." But when he started to take off the afghan, she grabbed his hand away.

"What, are you worried you won't be able to control yourself?"

"Something like that." She tried to go for indifference, but the truth was her thoughts were running along the same line as his. Why not? It was Christmastime and a night with a man as virile as Boden would be a superb way to spend it. Just as quickly she tried to convince herself that a one-night affair with the enemy was reckless. Her brain got it, but her body was having trouble saying no. "Why don't we see if the Canadells have any board games or a deck of cards?"

"Seriously, you want to play Monopoly now?"

She didn't really, but it seemed safer than the alternative, getting naked on the bear rug with Boden and doing something she'd later regret.

CHAPTER 8

The frigid temperature had done nice things to Rachel's breasts and Boden tried with all his might not to laser in on them. Why was she cold when he was hot? The fire was throwing off enough heat to make him tight and uncomfortable. Hell, who was he fooling? It was Rachel making him feel that way.

Just drink your brandy, asshole.

"So tell me about your parents." It was a neutral conversation topic and, frankly, he was interested. "Both lawyers, huh?"

"My dad's an appellate court judge and my mom is a corporate attorney. My sister, Kate, and her husband are both medical malpractice attorneys. Nothing more to tell really."

"What's with Trial Lawyer of the Year? Is it some kind of family tradition?"

She laughed and moved closer on the couch so that their shoulders were touching. "No. It's a long, boring story," she said, and waved him off.

He leaned back and stretched out his feet on the coffee table. "Seems to me that we've got nothing but time." He wanted to know what her earlier reference was about. She didn't strike him as someone who was low on the confidence scale, but the way her face had dropped when she'd mentioned the subject made him wonder. Did Miss Perfect have an Achilles' heel?

She let out a sigh. "A guy I used to date was recently named Trial Lawyer of the Year. That's all."

"And your parents wanted you to marry this guy?" For no understandable reason he felt a wave of envy pass over him.

She did a double take. "Where'd you get that? No. They didn't even like him. He was a back-stabbing jerk."

"Back-stabbing?" He turned to face her. "What'd he do?"

She hesitated for a few seconds, then said, "He pretended to be in love with me and used my knowledge of Dole to steal my job."

"What do you mean he stole your job? He got you fired?"

"No. He was outside counsel. We hired his firm to take on the extra caseload. At the time, my boss had put in his resignation and I was the heir apparent to take his job. It had all but been promised to me. While I was dating Jeremy, I told him my plans for taking over the legal department, the changes I wanted to implement. Then he went behind my back and applied for the job, proposing all my ideas at the interview. And he got the position."

This Jeremy dude sounded like a real douchebag "You dumped him, right?"

"I would've if I'd had the chance. He sent me a text the minute he was named general counsel, saying that as my new boss we could no longer be romantically involved. Can you believe it?" She shook her head. "Needless to say, I quit the next day. I'm over it now, but that's what I get for trusting someone like him."

Jeremy sounded like he needed to have his ass whupped. And as far as being over it . . . Boden didn't think so. "Did he initially give you any reason to believe he wasn't trustworthy?"

She thought about it for a second. "No, I guess I'm just gullible. Not anymore, though."

Boden got up and put another log on the fire. "Or maybe Jeremy was a con man who you didn't see coming. It happens to the best of us."

"He's unscrupulous, that's for sure. And yet, he's Trial Lawyer of the Year."

"Were you in love with the guy?" Boden sat back down and again Rachel inched closer.

"No," she said, but Boden didn't believe her. And once more, he felt an unexpected jolt of jealousy. Jeremy was a jerk-off, but he had the kind of pedigree a woman like Rachel went for. Well educated, professional, a lawyer.

He refilled their brandy snifters and raised his glass. "Screw Jeremy."

She laughed. It was a nice musical sound. And she looked so pretty sitting there with her feet tucked under her butt, her cheeks rosy from the heat of the fire, that Boden couldn't help himself. He kissed her. Soft and slow at first, in case she wasn't into it. When she didn't pull away, he went in for more, covering her mouth with his. All day, he'd wanted to do this. Longer, if he was being truly honest with himself. There was a reason he went to her bakery every morning when he owned his own gastro pub. And there was a reason he continued to taunt her at catering jobs like a fifteen-year-old.

Rachel whimpered and Boden took it up a notch by slipping his tongue between her lips. She tasted like brandy and woman. He moved over her, sifting his hands through her hair. The warm pull of her mouth pleaded for more, so he took the kiss deeper, eliciting another feminine moan.

He untucked her blouse, inched his hands up her soft skin, and rested them just beneath her rib cage. "This okay?"

"What this is, is a dumb idea." She sighed.

"You think? Because you seem pretty into it. I am, that's for sure. But just give me the word and I'll stop."

She leaned up and kissed him. Probably a green light, but Boden kept his hands still, letting her call the shots.

"Just this one time, right?" She seemed to be rationalizing this . . . him . . . to herself. Boden should've been offended—later he probably would be—but his dick didn't have that much pride.

"Yeah, sure." He rolled on top of her and the blanket came loose in the process. "How about I get rid of this damn thing?" He tossed the afghan on the floor.

She propped up on both elbows to look at him. "Wow, you work out."

"Not really." He shrugged and checked out his arms. "Don't have time. I guess it's all the boxes I carry."

"I like this." She ran her hand over his beer mug tattoo.

"You do?" It surprised him. Inked-up guys didn't seem her speed, but apparently she liked to slum it every once in a while.

"It's very you." She smiled and he didn't know whether the comment was a barb or a compliment.

"Yes, it is." *And I'm proud of who I am, lady.* "You got any?" He rucked her blouse up and landed a featherlight kiss on her belly. She smelled sweet, like that perfume she always wore with a hint of cinnamon and sugar. "I don't see any yet." He pushed her shirt higher, exposing her bra, a see-through number that made him grow twice as hard.

She actually giggled, which ordinarily would've turned him off. With her, though, it had the opposite effect.

"Any here?" He tugged the cups of her bra down and cupped her breasts. They were plump and firm with pretty pink nipples that puckered to attention as he touched them with his thumbs. "God, you're perfect, Rachel."

Her eyes heated and she whispered, "Not as perfect as you."

"Yeah, you are." He dipped down and tasted her again.

She ground into him and slid her hands underneath the waistband of his boxers. "I wondered if you had underwear on."

"Disappointed?"

She nuzzled his neck. "You think we're crazy to be doing this?"

"That depends. Have you been naughty or nice?"

She giggled again, then threw caution to the wind and slid her hands lower until she was clutching his ass. He liked her this way. Sexy and a little greedy for him. He rubbed against the juncture between her thighs and he could've sworn she purred.

"Let's get some of these clothes off." He unfastened the clasp on her pants, dragged down the zipper, and struggled to pull them off one leg at a time. She lifted her butt and helped shuck them off with a few wiggles. The move drove him insane.

And wouldn't you know it, her teeny-weeny bikinis matched the bra, leaving nothing to the imagination. He wondered if she always wore sexy lingerie. Regardless, it was going to be hard to see her at Tart Me Up in a white apron and not remember this moment without getting a woody.

He cupped her through the diaphanous material and felt how wet she was. She dragged her shirt over her head, leaving her in nothing but her underwear.

"Let's get it all off." He unhooked her bra and tossed it on the floor somewhere near his blanket.

The fire crackled and he had a hazy thought that he should put another log on. But the thought of leaving Rachel, even for a second . . . wasn't gonna happen.

"You warm enough?" he asked.

"Hot."

"Mm-m, you don't know the half of it." He slid her panties down her legs and she kicked them off.

"Yours too." She tugged his shorts down and he did the rest of the work, leaving them both naked.

"Want to move to the floor?" He was a big guy, and while the sectional was roomy by most standards it wouldn't cut it for what he had in mind. Besides, there was a nice, thick rug near the fire. Romantic, even if this was supposed to be a onetime deal.

"Okay." But she didn't move and he really wanted to see her. Standing up.

He waited, then finally stood, lifted her, and laid her gently on the rug. She reached up for him to come down. Instead, he took his time taking his fill of her body. In the glow of the light, her skin was rosy. Her legs long and shapely, her stomach flat, and her breasts firm and high. God, she was beautiful.

"Stop staring and come be with me before I chicken out."

He lay beside her and turned on his side. "Why? Why would you chicken out?" He didn't want to rush her into anything.

"Because we're competitors."

They were both bidding on the same venue. In his mind that didn't have to make them adversaries, just fellow business owners, looking to expand. But he supposed after her experience with Jeremy she was always leery. Always afraid of being sucker-punched.

"This doesn't have anything to do with that," he said, and ran his finger along her arm. It was hard to think about anything other than touching her when she was spread out on the floor like that.

She covered his mouth with hers and said against his lips, "Let's not talk about it."

Not talking worked for him. He rolled on top of her and kissed his way down her neck and chest, sucking on her breasts. She made a sexy noise in her throat and he moved his hand between her legs. And just like that she froze.

"I don't have anything and I'm not on the pill."

Shit. Boden crawled to his pants, praying he had a condom—or two—in his wallet. It's not like he walked around all the time hoping to get laid. But he usually carried them because Gunny had hammered the importance of being safe and prepared into his horny teenage head and the habit had stuck through adulthood. And then there was the not-so-small responsibility of owning a bar and being everyone's mother. He'd had to come to the rescue more times than he could count. Hell, he'd put a condom machine in the bathroom if Old Glory weren't a family restaurant.

He rummaged through his wallet and said a silent thank-you when he found three shiny packets wedged inside his billfold. "I've got us covered."

He crawled back and pulled her on top of him. Like he'd done before, she kissed her way down his body, stopping to examine a few of his tattoos.

"Is this one for your friend . . . Gunny?" She ran her finger over his American eagle. After Gunny died, he'd gotten it inked onto his left shoulder with a ribbon that said: "You'll be with me wherever I go."

"Yep." He let her explore while he did a little exploring of his own.

He loved the way she melted at his touch and the sweet sounds she made as he caressed her breasts, hips, and ass. He'd never been with a woman so responsive. She was also kind of shy—subconsciously covering herself whenever he looked too long—which Boden found endearing. Rachel didn't seem to know just how gorgeous and sexy she was.

He rolled her under him, ripped open one of the foil packets with his teeth, and suited up. With his fingers, he brought her close to climax.

"Please, Boden."

"Please what?"

She rocked into him and tried to guide him inside her, but Boden continued to use his hands. "You know what?"

He grinned. "Tell me, just so we're clear."

"I want you inside of me."

He slipped a finger in.

"Oh, that's good." Her head fell back and she closed her eyes. "But that's not what I meant."

He laughed. "Patience is a virtue, you know."

"To hell with patience." Once again, she tried to take what she wanted, her hand squeezing around his dick, making it throb. It felt so good he thought he'd explode.

"All right, you win." And with one forceful thrust he was in, surrounded by warmth and a mind-blowing tightness that made him see colors.

She started to move and he held her hips firm. "Give me a few seconds. Otherwise, this is going to be very short-lived."

He reached under her and wrapped her legs around his hips so he could go deeper. "This okay?"

"Never better." Despite his admonition, she started to move.

"Can't get enough of me, huh?"

"It's been a while; I'm making up for lost time."

The fact that she hadn't had sex in a while stoked something in him. Pride. Protectiveness. Possessiveness. The last one wasn't typically his thing. He'd had a lot of girlfriends over the years and never felt the inclination to mark his territory. Having it come up now . . . well, he'd think about that later.

He slowly increased his thrusts until he found the perfect tempo. She held on to his shoulders, trying to keep up.

"Too much?"

"It's good," she said, her voice coming out in breaths. "So good. How 'bout for you?"

He brushed a lock of blond hair away from her face. "Good." Then he kissed her, long and slow, and something moved in his chest. Fearing that she sensed whatever he was feeling, he quickly broke the kiss and turned his head.

"I'm close," she said, and pulled him down, tighter.

Boden picked up the pace, reaching between her legs to take her higher. He wanted this to be good for her. He wanted her to remember this day; he wanted her to remember him. Another first, because usually he wasn't this sentimental about his liaisons. It was the holidays, he told himself. They messed with your head.

"Oh, Boden! Boden." She shuddered and tightened around him, climaxing.

He grunted out her name and the pressure began to build until it swamped over him like an eruption. For a second his head cleared and the euphoria was replaced by intense lucidity. And just like that it was gone.

He regained his breath and smiled down at her, nearly losing his shit at the way she looked up at him. Sort of like he'd hung the moon when all he'd done was give her good sex.

"You're welcome," he said to lighten the mood, because suddenly everything felt real intense.

"You too," she responded smugly.

Apparently, the old Rachel was back, which was fine with him, because the new Rachel scared the hell out of him.

CHAPTER 9

Sometime after Boden got up to put another log on the fire, Rachel had fallen asleep. When she woke up, the comforter was wrapped around her and Boden sat cross-legged next to the coffee table, eating cake.

"Is that my *bûche de noël?*"

"Yep," he said around a bite.

She clutched the blanket around her and sat up. The room seemed darker than before, so dark that she couldn't make out what was going on outside. "How long have I been asleep?"

"Hours. Merry Christmas, by the way."

She reached for her phone on the coffee table and checked the time. It was past midnight. "Whoa, you're not kidding." She couldn't remember what time it had been when she'd nodded off, but it couldn't have been too late. Great sex was apparently better than Ambien.

She watched Boden eat. He'd dressed, which was a shame, because he was pretty breathtaking naked. Then again, he was pretty breathtaking in jeans and a flannel shirt. And in bed . . . she'd never experienced anything like it. She'd felt a connection she'd never had with any other partner, not that there'd been a lot of them. In college, she'd had a long-term boyfriend, who'd broken up with her when she'd moved back to California to go to law school. Law school and studying for the bar had been too taxing for serious dating, though she'd had a few sporadic affairs. There'd been boyfriends since, but nothing serious. And then there'd been Jeremy.

"Want some?" Boden lifted his fork.

It seemed like a sacrilege to eat the bride and groom's cake after their wedding had been spoiled, but she was hungry. And curious how the cake came out. She inched closer to Boden. "Is it good?"

"It's out of this freaking world. You should really try it." He held out a forkful and she scraped it off with her teeth, letting the white chocolate and buttercream frosting melt in her mouth.

"Mm-m. Delicious, if I do say so myself."

He chuckled. "You learn how to make it in culinary school?"

She was surprised he knew that she'd gone to culinary school. Not every baker took that trajectory. "How'd you know about culinary school?" Rachel couldn't remember ever having talked to him about it. Until this weekend, they'd hardly talked at all other than to grouse at each other.

He shrugged. "I don't know. I think it's on your Web site."

"You looked at my Web site?" She arched a brow. Was he spying on her to build his case to get the Old Watermill House?

"Sure." He hitched his shoulders again as if it wasn't a big deal, which it probably wasn't. But she had a suspicious nature, especially after Jeremy. "You look at mine?"

"No." She probably should've, but it had never occurred to her.

"The same woman who did Garner Adventure's did mine. She's up in Reno . . . does great work."

Using a free template on one of the hosting sites, Samantha had created Tart Me Up's. When Rachel opened her restaurant, she'd do something more professional. For now, the one she had worked fine.

He made room for her at the coffee table and it struck her that this was a weird conversation to be having after mind-blowing sex. Web sites. But it would always come down to business between the two of them. For some reason that made her sad, like it was a lost opportunity.

Boden cut another piece of the Yule log and put it on his plate. "Here, have some more." He fed her another bite.

She picked up the fork and reciprocated.

"Damn, this is good." He caught a few crumbs that had fallen from his mouth with his hands. "Best wedding cake I ever had."

The compliment warmed her. People usually raved about her baked goods, but something told her Boden was a tough critic. He was certainly persnickety about his beer. And, inexplicably, she wanted to impress him.

He forked over another piece, sliding it into her mouth, and she laughed. "This is the strangest Christmas I've ever had . . . eating wedding cake at midnight."

He looked at her, and for a second something in his eyes flickered. Melancholy, maybe. "It's the best one I ever had."

She swallowed hard. It was either the saddest thing she'd ever heard or the best compliment anyone had ever given her. "You don't hear me complaining." She could honestly say she'd never felt this blissful, and she knew she had Boden to thank for that.

"Do you think it's stopped snowing?" She gathered up the comforter, wrapped it securely around her, and padded over to the bank of windows to peer outside. It was hard to tell in the darkness, but she couldn't hear the wind blowing like it had before.

"Well?"

"I can't see anything." She continued to press her face against the glass.

Boden came over to join her. "I think it's stopped. For now, anyway."

He was close enough that she could feel the warmth of his body and a shiver went through her. "What do we do now, besides eat cake?"

He glanced at her and held her gaze. "I can think of a few things."

Sunlight beamed through the windows and for a second Rachel forgot where she was. Then she felt Boden's arm around her and the breadth of his bare chest pressed against her back and she remembered. The storm, the Canadells' house, and the best night of her life. The fire had nearly burned out, yet she felt snug and toasty underneath the blankets with Boden. His body was like a furnace.

"You awake?" he asked next to her ear, and the vibration of his voice tickled.

She twisted around and came directly in contact with his chest. A very nice chest. He kissed the top of her head, letting his lips hover over her hair, and her insides squeezed. Sleeping with him felt natural. And glorious. A secret part of her hoped they'd be snowed in for a few more days.

"Mm-hmm. You want coffee?" She could heat the water over the fire and make drip.

There was a long silence as he pulled her closer, his strong arm across her back. "Just stay here a few minutes longer."

"Okay." She expected him to initiate sex—she could feel his erection pressed against her stomach—but he just held her with his eyes closed, resting his chin on her head.

She kissed the hollow of his throat, tasting a hint of salt and something distinctly Boden. The memory of their pre-dawn hours together flitted through her head and she could feel her breasts go heavy. She wanted him again.

He stirred slightly. "I'm gonna check the weather and see if we have any cell reception."

And before she knew it he was up and putting on his pants. It happened so quickly she didn't have time to protest. Alone on the floor, she felt bereft. She got to her feet, gathered her clothes on the hearth, and headed to the bathroom. There was enough natural light to see her way across the house without a flashlight.

"It looks like it's cleared!" he called after her. "When we finish our coffee, I'll check out the driveway!"

What was there to check? It's not like the tree could've moved itself. She supposed Boden wanted to feel useful, and nodded.

In the bathroom, she was able to get enough water from the sink to wash up a little and finger brush her teeth. She slipped into her yoga pants and sweater, put her hair in a twist, and made her way into the kitchen to search for ground coffee. She'd only brought beans. There was a bag in the pantry and she filled a kettle with bottled water and took it to the fireplace where Boden was stoking the flames.

"How do I do this?" She eyed the fire.

He took the pot from her, slipped the handle over an andiron, and held it over the flame. "Old school, baby."

"You were definitely an Eagle Scout, weren't you?"

"Nope, just went camping with Gunny a few times. And what do they say? 'Necessity is the mother of invention.'"

And Boden Farmer was a very capable man—in and out of the bedroom.

"I'll get a potholder." She returned to the kitchen and found an oven mitt in one of the drawers.

While she was there, she set up two mugs with filters and coffee grinds. Boden wasn't the only one who knew how to improvise. Sometime during the wee hours of the morning, Boden had put the *bûche de noël* back in the fridge. She got it out along with two plates.

By the time she returned to the living room with her tray of goodies, the kettle was whistling. Boden pulled it from the flames and Rachel took it from there.

"We're having cake again." She could feel her face heat, remembering exactly what they'd done with the cake during their second round of heart-pounding sex.

Boden's lips curved up. "I'm down with that."

She poured water into their cups and the smell of freshly brewed coffee filled the air. "The sun's out," she said, gazing out the window.

Boden let out a breath. "Yeah, but there's gotta be at least four feet or more of snow on the ground."

They'd certainly had that much snow before in Glory Junction. The city was a winter sports Mecca.

He took a sip of coffee. "That tree is probably buried by now, which is going to make it twice as hard to get out of here."

She wondered if he was regretting their time together and anxious to leave. Then she chided herself for being a moron. They had to leave sometime.

He watched her over the rim of his cup. "If it's at all possible I'll get you out of here in time to make it to your parents'. At least you might get there in time for Christmas dinner."

Her throat went dry. He was being incredibly considerate—and sweet. It touched her; it really did. "That's very kind of you, Boden, but I don't think it's going to happen and I'm okay with that. I'm more concerned with the bakery and what's going on there." She had hundreds of dollars' worth of ingredients that could be spoiling, unless Sam figured out how to work the backup generator. At this point, she'd lost faith in the stupid things.

He drained his coffee and rose. "Let me see what I can do with a shovel and a chainsaw."

She took their dirty dishes to the kitchen and watched through the window as he headed to the garage. Her socks and boots were still by the fire and Rachel put them on and bundled up. In the time it took her to get down the hill, Boden had made good progress shoveling a decent trail to the fallen tree.

"Can you believe this?" She held out her arms and looked up at the sky, where the sun shone like it was summer. Fickle weather. "How long until you think the power will come back?"

He leaned on the handle of the shovel. "No way to know. I'm sure PG and E's all over it, though."

"What can I do to help?"

"Not a lot. This tree is in here pretty good and it's a big sucker." He eyed the chainsaw. "It works about as well as the generator. These folks don't take care of their tools; the nose sprockets are gummed up."

The Canadells were rarely here, according to Tara. When they were, Rachel doubted they spent the time cleaning their chainsaw.

"You try your cell phone?" she asked.

"No signal."

She pulled hers from her jacket pocket and tried to make a call. Zero dial tone, zero bars. She attempted a text to her parents, which also failed. "Nothing."

Boden, who'd started shoveling again, stopped and stared at her. "We may have to spend another night here."

The words made her body tingle. *Another night.* Another night with Boden.

"You hear that?" he said, and whipped his head around.

In the distance came the sound of a motorcycle. Boden shielded his eyes against the sun and peered out over the forest. A snowmobile came over the knoll. It was too far away to make out who was driving it, but it looked as if help was on the way.

CHAPTER 10

There days had gone by and Boden hadn't talked to Rachel since they'd been rescued by the police chief. Colt had ferried them both on his snowmobile to the highway where his truck was parked and driven them home. Tuesday, after a crew had removed the tree, Boden had gone up to the Canadell house to collect his portable bar, supplies, and truck. Rachel's stuff, including her bakery van, was already gone. He figured she'd headed to the Bay Area to see her parents, because she hadn't been at the bakery. He'd checked. Just the kid, Samantha, and one of the other girls who worked there.

"Hey, boss, you're here early." Ingrid hung her jacket on a hook behind the bar.

"Yeah, I'm trying to figure out this new coffeemaker. You need a freaking Ph.D. just to pull an espresso." He wanted to have it ready by New Year's Eve for the rush. Colt's band was playing and Boden expected a crowd.

"Congrats, by the way. I was just over at the Morning Glory and everyone's talking about it."

"Thanks. Rita Tucker called me this morning with the news. I'm hoping you're down with a promotion, because I'm gonna need help getting the brewery up and running and the restaurant going over at the mill house."

"I'm in." Ingrid rubbed her hands together enthusiastically.

Boden wished he could feel better about having won the bid. He wondered if Rachel even knew yet. With any luck, she wouldn't hold it against him. Since their night together, she'd been all he could think about, and he hoped they could start seeing each other, despite her edict that it was a onetime deal. But his getting the Old Watermill House would likely stick a fork in those plans. He had a sneaking suspicion that she'd lump him in with the likes of Jeremy, even though their situation was completely different. Boden hadn't used her to climb the corporate ladder. He got the mill house fair and square.

"You mind watching the place while I take a quick break?" He planned to run over to Tart Me Up to see if the elusive Rachel had shown up.

"Nope. Do what you need to do."

Boden shrugged into his coat. As usual there was a line at the bakery. But it didn't take long for him to get inside, where Samantha was working the counter.

"Rachel here?"

"She's in the kitchen." Sam took her time making a latte for a customer and didn't seem in any rush to get her.

Yep, they knew.

"Should I go back there or wait?" he asked, a hint of impatience in his voice.

Sam looked over her shoulder and called into the kitchen, "Rachel, Boden's here!"

Rachel came out a few minutes later, covered in flour. "I can't talk to you now. I've got a situation."

She turned around and Boden followed her into the kitchen. There was a broken flour sack on the floor and flour everywhere.

"I'll help you clean it up," Boden said.

"I don't need help and you shouldn't be back here without a hairnet."

Funny, because she didn't have one on. Her hair was tied back and her cheeks were filled with color and all Boden could think about was taking her face in his hands and kissing her. But he didn't think that would go over too well.

"Come on, Rach. I know you're disappointed, but—"

She whirled around. "You don't know anything, so please don't tell me how I feel."

"Okay." He held up his hands. "Could we at least talk about it?"

She nudged her head at the mess. "Not now, obviously."

"When, then?"

"When I've had time to process it and don't feel like biting your head off." She tried for a smile, but Boden could see it was strained.

"Fair enough." He started to leave and stopped. "I'm not Jeremy, Rach."

"No, you're not, but this still feels like déjà vu all over again."

There was nothing he could do about that. He'd made an honest bid for the building and had been awarded the lease based on his proposal and projected revenue. The way he saw it, what happened at the Canadells' Christmas Eve was totally separate.

He left, frustrated. Two days later, he was angry. Rachel had done everything possible to avoid him, including holing up in Tart Me Up's kitchen every time he went over there. He'd wanted to invite her to Old Glory's New Year's Eve party. Although he had to work the bar, he'd hoped to have a couple of dances with her. And after he closed . . . well, perhaps they could've started the new year together. Since the party was the next day, it didn't look like that was going to happen.

"What's with the long face?" Colt pulled up a stool to the bar.

"Nothing." Boden assumed Colt was off duty because he wasn't in uniform or wearing his sidearm and he filled him a pint glass. "Rachel Johnson's a real piece of work."

Colt laughed. "You seemed to like her just fine the other day."

"That was before the city awarded me the lease on the Old Watermill House." He wiped down the bar.

"Yeah, I heard she was going for it, too. Her and about a dozen other people. So there's some hard feelings, huh?"

"She wanted it pretty bad."

Colt shrugged. "Only one business was going to get it. She had to know there was a chance she'd lose out."

Colt was right of course, but Boden still felt a pang of . . . not exactly guilt but something. "I wish there was another place she
could get, but spaces the size of the mill house are non-existent in
Glory Junction."

"That's for sure. The last big building available that I can remember is the one my family got for Garner Adventure." Colt took
a swig of his beer. "You still looking for investors for the brewery?"

"Besides you?"

"A friend of Delaney's might be interested. He lives in LA and is
a big craft-beer drinker."

"If you and Delaney vouch for him I could make room for his
money." Boden wanted to keep the circle small, though. Too many
investors equaled too many bosses. He was his own man.

"I'll talk to him and let you know. He's coming up for New
Year's Eve. In fact, you'll meet him; he's coming to my show."

"It's gonna be a full house, buddy boy." Boden leaned over the
bar and patted Colt on the shoulder. Half the town was coming,
everyone but Rachel.

Colt finished his beer and took off, leaving Boden in a nearly
empty bar. He spent the time before the evening rush polishing
glasses, mopping floors, and convincing himself to stay away from
Tart Me Up. He'd made the first overture. It was up to Rachel to
make the next one. She said she would as soon as she cleared her
head and got over her disappointment.

The problem was Boden didn't want to wait. Something had
clicked between them the night they were stranded together and he
wanted to see where the two of them could lead. The feelings were
new to him. He wasn't usually overcome by a one-night hookup.
But Rachel was different. For the first time since Gunny died, in her
he had found someone he could talk to. Really talk and tell things to.
And then there was the undeniable attraction he felt for her.

By the way they poked at each other during catering gigs, he
suspected she felt the same attraction. And the night they'd spent
together . . . he didn't think he'd imagined her reaction. Pure chem-
istry. But he'd miscalculated situations before and for all he knew
she'd just been scratching an itch. Besides, whatever hope they had

of starting something ended with him getting the Old Watermill House.

He told himself to let it go and kept mopping.

Rachel shoved a sheet of already-baked buns into the oven. "What am I doing?" she chided herself aloud and quickly replaced the pan with the unbaked buns.

It had been like that the last couple of days. Her head barely screwed on. She told herself it was over the disappointment of losing the bid for the mill house and having her grand plans derailed. But that was only half of it. The other half was six foot two with arms of tattoos.

She debated whether to march over to Old Glory and apologize to Boden for her rude behavior. It wasn't his fault that the council had chosen him. His proposal was simply better than hers and a brewery was a stronger revenue generator than a bakery. On an intellectual level, she got that. On an emotional one, she was a wreck and didn't really want to explore all the reasons why. So she went with the easy one—the Old Watermill House. She'd wanted it and had lost it to the competition. Boden.

It all felt vaguely familiar, yet different.

"You still brooding?" Sam popped her head into the kitchen. "We've got at least twenty people lined up out here waiting to pick up their New Year's orders."

They were closed Sunday and customers were anxious to get their errands done so they could begin their New Year's Eve revelry. Everyone was celebrating at Old Glory tonight. Colt's band was playing and Boden was serving specialty drinks to ring in the new year. Friends had invited her to go with them, but she planned to avoid the bar and spend a quiet night at home in front of a fire.

It wasn't because she didn't enjoy a festive crowd; it was because she was avoiding an inconvenient truth. She felt something for Boden that she didn't want to feel. While she wanted to slough it off as reading more into a night of hot sex than the act deserved, she and Boden had been dancing around these feelings for some time. The juvenile jabs they took at each other during catering jobs, the way she pretended not to notice him when he came in for his morning coffee, the way he pretended not to notice her when she'd go to Old Glory for happy hour with some of the locals. Classic denial.

But after their snowbound night together . . . well, a lot had changed.

"I'll be right out," she told Sam. "I just have to pull the buns out of the oven."

"I did it."

Rachel stared at her quizzically. "You did what?"

"I filled out my application for CalArts. Just have to drop it in the mail."

Rachel had been so wrapped up in herself, she'd forgotten all about Sam and art school. "Oh, Sam, that's wonderful. I'm so proud of you."

"Will you do it with me?"

"Go to art school?" Rachel asked, flummoxed.

"Walk to the post office with me . . . for luck . . . and moral support."

"Of course. I'd be honored to." She pulled Samantha in for a hug. "This is going to be a great year for you, Sam."

The thought of losing her, though, almost made Rachel cry. Despite the age difference, they'd become close, and Sam was the best employee she had.

"For you, too," Sam said. "I know it doesn't seem like it right now, but I think things work out for a reason. Maybe you'll find something better than the mill house, something that will be hugely successful."

Rachel didn't think there was anything out there better than the mill house—Lord knew she'd searched—but she nodded, trying to put on a good face. There was no need to bring Sam down, not when she had such exciting prospects for her future.

"Let's finish up here and go mail your application."

By the end of the day, Rachel was exhausted. She kicked off her shoes, flicked on the gas fire, and headed to her bedroom to change into something warm and comfortable. At least the holiday rush was officially over. And without a new venture in the works she was no longer desperate for capital, which meant she could cut back on catering. She tried to tell herself that was the silver lining of not get-

ting her dream. Instead, she poured herself a glass of wine and decided to get shitfaced. Why not? It was New Year's Eve and she
didn't have to drive.

Two hours later, she was startled awake on the couch by the
sound of gunshots. Jolted upright, she searched the coffee table for
her phone to call 911. When the explosions went off a second time,
she jumped to her feet, ready to take cover. That's when it struck
her that the loud noises weren't gunshots but fireworks.

She glanced at the clock on her wall. Midnight. Awesome. Let
the new year begin, she said to herself without much enthusiasm,
and padded into her bedroom to go back to sleep.

The next morning, she got out of bed with a hell of a headache
and tried to cure it with a hot shower. When that didn't work, she
downed two cups of coffee, looked at herself in the mirror, and
made a couple of gagging noises. Thank goodness Tart Me Up was
closed today.

But it was time to make amends for acting like a petulant child,
so she grabbed a concealer stick and tried to work some magic. An
hour later, she looked presentable and drove the short distance to
Old Glory. She checked her reflection one more time in the rearview
mirror and got out of the car. A combination of nerves and anticipation pooled at the pit of her stomach. It was more about seeing
Boden again than it was about making an apology. She'd behaved
like a spoiled brat and was willing to eat crow. The hard part was
navigating her feelings—or whatever this was—when it came to
Boden.

It was still too early for the bar to be open, but she knew Boden
got there in the morning to prepare for Old Glory's lunch service.
She'd taken a chance that the place would be open at all on a holiday. But sure enough, the jukebox was on and Ingrid was stocking
the shelves.

"Hey, Happy New Year." Ingrid waved.

Rachel scanned the dining room. It looked like there'd been a
heck of a party and they'd only half cleaned up. "Big night, huh?"

"It was crazy. I think everyone in town was here, including the
fire marshal." She laughed and followed Rachel's eyes around the
room. "We're still recuperating."

"Where's Boden?"

"He's over at the new place...said he had something to do there." Ingrid shrugged. "How come you didn't come by last night? Did you have other plans?"

Rachel's eyes dropped to her shoes and she let out a breath. "Oh, you know, the holidays knocked me out."

"I think the boss was disappointed. I was in charge of the door, and between you and me, he kept asking if you'd come in."

"He did?" Boden hadn't specifically asked her to attend. Then again, the whole town was coming, so he'd probably assumed that she would, too. But disappointed?

"I know, right? I've never seen him that way before. It was sweet. So are you two an item now?"

"Uh...no." Since that night, they'd barely said two words to each other. But that had been her fault, not Boden's. "You said he was at the Old Watermill House?"

"Yep."

"Thanks, Ingrid. And Happy New Year." Rachel dashed out of the bar and back to her car.

When she pulled up in front of the mill house five minutes later, Boden was up on a ladder, hanging something on the front of the building. It was too windy to be up that high and Rachel feared that one good gust and Boden would get blown down.

He twisted around at the sound of her engine and squinted. Her stomach dipped at the sight of him. A ski jacket hugged his wide shoulders and a pair of well-worn jeans rested low on his hips. And here she was ogling him when what she should've been doing was telling him to get down from the ladder before he broke his neck.

He continued to look at her car, curiously. It was clear to Rachel that he was blinded by sunlight and was having trouble identifying who she was. She got out and walked closer. It was a beautiful building with an old-brick façade that had been weathered from more than two hundred years of rain and snow and the summer heat. The waterwheel had been cleaned up and refurbished by the city, the gears gleaming off the river. Rachel took in a breath, staring at what might've been, willing to concede that the place would make a gorgeous taproom.

Obviously, Boden wasn't wasting any time putting his stamp on the building. She stared up at where he was working and noted that he was attaching a sign to the top of the building. She couldn't yet make it out. Something that said "Old Glory," no doubt, though she wasn't even sure that's what he planned to name it. Perhaps Old Glory II or something after his mentor, Gunny.

She pulled her coat tighter, trying to ward off the cold. At least it was clear and sunny. She yelled up, but from his precarious perch Boden couldn't hear her through the sound of the howling wind. Or his drill.

She stood there for a while, just watching, waiting for the seed of regret to bury itself deep inside her belly. But all she saw was Boden and how much it meant to him to carry out Gunny's dream, and something in her chest moved.

He continued to fuss with his tools, drilling and hanging, despite the wind. Twenty minutes later, he came down the ladder, giving her a clear view of the side of the building where he'd been working. And that's when she saw what the sign said.

CHAPTER 11

"Buns and Beer?" She looked at him quizzically. What kind of name was that for a brewery? "You riffing on the whole Hooters theme?" Boden didn't strike her as the type to sell T and A; at least Rachel certainly hoped not.

He laughed, but it sounded kind of mirthless, like he was disappointed in her for coming to that conclusion. "No," was all he said, and he watched her closely. "Didn't expect you to show up here."

She stared up at the sign, shielding the sun with her hands. The marquee was made up of three-dimensional rusted steel letters that lit up. Very vintage and industrial, like it had been there forever. She wondered when he'd had time to have it made.

"I owe you an apology," she said. "Can we start over?" She stepped closer and stuck out her hand to shake his. "Congratulations, Boden. I wish you much success and happiness in"—she stared up at the sign again—"Buns and Beer. I'm sorry I acted like a sore loser. It was low of me and really cruddy. You're carrying out Gunny's legacy and I think it's amazing." She squeezed his hand.

"Yeah?" He leaned against the door of his truck. "Why didn't you come last night?"

She hitched her shoulders. "It's not because of this." She nodded at the old building. "I've made my peace with it. You were the better candidate and I'll find something else. The truth: I'm still trying to work out what happened between us at the Canadells' Christmas."

"Are you having regrets?" He frowned and she swore she saw disappointment in his eyes.

"No, not regrets." Just the opposite, it was all she could think about.

"Then what's the problem?"

Spoken like a true guy, she thought. "So we just move forward as if it's business as usual?"

He gave her a solemn look. "Those were your rules, sweetheart, not mine." He gazed up at the sign and pointed. "You're the buns."

"Huh?" she asked, confused.

"I want to share the space with you." He paused while Rachel let it sink in. "I'll do my brewery and taproom; you'll have your bakery and restaurant. There's enough square footage to do both and we'll split the cost of the lease. It makes good business sense."

She looked at him, really looked, because giving her half the space would significantly reduce his profits. It would change his entire plan. As far as cutting costs, he'd never indicated the rent was an issue. So why would he do this for her? It was crazy.

"Boden? What are you saying?"

"What I'm saying is I think we'll make a hell of a team." He waited for her response.

"It's beyond generous, Boden. And it's also insane. You were the city's choice. I accept that and will figure out a way to do my restaurant somewhere else in Glory Junction."

"If that's what you want to do . . . it'll mean I have to get a new sign . . . but whatever." One side of his mouth tipped up. "Come on, Rach. I've given it a lot of thought and I wouldn't do it unless it made sense. Seriously, I'm not that nice. Think about it. Together, we can turn this place into a food and beer destination. With both of us, we'll have twice the capital, twice the appeal, and can do twice the marketing as what we could've afforded on our own. It's a solid plan."

She huffed out a breath, still trying to process the offer he was making. Yes, it made sound business sense. But how would it be working with him every day? Especially with all these new feelings she had for him. What if he didn't share those feelings? "We can't even get along at catering jobs. How do you propose we work side by side?"

He chuckled. "Every time we get angry, we kiss?"

"Be serious, Boden. This is a big commitment."

"You bet it is. It's a partnership. A *business* partnership." He emphasized the word "business" and a sharp prick of disappointment stabbed her in the chest.

Ridiculous, she thought to herself. They'd barely had two kind words for each other before Christmas, let alone an actual date. And here she was wishing for more than the incredibly generous offer he was making her. A proposal she'd be a fool to turn down.

"We'd have to draw up some kind of contract . . . put the details in writing," she said.

"I know a good lawyer." He winked and her treacherous heart fluttered.

"We should each have our own attorneys, someone looking out for our individual interests," she said.

"Seems like a waste of money to me. I trust you. But if it'll make you feel better . . ." He rubbed his hands together. "It's freezing out here. Let's continue this in my truck with the heater turned on."

She sat next to him in the cab. His legs rubbed against hers and a hot rush of desire hit her like a thunderbolt when she needed to focus.

She inched away, trying to put a little distance between them. "Boden, are you sure you want to do this?"

His brown eyes held her gaze. "Yep. I'm also interested in pursuing other things with you, but this has to be separate."

Her heart hitched. "What kind of other things?"

He reached over, pulled her closer, and covered her mouth with his. "This."

His tongue tangled with hers and he cupped the back of her head. She held him, luxuriating in the warm pull of his mouth, the smell of his aftershave, and the strength of his arms. It didn't get any better than this and that was the problem. Yet she couldn't stop herself.

He changed his angle, pressing her against the padded seat, moving over her, hungry and frenzied. She, just as feverish, gripped the hem of his jacket and tried to pull it over his head. He saved her the trouble by unzipping it and she touched his chest, feeling his heart thunder. Hers was hammering in her chest. The windows were fogged up and he reached for the button on her jeans.

"Boden, what are we doing?" Feeling dizzy and a little overcome, she broke the kiss.

"I thought it was pretty obvious." He grinned. "You want to stop?"

"Nope." She nibbled on his bottom lip. "I just want to know the rules."

"You and rules." He reached over and opened her door. "Stay there." He got out of the driver's door, rushed around the front of the truck to the passenger side, got down on one knee, and took her hand. "Will you, Rachel Johnson, go into business with me?"

She stared down at him, touched beyond words. "I'd be honored to," she said, and leaned out of the truck, craning her neck to have another look at the sign. "Buns and Beer, huh?"

"I thought it was pretty clever. You don't like it?"

"I like it. And I like you." She held his face and rubbed her hands over a day's worth of scruff. A week ago, the admission would've made her feel vulnerable. But today she had nothing but trust. In him, in them, and in their future venture together.

"I like you, too. A lot," he said, gazing up at her with such tenderness in his eyes it made her breath catch in her throat. "You think we can see where this goes?"

Rachel launched herself at him, knocking them both to the snowy ground. "Let's see where it goes."

But in her heart, she already knew he was the one.

Epilogue

One year later . . .

"We made the list." Rachel twined her arms behind Boden's neck and wrapped her legs around his waist.

"What list?" He walked them to the bar, dropped her on a stool, and dipped down to steal a kiss.

"Oprah's Favorite Things. She said Buns and Beer was the perfect getaway stop for people who love artisan baked goods and craft beer."

"Does that mean more business?"

"You bet it does." She pulled him down for another kiss. One was never enough for her when it came to Boden. In fact, she could kiss him all day.

"You know what made my list of favorite things? You. It's a list of one."

She laughed, which she found herself doing a lot these days. "I don't know, with all the wedding plans I've been a true bridezilla."

"Nah, you just want everything perfect." He nuzzled her neck. "Me too."

She gazed out the window into the dim light where the white-flocked trees shook from the wind. In an hour, she and Boden would be opening for breakfast. "They're predicting more snow this weekend. At this rate, we may wind up like the Canadell wedding."

"Snowed in?" He followed her line of vision to the choppy river. "I doubt it, since we're doing it here. Easy access, even in a storm. But would it be so terrible?" He waggled his brows. "Last time we were snowbound I recall it working out pretty well."

She stroked his face. "Me too. I heard Tara and her fiancé wound up tying the knot in Hawaii. Sounds nice, huh?"

"No," Boden said. "I like Glory Junction in winter for a wedding, surrounded by all our friends."

She nodded, because she adored the idea. The last year had been a dream come true. Buns and Beer was thriving as well as their other businesses. They'd sidelined catering opportunities to have more leisure time together. And Boden had moved into her town house. Recently, they'd started scanning the real estate listings for a bigger house with property to eventually raise a family. A family. Sometimes Rachel had to pinch herself.

"I better get to work." Rachel let out a contented sigh. "The staff will be here soon. Why don't you turn on the Christmas lights?"

In between running their respective businesses and wedding appointments, they'd decorated the entire building for the holidays. Boden's friend, who'd made the last-minute Buns and Beer sign, had constructed a giant lighted reindeer out of the same rusted metal, which they'd mounted to the side of the building. They'd put a Christmas tree and menorah in the lobby and boughs of holly everywhere. The restaurant and taproom looked so festive that tourists and locals crowded the place every night. Buns and Beer had become exactly what she'd wanted, a warm and inviting culinary destination.

Best of all, she and Boden got to work side by side every day. They didn't even fight anymore . . . well, sometimes they disagreed. Adamantly. But then they got to make up, which they'd perfected to an art form.

He got up and flicked on the Christmas lights. "Come here." He crooked his finger and opened his arms.

She walked into them and nestled her head against his chest. "Do you know how much I love you?"

"This much?" He held his arms wide.

"More," she said. "Way more."

"No more than I love you." He pointed above her. "See that? It's mistletoe."

She stared up. "No, it's not. It's a cobweb."

"Why do you always have to be so contrary? Shut up and kiss me."

A COWBOY WEDDING
FOR CHRISTMAS

NICOLE HELM

CHAPTER 1

Lindsay Tyler remembered exactly what she'd said to her oldest brother when he'd asked if she'd feel weird about him getting married at her ex-boyfriend's family's Christmas tree farm.

Why would I care about that?

No matter that Cal still lived in her head as the paragon of boyfriend-ness that no other man she'd dated had come close to. It had been *years* since she'd decided she wanted more than Gracely, Colorado, and Cal Barton.

Why would I care about that?

As she turned onto the lane that would lead to the Barton Ranch and Christmas Tree Farm, she realized why she would care. Too many memories, sweet and increasingly nostalgic with time. There had been years of her life when she'd been so sure she'd marry Cal, move into the house at the end of this lane, and that would be it.

But he hadn't wanted her *more*, and she hadn't been willing to sacrifice seeing a different world for him.

A different world that hadn't fit her like the glove she'd expected it to. A different world that never quite lived up to *home*. Oh, she was glad she'd done it. Six years of independence and learning to be Lindsay Tyler outside of her wonderful but overbearing family. She'd *needed* that.

But coming home. . . Well, it was the right step now. Adult, twenty-four-year-old Lindsay needed home. And for good.

She still couldn't believe herself. Instead of traveling the world or being a famous artist, she was going to student teach and then ideally get a job in the fall where she'd once been an elementary school student.

It was such a joke after all her grand proclamations when she'd left the Tyler Ranch. An embarrassing one. So embarrassing she still hadn't told her family she wasn't just coming home for Christmas vacation. She was home for good.

The thought of telling them made her a little sick, so she was more than happy to fall into wedding plans for her oldest brother and his soon-to-be wife. Even if it meant driving up to the Barton house.

The arching sign over the entryway to the Barton Ranch and Christmas Tree Farm read just that in block red and green letters and had for something like a century. She'd always liked that, that Cal had roots just like hers. Old and settled into the land, but unlike her family's straightforward cattle ranch, Cal had this amazing, festive, and unique history.

Cal was none of those things, which had always pleased her. Her gruff, taciturn cowboy whose smile was mostly just for her because he didn't smile for much else.

She needed to get over the nostalgia train and focus on what was ahead of her. Her brother's wedding. Christmas with her family. And, at some point, swallowing her pride and telling them she was back for good.

Merry Crappy Christmas.

She pulled up behind a line of her family's trucks. The Barton house was decked out with an impressive light display. Before Cal's mother had abandoned the family, Cal's dad always spent days and days getting it just right. After that, the task had fallen to Cal and his sister, much to Cal's consternation. He'd bitterly resented the Christmas tree portion of his family's legacy, especially after his mother had left a second time, but Gracely depended on Barton's for a festive Christmas tree getting experience, and Cal couldn't say no to the influx of cash in the cold winter months.

She really had to stop thinking about Cal. Tonight was about

Shane and Cora's wedding. The coming days were about celebrating that and Christmas with her family. Being on Barton property didn't really matter.

She stepped out of her car, finding her footing on the slick, snowy ground. The quiet of rural Colorado wrapped around her like a warm blanket. No matter that coming home involved swallowing her pride, she was happy to be here. Happy to be back where she could see the stars spread out like a canvas of joy above her, where she could go outside to feel perfectly alone and perfectly safe.

"I've missed you," she whispered fancifully into the dark. She carefully walked up to the porch stairs, then crested the gorgeous wrap-around porch that was lit up to blazing with glowing white lights. Wreaths hung in every window and two small Christmas trees sat in pots at the corners of the porch. It was the picture-perfect place to have a Christmas wedding. That was for sure.

Footsteps and grumbling interrupted the picturesque quiet. Lindsay lifted her arm to knock on the front door, but then the source of the noise came around the corner and Lindsay forgot to hit her fist against the door.

Because bathed in the warm glow of the Christmas lights, the cowboy hat low on his head, was a man who could have been any ranch hand or friend of Sarah's.

But he lifted his gaze.

"Cal." She said his name on a whoosh of breath, because he'd always taken away her breath a little bit. Something about the midnight black hair and the shock of summer sky blue eyes.

And now he wasn't just tall and lean. He was broad. Sturdy. She'd always thought he was the most handsome man in Gracely County, but now that she'd spent some time outside of Gracely she understood the truth.

He was one of the most handsome men *ever*, anywhere.

Crap.

"You seem surprised to see me on my own porch," he said, and she didn't remember his voice being that low and deliciously raspy. She didn't remember that hard, mean line to his mouth geared at anyone except his stepmother.

To be on the receiving end was more of a blow than she expected it to be. Still, she cleared her throat and forced her mouth to curve. "No, no. I just . . . You look so much different than the last time I saw you."

"Funny," he returned, giving her a quick once-over. "You look exactly the same."

Which shouldn't sound like an insult considering he'd once considered her *the prettiest girl in Colorado*—his words. But the way he said it now . . .

Well, humph.

"Well, I, uh, my family is here. I'm meeting them. Shane's . . . wedding."

He grunted in assent, moving for the door. Except she was standing in front of it, her hand still raised and ready to knock.

Cal. Cal was standing there in front of her, and she didn't know what to say or even feel. She'd avoided him at all costs on visits home for six years. At most, she'd seen him across the street in Gracely proper once or twice, but Cal was happiest on his ranch and she'd avoided anything and everything to do with the Barton ranch.

Now he was right there. Right. There. He clearly wasn't the boy she'd loved six years ago, but somehow standing on the same porch with him made her feel like that girl again. Naïve and so desperately in love.

"Darlin', either knock on the door or get out of my way."

Darlin'. He only ever pulled out that drawl with people he hated, but that didn't make sense. It had been six years. Surely he didn't still *hate* her. "I . . ."

"Did I sprout devil horns?"

"No. No. I just . . . No." Heat infused her cheeks and she finally got herself together enough to step out of the way, drop her hand, and not be a complete and utter dope.

Cal moved into the space she'd evacuated and pushed the door open. She could have done that. She *should* have done that. Instead, she followed timidly after him into the warmth of the Barton house.

Not that her face needed to be any warmer.

"Straggler," Cal announced simply, gesturing vaguely at Lindsay. Her family were sitting in various seats around the Barton living room, Cal's sister, Sarah, standing in front of all of them.

"Lindsay!" Sarah squealed, and rushed over to envelop her in a tight hug. "Oh my gosh, you look *amazing*."

Lindsay laughed uncomfortably, though she hugged Sarah back. "Me? You're all grown-up."

Sarah beamed and released her. "Come on in. You didn't miss much. We were just chitchatting waiting for you to get here." Sarah ushered her to a couch where Molly and Gavin were sitting.

Lindsay took the seat in between her siblings. "So, let me guess, you're the driving force behind the Barton Christmas Tree Farm as a wedding venue?"

"Er, well, sort of." Sarah looked back at Cal, who was standing there stoically in the corner. At his sister's glance he shook his head and disappeared down a hall Lindsay knew would take him to the Barton kitchen. "It was Cal's idea," Sarah said, overbrightly. "But I do most of the work on that front. But Shane and Cora's wedding is going to be our first."

"It's perfect," Lindsay said, grinning at her future sister-in-law, Cora. She didn't let that grin or cheerfulness die, even though her head was anywhere but on weddings or Christmas.

No, her thoughts were full of Cal.

Cal tossed a frozen meal into the microwave and took out at least some of his irritation on the microwave buttons.

Tylers in his house. Since he was alone, he could scowl. He had nothing against the Tylers in theory. Deb Tyler had been like a mother to him growing up, and Shane and Gavin were good ranch neighbors and decent men.

But no matter that he might like each person individually, they were all blood ties to the one person in the world he expressly did not like.

Lindsay Tyler.

Pretty as ever, too. He hadn't been lying when he'd told her she hadn't changed. She looked exactly the same as she had the day she'd effectively shoved a dagger into his heart.

Since he was not a man prone to hyperbole, the fact he'd even think that comparison proved what a betrayal it had been. Cal Barton was well acquainted with desertion and betrayal.

The microwave dinged and Cal scowled at it. A burst of laughter from the living room invaded the quiet of the kitchen.

He wasn't a particularly *fun-loving* guy, but the laughter normally wouldn't bother him in the least. Especially if it meant Sarah was building a little side business for herself. Except *this* laughter was *Tyler* laugher and he was almost certain he could pick out Lindsay's tinkling laugh in the midst of all the other people's.

He plopped himself onto a kitchen chair and attacked the microwave meal. It was only half-hot, half still cold. He choked it all down anyway. The sooner he was done with dinner, the sooner he could head back outside. He didn't have any necessary chores left, but there were always extra chores to be scrounged up when he didn't want to be around people.

Especially Tyler people.

He would have avoided dinner altogether, but when he did that Sarah scolded him and pecked at him like she'd decided to be his mother, and he'd rather avoid watching her childhood issues bleed out all over him.

After all, he had plenty of his own.

He got up from the table and tossed the remnants of the meal. More laughter from the living room, and with all the damn Christmas lights twinkling around him, he really just wanted to punch something.

He hated Christmas.

He hated Lindsay Tyler.

He hated this ugly, black feeling inside of him. He always wondered if it was the same one that had caused his mother to leave them. Twice.

Always on Christmas.

Cal needed to get out of here, but instead he stood and stared at the cabinet of liquor. It was tempting. A Barton Christmas tradition, after all, to get drunk and wax poetic about the woman who'd left you.

But Cal had decided a long, long time ago to be nothing like his father. That liquor cabinet was a reminder.

"You could have said hello."

Cal glanced back at his sister. She was only nineteen, and Dad had let wife number three (marriage number four since he'd married Mom twice before moving on) talk him into traveling the world, leaving Sarah without the means or opportunity to go off to college.

She was stuck here, and Cal was determined she have something. Something that would fulfill her. Something that would make her happy.

Something that will keep her here.

"I did say hello."

"No, you didn't. You said exactly one word, which was 'straggler,' and then you stomped back here."

"I did not stomp. That's called a manly cowboy swagger."

She snorted in disgust but grinned nonetheless. Then her smile died. "You know I'm going to ask her."

"I know." He didn't have to like it to know.

"She's going to say yes."

"Of course she is. I don't know how long she's in town, but Lindsay would never refuse you. No matter what . . ." Which was why he hated Lindsay Tyler after six years, because he knew with everything he was that she was a good person. Pretty and good and helpful, and they belonged together.

But she'd needed more than him and this, and how could he ever forgive her for that?

The fact Sarah needed some help with graphics and whatnot for advertising the Christmas tree farm as a wedding venue had nothing to do with him. Asking for Lindsay's art help had nothing to do with him. So, he wouldn't stand in Sarah's way. No matter how much he didn't want Lindsay hovering around, even for a short period of time.

"Okay . . . Well . . ." she trailed off, then shook her head and went for the pantry. "The chocolate ones went fast." She grabbed a cookie tin and opened it. She took two out and placed them on the table. "That's for being a good little rancher boy."

"Ha. Ha." But he took his sister's cookies, because she was a hell of a baker. Whether it was Christmas or old bad memories swirling, he found himself swayed by an unusual wave of sentimentality. "You're really good at this. The whole entertaining thing. I'm not. I never will be. Lindsay or no. So, just ignore my manly cow-boy swagger and focus on this thing you're really good at."

For a second she looked like she was about to cry, which horri-fied him enough to start edging toward the back door. But she straightened her shoulders and blinked a few times.

"You're not that manly," she offered gravely, before bursting into laughter as she headed back out to her waiting guests.

On a sigh, he ate the Christmas cookies and listened to the faint laughter of another family in his living room. Tylers. The whole lot of them. Up in his house and ranch for the next few days.

Christmases were never very merry around the Barton spread, but it couldn't be worse than waking up to finding Mom or Dad gone, so he supposed he'd survive.

He'd just do everything in his power to avoid Lindsay. It shouldn't be a problem. She couldn't possibly want to see him any more than he wanted to see her.

So, that was settled, and he'd eaten his dinner and talked to his sister, and now he could go back to the solitude of the barn and do something that didn't feel like a knife being shoved in his heart.

CHAPTER 2

Lindsay woke up in the twin bed of her childhood. This was the first time she'd been home in a few months, and the first time coming home knowing she was staying. She had no doubts about staying, but the view from her tiny childhood bedroom was a bit stifling. Remembering all those dreams she'd made to escape.

Dreams that turned out to be little more than mirages. Mirages that disappeared into just wanting to be home. For good.

Bleh.

She got out of bed and glanced at the time and scowled. She was supposed to be able to sleep in on Christmas vacation. She'd have to be up early all semester, and this was her last chance to just relax. But she was wide awake.

Bleh again. Still, she got up and went through the shower. She was meeting Sarah over at the Barton house at eight to discuss some mysterious thing Sarah hadn't wanted to go into details with everyone around last night.

That gave Lindsay a few hours to kill first, so maybe she'd make breakfast for everyone. If she beat Mom or Grandma to the kitchen anyway.

But of course, Mom was already at the stove flipping pancakes while Grandma cut up strawberries and blueberries. Gavin was sitting at the table, a mug of coffee in front of him. Boone and Molly were probably still asleep, and likely Shane was already out doing chores while his soon-to-be wife and soon-to-be stepson still slept.

For a brief moment, Lindsay felt that wave of rightness she'd been chasing since she'd decided to move home. This, *this* was where she belonged. Home. She almost opened her mouth to tell them all she was here for good, but then her brother opened his big, obnoxious mouth.

"Just waking up, sleeping beauty?"

She scowled at him. "It's six in the morning."

Gavin glanced at his watch. "It's six-forty-five. How long were you in that shower? Jeez, Linds. Didn't you ever learn to share?"

She wanted to punch him in his already-crooked nose, but Mom tsked.

"Lindsay doesn't live here anymore, Gav. You have to give her a break if she's a bit out of practice."

Lindsay didn't scowl at her mother, but she wanted to. *Doesn't live here anymore.* Being away at college didn't mean *not living here.* And maybe she'd spent the past two years not coming home for the summer because she'd been working on getting all her education courses in after spending her entire bachelor's degree on art, but . . .

Well . . .

Ugh. Her family always knew how to make her feel like an outsider. Just because she wasn't as into horses as Molly or Boone or didn't want to be involved with the ranch like Mom, Shane, and Gavin were. Just because she loved art and was damn good at something creative.

"Sit. Eat," Mom ordered.

"I can't eat with you guys. I agreed to have breakfast with Sarah."

"At the Bartons'?" Mom asked, and though no one outside their family would have heard the censure in her tone, Lindsay could read it. Mom did not approve.

"It's a business breakfast. I'm sure Cal will be out working if that's what you're worried about."

"He's had it rough."

Twist that guilt knife, Deb Tyler. "And I'm part of that rough?"

Mom sighed. "I'm just asking you to be careful, sweetheart. Hearts are a little more tender around Christmas."

And I'm a trampler of hearts. That's what her mother thought of her. The one who'd insisted on leaving. The one who'd broken Cal Barton's heart right along with her mother's. Lindsay knew that's how her family saw her. Careless and a little selfish.

Why are you coming home to that, then?

Lindsay blew out a breath as she headed out of the kitchen. She wasn't going to sit around for a pissing match with Gavin. Maybe *her* heart was a little tender around Christmas, too. Especially when more and more she realized how little her family respected her.

When she'd finally grown up and learned to respect herself. *Humph.*

She pulled on her coat and shoved her feet into her boots before stepping outside. She'd take a walk. Remind herself why she'd come home. Not for Mom or Gavin or anyone else. Just for herself. Twenty-four years old and she had some work to do to prove to her family she wasn't still the little baby. She'd done all her growing up away from them, so now she had to show them. It would take time to prove it.

Proving didn't mean sniping with Gavin or arguing with her mother. So, she needed to find some self-control.

She stomped out onto the porch and hugged herself against the cold. The world was white and vast and the tension inside of her immediately loosened. Oh, she'd always, *always* loved this view. Loved winters at home.

She still hadn't untangled how she could have this much love for it and had still wanted to escape, to see what else was out there. Eighteen years old and she'd *loved* this place, but she'd never dreamed of actually making it home.

"But now you are, and that's what matters."

"Talking to yourself? Don't you remember what Miss Perdue told you about that?"

Lindsay glared over her shoulder at her brother Boone. Of the three Tyler men, he was the closest in age to her—only two years older. Shane and Gavin were a respective eight and six years older, and since their father had died when she'd been a toddler, the two older brothers had been more like adult, supervisory figures.

But Boone had been a kid with her, wild too. He'd left Gracely to join the rodeo, and so they often fell into the same irresponsible pool of Tylers who didn't do what they were supposed to.

"Can I ask you something, Boone?"

"If I said no it wouldn't stop you."

She sighed heavily. "Why'd you come home?"

Boone adjusted the hat on his head, squinting at the mountain-laden horizon. "Didn't have much choice. Can't rodeo when you've gotten the piss shattered out of you by a bull."

"But you're still here."

Boone gave her a sideways glance. "If you're asking for the deep, heartfelt reason I'm home, I don't have one for you. I came home because I didn't have a choice. I've stayed home for the same reason."

She laid her hand on her brother's forearm. "You absolutely have a choice." It was the one thing she'd finally learned out there on her own.

She had a choice. No matter how her family treated her like the baby or how running into Cal last night still vibrated through her. She could have chosen to chase art, could have chosen to settle anywhere but Colorado, but she hadn't wanted to.

She'd come home because that's what she'd wanted, what she'd chosen. So, she couldn't get her nose bent out of shape if Mom or Gavin said something dismissive or Cal looked at her with blank eyes.

All that mattered was that she was home. To build the life *she* wanted. Make the choice she needed to.

"I think you should find a reason, Boone. A reason to stay, or a reason to go. But either way, you have a choice."

"That so?"

She nodded sharply. "Very, very *so*."

Cal drained the last drops of coffee out of his thermos. The sun was had risen over the mountains in the distance, but a few low, flat clouds held that tinge of pink of sunrise. A good morning, he decided, willing himself to feel it.

His cattle were weathering the hard winter. The neat rows of Christmas trees sparkled with overnight snow in the distance. They'd had a good season, with a few days left to go, and Sarah's little wedding location side business was promising to pad their savings a bit. Sorely needed after Dad had taken off.

Cal sucked in a deep, icy breath and willed himself to find a little levity. Sarah only had him, which meant he needed to find some Christmas cheer. Somewhere.

Except when he marched back to the house intent on filling up his thermos and maybe grabbing a bite to eat that was more than the protein bar he'd had upon waking, there was Lindsay's car rolling up the drive.

Cal tried to remind himself of levity and Christmas and bullshit, but all he could think about was the nerve of this woman. Coming to his house *again*. He'd wanted to tell Sarah to conduct her business with Lindsay elsewhere, but that had seemed a little cruel when he spent so much time out of the house.

Lindsay just *had* to show up when he was in search of coffee. Since she'd already ruined his life once, he wasn't about to let her get in between him and coffee. He kept marching.

Unfortunately, the back door was broken, which meant Cal had to go around the front. Which meant meeting her on the porch again. This time in daylight. No Christmas lights to hide how much he didn't want her here.

"Morning, Cal," she offered. Even her voice hadn't changed. He could hear every *morning, Cal* she'd ever greeted him with. And some pieces of all those feelings of contentment and love fluttered through him like ghosts he couldn't eradicate.

He grunted.

"I'm meeting Sarah. For breakfast. For . . . business."

"I'm aware."

She smiled tightly, but the fact she would *smile* at him was really damn grating.

"We don't have to be friendly."

Her jaw dropped. "What?"

"I'm just saying, we don't have to chitchat or smile at each other. We can just not."

Her mouth was still hanging open, but since he didn't want to continue having this conversation, he brushed passed her and went for the door.

"Cal."

He didn't stop, because what else was there to say? He didn't want to continue to be on the end of her stilted smiles when this was a few days of annoyance before he could go back to his normal life.

"Cal Frederick Barton, don't you dare walk through that door."

He turned, slowly, very, *very* slowly. "Did you just middle name me?" he demanded, his voice low as he tried to control the anger spiking through him.

She stood on *his* porch, her hands on her hips and a familiar frustration snapping in her big blue eyes. Familiar, and that only pissed him off more.

He'd listened to her complain about Gracely or school. He'd soothed her as she'd ranted about how her family treated her like a brainless baby. He had done all that while trying to understand the exact same frustration that flashed in her eyes now, and he didn't want to be reminded of how stupid *he* had been.

"You can't just . . ." She heaved a sigh. "We should be able to have a polite conversation. We're going to run into each other."

"For a few days. A few days we *don't* have to have polite conversation," he said firmly.

Her eyebrows drew together and she pulled her bottom lip between her teeth as though struggling with some important thought.

Which reminded him of things he really, really didn't want to remember.

"It won't just be for a few days," she finally said, her voice quiet but sure. Oh, how he remembered that surety in her.

"What the hell does that mean?"

"It means I'm staying in Gracely. For good."

"You . . . can't. . . ." She couldn't. She . . . She couldn't *stay*. That was the whole entire reason she'd upended his life. Because she couldn't stay. Because not Gracely, not the Barton or Tyler ranch, not *him* could be enough to keep her here. She'd made that decision. She couldn't take it back after *six years.*

"I am. I am staying, and I think—"

"Don't finish that sentence. Do not finish that sentence. I don't care what you think. I don't care if you're back for some supposed long period of time. We will not be spending any time together."

"I'm not your mother."

He took a step toward her, wanting to intimidate her right off his porch, his land. But she didn't budge. Even after he took another step, towering above her with what had to be a god-awful expression on his face, she just lifted that stubborn chin.

Why wasn't anything about her *different*?

"Don't you dare, ever, bring up my mother to me. Don't you dare assume to know why I don't want to be around you, and don't you dare think you're going to fit yourself back into my life. Sarah wants your *temporary* help with some business, and that's fine. But that's got nothing to do with me. None of you has anything to do with me. Ever again."

"I don't know why you're so angry. It's been so long."

For a brief second he thought about telling her. That no matter how he'd tried to get over her, the women he'd dated had just been pale comparisons. That she haunted him no matter how desperately he tried to exorcise her. That she'd put the final nail in the coffin of his being able to trust anyone with anything. He couldn't even trust his sister to stick around.

It wasn't *all* her fault, but he wasn't too keen on forgiving his parents, either, so why would he forgive her? Why would he want anything to do with her?

"Stay away from me, Lindsay. That's a demand, not a request, since you apparently haven't gotten any brighter with age."

She balled her fist and hit it against his chest. It didn't hurt, per se, but he did take a step back.

"And you apparently turned into a giant asshole," she retorted, all her frustration and confusion turning to straight rage.

Good. It matched his. It lit something inside of him he didn't want to analyze. He wanted to dive into it. Anger felt so much better than wallowing.

"Well, just another reason to stay the hell away from me."

"Oh, but I haven't changed at all, which means I'm going to stick to you like glue just to piss you off."

Cal laughed bitterly. "Oh, darlin', you can try."

"Save your 'darlin's' for someone who's afraid of you, Cal. But I know you. All your secrets. All your insecurities. Every last inch of you. I can make it hurt real good."

She was probably right, but that only meant he knew the same things about her, and he could make it hurt, too. "That how you want to spend your life, Lindsay? Turning the knife in someone you already stabbed."

"I didn't do it *to* you, Cal. Breaking up with you was *for* me."

"Yeah, Lindsay Tyler, center of the universe."

"I guess I'd rather be selfish than the victim of everyone else not loving you quite enough."

Ouch. Yeah, she knew his weaknesses. "We all make our choices. Now, if you'll excuse me, my choice is to work for a living, not doodle."

"Is it your choice? Or was it just what you got stuck with because you couldn't do anything else?"

"Lindsay."

It was Sarah's voice and Cal didn't miss the fact they *both* winced at it.

Lindsay opened her mouth to say something, but she couldn't seem to get any words out.

Which meant Cal had to fix this. Not for Lindsay, but for Sarah. "Don't worry about it, Sarah. We were just reminiscing about old times. I'm going to fill up my thermos and be out of your hair." He clenched his teeth together. He didn't want to apologize. He certainly didn't mean it, but he'd swallow some pride for his sister. She was the only one he'd do it for.

"Sorry, Lindsay. Things got out of hand. Let's avoid each other for both our sakes." He didn't wait for her to agree before he went inside.

If she wouldn't avoid him, he'd just have to work harder to avoid her.

CHAPTER 3

Lindsay was a swirl of all the worst emotions. Anger. Frustration. Confusion. Hurt. She didn't like that Cal had pulled out those old insecurities and, worse, she'd fallen into the trap of defending them. Like she didn't know exactly what he was doing.

She wasn't a teenager anymore and getting worked up like she was only proved Cal's point. *Lindsay Tyler, center of the universe.* How many times in her life had she heard that one? And how many times had it been true?

But what no one seemed to understand was that being on her own, mostly, for the past six years had taught her how to be less selfish. She'd found a balance in going after what she wanted and also being cognizant of how that affected other people. She wasn't a girl anymore, childish and peevish.

Except Cal had so easily shoved her back into that place.

She forced herself to reach out and take Sarah's hand. "I'm so, so sorry you walked into the middle of that."

Sarah looked patently miserable, but she shook her head. "You don't have to be sorry. It's my fault. I should have had us meet in town. Cal works so hard, I figured we'd be able to avoid him here, but . . ."

"I don't understand how he can still be so angry when it's been so many years." She'd never meant to hurt him. She hadn't wanted to break up with him, but they'd wanted completely different things. How could he blame her for needing to go after what she wanted? Still.

"Unfortunately, they've been rough years around here." Sarah smiled warily. "Let's go inside. I made cinnamon rolls."

"I missed your cooking," Lindsay said, giving Sarah's hand a squeeze before she dropped it.

Sarah led her inside. "You have your mother's and grandmother's cooking. Theirs is far superior to mine."

"Don't be silly. My mom taught you everything she knows, which means you're just as good as her."

"I'd like to see you say that to her face."

"Only if you want to see me die." Lindsay was relieved they could move on from the awkwardness of the porch. Sarah led her to the dining room, purposefully no doubt, since the dining room attached to the kitchen but also allowed whoever was in the kitchen to go through a separate hallway to leave the house. Giving Cal the opportunity to leave without having to see her again.

It hurt. Lindsay didn't know quite why it hurt that Cal was still angry with her. Those were his issues and had nothing to do with her. But it still hurt. A nagging ache in the pit of her stomach.

Cal was so good. He could be grumpy and mean, but she knew he'd developed that as a protective armor. He'd been dealt so many unfair blows, and still he was loyal to those he loved. A protector, fierce and determined to make right in a very wrong world.

She hadn't broken up with Cal because she'd stopped loving him. She'd just needed to see the world so that curiosity didn't eat her alive.

Lindsay took a seat at the table and thought about what Sarah had said out on the porch. "What's been rough about the past few years?"

Sarah smiled thinly. "Oh, you know. I'm going to go get the cinnamon rolls and coffee." With that, she left the dining room area for the kitchen.

Which left Lindsay alone. Despite over four years of dating Cal, she'd only eaten in the dining room twice. She remembered both times with awful clarity. One involved his drunk father going on and on about how his children were the reason his wife had left him. The other had been their last Thanksgiving. Cal's stepmother had pushed and picked on Sarah so horribly, he had told her to stop, which then resulted in a fistfight with his father. Right here in this very room. They'd broken dishes and glasses, and Lindsay and Sarah had both watched in horror, crying.

It was hard to keep her anger at Cal when Lindsay remembered things like that. He'd had a rough go and it had been cruel of her to think he could ever understand why she'd had to leave. When he'd suffered so much leaving, truly suffered at the hands of it.

She'd had to leave. There was no denying that. But in retrospect, Lindsay felt a certain amount of shame at how she'd handled it, and how she was handling her return.

Sarah came back to the dining room with a beautifully decorated tray of cinnamon rolls and a big carafe of coffee. She'd already set pretty Christmas-themed dishes out on the table and Lindsay smiled.

"You're so good at this hosting thing. It's like you were meant to do it, Sarah. I'm so impressed at how mature you've gotten."

Sarah smiled, a little shyly, and that was more the little girl Lindsay remembered. "Cal said the same thing to me last night. That I was good at this."

"Cal and I might not agree about a lot anymore, but I think we can agree on that. And maybe partly it's because I still see you as thirteen and shy."

"I really like it. I didn't expect to, either."

"Then why did you do it? Weren't you going to be . . . an accountant, was it? Yes, you were so good with numbers."

"Yeah, well. Maybe I'll get a chance someday, but right now I have to stay home with Cal."

Which didn't sit right with Lindsay at all. "Sarah, you don't have to stay home with Cal. You can't let him make you think you do. If you want to get out and—"

"Save me the lecture, Lindsay," and there was an adult finality to that tone that stopped Lindsay in her tracks. "I know you mean well, but you don't understand anything about what's happened around here for the past few years."

"So why don't you tell me," Lindsay said gently, because it seemed like this girl—no, woman—wanted someone to tell.

"Cal wouldn't want me to spill it all, and I don't really want to, either. Maybe you don't understand why he's still angry with you, but . . . I . . . I do. I may not understand everything that went on between you two. I was a kid and I kept my nose out of it, but it did hurt that you just left. I looked up to you so much. Your mom tried to help us, but that hurt Cal, too."

Lindsay opened her mouth to pose some argument or offer some excuse or apology, but Sarah stopped her.

"You broke his heart. I'm not about to tell you that you were wrong, that you shouldn't have done what you did. I don't have that kind of insight. But I'm the one who's been living with him the past six years, and I've seen him weather all of the storms. All of the broken hearts. Dad got married again last year, and this one wanted to travel the world. Dad drained our savings, including my college account, and took off for Europe."

"Sarah."

"It wasn't terrible. The ranch does well and we were both kind of relieved he was gone, but the savings . . . I couldn't put the burden of college expenses on Cal. I couldn't leave him like everyone else already had. So, I came home to run the Christmas tree stuff and to take care of him. I can't regret that. He basically raised me, and loved me when no one else did. So please don't ever lecture me that I need to look out for myself over Cal. Cal is always looking out for me, not him, and I can't be happy knowing I'm hurting him. And, you know, taking care of him and this place *does* make me happy even if it wasn't my dream."

Lindsay blinked back tears, because she'd come to some of those conclusions, too. That dreams didn't have the power to make you happy. Sometimes the thing you wanted fell short of being what you needed. It was why she was home, learning to teach instead of spending her time painting.

It had just taken her a lot longer than it had taken Sarah.

"I'm sorry, Sarah. Sorry that I stuck my nose where it didn't belong."

"I have a great future with a really cool job. But my job needs help. Some art help." She glanced at her watch. "And I've got about two hours to talk to you about it before I have to go man the tree customers."

Lindsay nodded, and she spent the next two hours having breakfast with an old friend and coming up with ideas on how to use her art skills to help a Christmas tree farm wedding venue.

When they were done, Lindsay knew she should head home. She should go tell her family she was staying in Gracely for good and throw herself into Shane and Cora's wedding preparations.

She should do what Cal asked her and just stay out of his way. She stepped onto the Barton porch and looked out over the ranch and Christmas tree rows.

Instead of walking to her car, she started walking toward the stables of the Barton ranch.

There were few things a late winter morning on horseback couldn't cure. Apparently Cal's bad mood was one of them.

He just kept thinking about Lindsay. In his house. Talking and laughing with his sister and eating her cinnamon rolls. Lindsay was at his dining room table helping Sarah and likely having a grand time.

Staying. She was staying in Gracely. Oh, she thought it was for good, but Cal knew better. Mom had come back, ready to be a mother and wife again. It had lasted two years. Why wouldn't Lindsay be exactly the same? Come back. Convince everyone she was going to stay, and then hightail it out of here for bigger and better. Again.

He was too old and too hard to get clobbered again, but Sarah . . . Chances were Sarah was going to fall for it hook, line, and sinker. Cal would be left to clean up that mess again.

Maybe he should force her to go back to school. What was some crippling student loan debt? The news was always saying everyone had it.

Cal dismounted his horse, tied it to the branch of a Christmas tree. He unloaded his tools from the horse's saddlebag and studied the platform he'd built for the wedding. Sarah had asked him to check to make sure it was holding up to the snow and ice.

He cleared off the surface and got to work checking nails and screws and making sure everything was still level for the rehearsal and wedding that would happen over the course of the next few days.

Two people would get up here and pledge their lives to each other. Cal wanted to believe that marriage was a joke and that no one stayed. Sadly, the truth wasn't that everyone left. It wasn't that people didn't love wholly and forever.

He, in particular, wasn't good enough to inspire that kind of lifelong commitment. From parents or significant others. Cal wasn't even sure Sarah would stick around once she figured out she had other options.

He'd stopped feeling sorry for himself over it. He liked his solitude quite well, but Lindsay's reappearance reminded him of what it was like to be part of a partnership. Just her existence in his world reminded him what it was like to have someone he could confide in. His problems, his worries, his fears. All things he'd only ever been able to confide in her.

Christmas was always a little harder than the rest of the year, but Lindsay really was salt in that wound. He didn't even have January to look forward to, because she'd be hanging around like a ghost of When Things Were Okay.

Well, he had this place and he had Sarah. Once Christmas was over, he'd find a way to numb that hurt and those reminders.

Cal noted the faint sound of hooves in the distance. He stopped his work and frowned. If Sarah came out to find him, she usually did it in one of the four-wheelers.

The rider who came into view wasn't his dark-haired sister, though. No, Lindsay's blond hair was flying in the wind as she advanced on him. She used to tease him that his heart skipped a beat when he saw her, and she'd always been right. There was a stutter in its normal beat, and time hadn't stopped it. He felt it again, but her on horseback only reminded him of all the riding they'd done together, planning for a future she was never, ever going to be a part of.

Honestly, he shouldn't blame her. He should thank her. She'd left before they could get married and have kids and ruin someone else's life.

She was a goddamn saint.

Lindsay dismounted gracefully, and there was none of the anger from before on her face. She looked around the space he was working in with a certain amount of awe in her expression.

"This is amazing. It's going to look so beautiful on Saturday."

"That's the plan." He was not going to argue with her. He owed his sister at least civility to this woman whose very existence felt like an assault.

"I hope you don't mind I borrowed one of your horses for a little ride."

"Minding wouldn't matter, since you already did it."

She took a step toward the platform he was standing on. "Well, I came to apologize for this morning."

"We already did that," he returned, resisting the urge to edge away from her.

"No, you apologized to me to make your sister feel better. But I actually want to apologize to you because I reacted poorly."

Cal shook his head, trying to keep a handle on his temper. Clearly Sarah had told her about their sob story and now she felt pity for him. *Fantastic.*

"Lindsay, please, I am begging you to just leave me alone. I have nothing to say to you. I have no desire to be around you. I don't care if you're staying or going. Let's just leave each other alone."

She looked so damn hurt he almost felt guilty.

"Can't we be friends?" she asked timidly.

"Friends? No. God . . ." She didn't get it. She just didn't get how irreparably she'd hurt him, and he didn't know what to do with that. He'd always assumed she understood that what she'd done, echoing everything his mother had ever done, was a betrayal, regardless of how much she'd needed to leave.

But she was clueless. She clearly thought they'd had some childish relationship and he should just get over the inevitable breakup to go be adults.

"It must be nice," he said, and then tried to remind himself he was going to be civil. For Sarah. "It's nice that you feel nothing but goodwill for me, but I do not feel the same. I don't say that to be mean. I don't want to hurt you, Lindsay. But you being here causes me to suffer, so I cannot be your friend."

"But . . . It can change. It should change. Maybe if we tried to be friends—"

"No! No. Don't you get it? I was stupid enough to trust you. Stupid enough to think we had a future, and all you are from this day forward is a reminder of that future that was never meant for me. I don't hate you, Lindsay. I hate what you represent. And I want nothing to do with it. I'm happy here, and I'm happy alone, but I don't need you flaunting that aloneness in my face."

"You're not alone. You have Sarah. I'm not trying to—"

"I don't care what you're trying to do. You have nothing to do with me. We have nothing to do with each other. What we had isn't just gone. It's dead. I don't want to build anything on that gravesite. Not friendship. Not goodwill. Not anything."

Still she didn't leave. *Still* she didn't get the picture, and it felt like his heart was breaking all over again. This woman who'd been his rock and partner as they'd grown up toward adulthood, and she'd ripped the foundation out from under him.

Now he'd built a life on that missing foundation and she wanted to rip it away again? He wouldn't let her.

"Sarah told me your dad left."

Cal simply stood there and waited, but she seemed to be waiting for him. "And?"

"And . . . I just wanted to say I'm sorry."

"What's there for you to be sorry about?"

"I'm sorry that he did that. That he hurt you both. I'm sorry that it means Sarah can't have the education she deserves."

"I promised myself I wouldn't fight with you anymore for Sarah's sake, but my God if you start lecturing me about what Sarah deserves, I will . . ."

"You'll what?" she demanded, crossing her arms over her chest.

"What do you want from me?" he demanded, dropping his tools on the platform. "Why are you torturing me?" he said, too broken to be ashamed that his voice broke, too.

"I'm not saying any of this to torture you. I want to be your friend."

"I want nothing to do with you, Lindsay. Someday, I will get what I want." He hopped off the platform and jabbed a thumb into his chest. "It's starting with not having anything to do with you."

"Why . . . Why are you so *angry*? I know I hurt you, and I'm sorry, but I did what I had to do. If you're happy being alone, why are you so *angry*?"

He didn't have it in him to fight her. Not when his heart felt like it was being squeezed in a vice and he was losing her all over again when he didn't even want her. He had to end this once and for all. "Okay. Fine. You win. Let me spell it out. I still love you. I will always love you. Nothing in my life and no one in my life matches up to that love. I have *tried* to find someone else. I have *tried* to forget you were ever mine. I cannot kill this awful, painful love I have for you no matter how much I want to. You being here is nothing but a constant reminder of all the things I am not good enough for."

She moved for him, even reached out for him, but he sidestepped it because the stupidest, most beaten part of his brain was whispering for him to let her touch him. Hold him again. Be that thing he wanted.

"Me leaving had nothing to do with what you're good enough for, Cal," she said on a broken whisper.

But of course it did. Of *course* it did.

"I don't want you here," he choked out.

"I'm . . . sorry." She was crying now, fat tears falling down her cheeks.

"I don't care if you are," he returned, willing himself to harden against her tears, against her confusion.

He loved her, but he didn't want anything to do with her, and that was that. So, he picked up his tools and shoved them haphazardly into the saddlebag.

"Cal, please, I—"

But he couldn't listen. He mounted his horse and rode off as fast as the horse would go.

CHAPTER 4

Lindsay cried the whole way back to the stables. She managed to get herself together to clean up the horse and lead it back into its stall. Then she drove almost the whole way home without crying.

But something about driving under the arch of the Tyler Ranch had her sobbing all over again.

I still love you. I will always love you.

It should have been romantic. It should have led to her rushing into his arms and saying she felt exactly the same way.

Because she did. She'd *tried* to find someone else. Had convinced herself eventually the right guy would come along to turn Cal into a pleasant memory, not this yardstick she held every other guy up to.

But the truth was Cal was the man she'd always loved and it hadn't gone away with time. His saying the same to her only made her more sure. Maybe she wasn't exactly the same as she'd been at eighteen, but the heart of her was. She was older, wiser, and stronger, but she was still herself.

He was harder, meaner with age and tragedy, but the heart of him was still the same. He protected what was his. He loved so fiercely it didn't die out.

She parked in front of the house and she knew she had to get a hold of herself before she went inside. In a house of ten people, someone was bound to find her with blotchy cheeks and a stuffed-up nose and demand to know what the problem was.

She pulled some tissues out of her purse and tried to mop up her face up and then wondered why. What did it matter if someone asked her what the problem was? What did it hurt if she told them?

Wasn't that half the reason she was home? To have people who loved her and cared about her and supported her around? She missed having her sister to talk to and she'd missed having her mother's gentle love. They might treat her like the brainless baby sometimes, but they had always, *always* loved her and been there for her.

She trudged inside, and as if Mom had some sort of *your child is distressed* alarm in her head she appeared in the hallway almost immediately.

"What's wrong? What is it?"

"I talked to Cal. 'Fought' would probably be a better word."

Mom's expression was grave, but she held out her arms and pulled Lindsay into a fierce hug.

"Mom. He said he still loved me," she whispered into her mother's shoulder.

Mom was quiet for a few moments, but she didn't let go. "How do you feel about that?"

"I might have been happy about it, if he thought it was a good thing." She blew out a shaky breath and wrapped her arms around her mother. Her mother who wouldn't ever have willingly left them. Not in a million years, for a million opportunities. Deb Tyler was dedicated to her children, no question.

Poor Cal. Who was dedicated to him, no question? Sarah, at most. And she might be nineteen now, but for a lot of years she'd been a kid dependent on him.

"He said he loved you, but thinks it's a bad thing?" Mom asked, guiding her toward the formal sitting room.

"He wants nothing to do with me. And I mean nothing."

Mom deposited her on the couch, and as if she'd sent out some familial homing pigeon Grandma and Molly appeared at the door. Grandma had a plate of cookies in her hands.

A hiccuped sob escaped Lindsay's mouth and she knew that there would be no perfect moment beyond this one to tell them.

"I'm home. For good."

Grandma, Molly, and Mom made identical expressions of surprise without saying a word. Lindsay laughed through her tears.

"I haven't just been working at an art gallery for the past two years. I've been getting my education degree. I decided I wanted to be an art teacher, and then I decided I wanted to come home. So, I'm student teaching at Gracely Elementary next semester, and the teacher is retiring at the end of the year, so as long as things go smoothly I should be a shoo-in for the job."

Still the women in her family just stood there with matching expressions of shock.

"I'm sorry I kept it from you, but I didn't want to hear 'I told you so.' I didn't want crap for wanting to come home. I just wanted to do it. But you were all right. Leaving was stupid, and I should have just stayed, because being here is all I want."

Molly took a seat next to her and pulled her into a hug.

"Speaking as someone who left home for all the wrong reasons, and came back for all the right ones, I don't think you made a mistake, Linds. You grew up. You figured out you wanted something different than you originally thought and you went after it. That's nothing to be ashamed of."

"So you wouldn't have said 'I told you so,' you would have just supported me, if I'd told you two years ago?" She looked up at her mother.

"I think it was more the crying than the timing that kept me from saying I told you so. Except Molly's right. Much as it pains me to admit, you were right to leave. You needed to get away from us for a few years and find yourself. We sheltered you and you knew you had to get away from that and find something else. I'm glad it ended up being coming home, but I'm also glad you left and found what you needed to find."

"Everyone has to learn their lessons in their own way, in their own time." Grandma thrust a cookie at her. "Now have some sugar."

Lindsay managed a watery smile and took the cookie, but it only reminded her of the Bartons.

"Cal told her he still loves her," Mom announced.

Molly screeched so loud Lindsay thought she felt her eardrum vibrate.

"It wasn't a good thing, though," she assured her sister. "He'll never trust me again. He said too many people hurt him and he doesn't want to love me."

"That's a hard thing to overcome," Mom said, as if it was hard and not impossible.

"I can't overcome it. You should've seen the way he looked at me. Like I was the source of all of his problems or his worst nightmare or I don't know. He hates me. He said he didn't hate me, but he does."

"I suppose he might feel as though he hates you because he can't stop loving you, but I don't think he can hate *and* love you."

"Why not?"

"It's all moot," Molly said, frowning. "It's been six years. He might think he loves *you*, but what he really loves is who you used to be. He loves the image of you he has in his head. Six years changes a woman. It changes a man. I know that sometimes you can convince yourself you love anything if you try hard enough, but you've been apart too long for it to still be love."

"I know it's a little different," Mom offered gently. "But no matter that I've married Ben, I still love your father. I suppose if he'd lived I might have fallen out of love with him, but I can't imagine it. He was a good man and that center of goodness never changed, even as we grew up and had kids and worked hard at this ranch. Sometimes you change at the core of who you are, but baby girl, I know you both. The core of you hasn't changed. The core of Cal hasn't changed. That doesn't mean you should plan to get married and have kids this very second, but it means that you both still feel some love for each other—"

"It doesn't matter. He wants nothing to do with me. He said my existence hurt him." The way he'd looked at her like she was physically driving a stake into his heart. It would haunt her.

"Maybe your existence does hurt him, and maybe you can change that," Mom said, as if it were simple. Possible.

"I can't. He said there was nothing I could do to change what he felt."

"Baloney," Grandma said. "If he loves you, truly and not just the idea of you, then there are a million things you can do to patch up what went wrong. That's what love is. The patching up."

"You know what that boy has never had? Someone willing to fight for him," Mom said firmly. "No, it won't be an easy fight because he has been taught over and over again no one will. But if you love him, if you want a chance to build something as adult Lindsay and adult Cal, you have to be willing to put up that fight."

"Even if he doesn't want me to?" Lindsay asked. She didn't want to hurt him. She wanted to give him whatever he wanted. He deserved some peace, some goodness. If she pushed this, oh, she wasn't sure she could watch that naked pain on his face again.

"Did you *want* to leave us years ago or did you feel like you *had* to? Did you come home to face the inevitable 'we told you sos' because you wanted to or because it was the best thing for you? The things we want are not always the things that'll make us happy."

"Oh, crap, Mom's dropping wisdom. We're all going to be crying at the end of this," Molly muttered.

Mom gave her a sharp look but then continued talking. "I'm not saying you can force that boy's hand to give you what you want or even what you need. You can't. He has to make the choice to trust, and he might not. So what you do is decide what you want, and what you're willing to fight for. Maybe it's him. Maybe it's not. But you have a choice."

Choice. The thing she'd been talking to Boone about this morning. *She* had the choice, and Cal had his own, but she didn't have to let his change hers.

"You know, I talked to Boone this morning. He said he was home because he didn't have a choice, and I told him we always have a choice and he needed to make his."

Mom sniffed, and then Molly was dabbing at her eyes, and Grandma had suspiciously turned away.

"You have become a very wise woman, darling daughter," Mom said with a scratchy voice.

Lindsay smiled up at her mother, and squeezed her sister's hand, and made sure her voice was strong enough to reach Grandma's retreating form. "I learned from the wisest."

CHAPTER 5

Running away was not an option. Cal had lived by that simple, steadfast rule since the second time his mother disappeared.

This morning he'd run away from Lindsay, and it had eaten at him all day. Real men didn't run away from their problems. They faced them. If the other party ran away, well, you dealt, but you never turned tail and ran.

Ever.

The problem was, it wasn't a mistake he could apologize for. The person he'd hurt hadn't been Lindsay. It had been himself. He'd broken his own code, and how was he supposed to fix that?

He didn't want Lindsay anywhere near him. It ate him alive. What had she been doing for the past six years? Who had she touched? Did her skin and lips and body feel the same as they had? Did she still laugh at puns, and eat far too much sugar, and want to change the world with her art? And if she didn't . . . he wanted to know every last inch of what was new.

Staying. In Gracely. In his orbit. Forever circling around a single source of pain.

"It won't be forever," he reassured himself. If her leaving hadn't lasted forever, why would he expect her staying to? Why would he expect anything from her except all the things he'd always known?

He blew out a breath as he pulled the stable doors closed. Across the yard the house was lit up like a damn carnival. Dad had always gotten into the whole thing, believing Christmas was magic and pulling in Gracely-ites and tourists alike to cut down trees or drink warm cider or do whatever other shit depending on the year.

Business! he'd proclaim cheerfully. Then when Mom or whoever didn't show up on Christmas Eve he'd get so piss-poor drunk Cal would have to search the whole house for things he could wrap so Sarah would still believe in Santa.

Belief. He knew what belief got a person.

He stomped toward the house, his mood somehow fouler than it had been after running away from Lindsay like a coward.

There was a car he didn't recognize parked near the house. Probably someone to do with the wedding, since the rehearsal was tomorrow. He couldn't wait for it to be over. Of course, then he had to face Christmas.

But in one week, one hellish week, things would go back to normal. Another Christmas behind him, and not another wedding to worry about for the foreseeable future. He could certainly survive one week.

Even if it's full of Lindsay?

He grimaced as he shoved the front door open, and then he stared in openmouthed shock as he watched his baby sister jump out of the arms of some man.

A *man*. Not a boy. A *man*.

"What the hell is this?" he demanded.

"Cal. You're . . . you're back early."

"Am I?" He glared at his sister, temper boiling. Maybe he was spoiling for a fight, and God had presented him with this gift. Some *man* touching his baby sister.

"Th-this is—"

The *man* stepped toward him, hand outstretched, polite smile on his face. "It's good to meet you, sir. My name's Bill Gower."

He looked down at *Bill's* outstretched hand, then at his sister, most assuredly not shaking this *man's* hand. *Sir.* This man who'd been molesting his sister's face had called him *sir.*

"And who the *hell* is Bill Gower, Sarah?"

"He runs a company that rents out chairs and heaters and other outdoor wedding necessities." She swallowed, forcing a bright smile at Bill, then at Cal. "We've been working together for the past few months. Obviously, wedding venues need chairs, but I didn't want to store the chairs, so we've come to an agreement on... chairs."

"Are there chairs stored down your throat?"

Sarah's cheeks turned bright red and Bill made some move to speak, and Cal was determined right then and there if *Bill* spoke one word he would punch him straight in the nose.

But Sarah held up her hand, and Bill nodded, some unspoken conversation going on between them. The kind of unspoken conversation you had with someone you'd been intimate with.

Oh, Bill Gower was going to meet his maker.

"Kitchen," Sarah stated through gritted teeth.

"You will not order me around, Sarah Barton."

"Kitchen," she repeated, and he knew if he didn't acquiesce he'd be eating a microwave meal for Christmas. With no cookies. Sarah really did make the best cookies.

She stalked toward the back and Cal stared at Bill. The man didn't say anything, but he held Cal's murderous gaze.

"I could kill you with one hand."

"I hope you won't," he replied gently.

Gently. As if Cal was completely off his rocker. As if Cal was acting like some petulant child.

He stalked after Sarah and into the kitchen. "I don't know what the hell—"

"Stop. Stop." Sarah wrapped her arms around herself looking wounded somehow, though he didn't know what she had to be *wounded* about.

"That wasn't a business meeting in there."

"No, it wasn't. Bill and I have been dating, and I invited him for dinner so I could introduce you two. I've been trying to tell you for days, but ... Well, Lindsay has made you rather grumpy."

"My moods have nothing to do with Lindsay."

She snorted. "Sure, and I have chairs stored down my throat. Cal, listen to me. I like him. I ... I think I *love* him."

"No."

"You don't get to decide that."

"Haven't you learned a damn thing?" he demanded, panic at the fact she'd even utter that horrendous word beating through him. "Love is poison, and it will only leave you hurt and alone."

She let out a breath, almost like she'd had it punched out of her. "You don't really think that, do you?" She looked so pained, as though *she* felt sorry for *him*. "Cal . . ."

"What could possibly give you the impression you can trust him? You can love him? You're nineteen and—"

"And you've been in love with Lindsay since, when? Eighth grade? It isn't about how old I am, or how old he is—"

"Just how old is—"

"Cal, I love him. Nothing you can say is going to change that. We're dating. Maybe . . . It's possible at some point we'll be more than dating. I don't need your permission, but I'd like your support."

"You will end up hurt. You will end up like the rest of us. You can't trust this. You can't want this." He had to convince her of that. For her own good. He couldn't stand it if she was hurt. It would kill him.

She crossed the room and put her hands on his shoulders. "Oh, Cal. You make me so sad sometimes." Then she wrapped him in a hug as if . . . None of this made any sense.

"Maybe your cynicism is warranted," she said, giving him one last squeeze before releasing him. When she looked up at him, there were tears in her eyes, but she was smiling. "But I don't want to be cynical. I want to be in love."

He was pretty sure she could have stabbed him and that statement would have hurt less. She was going to get clobbered. By love. Just like Dad. Just like him. And he didn't know how to save her from it.

"Please have a civil dinner with us. Because if you can't, you need to go back to your stables. I'll leave you leftovers, but I'm not eating dinner with . . ." Her eyebrows drew together. "I know you want to protect me, and I know you'd never leave me, Cal. You would and have sacrificed yourself for me. Maybe that's why it isn't so hard to want to be in love. I've always had yours."

Now she was twisting the knife. He nearly doubled over from the pain of it.

"Of course you've always had mine. So, maybe you should try a little faith. You might be happier for it." She smiled thinly. "I'll leave you alone for a few minutes to decide." But she didn't just leave. She rose to her tiptoes and brushed a kiss across his cheek. "I love you, Cal. And I always will."

Then she left him alone in the kitchen with that impossible, impossible task.

Lindsay stared at the lit-up Barton house and tried to ignore the nerves fluttering in her stomach. She could have called Sarah and asked if it was a good time. She could have made an appointment to meet Sarah in Gracely.

But she wasn't really here for that. She had her laptop with her designs for some marketing material for Sarah, but she was absolutely, truly here to see Cal.

Still, she *did* have things to show Sarah, so that's what she'd do first. She pushed out of the car, allowing herself to enjoy the pretty starlit night, the snow under her feet, and the magic of Christmas all around her.

"Give me some of that magic," she whispered into the evening before cresting the stairs of the porch. She knocked on the door and waited for someone to answer.

When Sarah finally did, her cheeks were flushed and she was grinning. "Lindsay! Oh, gosh . . . Did I know you were coming?"

"No. I . . ." She noticed there was a man sitting on the couch, and based on Sarah's flushed face, Lindsay didn't think they'd been chatting.

"I'm interrupting."

Sarah's grin all but split her face. "Just a little bit. But um, come inside for a sec. I want to introduce you."

"Sure."

"Lindsay, this is Bill. Bill, this is Lindsay. She's one of the Tylers. She used to date Cal a long time ago, so she was like a big sister to me. I've told you about her."

Bill got up off the couch and held out his hand. "It's good to meet you. Sarah really looks up to you."

"Oh, that's sweet."

"Bill's my . . . fiancé," Sarah said, still grinning.

Lindsay dropped Bill's hand and turned to face Sarah. "Your ... what?"

"He just asked." Sarah held out her hand, where a pretty little ring glimmered. "I mean, not *just*, but tonight he asked and ... Well, yeah."

"I ..." Lindsay was speechless, for a lot of reasons, but Sarah looked so damn hopeful all Lindsay could do was engulf her in a hug. "Congratulations, Sarah. Oh, I'm so happy for you."

Sarah squeezed her tight. "Thank you," she whispered. "Thank you so much." She pulled back a little but kept her arms tight around Lindsay. "Maybe you could ... Maybe you could check on Cal for me."

"Oh, Sarah." She couldn't even imagine what this might do to Cal. Cal wanted what was best for Sarah, but this would still be difficult for him. A very complicated kind of difficult.

Just like Lindsay was to him. "I ... I don't know if I'd be the right person for that."

"No." Sarah smiled and released her completely, holding out her hand for her fiancé. "But I'm not the right person, and he doesn't have anybody else."

Oof. "Okay. I ... can let him yell at me. It might be cathartic for him."

Sarah laughed, but it was tinged with sadness. "I wish—"

"Don't wish. Celebrate with your fiancé. Enjoy your night, and I will ... I will figure out a way to handle Cal."

"You are the best, best, best."

"I know," Lindsay joked. "Remember that when picking out my Christmas gift. Now, let me guess, he's out in the stables?"

"I'm not a hundred percent sure, but that'd be my guess."

Lindsay nodded and adjusted her scarf to head back out into the cold. "Congrats, you two." She walked outside and tried to form some kind of battle plan. It just about broke her heart that Sarah had said he didn't have anyone else.

She couldn't regret leaving Gracely. Those six years away had been necessary to learn and understand home was not the prison her teenage self had imagined it to be, but she wished ... She wished she'd had the kind of adult fortitude to have made it hurt less for Cal.

She trudged over to the stables and she had no plan, no clever or sympathetic words. She didn't have a clue what to say or do for him, but she couldn't very well leave him alone.

The stable doors were open and Cal stood right there in the entry, staring up at the sky. It was a pretty winter night. The kind of frigid air that made the moon and stars really glow. Everything looked sparkly and silver, including Cal himself.

"Hi," she offered.

He didn't move. Not a stiffening, not a sneer. He stood exactly as still as he'd been on her approach, with the exact same blank grimness to his expression. She moved closer, tightening her fingers into fists so she wouldn't reach out to touch him like she wanted to.

"What are you doing here?" he asked, his voice raspy, his breath puffing out like smoke.

"I brought by some designs Sarah had asked for and she told me... Well."

Cal stood there, so absolutely still, staring up at the sky. How long had he been standing in the frigid cold with only a coat to keep him warm? He said nothing. She said nothing. He watched the sky. She watched him.

After a silence that had to be minutes, if not hours, he finally spoke, his voice a quiet rasp against the dark.

"I understand why my dad was drunk all the time."

She reached out, even knowing it wouldn't be wanted. She touched her gloved fingers to his cheek until he finally moved that blue, piercing gaze to her face. "You are not your father," she said fiercely. "You care. You *try*. You would never hurt that girl out of your own misery."

He shook his head, moving away so her fingers fell away from his face. "Except I did. Because I couldn't cheer and celebrate and find any fucking joy in the fact she's going to *marry* someone. He asked me... He asked my permission. Did you know that? After this stale, stilted dinner he asks to speak to me alone and asks *permission* to ask to marry her. This man she's been keeping a secret from me. This *man*."

"I think that's sweet."

"Of course you do," he muttered disgustedly. "You probably think she won't get her heart crushed, either."

Lindsay gave herself a few seconds to consider her words. To try to find the right ones. "Maybe she will. Maybe she won't. Either way, she'll have you to wipe up the tears, so I think she'll live."

He looked down at her as though she'd cursed him instead of given him a compliment, but that confusion and irritation faded into something else the longer he looked at her. The shimmering air seemed to warm, and somehow they were closer than she'd thought they were.

She sucked in a breath as Cal's gaze moved down to her mouth. He wasn't going to kiss her. Of course not. But he'd at least *thought* about it for a second. What it would feel like now. He looked at her mouth and he remembered what it had been like between them.

She *knew* he did, because she could bring so many of their old kisses to mind. So many memories of the different ways he used to touch her, kiss her, love her.

She hadn't come here to kiss him. Or tell him she still loved him. She hadn't come here to beg for a second chance. She'd wanted to lay the foundation first. To start with friendship or reminders or at least him not *hating* her.

But this close to him, this close to kissing him, it was all she wanted. Screw plans and foundations, she wanted this man who'd spent six years haunting her.

With shaky hands, she pulled a glove off. Then she reached up and pressed her fingers to his cheek. His skin was near frozen, but she felt heated. She wanted to share that heat. She wanted . . .

He was still simply standing there staring down at her, but he wasn't pushing her away or telling her to stop and she wanted to remember what it felt like to have his mouth on hers. No man she'd kissed since had ever come close to those memories.

So she lifted onto her toes and pressed her mouth to his. He let out a shuddering sigh against her mouth, and then she was wrapped firmly in his arms, against his hard body. There wasn't a second of gentleness or kindness in this kiss. It was hard and desperate and oh, *oh.*

It was exactly the same, and somehow a little better. Like they'd been made for each other in the stars, stitched together to fit each other perfectly. Because her memories of Cal hadn't been nostalgia. His kiss was just as potent and meaningful as it had ever been.

She melted into it, softened the kiss, poured all of that *care* she'd held in her heart for him even in six years apart. Because she'd never wanted to leave *him*. She'd wanted to leave home. She'd wanted to leave the Tylers and find Lindsay. She'd *needed* to.

But she'd loved him then, and the whole time in-between, no matter that she'd tried to convince herself that wasn't possible.

His grasp on her loosened, his arms slowly letting her go, then nudging her away from where she'd plastered herself against him. He looked down at her, and she couldn't read that expression. The furrowed eyebrows, the flat mouth, something like chaos in his blue eyes.

"Cal, I still—"

He released her so abruptly she stumbled.

"No." He laughed, the sound caustic and ugly on such a pretty night. "No. None of that."

"But you—"

"Good night, Lindsay." And he left her there, in the silvery moonlight, the heat of that kiss still moving through her even in the cold.

CHAPTER 6

Cal felt as though he'd spent the next two days with a hangover even though he hadn't touched a drop of liquor.

He'd wanted to. Lord, how he'd wanted to after that kiss with Lindsay. But he hadn't. Still, it was as if Lindsay's kiss had intoxicated him to the point of illness. That was still going on even forty-eight hours later.

Sounded about right.

He spent the morning dragging ass through chores, then some of the afternoon selling trees before he'd settled in to help Sarah with the preparations for the wedding rehearsal that would go on tonight. He'd even tried to talk with Bill the Chair Guy without threatening to kill him if he ever hurt Sarah.

All in all, a very shitty day. But one day closer to it all being over. Weddings and Christmas. He'd feel normal again after all this.

Had to.

"It looks great. Doesn't it?"

Cal opened his mouth to reassure Sarah that it did indeed look great, but she wasn't looking at him. She was looking at *Bill*.

"It looks amazing. We make a good team."

Cal just barely stopped himself from making a finger down his throat gagging motion.

"I better get up to the house to meet the wedding party when they get here. You two stay here and finish lighting the lanterns, okay?"

"I could go up to the house and meet the wedding party," Cal offered. Anything to get away from these two lovebirds.

Sarah looked at Cal as if he'd spoken in a foreign language. "You ... could ... You could, what?"

"I can lead people to the right place, Sarah."

"You'd have to smile. Be welcoming. You know, personable."

Cal straightened his coat. "I can ... I can do those things."

"No," she said shaking her head, her tone firm. "You can't."

"I could if I tried to. I just never try to."

"Bill won't bite," Sarah returned, heading for the four-wheeler she'd ridden down earlier.

"I know Bill won't bite," Cal muttered. He looked over at the man in question. *Man.* "I was trying to help, not avoid you."

Bill smiled. Cal wanted to attribute some oozing charm or fake bullshit to that smile, but every interaction he'd had in the past few days had been fine. The *man* was polite, deferential even, and he always looked out for Sarah.

It irritated the piss out of Cal.

"So, um, we haven't had much time to talk privately since Sarah said yes."

Cal wanted to say *thank Christ*, but he kept it to himself.

"Sarah ... Well, she'd like to stay here. Have me move in with you guys. That way she could still work the tree farm and I could still work the chair business. Once we're married of course."

Chair business. Apparently that was a business. Married. To his sister. This *man*.

"Obviously, it's up to you. I just thought I'd put it out there since I think Sarah's hesitant to bring it up."

"You want to move into my house," Cal repeated.

"I want to make Sarah happy," Bill said firmly. "She's worried about leaving you, and she doesn't want to leave the business. It makes sense for us, and it makes sense for you, but if it's not what you want ... Well."

"Well what?"

"I don't know you very well, Cal. I just know what Sarah's told me. I think you'd do anything for her. Even let a stranger move in with you. But maybe I'm wrong."

"You're not fucking wrong," Cal returned, jabbing his hands in his pockets as Bill carefully and methodically lit the remaining lanterns.

Cal watched him work for a few minutes, trying to figure him out. Trying to figure this brand-new world out he hadn't even seen coming because Sarah had kept *Bill* a secret.

"Let me ask you something, Bill. If she decided she didn't want to get married. If she wanted to leave you and go back to college, what would you do?"

"I'd follow her."

Cal could only frown at the simple, sure way Bill said that as if it was the only response. "You have responsibilities here. You can't follow her."

"I'd find a way. I'd find a way to make something work. My parents lived in two different countries for over a year. They made it work. That's what love is."

"Even if she wasn't willing to compromise what she wanted? You'd just do whatever she wanted?"

"Depends, I suppose. My mom always told me relationships are a balance, but that doesn't mean you're always giving fifty-fifty. Sometimes the other person needs eighty, and you only get twenty. Then you need eighty and they give up their sixty for you."

"That doesn't make a lick of sense." Except that it did. He just didn't want it to.

It was something like bedlam. Between her large, overloud family and Cora's large, overloud family—complete with baby niece and nephew twins—rehearsal was chaos. Loud, beautiful, *loving* chaos.

Lindsay tried to pay attention to the rehearsal and what she was supposed to do as one of Cora's bridesmaids, but she kept looking back to where Cal stood stoically with Sarah and Bill, who happily whispered things to each other.

Cal. Solitary and alone even when he wasn't.

He expressly didn't look at her. Not once the whole evening. She didn't know how he managed it. Well, she supposed pure hate was how he managed it.

Except he had most definitely not kissed her with *hate* in his heart the other night. No. No hate at all.

She smiled a little to herself at the memory.

"Lindsay?"

"Oh, what?" She blinked at her mother, who glanced once at Cal, then back to her, then sighed. "You're first back down the aisle. When the minister says—"

"Right. No, I remember." She smiled reassuringly at Shane's disapproving frown. "I'll be in tip-top shape tomorrow and listening to every word and following every command." She saluted him, which only sent his frown deeper, but she'd been kind of going for that.

She walked back down the aisle as she'd been instructed, marveling at the way lanterns flickered against the snow and garland to make this absolutely magical wedding venue. It'd be even prettier tomorrow, fully decorated, right at sunset, her brother and Cora pledging their lives to each other.

She'd be home to witness the way they came together to build a life for themselves and Cora's son. It infused her with joy, and hope, and that rare, amazing feeling she was exactly where she was supposed to be.

Cal's gaze met hers as she finished her walk back down the aisle and she didn't temper her smile.

He didn't look away, even if he didn't smile back. She'd count that as progress. Progress was all she needed. Inch by inch, heck, millimeter by millimeter. She wasn't the spoiled little girl who needed it all now and exactly like she wanted anymore.

She could wait. She could put in the work.

The rehearsal ended in the same kind of chaos as it had begun, and once they were all back at the cars that had ferried them over Lindsay held back, watching the Barton house and trying to figure out a way to be left behind without raising any questions or causing any concerns she would miss tomorrow's all-day-wedding-readying chore list before the actual wedding Saturday.

Keys suddenly appeared over her shoulder, and she glanced back at her soon-to-be sister-in-law.

"Take these," Cora offered.

"But—"

"Micah and Shane are heading back with your mom, and Lou's coming up to fix a few issues with the garland. She can drop me off at the ranch. You take my car and do whatever you need to do."

"You know you're my favorite sister-in-law, right?"

Cora rolled her eyes, but she pressed the keys into Lindsay's palm. "I'm a sucker for love these days, and . . . Well, I don't know anything that's happened between you two aside from what little Shane has told me, but I do know fear when I see it."

"I'm not afraid."

"No, but he is."

Lindsay curled her fingers around the keys. Yes, Cal was. She'd never seen that in him when they'd been together. She'd understood his insecurities to an extent, but she hadn't really empathized with them because she'd been so wrapped up in herself. In the future. "Thanks, Cora."

"Just don't be late tomorrow, huh?"

"Aye, aye, Captain."

Cora and the rest of her family scattered, heading home. Lindsay made a fake effort to find Sarah to talk business, but really she was looking for Cal.

It was no surprise to find him in the stable. What *was* a surprise was finding him in the little back room surrounded by wrapping paper and ribbons.

"Did I stumble into an alternate dimension?"

Cal sighed heavily. "I'm too irritated to even be surprised you're here. Are you stalking me?"

" 'Stalking' seems like a harsh word. But I was looking for you."

He shook his head, dropping a knotted pile of ribbon on top of crumpled piles of cheerful wrapping paper. He raked fingers through his already-wild dark hair. "Sounds about right."

"We kissed, Cal."

"We've kissed lots of times, Lindsay."

Oh, he could be such a pill. Still, she looked around at the mess he'd made no doubt trying to wrap a few pretty packages for Sarah to open on Christmas morning. But Sarah had Bill now and . . .

Lindsay knew Sarah wouldn't desert Cal completely, but he'd certainly feel a little deserted no matter what.

"I could wrap them for you."

He looked up at her suspiciously. "What's your angle?"

She smiled sweetly. "You have to keep me company while I do it."

He grunted and surveyed the mess. "I'd keep company with the devil to get this done. Go ahead."

Lindsay got to work, cleaning the mess, reorganizing the three rolls of wrapping paper and one of those big bargain spools of cheapo ribbon. Still, it was adorable he'd tried this hard. A mushy heart of gold underneath all that gruff sternness on the outside.

She used to think that's just how he was, but with a slightly more mature outlook she could see that wasn't accidental or even just his personality. His soft heart had been broken so many times he'd tried to build himself the hardest, thickest shell he possibly could.

She wanted to get underneath that shell again, but she had to admit it was going to be an uphill mountain climb. In an ice storm. In the dark.

Still, she got to work wrapping Sarah's gifts, humming "White Christmas" to herself, and occasionally sneaking glances at him or even the room around them. It was a small office-type room that Cal said had once been used as a ranch manager's quarters. So, it had heat, lousy, though it was. And it had a bed.

She snuck a glance at the bed. They'd spent some time on that bed, in this room, playing at being grown-ups. She sighed at the odd mix of nostalgia and the wanting to actually build that future they'd always planned. It'd be different, sure, but she didn't want the trappings anymore. The *life*. She wanted him. The *partnership*.

"A lot of firsts happened here," she offered, sneaking another glance at him.

His expression was blank, but she knew he remembered. He had to remember everything just like she did. They were good, sweet memories no matter what came after, too. She wouldn't let bitterness coat them, and she hoped he wouldn't, either.

"You made me wait forever," he said after a very long pause.

"We were sixteen."

He shrugged. "Even more reason it felt like forever."

"I wouldn't make you wait that long now." She finished tying the bow and making it sure it looked pretty and perfect before she dared look up at him.

His blue gaze blazed hot, and she felt it wash through her like wildfire. A need she hadn't felt ignite inside of her with that intensity since *him*. No date, no boyfriend, no other man on this planet had ever made that pang pull sharp and sweet that fast or that desperate.

It was a *need* to touch him, to feel him, to be with him. She suddenly didn't care about foundations anymore, or building or waiting or trust. She only wanted.

Because they weren't teenagers anymore, and that promised so much...more. More than sweetness and exploration and just being excited to see someone naked. They'd been with other people, and she assumed he'd learned the same lesson she had.

Only the two of them together ever caught that spark into true fire.

She carefully placed the wrapped gifts in the corner and pushed the supplies over in the same direction. Then she got to her feet and smoothed her dress out. He was still sitting behind the falling-apart desk shoved in the corner, but she sidestepped the desk and stood next to his chair.

Swallowing against the way a mix of nerves and desperation pounded through her, she reached out and brushed her fingers over a lock of hair at his temple.

"Cal."

He shoved to his feet. "I'm not going to—"

She blocked his exit, pressing her hands to his hard chest where his coat was open. She could feel his warmth, the strength in him. A new strength since she'd touched him like this, and a much harder shell to crack.

But underneath all that he was still her Cal.

"You don't have to make me any promises," she said, spreading her fingers wide.

"I'm not promising—"

"Or believe any of mine," she continued, dragging her fingertips down his abdomen. She met his hard, blazing gaze with an imploring one of her own. She stopped her fingers' journey at his belt buckle. "Let's just remember," she whispered. Though her hands shook, she undid the clasp of his belt.

And he didn't stop her.

CHAPTER 7

Somewhere in his brain, a dim voice was telling him to move. But it was such a quiet demand, and it had nothing on the pleasure of a woman's hands just barely brushing his very, very, *very* hard erection.

Which was at least in part because it was Lindsay. *Lindsay.* Those luminous blue eyes, that lush mouth parted slightly. He had memorized every sigh, every moan, every slide of their bodies together.

Then he'd tried to burn it all from his memory. For that first year or two, he'd tried to drown it in other women. He'd been determined to forget Lindsay and love and lose himself in someone else and sex. Anything, *anything* that felt better than the bleak emptiness of life on his father's ranch with a horrible stepmother.

Then the stepmother had gone, and there had been a relief in that. An opportunity to take over the aspects of the ranch Dad didn't like or was too drunk to handle. Not feeling like a failure every time he found out that woman had gotten to Sarah when he'd tried so hard to protect her.

In that year of freedom, he'd come to a dire kind of acceptance. Other women didn't do anything to solve his actual problem. And until he could get Lindsay out of his head and heart, other women couldn't fit into either.

So, it had been a long time. And with this look on Lindsay's face, cheeks flushed with desire and hands slowly and deftly opening his jeans, every memory of them together roared back through him like a freight train. As if he hadn't eradicated them at all but had just found a way to make them dormant.

Now they were alive again, and there was no turning back. There just wasn't. She didn't make promises and he didn't fool himself into thinking this was the *start* of something even if she did.

It was just sex. Maybe it'd mess him up a bit, but he was already a mess. A mess *without* sex.

So.

He grabbed her wrists and pulled them from his now open jeans. She made a noise of protest, but he covered it with his mouth. He poured years of wanting her into that kiss and propelled her back toward the bed.

She wrapped her arms around his neck, pressing her long, lean body against his. He groaned an oath into her mouth, then sank deeper into it, tangling his fingers in the silky strands of her hair.

She was all she'd ever been—sweetness and light, and a balm to his fractured soul. He didn't want her to be any of that, but she was. She just was. She shoved the coat off his shoulders as he unzipped hers. He nudged her onto the bed and she sat with an audible squeak of the old, rusty frame.

Firsts. Yes, they'd explored a million firsts here and he should probably shove them firmly in the *lasts* column of his life. Maybe that's what this was. A good-bye. A last hurrah. An exorcism.

He didn't believe it, but it at least gave him a reason to move forward, to pull his shirt off and drop it on top of his coat. It gave him enough mental excuses to reach behind Lindsay and unzip the back of her dress.

She wriggled out of the sleeves and the fabric pooled at her waist, the colorful bra she was wearing a bright contrast to the pale acres of skin. She stood up, letting the dress fall off completely, and then she stepped out of the shoes she'd been wearing. So, she was standing in front of him in this chilly room in nothing but her underwear.

Lindsay Tyler. The ghost he couldn't exorcise. Flesh and blood and offering herself up to him. No matter how many times he'd dreamed of this, and his inevitable refusal, he'd understood even in those fantasies of rejection it was just a fantasy.

For all the ways it made him weak, pathetic, and a damn useless human being, he was inextricably linked with Lindsay Tyler for the rest of his life, and he didn't have it in him to say no to this.

She reached out and pulled at his jeans, so he toed off his boots and let the pants fall. She smoothed her hands over his abdomen and chest and then over his shoulders, till she was pressed against him, holding on to him, taking his mouth with hers.

No matter that he didn't want it to be sweet, her skin was smooth and warm and her mouth was like honey and hope. He had nothing left to hope for, but he'd take it anyway. He unclasped her bra, pulling the straps off her arms even as he didn't break the kiss. When his hands closed over her small, firm breasts, they both groaned against each other's lips.

She deepened the kiss, everything between them going something closer to wild. Her fingers slid inside his boxers and grasped him, sighing as she did. Still his fingers explored the perfection of her breasts. The tight buds of her nipples, the soft skin around them. The way she arched against him when he applied pressure.

Then his hands weren't enough. He lowered his head to taste the sweet perfection of her nipple. She squeaked, and then she moaned, and he spent precious minutes simply tasting her, from one side to the other. Until she was gasping, scraping her nails through his hair, her hand gripping and stroking him with increased fervor.

"Cal, please."

It ricocheted through him. Lindsay pleading for anything from him. So he tumbled them onto the bed. Not because she'd pleaded, but because that "please" made him desperate and desperate would only end everything far too soon.

The aftermath would be ugly. The sex had to be fan-fucking-tastic to make up for it.

She wiggled out from under him and maneuvered on top of him, and before he could offer up, well, anything she guided him inside of her.

He swore between clenched teeth because it blew him off his axis. He used to prepare for that. The moment when everything else ceased to exist except her. Them. But he'd forgotten how potent being inside Lindsay could be, and he hadn't thought he'd forgotten anything.

"Lindsay," he managed to say in the best warning tone he could muster.

She grinned down at him, trailing her fingertips down his chest. "What? You used to like me to lead." She moved her body slowly, torturously taking him deep, then moving away.

It was hard to say anything to her words, hard to think of anything beyond the movement of her body against his.

Used-tos hurt, and yet used-tos were why he was here. So, he didn't say anything at all. He gripped her hips, hard enough to keep her still as he moved deep into her.

She said his name on something like a gasp, so he kept it up. Holding her and moving against her and leading the whole damn thing even from his back. He kept an iron grip on his control and ruthlessly drove her to her peak.

She chanted his name, she held on to his shoulders as he thrust inside of her, with a slow, methodical pace that had her begging all over again.

"Please, Cal, oh God, go faster."

So, he did, until she was shuddering apart, clinging to him. His, again.

Temporarily.

Somewhere in the back of his mind he thought he heard bitter laughter.

He let her catch her breath. It took a few seconds, maybe a few minutes, but slowly the knowledge he was still hard inside of her burned through the glorious aftermath of orgasm.

Lindsay moved her body against him, watching him narrow his eyes at her. His mouth seemed carved out of granite he clenched his jaw so hard, and this time as she curled her body against him she brushed her fingers down his abdomen, reveling in the hard rigidness of his body.

Then without any warning whatsoever, he flipped her onto her back, looming above her. She shivered in anticipation at the determined, chaotic look in his expression. He wanted her. He needed her.

It was everything those other boyfriends hadn't been. Her friends had always made fun of her for that—for saying Cal was by far the best sex she'd ever had. They'd always told her sex was sex, no matter who the sex was with, and she only needed to find a more skilled partner if she wasn't getting off.

But that wasn't true, because being with Cal wasn't just simple biology. It was love and hope and knowing another person. It was being connected not just physically, but emotionally, maybe even spiritually.

No one else could give her what Cal gave her, because no one else was Cal.

He simply watched her with that inscrutable expression as she moved underneath him, trying to get him to move with her, until she felt less languid and more needy. Until he took her hand off his shoulder and held it above her head, then took her other hand from his back and did the same.

So that he was in charge. He was above her, setting the pace. Nothing languid or slow. No, everything sped up. She shouldn't be this desperate for more when she'd only just had *some*, but she needed it. Her own again. His. She needed everything, and it all sparked into brilliant life when he dipped his head to hers and kissed her.

Not soft or sweet, but not the desperate clashing from earlier. She could almost believe this was a start. Right here. Right now. He'd just needed time and they could start right here.

She loved him with all she was, and this was her chance.

He pushed deep inside of her, breaking the kiss on a groan, and she held him as he moved against her a few more times, deep and deeper still.

He collapsed on top of her, and she held him tight. She felt like crying, like making him all those promises she'd said she wouldn't.

But this hadn't just been remembering. It *hadn't*. It had been both the same and new. It had been both nostalgia and just beautiful present. It was the same as that kiss. Perfect and everything she wanted to build her new life on.

But slowly tension crept into his shoulders, and he shifted his weight off of her. She couldn't let that happen, so she held on to him, moving with him as he shifted to his side. She kissed his cheek, then his mouth, but still he stiffened, rolling onto his back, his eyes going up to the ceiling.

She blew out a breath and looked up at the ceiling, too. Okay, so . . . Maybe he didn't feel all those same things she had.

Except he had to. He *had* to. The thought that he might not made her want to cry for a million reasons, but she stared at the ceiling and blinked back tears. When she finally found words, they weren't exactly romantic. "I'm . . . on birth control. So."

"Christ," he muttered, and she didn't know if he was swearing over the awkwardness at announcing it or the fact they hadn't discussed it beforehand, but she wasn't sure she wanted to know. Not with the temperature cooling degree by degree.

She couldn't . . . she couldn't bear it. Before she thought she could stand it even if he still didn't want to try again. She thought she could be brave and certain he'd come around eventually. Fight for him, like her mother said, and eventually it would work out.

Eventually currently scared the hell out of her. She wanted him now. She wanted this *now*. If he walked away after *that* . . . Well, then she didn't think they felt the same things at all.

She turned onto her side, looking at him desperately. "Cal, I love you. I do. It hasn't changed for me, either. The things you said about . . . I tried, too, to move on, but I couldn't. Because I will always, always love you."

He rolled off the bed immediately and began to pull on clothes. She needed something else to say, but she struggled to find words.

He pulled on his pants, shoved his feet into his boots.

"Cal."

"I love you, too," he finally said, not looking at her as he pulled his shirt over his head.

Elation welled inside of her chest. Even though she was cold, she didn't move for her underwear or her dress. This was too important. "So . . . We should start again." She grinned at him, even as he pulled on his coat and expressly avoided her gaze. "Cal, we can start over. We could. We love each other. We *belong* together. Give us a chance to—"

"I can't, Lindsay." He zipped his coat, and finally those ice blue eyes met hers. Flat and certain and, worst of all, pained. "I love you. I do. But I could never trust you. I'd always be waiting for you to leave and I'd make us both miserable. I don't know how to change that. Whatever we have, it doesn't work anymore. Ever."

She could only stare.

"Do you need a ride home?"

"No," she managed to whisper.

Then he left her alone with the terrible understanding she had nothing to fight his words. He couldn't trust her and she couldn't make him.

And that was just . . . that.

CHAPTER 8

Cal had felt a lot of things regarding his relationship with Lindsay over the years. They ranged the gamut, too. From happiness and certainty and love beyond measure to a vile, black hatred of what she'd done to him.

But in all those times, he'd never felt this low-level beat of panic that was threatening to swallow him whole. He hadn't slept all night. Sex for the first time in *years* and he hadn't slept at all.

Now it was the day of the wedding and after struggling through his ranch chores he had to help Sarah make sure everything was in place. And *Bill* would be there.

Never mind that much as he hated to admit it, he liked Bill, he didn't like watching his *nineteen-year-old* baby sister fawn all over a *man* she was going to marry.

Marry. The word itself left a sick feeling in his gut, and he couldn't escape the word because there would be a wedding on his land today. A Tyler wedding. A Christmas-themed Tyler wedding, because life had a way of really clubbing you over the head hard and over and over again.

He blearily poured the last dregs of the coffee into a mug and looked around the kitchen. Sarah had spent all morning decorating little wedding-themed cookies, and while she'd cleaned up most of the debris, there were trays and trays of goodies.

Cal was too tired to work up the energy to poach a few. Which worked in his favor as Sarah bustled into the kitchen at that moment. So, instead of being caught red-handed he was just standing there.

"You can have as many as you want," she offered with a grin. "I made enough for twenty people and the only people here will be the ladies. The female wedding party is getting ready here, which will be..." She counted off on her fingers. "Four. Although the florist and baker might come up here, too, but even so, six won't eat all these. So help yourself." She frowned at him. "Are you getting sick?"

"No. Why?"

"You look awful. You didn't shave, which isn't like you. And you haven't stolen one cookie." She reached out and placed the back of her hand against his forehead.

"I'm not sick."

"Then what's wrong?" She moved her palm to press to his cheek.

"Nothing a few cookies can't cure."

Her frown dug deeper. "That's a lie."

"What do you need me to do for today?" he asked, because he couldn't get into Lindsay with Sarah and he couldn't dump on her when she felt like she had everything riding on this. When she deserved a happy, uplifting Christmas.

It'd probably be their last full Christmas together. She'd get married, and even if Bill did move into this house with them, he and Sarah would spend at least some time with his family. And Cal would be truly alone.

Which was probably how it should be.

"I told you I'd take care of everything, well, except building the platform, but that was all I needed. I've got today handled. I'll take care of the women up here, Mrs. Tyler's in charge of the men and pastor and getting them set up down at the site. Bill's doing his chairs and heaters and handling any tree stragglers. The bridesmaids are going to use their trucks to get down to the site, and I'm going to drive the bride down in the old Ford."

"So..."

"You can do whatever ranch stuff you want to do, or you can take the afternoon off. I've got it all covered."

"There aren't... lights you need stringing or chairs to— I could handle the Christmas tree crowd."

"Bill and I have it covered." She gave him a hug as if that weren't like shoving him clear through with a meat cleaver. "You get to relax. When was the last time you did that?"

Technically, last night. Sex was very relaxing for as long as it lasted.

It was all the mental rigmarole *after* that wasn't relaxing. And not working meant thinking more about it. Meant constantly beating back that little flicker of hope things could be different.

He would literally never learn.

"You don't even have to be here if you don't want," she said carefully, not meeting his gaze and nibbling on a cookie delicately.

"Not be... Where would I go?"

She shrugged, still looking at the cookies instead of him. "Wherever you wanted. A drive. Into Benson. You could go to a movie!"

"Alone?"

Her gaze slid to his, something like hurt in her pitying gaze. Because alone was what he'd always be, and she knew that as well as him.

She swallowed her bite of cookie and took a deep breath. "Don't take this the wrong way, but you've... You've made yourself alone. I figured you either liked it, or you'd eventually snap out of it, *grow* out of it, and sometimes I think you have, but Christmas comes and you always turn into this." She gestured at him as if he knew what she was referring to. "Gruff and a little self-pitying, though Lindsay being here has brought that to a lot of self-pitying this year. And I get it, I do, I've felt some pity for myself, too, but... you can't keep at it."

"I'm struggling to see how I'm not supposed to take this the wrong way."

"The wrong way is thinking I'm accusing you of doing something wrong, or bad, or that I don't understand. I *do* understand. I think I was in that cycle myself for a while, but Bill—"

"You're in love and getting married, to a guy you didn't want to introduce me to but now want living under my roof—"

"*Our* roof," Sarah interrupted, suddenly looking closer to tears. "You always said it was *ours*. I don't want that to change. Did you?"

"No, I don't want it to change," he managed, though his throat felt tight and all that panic from this morning was clutching at his throat. Didn't this just prove his point? "This is just who I am. The guy who says the wrong thing and makes you cry. No one wants this," he said, mirroring her move and gesturing toward himself. "I wouldn't wish this on my worst enemy."

"I would." She hit him on the chest. Hard. "You are kind and generous to a fault and I know you'd *die* for me, Cal Barton. This isn't about who you are. It's about how you see yourself. And how you've let . . . Mom and Dad don't define who you are, Cal. Not their shit and not their leaving. Lindsay doesn't define who you are. You've let your grief over those things define yourself to yourself, but no one else sees you the way you do. What does that tell you?"

"That you're all too softhearted."

"You know, Bill asked me out five times before I said yes."

"Sounds like a stalker."

She hit him again. "Finally I said, '*Why* do you keep asking me out? What could you possibly see in me that makes you so damn persistent?' And you know what he said?"

"No, but I don't think I want to know."

"He said, 'What don't I see in you, Sarah?' "

She left that there as if it was some amazing thing and Cal tried to rearrange his face to somehow look receptive and understanding instead of what he felt—which was baffled.

She sighed and shook her head and Cal could only hope he'd be dismissed and this horrible delving into personal matters could be over—because they took care of each other, but they didn't have heart-to-hearts. Cal didn't *do* heart-to-hearts.

"Do you love me, Cal?"

He winced—both at the fact this wasn't over and the fact she could even ask. "You know I do."

"Do you think I'm stupid?"

"Of course not."

"Then don't presume people loving you is stupid. I love you with my whole heart, and I am not stupid. I am not wrong."

"Okay," he returned, figuring agreeing with her would end it. But she only fisted her hands on her hips looking more irritated.

"It's not okay until you get it through your head that these things you think you are—unlovable, insufferable, whatever—are things we all are at some point or another. They can either define you, become your day-to-day, hour-to-hour, or they can just be low points you have every now and again."

He still didn't know what she wanted from him. Maybe the belief he was okay. That he could take care of himself, because she wanted out. That had to be it. She didn't want Bill to move in here with him. She wanted Cal to be okay so she could leave.

He wasn't, and he wouldn't be, but he'd die before he let her know that. "You don't have to worry about me. I don't want you to feel like you have to stay here for me. I want you to go wherever you want to go, do whatever with Bill that would make you happy. I don't want my shit to be the thing keeping you here. I'll be okay. Once Christmas is over, I'll be okay."

"I don't want to leave, dumbass. The thing keeping me here isn't your *shit*. It's you. It's the Christmas trees and having weddings here, which has been so *cool*. It's the fact this is my home and I've always loved it and taken great solace in its existence no matter who came or went. I don't *want* to leave, Cal. Not everyone does."

The doorbell sounded from the front of the house and Sarah hefted out a sigh. "This conversation isn't over," she said on her way to answer the door.

"Yes, it is," he said, to an empty room, his own stupidity echoing back at him.

Lindsay wasn't exactly *thrilled* to be getting ready for this wedding in Cal's house. She wasn't exactly *thrilled*, period. She was gritty eyed and exhausted.

But her big brother was getting married today, to a woman he adored, a woman the whole Tyler clan adored. It was a good day even if she was a little raw from last night. Memories of being a teenager in this house, of watching Cal valiantly trying to shield Sarah from their awful stepmother or their drunk father.

In this house she remembered too much of the good man she'd left. It wasn't that she regretted leaving. It was just . . .

As an adult, she could look back and see how she might have handled things differently. How she might have found a compromise between leaving *everything* behind and never finding herself the way she had.

But she couldn't go back, and she couldn't let herself dwell on old mistakes. Not today. Today was about Shane and Cora and happy beginnings for people who truly deserved them.

Cal deserves one, too.

She rolled her eyes at herself. Today was not the day to obsess about Cal or anything. Today was for Shane and Cora.

Cora, who looked so giddily nervous as the hairdresser worked on her hair. Molly and Lilly were oohing and aahing over the bouquets Lou had dropped off. Lindsay looked around desperately trying to find something, *anything,* to lift her out of this crappy mood.

Cookies. Christmas cookies solved everything, she was pretty sure. And Sarah was a fine baker. She sidled over to the table where Sarah had set out piles of delicious cookies and went to town.

Sarah entered from the kitchen, carrying another pitcher of lemonade. "Everything going good?" she asked cheerfully.

Lindsay nodded through a mouthful of cookie. Sarah narrowed her eyes at her, studying her face with a weird kind of suspicion. Lindsay forced herself to smile. "What?"

"You look about as with it as Cal does."

It was awful to hope he was miserable, too. Of course he was miserable. He'd decided to be, hadn't he? Lindsay cleared her throat. "What about Cal?" she asked, trying for clueless innocence.

"Did . . . Something happened, didn't it?"

Lindsay shoved the rest of the cookie in her mouth, buying some time to think while she chewed. "Oh, you know. I just . . . helped him with his Christmas wrapping." *And had hot, sweaty sex in the stable room, confessed all of my feelings, was rejected in the worst possible way.* The kind you couldn't fight.

Sarah pulled a face. "That's not a euphemism, is it?"

Lindsay's face heated against her will. "I mean, I *did* wrap your gifts."

"Oh God, you guys—"

Lindsay slapped a hand over Sarah's mouth, glancing back at where her sister and just-about-to-be sister-in-law stood with Cora's sister. She could *not* let Molly get wind of it. Not yet. Lindsay just wasn't emotionally stable enough to listen to her older sister's lectures. Not yet.

Sarah pulled Lindsay's hand away. "But you did?" she whispered.

"I shouldn't be discussing this with you," Lindsay whispered back, still keeping an eagle eye on her sister.

"But you did?"

"Stop asking me that!"

"So, you did."

"Sarah."

Sarah sighed, looking more than a little miserable herself. "I just want him to be happy."

"Me too." Lindsay swallowed and reached out to squeeze Sarah's hand. "But he has to choose it, or he's never going to be it. I can't— *We* can't make that choice for him."

"I know. I know. But something has to push him, doesn't it? Someone?"

"I've done my fair share of pushing, Sarah. I don't know what else to do."

"Well, I do."

"You do?"

"You don't give up," Sarah said firmly, so much nineteen-year-old surety shining in her eyes.

It was Lindsay's turn to sigh. "I hurt him. Then and now. It all hurts to him. I think giving up is the . . . it's the generous thing to do."

"No, it's the cowardly thing to do. If you love him. If you want to make it work this time. And you do, don't you? You wouldn't have . . . Well, you know, if you didn't want him. You're not cruel. You love him."

"Yes." Lindsay turned away from her family, because if they even glanced at her they'd see all the emotion on her face. The sadness and the hurt and the despair, and that didn't belong here today. She'd have plenty of other non-wedding days to feel sad over it and him. "I do love him. I'll never stop, I don't think. It's been this long. But I can't force him to accept that love. I can't make him believe he deserves it."

"But we can keep loving him until he does."

Lindsay couldn't bear to voice her greatest fear, though it lingered there in the silence.

What if he never did?

CHAPTER 9

Cal couldn't bring himself to leave. Not after his conversation with Sarah this morning. She wanted to stay because she loved him, and she loved this place, so maybe he wanted to help for the same reasons.

Damn it.

He shoved his hands in his coat pockets and headed over to Bill, who had some strange-looking contraption that seemed to make sure the chairs were all lined up perfectly.

"You, uh, need any help?"

Bill didn't look up from his chairs. "Got it. Thanks, though. I just put up the Closed sign, so we shouldn't have any more tree customers."

We. Cal was going to have to get used to that and not wince at it. "Yeah. Gre—"

"Bill, it looks perfect. I swear to Pete if you measure one more time I'm going to beat you with the tape measure."

Cal swallowed at Mrs. Tyler's voice. Lindsay's mom had been such a part of his life growing up and then . . .

Maybe it was Sarah's words, or maybe it was Bill's from the day before. Maybe it was all the words and all the people poking holes in all the barricades he'd built around himself in the aftermath of all that abandonment, but he could see something with a startling clarity he hadn't before.

He'd pushed Mrs. Tyler away after Lindsay had left. Made clear in no uncertain terms she wasn't his mother and he didn't want her help or her support. Because he'd been afraid. Afraid of support. The very same panic he'd felt this morning.

He hadn't understood it at nineteen, and he wasn't sure he understood it now, but he was beginning to fully comprehend it was *him*. Not his parents. Not Lindsay. Not anyone's betrayal or disappearance, but his reaction to it.

Because Mrs. Tyler had never really disappeared. She'd given him space, but there'd always been gestures. Hugs when she bought her Christmas tree. She'd taken Sarah shopping on occasion. He hadn't let her be a mother to him, but she'd been a presence no matter how much of a petulant asshole he'd been.

"Hi, Mrs. Tyler."

She crossed her arms over her chest and studied him. "I think we need to have a little talk, boy."

She'd said those exact same words to him after Lindsay had confessed to her they'd had sex for the first time. Then she'd proceeded to give him the safe sex talk his father had never bothered to bestow. And even then, in the miserable embarrassment of his girlfriend's mother offering to demonstrate condom usage on a banana (he'd refused, politely), he'd known that was something she was doing because she cared.

"I'm not really a boy anymore, Mrs. T."

"Aren't you just, though."

Slightly insulted, he straightened and frowned down at her.

"When you get to be my age, twenty-five is still pretty young, sweetheart." Then she smiled at him and sighed. "What are you doing to my baby girl?"

"I'm not—" He glanced at Bill, who seemed so lost in chairs he wasn't even listening. Cal stepped forward trying to create some space. He spoke quietly. "*I* was minding my own business. Whatever happened, happened because she wasn't minding hers."

Mrs. Tyler laughed, that big, booming laugh she had that always put him at ease, gave him a few seconds of forgetting he didn't really belong.

He'd never let himself.

"Tylers minding their own business? When has that ever happened?"

The smile was inevitable, but it came with a crushing weight of regret. For once it wasn't someone else's actions causing that regret. It was his own.

It was easy to blame Lindsay for everything that had happened. She *had* left. It was easy to blame his parents. They were assholes, no question. But Mrs. Tyler . . . what had she ever done to him?

"I'm sorry," he said, before he could think better of it.

Mrs. Tyler looked at him quizzically. "For what?"

"I know you wanted to be there for us, and I wasn't kind or grateful about it. But I am grateful. You were always good to Sarah."

"And I always will be. She's a sweet girl. But I also knew she was in good hands with you."

"A surly asshole?"

"A kind, loving, sacrificing older brother. Who's a little bit of a surly asshole, yes. But not to her. Never to her."

Cal didn't know what to say to that. He looked uncomfortably over at Bill, but he'd moved to the top of a far-off hill and seemed to be analyzing the chairs from way over there. Cal shook his head.

"You could talk to me."

He looked at Mrs. Tyler dolefully. "About your daughter? I don't think—"

"I didn't say I'd give you advice or solve your problems or take your side. I only said you could talk to me if you needed to talk to someone. It isn't any good, you know, bottling it all up. Believe it or not, I've been there myself. After Lindsay's father died, my amazing mother was smart enough to tell me to let it out on occasion. So, what I'm saying is, let it out. You won't on Sarah. You won't on Lindsay. So." She gestured at herself.

"Your son is about to get married."

She glanced at her watch. "I have a full hour before I have to go get dressed." She situated herself on one of Bill's chairs and pointed to the one next to her.

He knew Mrs. Tyler well enough to know that there was no refusing or turning away. She wanted you to sit, you sat. So he did, uncomfortably.

"Get it out, boy."

"I just . . ." He thought about last night. About saying "I love you" and knowing it didn't matter, because he couldn't get over what had happened. It was hardly Lindsay's fault, but that made it worse. He didn't know how to fix it. It felt foolish to talk about an unfixable problem. Especially with Lindsay's mother, but she was looking at him expectantly.

She was right, too. He couldn't unload on anyone else. Mrs. Tyler might not be an unbiased party, but she'd listen. He hadn't thought he wanted anyone to listen until right this second.

"I love her. I'll always love her. And maybe she feels the same way." Maybe. He kept trying to convince himself of that maybe, but he'd never doubted Lindsay had loved him before and he wasn't certain he doubted it now. After all, he felt it this deeply. Why shouldn't she? But love wasn't the issue.

"She told you she was staying?"

He nodded, looking at his gloved hands. *Staying. Such a strange word.*

"You know how she hightailed it out of here. Destined for bigger and better things than Gracely, Colorado."

And me.

"So, she had to swallow her pride a bit to come home. To realize this was where she belonged and admit it to her whole family. Trust me, my children don't swallow their pride easily."

"I know, but . . . I can't . . . It'd always be hanging there. That she left. That she could again. I've had too much of it. I don't know how to . . . I don't know how to believe it changes."

Mrs. Tyler nodded, squinting off into the distance. "I understand that. It's hard to believe in good things when bad things happen. But . . . Well, if there's anything I've learned in this life it's that belief is a choice. Belief in the good. Belief in the bad. The world around you has both, and you'll never get to decide which one wins on any given day, but you do get to choose which one defines you. The world will turn on either way, regardless of what you choose to believe in. So, why not believe in the good?"

He shook his head. "I don't feel like I have that choice. Not with this."

"Your feelings are wrong, Cal." She smiled kindly. "I know, I know, I'm supposed to say that all feelings are valid, blah, blah, blah." She rolled her eyes. "My boys used to play that old 'why are you hitting yourself?' game. You know where they take your hand and make you slap your own face?"

"Um, sure."

"Cal, sweetheart, stop hitting your damn self."

Much like the other day with Bill, he didn't want to admit the words made sense, but of course they did. The kind of sense that rearranged your whole life, and he really didn't want to.

But he was starting to think he had to.

"See what the rest of us see. Believe in the good, and my God, believe in yourself." She reached out and cupped both his cheeks. "You're a good man. But it doesn't matter how good you are if you don't believe it. It doesn't matter how much you love if you don't choose it." She patted one cheek, not exactly lightly, then hopped to her feet. "That's my drop of wisdom for the day. What you do with it is up to you."

Up to him. *Well, shit.*

The wedding was beautiful. Lindsay didn't think there was a dry eye in the house when Cora and Shane exchanged vows, including her stoic oldest brother's. Which only made her more teary. When the pastor announced them as, not just husband and wife, but a family as they engulfed Micah in a hug onstage, she downright sobbed.

The small reception was a magical winter wonderland. There were industrial heaters and little pitted bonfires surrounding the small space, plus plenty of cozy places to sit and piles of heavy flannel blankets. Micah was pulling around Cora's niece and nephew in a sled, and Christmas music crooned from the speakers on a beautifully decorated table.

A beautiful Colorado night sky stretched out above, perfectly clear and glowing gloriously. And Lindsay was eating some of the best wedding cake she'd ever had.

It was perfect and beautiful and Lindsay was so, so glad she'd decided to come home. To be a part of not just weddings, but the everyday. To exist in this wacky world of Tylers. Her blood, her roots, her hope.

She finished off the cake and looked out at the small dance floor. Shane was dancing with Cora. Molly had clearly coerced Boone out there, since he was standing and scowling as Molly laughed and tried to get him to move. Gavin was sitting in between Em and Lou Fairchild, making them both laugh. Lindsay's mom danced far too close with her new husband, Ben. A few more couples from Cora's side danced to the happy tune of "Rockin' Around the Christmas Tree."

She was about to get up and convince Gavin to dance with her, to give up the little sliver of lingering melancholy that everything hadn't worked out *exactly* the way she wanted and focus solely on the joy of it all.

Then Cal appeared. He stood next to the hay bale she'd been sitting on with a few heavy blankets over her lap and around her shoulders. He was mostly still shrouded in the dark, since she'd chosen the most faraway seat she could when she'd gotten her piece of cake.

"Hi," she offered, peering up at him.

"Hey."

"Crashing the party?"

"Something like that."

"You want to sit?"

He gave a little nod, then took a seat next to her. She offered up a bit of blanket and he nodded again, so she moved it over his lap. They sat there like that for a few moments, watching the wedding reception in front of them.

"I talked to your mom today," he finally said.

"Oh yeah?"

"Yeah. Is she always right?"

"No. But she's right an annoying lot of the time."

His mouth quirked at that, even as he watched the goings-on in front of them. But she watched him. The soft cast to his mouth, that hint of something hopeful in his blue eyes.

"You know, she didn't want me to leave back then. She thought I'd regret it, and she was wrong." He stiffened, but she plowed forward, because hope and truth was the only way. "I can't regret leaving. I really needed that. It gave me a confidence being the Tyler baby was never going to allow me, but I regret the way I did things.

I wasn't thinking about you. I was eighteen and self-involved and all that mattered to me was escaping and making my mark and I didn't think about how you might see that. There were so many things we could have tried, or done differently, but I was too selfish to see them."

"Me too."

She whipped her head up. He'd never . . . never once taken even a shred of responsibility for anything that had happened when they'd ended things. "What did my mother *say* to you?"

He chuckled at that, and it wasn't even a bitter sound. It was a bit more like the Cal she remembered.

"Actually that realization didn't come from anything she said. She just . . . was there and I had to realize . . ." He blew out a breath. "You might have left, my parents might have left, but there were plenty of people who stayed, even if I was an ass to them for it. I should have focused on what I had, instead of what I didn't, but I was young and . . . what was your word? Self-involved. I was very, very self-involved."

Lindsay didn't know what to say to that. Even less so when he finally turned his head to meet her gaze.

"But I loved you. I still love you. And I'd like to think I'm not quite as self-involved as I used to be. Or at least, I'm taking the steps not to be."

"I love you, too." She tried to breathe normally. Was afraid to make sudden movements or more begging proclamations for fear he'd evaporate in front of her very eyes. "I'm waiting for your but."

"I don't have one." He hesitated for a second. Then his hand reached under the blanket and grasped hers. "I'm scared. It's hard to weather, being left behind. It's hard to get over that fear. I'm not even sure I can. But . . . I have a choice to believe, and to build a foundation, and to build it with you."

She couldn't say anything. She wasn't even sure she was breathing. She thought she'd need to put in so much more work, so much more *proving*, and she would. She still would, but . . .

"Well, are you going to say anything?"

"Cal." Cal. Her Cal. Her future. Tears spilled over onto her cheeks and she didn't have any words. Not any. So she just launched herself at him, knocking them both to the snowy ground. But he laughed and the blanket was still tangled around them and today really *was* perfect.

Which finally gave her the words she needed to say. "I love you, Cal, and I'm not ever giving up on us again. I'll prove it to you. Over and over again. I'll never walk away like I did. Not ever. I will fight and I will stay and I will give *us* everything I am."

"Yeah?"

"Yeah. And you are going to do the damn same, do you hear me?"

"Yes, ma'am."

And on the frigid ground in the midst of her brother's wedding, she kissed the man she'd loved and lost, and now got to love again. Forever.

Epilogue

One Year Later

Lindsay loved teaching. Even with a headache brewing and her favorite top stained with paint from one child's enthusiastic thrusting of his overly painted paper at her, she was pretty damn happy.

It was hard. Some days she wanted to scream—whether at the kids or the administrators—but some days she felt so damn fulfilled she could barely catch her breath. The learning to deal with both was making her a better person, step-by-step. The handful of handmade presents she had in her bag was a bit of the icing on the cake.

But the best part of all of it was that she got to come home, to the Barton ranch. There'd been an attempt to just date at first, but it had been silly when you knew you wanted to be with the other person every night forever. So, Cal had started remodeling the old barn to be their new home. Sarah and Bill would live in the big house and handle Christmas trees and weddings, and she and Cal would live in the barn. He would ranch, she would teach, and life felt . . .

Well, a bit like a Christmas miracle.

They'd spent the past year building. It had included ups and downs, fights and makeups, and a million other things Lindsay had finally come to realize were simply life. Regardless of dreams or the whole big world out there, the bulk of her life would always be this: Cal and her, happy or fighting, struggling or marveling at their success. It was *all* her life, and nothing better awaited her.

It was a far more beautiful life than her wildest imagination had been able to dream up as a teenager.

She parked outside the barn. They had a working bathroom and working heat at this point. The kitchen was still in progress, so they ate a lot of meals up at the main house, but most nights they then cozied together here and it felt like home.

Humming "Jingle Bells," Lindsay let herself in through the front door. Sometimes Cal was here when she got home, but sometimes he was still out with the cows. This afternoon, though, he was home, and he even looked like he'd showered and put on his nice clothes.

"Are we going somewhere?"

He uncurled from the couch, and since she was feeling the Christmas spirit, she allowed herself a dreamy sigh, because she was a very lucky woman indeed to be so desperately in love with a man that handsome.

"I thought since you're off work for the next two weeks we could drive into Benson and have a nice dinner."

"Steak?"

"Most definitely. I may even splurge on wine."

"I think you're trying to get lucky tonight, Cal Barton."

He grinned. "Indeed I am."

"Just let me change. I got paint attacked by Jaxon the Enthused."

"Again?"

She sighed heavily. "Again." But as she made a move for their bedroom, Cal took her by the arm and gently pulled her toward the tree. "Before you do that, why don't you have a look. I added a new ornament."

"You, Cal Barton, hater of Christmas and begrudger of this very tree—"

"I did not begrudge you this tree. I begrudged you the amount of junk you put on this tree."

"Humph."

"Look at the tree, Linds."

She peered at the well-lit branches, trying to sort through the parade of sparkling ornaments she'd perhaps oversplurged on. "I don't see anything—"

But then she did, and her bag fell to the floor with a thump and she sort of thought she might fall because she couldn't feel her legs. She couldn't breathe.

Cal watched Lindsay stare at the very modest ring that hung from a red ribbon on a branch at eye level. And she just stared, openmouthed, maybe shiny eyed, but there was no immediate answer.

But then he supposed he hadn't asked the question.

It was a lesson he was learning, bit by painful bit, that people could not read his mind. That they'd never automatically give him what he wanted if he didn't *ask*.

All those years ago when Lindsay had broken up with him, he'd never asked her for different. Not to stay, not to compromise. He'd simply been furious and determined she'd done everything he'd ever feared.

Those fears didn't disappear, but he'd found in asking he often got the answer he wanted, and it always, always alleviated the fear.

So, instead of waiting any longer, Cal did what he should have done in the first place. He got down on one knee. "Lindsay, I love you. We've started building this life together, and I want to keep building it. Will you marry me?"

Finally she breathed, moved, escaped that frozen shock. Much like she had that night a year ago, because he had definitely picked this day for a reason, she launched herself at him and knocked them to the ground in the process.

"You delight in causing me bodily injury, so that better be a yes."

"It's a . . . It's a . . . Whatever's bigger and better and more beautiful than a yes."

"There is nothing bigger or better or more beautiful than you saying yes to this particular question."

She nuzzled into his neck and he figured she was probably crying. So, he let them lie there on the hard ground for a few uncomfortable seconds before he nudged her off him and helped her up. "Come on. You have to put it on."

She laughed through the tears, and when he tugged the ring off the tree his hands were shaking too hard to untie the ring from the ribbon.

"Let me try," Lindsay said, but her hands were shaking, too, and in the end she just shoved the ring, ribbon and all, onto her finger. "There," she said, holding it up so he could see, tears streaming down her cheeks.

He felt a little choked up himself. "Feels kind of silly to be this worked up," he managed to say.

She pressed her palm to his cheek, her eyes still bright with tears, but her hands weren't shaking anymore. "We worked hard for this. And we have a lot of hard work ahead of us. I'm going to be worked up about every good thing, because it feels damn good to work hard and get what you want."

He pulled her into a hug and just held her there for a moment, because it reminded him of what Mrs. Tyler had told him that day a year ago. That good and bad happened, but you got to choose what you believed in. There would be hard times and hard work ahead, and he would always, *always* choose to believe in the woman in his arms.

So, he swept her up and against him and started carrying her toward the bedroom.

"I thought you were going to take me to Benson," she murmured, planting a kiss on his neck, then his jaw.

"There's still time."

She laughed at that and sank into a kiss that nearly had him running into the wall. Instead, they made it to the bed and celebrated the best way Cal knew how to celebrate. Together and naked.

Later that night, instead of heading to Benson for a nice celebratory meal, Lindsay insisted they go to the Tyler Ranch and tell her family. There were cheers and hugs and toasts and eager wedding plans already being made. Thankfully Shane, Gavin, and Boone helped him escape and they went out to the barn and taught Shane's stepson how to throw darts.

Then they headed back to Barton house. "We should stop by and tell them, too," he said, turning onto the drive that would lead them there.

Lindsay leaned her head against his shoulder as he drove. "Of course we should."

Bill and Sarah had gotten married at the tree farm in the summer at a very small ceremony. This winter they'd made the Christmas tree farm an even bigger success than it had ever been, adding sleigh rides and Santa visits and hot chocolate stands.

Cal had even admitted to Bill that seeing him take such good care of his sister made him up his own game. He'd been a little drunk at the wedding when he'd confessed it to his new brother-in-law, but he felt rather proud of himself for saying it all the same.

It was still weird to knock on his own front door, but there'd been an unfortunate not-knocking incident a while ago that had made them all agree knocking was the best policy if anyone wanted to keep their eyeballs.

So, he knocked, and Lindsay slid her arm around his waist and it didn't matter that some parts felt weird, because most parts felt beyond right.

Sarah opened the door, a bright smile on her face. "There you are! I've been looking for you!"

"You have?"

"We have some news we wanted to share," Sarah said, moving out of the way so they could step inside. She looked downright giddy, which Cal found very suspicious.

Lindsay shrugged out of her coat, looking just as giddy, though that only made him happy, not suspicious. "We have news, too," she said grabbing Sarah's hands.

The women held on to each other as they progressed into the living room, where Bill was. He had two bottles and four champagne flutes on the table.

"There you are!" he greeted exactly as Sarah had.

"Here we are. So, whose news are we going to—"

"You have a *ring*!" Sarah screeched, dropping Lindsay's right hand and using both hands to grasp Lindsay's left. "Oh my God! Oh my God!"

"Please don't cry," Cal murmured. He could take Lindsay's happy tears, but both of them at the same time was too much.

"It's just..." Sarah sniffled and took a hitching breath. "I'm...I..."

Bill slid his arms around Sarah's shuddering shoulders.

"We're having a baby," Bill said, big chested and proud.

Lindsay's shriek nearly deafened Cal and he could only stare at his *baby* sister having a baby. An actual baby.

Sarah looked up at him, tears streaming down her face, and he didn't have words, so he just pulled her into a hug.

She hugged him back.

"I guess tonight is quite the celebratory night," Bill offered. He handed Lindsay a glass of champagne, and then Cal understood the two bottles because the glass he handed Sarah was clearly sparkling cider. He offered Cal a glass, then took one for himself.

Cal looked around a room that had once held nothing but bad, ugly memories and a certain sense of loss. He'd known over the past year they'd worked on eradicating all that bad, but now he knew for certain the ghosts of an ugly past were gone.

They were starting a new Barton future. A really good one.

Cal cleared his throat and held up a glass. "How about a toast?"

"From *you*?" Sarah and Lindsay asked in unison.

"Yes, from me," Cal replied with a scowl. "The first and possibly last one I'll ever give, so have some respect."

"He's so cute when he's grumpy," Lindsay said, probably to irritate him further.

"He's not half as grumpy now as he used to be," Sarah returned. "Thanks to you."

Cal sighed heavily. It was his great lot in life that his future wife would be far too good of friends with his sister. But Sarah would have the kind of sister she deserved, and he couldn't ask for more.

"To family," he said, hoping he wouldn't always be moved to

this kind of sentimentality on Christmas. "To love. And to as many Merry Christmases as we can shove into a lifetime."

Which earned him enthusiastic "hear, hears" from the small group, and an even more enthusiastic kiss from his future wife.

Wife. Lindsay Tyler was finally, *finally* going to be his wife, and he had no doubt he would make every moment of that dream finally coming true count.

Praise for Nicole Helm's Mile High Romance series:

"A classic small-town contemporary with extra angst, perfect for fans of Susan Mallery and Jill Shalvis."
—*Kirkus Reviews*

"A deeply moving contemporary. . . . The protagonists are refreshingly willing to be up front about their feelings and listen to each other, and readers will want to revisit their story often."
—*Publishers Weekly* (starred review)

A Baby for Christmas

LISA JACKSON

Prologue

December 1995
Boston, Massachusetts

I'll have a blue Christmas without you . . .

"Oh, no, I won't!" Angrily, Annie McFarlane snapped off the radio. She wasn't about to let the sad lyrics of that particular song echo through her heart. It was the Christmas season, for heaven's sake. A time for merriment and joy, not the dull loneliness that caused her to ache inside.

She unwound a string of Christmas lights and plugged it into the socket. Instantly the dreary living room of her condominium was awash with twinkling bright color. Red, blue, yellow, and green reflected on the carpet and bare walls, giving a hint of warmth to a room littered with half-filled boxes and crates, evidence of the move across country she was planning. Pictures, mementos of her life as a married woman, clothes, knick-knacks, everything she owned was half-packed in the boxes strewn haphazardly through the condo.

Her throat tightened and she fought back another attack of hot, painful tears. "Don't do this," she reprimanded herself sharply. "He's not worth it. He never was."

So what if David had left her for another woman? So what if this was the first Christmas she would spend alone in her entire life? So what if she was truly and finally divorced, a situation she'd never wanted?

Women went through it all the time. So did men. It wasn't the end of the world.

But it felt like it. The weight on her shoulders and pain deep in her heart wouldn't listen to the mental tongue-lashings she constantly gave herself. "Get over it," she said aloud and was surprised that her words nearly reverberated in the half-empty rooms. Her dog, a mutt who looked like he had his share of German shepherd hidden somewhere in his genes, thumped his tail against the floor as he lay, head on paws, under the kitchen table.

"It's all right, Riley," she said, her words sounding as hollow as she felt.

Sleet slashed against the windows, the old Seth Thomas clock still mounted over the fireplace ticked off the seconds of her life, and the gas flames in the grate hissed steadily against ceramic logs that would never burn. Outside, the city of Boston was alive with the festivities of the holiday season. Brilliant lights winked and dazzled on garland-clad porches while bare-branched trees were ablaze in neighboring yards. Wreaths and pine-scented swags adorned doors and electric candles burned in most of the windows. Children in those other houses were too excited to sleep. Parents, frazzled but happy, sipped mulled wine, planned family dinners, and worried that their hastily bought, last-minute presents wouldn't bring a gleam of gladness to their recipients' eyes.

And here she was, stringing a single strand of lights over a potted tree she'd bought at the local grocery store, knowing that tomorrow she would eat alone, put in some hours down at the local women's shelter, and come home to pack the rest of her things. She only wished that she'd been able to move before the holidays, but her timing—or, more precisely, David's timing—hadn't allowed for Christmas.

Three months ago she'd called her real estate agent about selling the condo, watched through her tears as David had carried his half of their possessions out the door, smiled bravely when he'd casually mentioned that Caroline, his girlfriend, was pregnant, and then had fallen apart completely as she'd reluctantly signed the divorce papers.

Annie had never felt more alone in her life. Her mother and stepfather were spending the holidays cruising up and down the west coast of Mexico; her sister Nola, forever the free spirit, was again missing in action, probably with a new-found lover. Annie remembered Nola's last choice, a tall, strapping blond man by the name of Liam O'Shaughnessy, whom Nola professed to adore for all of two or three weeks. Since O'Shaughnessy, there had been others, Annie supposed, but none she'd heard of.

Then there was Annie's brother, Joel, and his wife. They were spending Christmas at home in Atlanta with their three kids. Though invited to visit them, Annie hadn't wanted to fly down south with her case of the blues and spoil everyone's Christmas so she'd decided to stick it out here, alone in the home that she and David had shared, until she moved to Oregon after the first of the year.

Thank God the condo had sold quickly. She couldn't imagine spending much more time here in this lonely tomb, which was little more than a shrine to a marriage that had failed.

She fished in a box of handmade ornaments she'd sewed and glued together only last year and placed a tiny sleigh on an already-drooping bough. As she finished looping a length of strung cranberries and popcorn around the little evergreen, she had to smile. The forlorn little tree looked almost festive.

There would be life, a more satisfying life, after David. She'd see to it personally. At least she still had Riley, who was company if nothing else.

With a glimmer of hope as inspiration, she walked to the kitchen, scrounged in a drawer for a corkscrew, and realized that, as she'd given the good one to David, she was forced to use the all-in-one tool they'd bought years before for a camping trip. The screwdriver-can opener-bottle opener was more inclined to slice the user's hand than open a can or bottle, but it was the best implement she could come up with at the moment.

She managed to open a bottle of chardonnay without drawing any blood, then found one of the wine goblets from the crystal she'd picked out seven years ago when she'd planned her wedding to David. She'd been twenty-three at the time, graduated from college as a business major and had met David McFarlane, a witty, good-looking law student, only to fall hopelessly in love with him. She'd never thought it would end. Not even during the horrid anguish and pain of her first miscarriage. The second loss—during the fifth month—had been no better, but the third, and final, when the doctor had advised her to think seriously of adoption, had been the straw that had broken the over-burdened back of their union. David was the last son of his particular branch of the McFarlane family tree and as such was expected, as well as personally determined, to spawn his own child, with or without Annie.

It was then, during the talks of surrogate mothers and fertility clinics, that the marriage had really started to crumble. Enter Caroline Gentry: young, nubile, willing, and, apparently, if David were to be believed, able to carry a baby to term.

"What a mess," Annie said to herself as she carried her bottle and goblet into the living room. On the hearth, she tucked her legs beneath the hem of her oversized sweater and watched the reflection of the colored lights play in her wine. "Next year will be better." She held up her glass in a mock toast and her dog, as if he understood her, snorted in disdain. "I'm not kidding, Riley. Next year, the good Lord willin' and the creek don't rise, things will be much, much better." Riley yawned and stretched, as if tired of her pep talks to herself. She took a long swallow and closed her eyes.

No matter what happened, she'd get over this pain, forget about David and his infidelity, and find a new life.

And a new man, an inner voice prompted.

"Never," she whispered. She'd never let a man get close enough to her again to wound her so deeply. "I'll make it on my own, damn it, or die trying."

CHAPTER 1

December 1996

Oh, the weather outside is frightful . . .

"Damn." Liam snapped off the radio and scowling, settled against the passenger window of the battle-scarred Ford.

"Not in the spirit of the season?" Jake Cranston snorted as he stared through the windshield of his car. "I guess jail will do that to you."

Liam didn't respond, just clamped his jaw tight. He'd been through hell and back in the past few weeks; he didn't need to be reminded of it. Not even from a friend. Tonight Jake was more than a friend; he'd turned out to be Liam's goddamned guardian angel.

Liam glared out the window to the dark night beyond. Ahead of them, red taillights blurred through the thick raindrops that the wipers couldn't slap away fast enough. On the other side of the median, headlights flashed as cars screamed in the opposite direction. Christ, he was tired. He needed a good night's sleep, a stiff drink, and a woman. Not necessarily in that order.

It seemed as if Jake had been driving for hours, speeding through this rainy section of freeway without getting anywhere, but the city lights of Seattle were beginning to glow to the north.

"Want to stop somewhere?" Jake, while negotiating a banked

turn, managed to shake a cigarette from his pack of Marlboros located forever on the dusty dash of his Taurus wagon. He passed the pack to his friend and shoved the Marlboro between his teeth.

He thought about lighting up. It had been six years since his last smoke and he could use the relief. He was so damned keyed up, his mind racing miles a minute even though he was dead tired. He tossed the pack onto the dash again. "Just get me home, Cranston."

"Why the devil would you want to go there?" Jake punched the lighter.

"Gotta start somewhere."

"Yeah, but if I were you I'd put this whole thing behind me and start over."

"Not yet."

"You're well out of it." The lighter clicked. Jake lit up and let smoke drift from his nostrils.

"Not until my name is cleared." Leaning back in the seat, Liam tried to forget the nightmare of the past few months and the hell he'd been through. But the days of looking over his shoulder and knowing he was being followed, watched by men he'd once trusted, still struck a deep, unyielding anger in his soul.

It had all started four months ago on a hot August night in Bellevue. In the early morning hours, there had been a break-in at the company offices where Liam worked. At first the police thought it was a typical burglary gone sour; the security guard on duty that night, old Bill Arness, had been unfortunate enough to confront the crook and had been bashed over the head, his skull crushed. Bill, a six-times grandfather with a wide girth and quick smile, had never awakened, but lingered in a coma for six weeks, then died before he was able to give the name of his attacker. His wife had never once left his side and the president of Belfry Construction, Zeke Belfry, had offered a twenty-five-thousand-dollar reward for anyone who had information that would lead to the arrest and conviction of the perpetrator. Zeke, a law-abiding, holier-than-thou Christian with whom Liam had never gotten along, was personally offended that his company had been singled out for any kind of criminal act and he wanted revenge.

Which he ultimately got.

Out of Liam O'Shaughnessy's hide.

Within a few months the police had decided the break-in was an inside job. Records had been destroyed. An audit showed that over a hundred thousand dollars was missing, all of the money skimmed from construction jobs for which Liam had been the project manager.

The police and internal auditors had started asking questions.

It had been nearly two months from the time of all the trouble until the police had closed in on him, slowly pulling their noose around his neck tighter and tighter while he himself was working on his own investigation. It was obvious someone had set him up to take a fall, but whom?

Before he could zero in on all of the suspects, one woman had come forward, a woman who held a personal grudge, a woman who had driven the final nails in his coffin. Nola Prescott, his ex-lover, had gone to the police and somehow convinced them that Liam was involved not only with the embezzling, but the death of old Bill Arness as well.

So here he was with his only friend in the world, trying to forget the sounds that had kept him awake at night. The clang of metal against metal, the shuffle of tired feet, shouts of the guards, and clank of chains still rattled through his brain. Prison. He'd been in prison, for Christ's sake. All because of one woman.

His teeth ground in frustration, but he forced his anger back. *Don't get mad, get even.* The old words of wisdom had been his personal mantra for the past few weeks. He'd known that eventually he'd be set free, that the D.A. couldn't possibly hold him without bail forever, that there wasn't a strong enough case against him because he hadn't done it.

"Okay, so what's the story?" he finally asked. "Why was I let go all of a sudden?"

"I thought you talked to your attorney."

"He just sketched out the details. Something about the prosecution losing their prime witness. Seems Nola chickened out. Didn't want to perjure herself."

Jake snorted and two jets of smoke streamed from his nostrils. "That's about the size of it. Nola Prescott recanted the testimony in her deposition."

Liam's guts churned. Nola. Beautiful. Bright. Secretary to one of the engineers at the firm. Great in bed, if you liked cold, unemotional, but well-practiced sex. No commitment. Just one body seeking relief from another. Liam had quickly grown bored and felt like hell after his few times in bed with her. Too much vodka had been his downfall. Their affair had been brief. "Why'd she change her mind?"

"Who knows? Maybe she got religion," Jake cracked and when Liam didn't smile, drew hard on his cigarette. He guided the Taurus onto the off-ramp leading to Bellevue, a bedroom community located north and east of Seattle.

"I think she might be protecting someone," Liam said, his eyes narrowing.

"Who?"

"Don't know. Maybe someone else she was involved with." He concentrated long and hard. "Someone at the company, probably. It would have been someone she was involved with six or seven months ago, before she left for her new job with that company in Tacoma."

"Christ, why didn't you tell this to the cops?"

"No proof. I'd look like I was just grasping at straws, but there's got to be a reason she set me up."

"You dumped her."

"So she accuses me of murder? That's even lower than Nola would go. She claimed to see me at the company that night. Why? She worked in another city."

"But still lived in the area."

"Too much of a coincidence, if you ask me." He stared at the streaks of raindrops on the windows. "It's just a matter of finding out who she was involved with." He drummed his fingers on the dash and thought of the possibilities—several names came to mind.

"Anyone you want me to check?" Jake offered.

"Yeah. Kim Boniface, one of her friends, but I wouldn't think she'd be covering for a woman. Then there's Hank Swanson, another project manager, Peter Talbott in accounting, and Jim Scorelli, an engineer who was always making a pass at her. Other than that,"—he shook his head, mentally disregarding rumors of financial difficulties of other friends and coworkers he knew at Belfry—"I can't think of anyone."

"I'll check."

"There's something else," Liam admitted, though he hated to bring up the subject. "I heard Nola was pregnant."

Jake's lips curled in upon themselves, the way they always did when he was weighing whether or not he should level with Liam. "So the rumor goes, but who knows? A woman like that—"

"Is it mine?"

The question hung in the smoky interior.

"How would I know?"

Liam squinted hard as the Taurus accelerated through the hills surrounding Bellevue. "Just tell me if the kid was born late in November or early December."

"Look, O'Shaughnessy, I wouldn't open that can of worms if I were—"

"Is it mine?" he repeated.

"For Chrissakes, Liam, who cares?" Jake growled.

"I do."

"Don't do this." He cracked his window and flicked his cigarette outside onto the pavement where the burning ember died a quick death in the gathering puddles.

"Do what?"

"Develop some latent sense of nobility. You had a fling with the woman. A *short* fling. Later she testified against you, tried to get you locked up for something you didn't do. She's no good. Leave her alone."

Liam's neck muscles tightened in frustration. "I just want to know if the kid's got O'Shaughnessy blood running through its veins."

"Right now, you should concentrate on getting a job. Just because you're exonerated doesn't mean that Zeke Belfry's gonna welcome you back with open arms."

That much was true. Ever since the old man had retired and his son Zeke had become president of the company, things had changed at Belfry Construction. Liam and Zeke had clashed on several occasions before all hell had broken loose. He'd already planned to sell his house, cash in his company stock, and start his own consulting firm. He didn't need Zeke Belfry—or anyone else, for that matter.

Jake nosed the Taurus into a winding street of upscale homes built on junior acres. Liam's house, an English Tudor, sat dark and foreboding, the lawn overgrown, moss collecting on the split shake roof, the windows black. The other houses in the neighborhood were aglow with strings of winking lights, nativity scenes tucked in well-groomed shrubbery, and illuminated Santas and snowmen poised on rooftops. The lawns were mowed and edged, the bushes neatly trimmed, the driveways blown free of leaves and fir needles.

Welcome to suburbia.

He fingered his keys.

"Your Jeep's in the garage. Mail on the table."

"Where's Nola?" Liam wasn't giving up.

Jake pulled into the driveway and let the car idle in the rain, the beams of his headlights splashing against Liam's garage. "Don't know."

"What?"

"No one does."

"Now, wait a minute—"

"Let it go, Liam." Suddenly Jake's hand was on his arm, his firm fingers restraining his friend through the thick rawhide of his jacket.

"Can't do it. Where is she?"

"Really. No one knows. Not even the D.A. She recanted her testimony and disappeared. A week ago. Your guess is as good as mine."

"She's got family," Liam said, remembering. "A brother in the south somewhere, folks who follow the sun, and a sister in Boston . . . no, she moved. To Oregon." Liam snapped his fingers.

"No reason to drag her into this."

"Unless she knows where Nola is and if the kid is mine."

"I knew I shouldn't have told you." Jake slapped the heel of his hand to his forehead.

"You had to," Liam said, opening the car door as a blast of December wind rushed into the warm, smoky interior. "Thanks."

"Don't mention it."

Liam slammed the door shut and saw his friend flick on the radio before ramming the car into reverse. Jake rolled down the window at the end of the drive and laughed without a trace of mirth. "Oh, by the way, O'Shaughnessy. Merry Christmas."

Feliz Navidad, Feliz Navidad . . .

Annie hummed along with José Feliciano as she sat at her kitchen table and licked stamps to attach to her Christmas card envelopes. Marilyn Monroe, Elvis, and James Dean smiled up at her along with the more traditional wreaths, Christmas trees, or flags that decorated her rather eclectic smattering of stamps. Her home, a small cottage tucked into the low hills of western Oregon, was decorated with lights, fir garlands, pine cones, and a tree that nearly filled the living room. The cabin was warm and earthy from years of settling here in this forest. The pipes creaked, the doors stuck, and sometimes the electricity was temperamental, but the house was quaint and cozy with a view of a small lake where herons and ducks made their home.

Riley lay beneath the table, his eyes at half-mast, his back leg absently scratching at his belly.

Annie had been lucky to find this place, which had once been the home of the foreman of a large ranch. The main house still stood on thirty forested acres while the rest of the old homestead, the fields of a once-working farm, had been sliced away and sold into subdivisions that crawled up the lower slopes. The larger farmhouse, quaintly elegant with its Victorian charm, was empty now as the elderly couple who owned it had moved to a retirement center. It was Annie's job to see that the grounds were maintained, the house kept in decent repair, the remaining livestock—three aging horses—were fed and exercised and, in general, look after the place. For free rent, she was able to live in the cottage and run a small secretarial service from her home.

"I wanna wish you a Merry Christmas, I wanna wish you a Merry Christmas . . ." She sang softly to herself as the timer on the ancient oven dinged and she scooted back her chair to check the batch of Christmas cookies.

Outside, snow had begun to fall in thick flakes that were quickly covering the ground. Supposedly, according to the local newspeople, a storm was going to drop several inches of snow over the

Willamette Valley before moving east. But there was no cause for concern—maybe a slick road or two, but for the most part the broadcasters were downplaying the hazards of the storm and seemed happy to predict the first white Christmas to visit western Oregon in years.

Annie planned to fly to Atlanta to spend the holidays with Joel, Polly, and her nephews. She'd come a long way from her dark memories of the past year, managing to shove most of her pain aside and start a new life for herself. Even the news of David's marriage and the birth of his son hadn't affected her as adversely as she'd thought it would, though her own situation sometimes seemed bleak. She wondered if she'd ever become a mother when she couldn't begin to imagine becoming some man's wife.

Well, as Dr. James had told her after the last miscarriage, "There's always adoption."

Could she, as a single woman?

The scents of cinnamon and nutmeg filled the kitchen as she slipped her fingers through a hot mitt and pulled a tray of cookies from the oven. She glanced out the window and saw snow drifting in the corners of the glass. Ice crystals stung the panes and a chill seeped through the old windows. A gust of wind whipped the snow-laden boughs of the trees and rattled the panes. The newspeople were certainly right about the storm, Annie thought, feeling the first hint of worry. She turned on an exterior light and mentally calculated that there were two inches of white powder on the deck rail.

If this kept up, she'd have a devil of a time getting to the airport tomorrow. "It'll be all right," she told herself as she snapped off the oven.

Bam!

A noise like the backfiring of a car or the sharp report of a shotgun blast thundered through the house. Within seconds everything went dark.

"What in the world—?"

Riley was on his feet in an instant, barking wildly and dashing toward the door.

"It's all right, boy," Annie said, though she didn't believe a word of it. What had happened? Had a car run into a telephone pole and knocked down the electrical lines? Had a transformer blown?

It didn't matter. The result was that she was suddenly enveloped in total darkness and she didn't know when the electricity might be turned on again. Muttering under her breath, she reached into a drawer, her fingers fumbling over matches, a screwdriver, and a deck of cards until she found a flashlight. She flicked on the low beam and quickly lit several candles before peering outside into the total darkness of the hill. Though she was somewhat isolated, there were neighbors in the development down the hill, but no lights shone through the thick stands of fir and maple.

Alone. You're all alone.

"Big deal," she muttered as her eyes became accustomed to the darkness. She wasn't a scared, whimpering female. Shaking off a case of the jitters, she found her one hurricane lantern and lit the wick. "Okay, okay, now heat," she told herself as she opened the damper of the old river-rock fireplace, then touched one candle to the dry logs stacked in the grate. The kindling caught quickly and eager flames began to lick the chunks of mossy oak while Riley, not usually so nervous, paced near the front door. He growled, glanced at Annie, then scratched against the woodwork.

"That's not helping," Annie said. "Lie down."

Riley ignored her.

"Just like all males," she grumbled. "Stubborn, headstrong, and won't listen to sound advice." Bundling into boots, gloves, her ski jacket, and a scarf, she headed for the back porch where several cords of firewood had been stacked for the winter. She hauled a basket with her and after twenty minutes had enough lengths of oak and fir to see her through the night. The batteries on her transistor radio were shot, and the phone, when she tried to use it, bleeped at her. A woman's voice calmly informed her that all circuits were busy. "Perfect," she said grimly and slammed down the receiver.

I wanna wish you a Merry Christmas from the bottom of my heart . . . The lyrics tumbled over in her mind, though the music had long since faded. "Right. A Merry Christmas. Fat chance!"

As firelight played upon the walls and windows, she drew the curtains and dragged her blankets from the bedroom. She'd be warmer close to the fire and could handle a night on the hide-a-bed. In the morning she'd call a cab to drive her to the airport, but for now she needed to sleep. Riley took up his post at the door and refused to budge. He stared at the oak panels as if he could see through the hardwood and Annie decided her dog was a definite head case. "It's warmer over here," she said and was rewarded with a disquieting "woof," the kind of noise Riley made whenever he was confused.

"Okay, okay, so have it your way." Settling under her down comforter, she closed her eyes and started to drift off. She could still hear José Feliciano's voice in her mind, but there was something else, something different—a tiny, whimpering cry over the sound of Riley's whine. No, she was imagining things, only the shriek of the wind, tick of the clock, and . . . there it was again. A sharp cry.

Heart racing, she tossed off the covers and ran to the front door where Riley was whining and scratching. "What is it?" she asked, yanking open the door. A blast of ice-cold wind tore through the door. The fire burned bright from the added air. Riley bounded onto the front porch where a basket covered with a blanket was waiting. From beneath the pink coverlet came the distinctive wail of an infant.

"What in the name of Mary . . ." Leaning down, Annie lifted the blanket and found a red-faced baby, fists clenched near its face, tears streaming from its eyes, lying on a tiny mattress. "Dear God in heaven." Annie snatched the basket and, looking around the yard for any sign of whoever had left the child on her stoop, she drew baby, basket, and blankets into the house. "Who are you?" she asked as she placed the bundle on her table and lifted the tiny child from its nest.

With a shock of blond hair and eyes that appeared blue in the dim light, the baby screamed.

"Dear God, how did you get here?" Annie asked in awe. She immediately lost her heart to this tiny little person. "Hey, hey, it's all right. Shhh." *Who* would leave a baby on the porch in the middle of this storm? What kind of idiot would . . . Still clutching the baby, she ran to the window and peered outside, searching the powdery drifts for signs of footprints, or any other hint that someone had been nearby.

Riley leaped and barked, eyeing the baby jealously.

"Stop it!" Annie commanded, holding the child against her and swaying side to side as if she were listening to some quiet lullaby that played only in her head. She squinted into the night and felt a shiver of fear slide down her spine. Was the person who left the baby lurking in the woods, perhaps watching her as she peered through the curtains?

Swallowing back her fear, she stepped away from the window and closer to the warmth of the fire.

The baby, a girl if the pink snowsuit could be believed, quieted and her little eyes closed. Head nestled against Annie's breast, she made soft little whimpers and her tiny lips moved as if she were sucking in her dreams. Again Annie asked, "Who are you?" as she carried the basket closer to the fire to peer into the interior.

A wide red ribbon was wound through the wicker and several cans of dry formula were tucked in a corner with a small package of disposable diapers. Six cloth diapers, a bottle, two pacifiers, one change of clothes, and a card that simply read, "For you, Annie," were crammed into a small diaper bag hidden beneath a couple of receiving blankets and a heavier quilt. Everything a woman would need to start mothering.

Including a baby.

"I can't believe this," Annie whispered as again she walked to the window where she shoved aside the curtains and stared into an inky darkness broken only by the continuing fall of snowflakes. The moon and stars were covered by thick, snow-laden clouds, and all the electrical lights in the vicinity were out.

Annie picked up the phone again and heard the same message she'd heard earlier. "Great," she muttered.

As the wind raged and the snow fell in thick, heavy flakes, she realized that unless she wanted to brave the frigid weather and hike to the neighbor's house, she and this baby were alone. Completely cut off from civilization.

"I guess you're stuck with me," she said and worried about the baby's mother. Who was she? Had she left the child unattended on the stoop? What kind of mother was she? Or had the baby been kidnapped and dropped off? But by whom?

For you, Annie.

The questions chasing after each other in endless circles raced through her mind. She placed a soft kiss on the infant's downy blond curls and lay down on the couch, where she held the child in the warmth of her comforter. "I'll keep you safe tonight," she promised, bonding so quickly with the infant that she knew she was going to lose her heart. "Riley will keep watch."

The dog, hearing his name, woofed softly and positioned himself in front of the door, as if he truly were guarding them both. Annie closed her eyes and wondered when she woke up in the morning, if she'd be alone and discover that this was all just part of a wonderful dream.

CHAPTER 2

"Is this an emergency?" a disinterested voice asked on the other end of the line.

"Yes, no . . . I mean it's not life or death," Annie said, frustrated that after finally getting through to the sheriff's department she was stymied. "As I said, a baby was left on my porch last night and—"

"Who does the child belong to?"

"That's what I'm trying to find out." Annie glanced at the basket—and at Carol, the name she'd given the child upon awaking this morning and discovering last night's storm wasn't a nightmare, nor was the basket part of a dream.

"Are you injured?"

"No, but—"

"Is the baby healthy?"

"As far as I can tell, but her parents are probably sick with worry—"

"Look, lady, we've got elderly people without any heat, cars piling up on the freeways, and people stranded in their vehicles. Everyone here is pulling double shifts."

"I know, but I'm concerned that—"

"You can come down to the station and fill out a report or we can send an officer when one's available."

"Do that," Annie said as she rattled off her address. A part of her felt pure elation that she had more time alone with the infant and another part of her was filled with dread that she'd become too attached to someone else's baby.

"Deputy Kemp will stop by and I'll put calls into the local hospitals to see if a baby is missing. I'll also see that social services gets a copy of this message. A social worker or nurse will probably contact you in the next couple of days."

"Thank you."

"As I said, an officer will stop by as soon as he can, but I wouldn't hold my breath. It could be a day or two. We're shorthanded down here with all the accidents and power outages. He'll call you."

"Thanks."

Annie hung up and sighed loudly. The frigid northern Willamette Valley was paralyzed. Sanding trucks and snowplows couldn't keep up with the fifteen-inch accumulation and still the snow kept falling. Annie had no means of communication except for the phone and her driveway, steep on a normal day, was impassable. She was lucky in that she had plenty of food and a fire on which she could cook. She'd even managed to heat Carol's bottle in a pan of water she had warmed on the grate.

She'd been awakened in the middle of the night when the baby had stirred and fussed. It took a while, but she'd added water to the dry formula she'd mixed in the bottle, then waited as it heated. The baby had quieted instantly upon being fed and Annie had hummed Christmas carols to the child as she suckled hungrily. "You're so precious," she'd murmured and the baby had cooed. She couldn't imagine giving her up. But she would have to. Somewhere little Carol probably had a mother and father who were missing her.

She fingered the note again, turning it over and studying the single white page decorated with a stenciled sprig of holly. Who had sent her the baby and cryptic message? Obviously someone who knew her and knew where she lived. Someone who trusted her with this baby. But who?

Was the child unwanted? Kidnapped? Stolen from a hospital? Taken from her cradle as her parents slept? Part of a divorce dispute? Her head thundered with the questions that plagued her over and over again.

She'd called the airport and found that Portland International was closed, all flights grounded. She'd tried to reach her brother in Atlanta, but all outside circuits had been busy and she figured Joel would eventually call her.

"So it looks like it's just going to be you and me," she told the infant as she changed her diaper and sprinkled her soft skin with baby powder. "You can have a bottle and I'll open a can of chili."

The child yawned and stretched, arching her little back and blinking those incredible crystal-blue eyes. "You're a cherub, that's what you are," Annie teased. She let her worries drift away and concentrated on keeping the fire stoked, the baby dry, clean, and fed, and allowing Riley outside where the snow reached his belly and clung to his whiskers.

Late in the afternoon while Carol was napping in her basket, Annie checked on the horses, then poured herself a cup of coffee and started writing notes to herself about the baby. The infant was less than a month old, Caucasian, with no identifying marks—no birthmarks or moles or scars—in good health. So who was she?

Though she tried to suppress it, an idea that the child might have been abandoned—legitimately abandoned—kept crossing her mind. Could it be possible? The note was addressed to her so . . . But why would someone who so obviously cared about the infant leave her in freezing weather? No, that didn't make sense—

"Stop it, McFarlane," she growled at herself as Riley lifted his head and stared at the door. He barked sharply, then jumped to his feet. "What is it?"

Bam! Bam! Bam!

Riley started barking like crazy as the person on the other side of the door pounded so hard that the old oak panels seemed to jump.

"Hush!" Annie hurried to the door. "Who is it?" she yelled through the panels, then smoothed away the condensation on the narrow window flanking the door so she could see outside.

She nearly gasped when she saw the man, a very big man—six feet two or three, unless she missed her guess. His face was flushed, his gaze intense, his long arms folded firmly across his chest.

Liam O'Shaughnessy. In the flesh.

"Oh, no—" she whispered and her stomach did a slow, sensual roll. Liam was the one man of all of Nola's suitors that Annie found sexy—too sexy.

And right now he was livid, his face red with fury—or the bite of the winter air. Blond hair, damp from melting snowflakes, was tousled in the wind. Wearing a suede jacket, jeans, and boots covered in snow, he was poised to pound on the door again when he caught sight of her in the window. His eyes, when they met hers, were as blue as an arctic sea and just as violent.

"Help me," she said under her breath.

Nervously, she licked her lips. Never in her life had she faced such a wrathful male. His jaw was square and set, his blond eyebrows drawn into a single unforgiving line. Power, rage, and determination radiated from him in cold, hard waves.

"Open the damned door or I'll break it down," he yelled as the wind keened around him and caused the snow-laden boughs of the fir trees near the porch to sway in a slow, macabre dance. "Annie McFarlane—do you hear me?"

Loud and clear, she thought, and swallowing against a mounting sensation of dread, she yanked on the door handle. Without waiting for a word of invitation, he stepped inside.

"Where is she?" he demanded, stomping snow from his boots.

"Who?"

"Your sister!"

"Nola?" Annie asked, remembering that he'd once been her sister's lover, but only for a little while, or so Nola had confided. Their brief affair had ended abruptly and badly. Nola had been heartbroken, but then she'd been heartbroken half a dozen times because she always fell for the wrong kind of guy.

"Nola isn't here."

He frowned, snow melting on the shoulders of his rawhide jacket as well as in his hair.

"What do you want with her? I thought you broke up—"

"There was nothing to break," he said swiftly. "But, it appears she and I have a lot to discuss."

"You do?" Why was he here, looking for her in the middle of this storm?

"So she isn't here, eh?" He seemed to doubt her and his restless gaze slid around the room, searching the shadowy nooks and crannies as if he expected to find Nola hiding nearby.

"No. I haven't seen her in months."

"Close relationship."

"It is—not that it's any of your business," she said, bristling at his condescending tone. "Now, was there something else you wanted?"

His eyes narrowed suspiciously. "Just to find your sister. She seems to have disappeared."

"No, she hasn't. She's just . . . well, she takes off for little mini-vacations every once in a while."

"Mini-vacations?" His laugh was hollow and the corners of his mouth didn't so much as lift. "I'm willing to bet there's more to it this time."

"I doubt it."

"Then where is she?" His nostrils flared slightly. "Where does she go on these—what did you call them?—mini-vacations. That's rich."

"Look, I don't have any idea. Nola sometimes just takes off, not that it's any business of yours."

He snorted. "It's my business, all right."

"Sometimes Nola goes to the beach or the mountains—"

"Or Timbuktu, if she's smart." He wiped a big hand over his face as if he were dead tired. "If you want to know the truth, I really don't give a damn about Nola."

"But you want to find her?"

"*Have to* is more like it." He raked the interior of the cabin with his predatory gaze once more. "Her beautiful carcass could rot in hell for all I care."

That did it. Annie didn't need to take insults from him, or any other man, for that matter. "I think you should leave."

"I will. Once I get some answers."

"I don't have any—"

Carol coughed softly and O'Shaughnessy's head snapped around. Without a word he crossed the living room, tracking snow and staring down at the baby as if he were seeing Jesus in the manger.

"Yours?" he asked, but the tone of his voice was skeptical.

She shook her head automatically. There was no reason to lie, though she felt a wave of maternal protectiveness come over her. "I—I found her."

"What?" He touched Carol's crown with one long finger. The caress was so tender, his expression so awestruck, that Annie stupidly felt the heat of unshed tears behind her eyes. "Found her? Where?"

"On the front porch. Last night."

He looked up, pinning her with that intense, laser-blue gaze. "Someone left her?"

"Yes. I guess."

"Who?"

"I don't know."

"Nola." He scowled and picked up the basket. "Figures."

"You think my sister brought a baby here?" Annie laughed at the notion.

"Not just any baby," he said, his expression turning dark. "Her baby. And mine."

"What?" she gasped.

"You heard me."

"But . . . Oh, God." He couldn't be serious, but she'd never seen a man so determined in all her life. He glanced down at the beribboned basket. A muscle worked in his jaw and when he looked up again, the glare he shot Annie could have melted steel. "Listen, O'Shaughnessy, I don't know what you're talking about, what you're saying. I—you—we don't have any idea if Nola did this."

"Sure we do."

"Nola's never been pregnant."

"Give me a break."

"Really. I know my sister and I'm sure . . ." Her words faded away. What did she really know about Nola? When was the last time they'd talked besides a quick chat on the phone? The last time Annie had seen Nola had been months ago.

"You're sure of what?" he spat out.

"She would have told me about a baby." Or would she have? Nola knew how much Annie had wanted a child, how crushed and forlorn she'd been after each miscarriage . . . was it possible?

For you, Annie. Sweet Jesus, was the note in Nola's loopy handwriting? Her knees gave way and she propped herself against the back of the couch. As if he'd read her thoughts, he nodded grimly and reached for the basket.

No! "Wait a minute—" But he was already tucking the wicker holder under one strong arm.

She was frantic. He intended to take the baby away! Oh, God, he couldn't. Not now, not yet, not after Annie had already lost her heart to the little blond cherub.

"O'Shaughnessy, you can't do this."

"Sure I can." His face was a mask of sheer determination. "If you hear from Nola, tell her I'm looking for her, that we need to talk."

"No! You can't. I—I mean—" She threw herself across the room and placed her body squarely between him and the door. Fear and pain clawed at her soul at the thought of losing her precious little baby. "Don't leave yet."

"It's time. Give Nola the message."

"But the baby. You can't just take her away and—"

"I'm her father."

"But I don't know that. In fact, I don't know anything about you or the baby or—" Oh, God. In such a short time she'd come to think of the baby as her own even though the notion was impossible.

"Look, Annie, I won't hold you accountable as long as you don't give me any trouble, but tell Nola this isn't over. When I find her—"

"What? You'll what?" Her heart was racing, her head ached, and she knew she'd never let him take the child. She reached for the basket, brushing his sleeve with her hand. "You . . . you can't just barge in here and take the baby and leave."

"Can't I?"

"No!"

His face was etched in stone, his countenance without a grain of remorse. Without much effort he sidestepped her, brushed her body aside, and reached for the doorknob with his free hand. "Watch me."

CHAPTER 3

"You're not going anywhere with that baby, O'Shaughnessy." Annie wasn't letting the baby out of her sight. Not without a fight. She squeezed between him and the door again. Riley, the scruff of his neck standing on end, growled a low, fierce agreement. "How do I know she's yours?"

"She's mine, all right. Just ask your sister."

Annie glared up at him and felt the heat of his gaze, the raw masculine intensity of this giant of a man, but she wasn't going to back down. Not to him. Not to anyone. He seemed to think that Nola was really Carol's mother. But it couldn't be . . . or could it? Was it possible? Who else would know that she desperately wanted a baby, that she would care for an infant as if it were her own, that in her heart of hearts, she would love the child forever? "Now why don't you back up a minute, okay? You're trying to convince me that you and Nola—who, as I heard it, only dated you a short while—that you had a baby together."

"Looks like it." Blond eyebrows slammed together and his jaw was hard as granite. But Annie wasn't going to let him buffalo her.

"Why didn't I hear anything about it?" she demanded.

"Why didn't I?"

"What?" She was having trouble keeping up with all the twists and turns in the conversation.

"You know your sister. Figure it out. Just like her to try and hide the kid here." He started to pull on the doorknob, but Annie pressed her back against the hard panels and put all her weight into holding the door closed. "Get out of the way."

"No! You just stop right there. I don't know that this baby has any connection to Nola."

"Sure."

"I *am* sure," she said, her anger elevating with her voice. "This child"—she jabbed at the basket swinging from his right arm with her finger—"was left on my doorstep in the middle of a storm and then you . . . you—how did you get here?"

"It was tricky. I have four-wheel drive," he conceded. "And a lot of sheer grit."

That much was true. She didn't know much about him, but she believed that with his determination he could literally move mountains.

"Just listen for a second," he insisted, and she notched her chin up an inch. "I thought you knew all about her pregnancy."

"I haven't seen her in months. She was . . . busy with something, something she wouldn't talk about."

A trace of doubt darkened his gaze. A musky scent of aftershave mingled with the smoky odor of burning wood. God, he was close. "But you knew Nola was going to have a baby."

Shaking her head, Annie sighed and rammed fingers of frustration through her hair. "Nola never said a word. For all I know, you could be lying."

"I *don't* lie."

"No, you just storm into a person's house and take what you want."

A muscle jumped in his jaw and every muscle in his body seemed tense, ready to unleash. His words were measured. "I don't know why Nola left the kid here, but—"

"You don't even know *if* she left the baby here."

He hesitated, his lips pursing in vexation. His gaze, icy-blue and condemning, narrowed on her. Obviously he was trying to size her up, to determine how much she really knew.

Annie swallowed hard and tried to ignore the rapid beating of her heart. "Didn't . . . didn't you say you never *talked* to Nola?" she pressed. He was so close that the rawhide of his jacket brushed against her breast. "How do you know that this baby is hers—or yours, for that matter?"

"Who else's?"

"I don't know, but until I do, the baby stays."

His smile had all the warmth of the arctic sea and yet she had the fleeting thought that he was a hot-blooded man. Passionate. Bold. Fierce one second, tender the next. *"You're* going to stop me from taking her?" That particular thought seemed to amuse him.

"Damned straight."

"You're half my size."

"I—I don't think this is a matter of physical strength." She'd lose in a minute to a man who was hard and well-muscled, all sinew and bone. "But I won't give her up without a fight, O'Shaughnessy."

"It's a fight you're gonna lose."

"I don't think so." She tried to appear taller as she looked up at him and tossed her hair over her shoulders. "If I can't convince you, then I guess I'll just have to call the police. They already know about the baby, anyway. A deputy by the name of Kemp is supposed to come and take a statement from me after they check and find out if there are any missing infants in the area. He could be here any minute. So—why don't you and I just wait for him?" She folded her arms over her chest. "I'll even make the coffee."

"We don't need the police involved."

"They already are."

"Damn!" He shook his head. "That was a foolish move."

"It wasn't 'a move.' I just wanted to find out where she came from."

"Sure."

"I did."

"Doesn't matter. What's done is done." His muscles seemed to stiffen even more at the mention of the authorities and the lines of his face deepened. For some reason he didn't want the police involved and for the first time Annie felt a niggle of fear. Who was this man? What did she know about him other than he'd seen her sister a few times, dropped Nola when he'd gotten bored with her, then landed smack-dab in the middle of Annie's living room with some ridiculous story about Nola having a baby—*this* baby! None of it made any sense.

"Fine," he relented. Muttering something under his breath about headstrong women who didn't know when to back off, he crossed the short distance to the grouping of chairs and couch surrounding the fireplace and set the basket on the floor near a small table. Throughout it all, Carol slept peacefully.

Annie breathed a long sigh of relief. Now, at last, she was getting somewhere and, fool that she was, she felt that she didn't have anything to fear from Liam—well, other than the possibility that he might take the baby from her.

She settled onto one of the arms of the couch while he warmed the backs of his legs by the fire. "So, now, why don't you start over and tell me why you came here—you said something about looking for Nola."

His jaw slid to one side and Annie was struck again at how sexy he was when he was quiet and thoughtful. "That's right. I need to find your sister. I just found out a couple of days ago that she'd been pregnant and had a baby—presumably mine, considering the timing. Jake found birth records. No father was listed, but I'm sure that the kid's mine."

Her heart plummeted. Obviously he'd done his homework and she knew in an instant that her short-lived chance at motherhood was over. "Who—who is Jake?"

"A friend."

"Oh."

"He's also a private detective."

Great. She'd hoped his farfetched story would prove wrong. "So you came here looking for Nola or information about her and just happened to stumble on the baby."

"Yep." He rubbed his jaw and avoided her gaze for a second, concentrating instead on the snow piling in the corners of the windowpanes. "There's another reason," he admitted.

"Which is?"

Leaning his hips against the side of the fireplace, he closed his eyes and pinched the bridge of his nose for a second as if he could ward off a headache. "Let's just say Nola and I have some unfinished business that doesn't involve the baby. I only found out about her"—he added as he cocked his head in the direction of the basket— "because Jake found out. I had no idea Nola was pregnant."

"She didn't tell you?" she asked, standing and walking to the basket to see that Carol was still sleeping.

"Nope."

"Why not?"

"Good question. One I can't wait to ask her, but let's just say that your sister and I aren't on the best of terms."

'Is that why you hired your friend?" What was Nola involved in? Normal, regular people didn't employ investigators—or even have their friends check up on old lovers. Or did they? Something was wrong here. Very, very wrong. He moved closer to her and she found herself so near this man she could barely breathe. The air in the little cottage seemed suddenly thick, the light through the windows way too dim.

"Nola lied. About a lot of things. Not just the baby."

"Such as?" Annie's heart was knocking, her breathing shallow as her gaze dropped from his to the contour of his lips, so bold and thin. Too much was happening, way too fast. She felt as if her life was spinning out of control.

"She set me up."

"For?"

He shrugged. "My guess is to get the blame off whoever she's protecting. She claimed she knew that before she left Belfry Construction, I was embezzling. One night, when she just happened to be driving by, she saw me go into the office. She concluded I'd gone to doctor the company books and was surprised by the security guard, so of course I killed him." He didn't elaborate, just stared at her with unforgiving eyes. "I didn't do it, Annie. I swear."

"But—but why would she lie?" Oh, God, what was he saying? Nola wouldn't . . . *couldn't* fabricate something so horrid. A man was dead. *Murdered* from the sound of it and Nola thought O'Shaughnessy was involved? "I—I think you'd better start from the beginning."

He did. In short, angry sentences he told her about his work, the projects he'd overseen, the discrepancy in the books, and Nola's suddenly recanted testimony that she'd known he was at the office that night. The problem was that he had been there, but when he'd left, Bill Arness was very much alive. Liam had thrown a wave to the old man as he'd stepped off the elevator and Bill had locked the door behind him. He finished there; he didn't tell her about being watched by the police, eventually hauled into jail, fingerprinted, and booked, only to have the charges dropped. Hell, what a nightmare.

Annie stared at him with disbelieving eyes. "On top of all this— which is damned incredible, let me tell you—you're sure that you're the baby's father and Nola's her mother?"

"I wouldn't put Nola in the same sentence with *mother.*" O'Shaughnessy glanced down at the basket as Carol uttered a soft little coo. The hard line of his jaw softened slightly and a fleeting tenderness changed his expression, but only for a moment. In that instant Annie noticed the wet streaks in his hair where snow had melted and the stubble of a beard that turned his jaw to gold in the dim fireglow. As he unbuttoned his coat and rubbed kinks from the back of his neck, Annie was nearly undone.

She had to think, to buy some time and sort this all out. Since he was bound and determined to take the baby with him, she had to entice him to stay. At least for a while. "Would you like something? I've got a Thermos of instant coffee I made on the fire this afternoon. It's not gourmet by any means, but I can guarantee that it's hot."

"That would be great." He shrugged out of his jacket and tossed it over the back of the couch as Annie hurried to the kitchen, twisted the lid of the Thermos, and quickly poured two cups. Her hands were trembling slightly, not out of fear exactly, but because she was a bundle of nerves around this man.

"So tell me again about last night," he suggested as she handed him a steaming mug. His gaze kept wandering back to the basket where the baby slept.

Quickly, she repeated her story of finding the baby, the note, seeing no one, not even footprints leading away from the porch, nothing. As she spoke, he sipped from his cup and listened, not interrupting, just hearing her out. ". . . So this morning, once I could get through, I started making calls. Everyone from the sheriff's department to social services and the hospitals around here, but no one seems to know anything about her."

"I do."

"You think. You really don't know that Carol—"

"Carol?"

"I named her, okay? The point is that there's no way to be sure she's your daughter."

The baby, as if sensing the tension building in the small room, mewled a small, worried whimper.

"Oh, great. See what you've done?" Disregarding the fact that he was a good foot taller than she and, if he decided, could stop her from doing anything, Annie hurried to the basket, gently withdrew baby and blankets, and held the tiny body close to hers. "It's okay," she whispered into the baby's soft curls and realized that the blond hair and blue eyes of this little sprite were incredibly like those of the irate man standing before her.

The baby cried again and Annie all but forgot about Liam O'Shaughnessy with his outrageous stories and damned sexy gaze. "She's wet and hungry and doesn't need to deal with all this . . . this stress."

"She doesn't know what's going on."

"I think that makes three of us!" Annie felt him silently watching her as she changed Carol's diaper, then warmed her bottle in a pan of water that had been heated in the coals of the fire.

"Here we go," she said softly as she settled into the creaky bentwood rocker and, as she fed the baby, nudged the floor with her toe. For the first time since O'Shaughnessy had pounded against her door, there was peace. The wind raged outside, the panes of the windows rattled eerily and a branch thumped in an irregular tempo against the worn shingles of the roof, but inside the cottage was warm, dry, and cozy. Even O'Shaughnessy seemed to relax a little as he rested one huge shoulder against the mantel and, while finishing his coffee, surveyed his surroundings with suspicious eyes.

"Okay," Annie finally said once Carol had burped and fallen asleep against her shoulder. "Instead of arguing with each other, why don't we figure out what we're going to do?"

"You think you can trust me?" he asked, trying to read her expression.

"I don't have much choice, do I?"

That much was true. He was here and definitely in her face. She couldn't budge him if she tried. Annie McFarlane was a little thing, but what she lost in stature she made up for in spirit. He cradled his cup in his hands and tried not to feel like a heel for barging in on her, for destroying her peace of mind, for intending to take away the baby that already appeared to mean so much to her.

"Nope, you don't."

"Great. Just . . . great."

Firelight played in her red-brown hair. High cheekbones curved beneath eyes that shifted from green to gold. Arched eyebrows moved expressively as she spoke with as sexy a mouth as he'd ever seen. A sprinkling of light freckles spanned the bridge of her nose and her hazel eyes were always alive, quick to flare in anger or joy.

What he knew of her wasn't much. She was divorced, had moved from somewhere on the East Coast, saw her sister infrequently, and did some kind of secretarial or bookkeeping work.

"Come on, O'Shaughnessy," she prodded as she carefully placed Carol into the basket. "Why would Nola lie to you and about you? Did she just want to get you into trouble?"

"A good question." He wasn't quite ready to tell her that he'd spent several days in a jail cell because of Nola and her lies. If he confided in her now he was certain she'd be frightened or, worse yet, call the police. There was no telling what she might do. Maybe she'd accuse him of trespassing or kidnapping if he insisted upon taking Carol—*Carol?*—with him. Good God, he was already giving the baby the name she'd put on the kid. She looked up to find him staring at her. "How'd you find me? Wait, let me guess. Your friend the detective, right?"

"Jake's pretty thorough."

"I don't like my privacy invaded."

"No one does," he admitted, "but then, I don't like being lied to about my kid." *Or lied about.* He finished his coffee and tossed the dregs into the fire. Sparks sputtered and the flames hissed in protest. "So why did Nola leave the baby here for you without so much as a word? It seems strange."

"I—I don't know."

She was lying. He could smell a lie a mile away.

"Sure you do."

"It's personal, okay?"

"So's my daughter."

She stopped cold, took in a long breath, and seemed to fight some inner battle as the baby began to snooze again. "I don't know what your relationship was with Nola," she said. "As close as my sister and I are, we don't share everything and she . . . she's been distant lately." Clearing her throat, she stepped over to the makeshift bassinet as if to reassure herself that the baby was still there. "I've been wrapped up in my own life, settling here, rebuilding, and I guess Nola and I kind of lost touch. The last time I called her apartment, a recording told me the number was disconnected. No one in the family—not even my brother or mother— has heard from her in a few weeks."

"Isn't that unusual?"

"For Nola?" A smile touched her lips and she shook her head, "Unfortunately, no."

God, this woman was gorgeous. Her eyes were round and bright, a gray-green that reminded him of a pine-scented forest hazy with soft morning fog.

"I've got to find her."

"Why? What good would it do?"

He considered that for a second. "First, I want sole custody of my child." He saw the disappointment in her features and felt suddenly like the scum of the earth. "And then there's the little matter of my innocence in Bill Arness's death. I want to talk to good old Nola and find out why she wanted to set me up. I've been cleared, sort of, though I think I'm still a—what do they call it when they don't want to say *suspect?*—a 'person of interest' in the case. I want to talk to Nola, find out why she lied about the break-in at Belfry and—" He jerked his head toward the basket.

"—The baby," she finished for him. "You know, O'Shaughnessy, you make it sound as if my sister's involved in some major criminal conspiracy."

As the fire hissed in the grate and the wind whistled through the trees outside, Liam leveled his disturbing blue eyes at her. "Your sister's in big trouble."

"With you."

"For starters. I think the D.A. might be interested as well."

"Well, if you think I can help you find her, you'd better think again. She's a free spirit who—"

"Is running for her life, if she's smart."

The baby let out a wail certain to wake up the dead in the next three counties.

"Oh, God." Annie jumped up as if she were catapulted by an invisible device, then carefully extracted the little girl from beneath her covers as if she were born to be this child's mother.

Liam couldn't hear what Annie was saying as she whispered softly and rocked gently, holding the child close to her breast. As if a fourteenth-century sorceress had cast a quieting spell, the infant instantly calmed.

It was damned amazing. Could he work this magic with the kid? Hell, no! Could Nola? At the thought of that particularly selfish woman, he frowned and plowed stiff, frustrated fingers through his hair. What was he going to do?

Carol—if that's what the kid's name was—sighed audibly and a smile tugged at the corners of Annie's mouth. For an instant Liam wondered what it would be like to kiss her, to press his mouth against those soft, pliant lips and . . . He gave himself a quick mental shake. What was he doing thinking of embracing her, believing her, wanting to trust her, for crying out loud?

He cleared his throat. "Look, Annie, the bottom line is this: You have my daughter. I want her. And I'll do anything—do you hear me?—*anything* to gain custody of her."

"Then you'll have to fight me," Annie said, her chin lifting defiantly and her back stiffening. "You don't have any proof that Carol is yours."

She tried to look so damned brave as she held the child and pinned him with those furious hazel eyes. For a second his heart turned over for her. She obviously cared about the baby very much.

No matter what her true motives were, she had strong ties to the child, probably a helluva lot stronger than Nola's. Nonetheless he was the kid's father and as such he had rights, rights he intended to invoke.

"She's mine, all right."

"Then you won't be averse to a paternity test."

"For the love of Mike. It's not like you could take a maternity test, right?"

"I've already talked to the powers that be. I'm not claiming to be the baby's mother."

"Fine. No problem. I'll take any damned test." He glanced out the window and scowled at the snow piling over his footsteps. Though he'd been inside less than an hour, the marks made by his boots were nearly obscured. In all truth, there was a problem, a big one. His four-wheel drive rig had barely made it to the end of the driveway because of the packed snow and ice on the roads. Without chains, his wheels had slipped and spun, nearly landing him in the ditch. Though sanding crews had been working around the clock, the accumulation of snow and freezing temperatures had reduced the snow pack to ice. As it was, driving any distance was out of the question, especially with an infant and no safety car seat.

Annie cast him irritated looks as she attended to the baby. Finally, when the child's eyelids had drooped again, Annie carefully placed Carol into the basket. She tucked a blanket gently around the baby and smiled when the infant moved her tiny lips in a sucking motion. "She's so adorable," Annie said. "If she is your child, Mr. O'Shaughnessy, she's darned near perfect, and you're one very lucky man."

He couldn't agree more as he stared at the tiny bit of flesh that sighed softly in a swaddle of pink blankets. An unaccustomed lump filled his throat. He'd never expected any kind of emotional attachment to the baby, not like this. Sure, he'd felt obligated to take care of the kid—duty-bound to see that his offspring was financially and emotionally supported. He planned on hiring a full-time nanny to start with and then, as the kid grew, employ the best tutors, coaches, and teachers that money could buy. If he had to, he had supposed, he could even get married and provide a mother of sorts.

He glanced at Annie and felt a jab of guilt, though he didn't know why. "However," Annie said, planting her hands on her hips, "if the blood tests prove that you're not her father, O'Shaughnessy, then you'll have a helluva lot of explaining to do. Not only to me, but to the police."

CHAPTER 4

The woman had him. No doubt about it. The last thing he wanted to do was get the police involved. She was smart, this sister of Nola's, and the firelight dancing in her angry green eyes made him think dangerous thoughts—of champagne, candlelight, and making love for hours.

"I've already told you I don't want to call the authorities. Not until I understand what's going on."

She lifted a finely sculpted eyebrow and desire, often his worst enemy, started swimming in his bloodstream. "And I've already told you," she said, poking a finger at his broad expanse of chest, "that I've talked to the police about the baby. I've got nothing to hide, so why don't you level with me?"

"I am."

Her hair shone red-gold in the dying embers of the fire. "I don't think so." Resolutely she crossed her arms under her chest, inadvertently lifting her breasts and causing Liam's mind to wander ever further into that dangerous and erotic territory. He couldn't seem to think straight when she was around; his purpose, once so honed and defined, became cloudy.

"I want you to help me find Nola."

"Why?"

"I need to talk to her and find out why she lied about the baby, why she lied about the break-in, why the hell she wanted to set me up for murder."

"If she did."

"She did, all right." Liam had no doubts. None whatsoever when it came to Nola Prescott. Annie was another story altogether. Her forehead wrinkled in concentration, but she didn't budge and he figured he should back off, at least a little. "Think about it and I'll do something about the heat in here, okay?" He didn't bother waiting for an answer, but threw on his jacket and walked outside. Firewood was already cut and stacked on the back porch, so he hauled in several baskets of fir and oak, restocking the dwindling pile on the hearth and adding more chunks to the fire.

Annie busied herself with the baby, feeding her, changing her, burping her, rocking her, cooing to her, and looking for all the world as if she were born to be a mother. *Idiot,* he told himself. *Don't be fooled. She and that sister of hers share the same blood.*

The phone jangled and they both jumped. Annie froze and just stared at the instrument, but Liam was quick and snagged the receiver before the person on the other end had a chance to hang up. "Hello?"

"Hello? Who is this?" a male voice demanded. Whoever the hell he was, he didn't sound happy. "I'm calling Annie McFarlane."

"Just a sec—"

Liam handed the phone to Annie and, without a word, took the baby. It was incredible how natural it felt to hold the kid, even though his hands were larger than the baby's head. Little Carol gurgled, but didn't protest as Annie, eyes riveted on him, placed the receiver to her ear.

"Hello?"

"Annie?" It was Joel, her brother. "For crying out loud, who was that?"

"A—a friend." Why she thought she had to protect O'Shaughnessy she didn't know, but somehow she thought it best not to tell her brother about his wild story and her plight.

"A *friend?* I don't know whether to be relieved or worried. I'm glad you're not pining over David, but from what the news here says, you're in the middle of one helluva storm. I've been trying to get through for hours."

"Me, too," she said and since she didn't offer any further explanation about O'Shaughnessy, Joel didn't pry.

"So you're okay?"

"All things considered." She watched Liam with the baby and her heart did a silly little leap. He was so big and the infant was so tiny, yet she sensed that this man who exuded such raw animal passion and fury would protect this child with his very life.

"Well, Merry Christmas."

"You, too."

"We all miss you."

"I know, but there's no way I can get to the airport." *Nor can I leave Carol.* At that particular thought her heart twisted painfully. How could she ever give up the baby?

"Yeah, I know." Joel sounded disappointed and they talked for a little while before she had the nerve to bring up their sister.

"You know, I haven't seen her since—geez, I can't remember when," Joel admitted, though there was some hesitation in his voice, a nervous edge that Annie hadn't heard earlier. "But then I didn't really expect to hear from her over the holidays. You know how it is with Nola—hit or miss. This year must be a miss."

"You don't have any idea where she is?"

"Nope. She did call, oh, maybe a month or so ago and said she was leaving Seattle, but that was it. No plans. No forwarding address. No damned idea where she'd end up. I can't imagine it, myself, but then I've got a wife and kids to consider." Annie could almost see her brother shaking his head at the folly that was his younger sister.

She noticed O'Shaughnessy studying her and turned her back, wrapping the telephone extension around herself and avoiding his probing gaze as she asked, "Do you know if she's been in any kind of trouble?"

"Nola? Always."

"No, no. I mean serious trouble."

There was a pause. "Such as?"

"Is it possible that she was pregnant?"

Another moment's hesitation and Annie knew the truth. "Joel?" Annie's heart was thundering, her head pounding, her hands suddenly ice-cold.

Her brother cleared his throat, then swore roundly. "I'm sorry, Annie, but Nola didn't want you to know." Annie closed her eyes and sagged against the kitchen counter. So it was true. At least part of O'Shaughnessy's story held up. Joel sighed. "Nola knew how badly you wanted a baby and with your miscarriages and the divorce and all, she thought—and for once I agreed with her—that you should be kept in the dark."

So the baby really was Nola's. "Did she say who the father was?" Annie's voice was barely a whisper.

"Nah. Some guy who was in and out of her life in a heartbeat. A real louse. She decided that the best thing to do was to . . . well, to terminate."

"No!"

"Annie, there's nothing you can do now. That was months ago. I tried to talk her into giving the kid up for adoption but she claimed she couldn't live with herself if she knew she had a baby out there somewhere with someone she didn't know raising it . . . I figured it was her decision."

"When was this?"

"Seven—maybe eight months ago. Yeah, in the spring. End of March or early April, I think. You'd just confirmed that David was about to be a father—the timing was all wrong."

"When . . . when was she due?"

"What does it matter?"

"When, damn it!"

"About now, I guess. No . . . wait. A few weeks ago, I suppose. I never asked her what happened. In fact, we never really talked again. I just assumed she did what she had to do and got on with her life."

"Did she say who the father was?"

"No."

"Just the louse."

She rotated out of the phone line coils in time to notice Liam wince.

"Right."

"Did she date anyone else?

"I can't remember. There was the guy with the Irish name—the father, I think."

"O'Shaughnessy?"

"Right. That's the bastard."

"No one else?"

"What does it matter, for crying out loud."

"It matters, okay?"

"Well, let me think." He sighed audibly. "I can't think of anyone. Polly—" His voice trailed as he asked his wife the same question and there was some discussion. "Annie? Polly thinks there was another guy. Somebody named Tyson or Taylor or what?" Again his voice faded and Annie's heart nearly stopped beating. Liam was studying her so hard she could hardly breathe. "Yeah, that's right. Polly seems to think the guy's name was Talbott."

"Peter Talbott?" Annie said and Liam's expression became absolutely murderous.

"Yeah, that's the guy."

"Good, Joel. Thanks."

"Are you okay?"

"Right as rain," she lied. The room began to swim. Annie's throat was dry. She brought up his kids and, for the moment, Joel's interest was diverted. Liam, however, seemed about to explode. His hands balled into angry fists and his eyes were dark as the night.

"Look, I'll see you after the first of the year," Joel finally said before hanging up. "And if I hear from Nola, I'll tell her you need to speak to her."

"Do that." She unwound the cord from her body and let the receiver fall back into its cradle. "So," she said in a voice she didn't recognize as her own. "It looks like part of your story is true. Joel knew about the pregnancy."

Liam's jaw tightened perceptively. "All of my 'story,' as you call it, is true, Annie. You've just got to face it." Carol was sleeping in his arms and Annie's heartstrings pulled as she saw the baby move her lips. Golden eyelashes fluttered for a second, then drooped over crystal-blue eyes.

"Here—let me put her down."

She took Carol from his arms and in the transfer of the baby, they touched, fingers twining for a second, arms brushing. As she placed the baby in her basket, Liam rubbed the back of his neck nervously, then shoved the curtains aside to view the relentlessly falling snow. He had to get out of the cozy little cabin with its built-in family. Not only was there a baby who had already wormed her way into his heart, but the woman who wanted to be the kid's mother had managed to get under his skin as well. It was too close—too comfortable—too damned domestic.

"So Talbott's the guy."

"Polly, my sister-in-law, seems to think Nola was involved with him."

"Figures," he said, conjuring up Talbott's face. Short and wiry, with blond hair, tinted contacts, and freckles, Pete was as ambitious as he was dogged. But Joel hadn't thought him a crook. Well, live and learn. "When's this gonna end?" he growled, staring through the frozen windowpanes. Anxious for a breath of fresh air and a chance to clear his head, he snatched up his jacket and rammed his arms through the sleeves. Snagging the wood basket from the hearth, he was out the door in an instant. Outside, the wind keened through the trees. Snow and ice pelted his face and bare head. He shoved gloves over his hands and wished he'd never given up smoking. A cigarette would help. Confronting Nola and Talbott would be even better.

What the hell was he going to do about the situation here? When he'd first stepped inside the cabin he'd planned to interrogate Annie, find out everything he could about Nola, grab his kid, and leave. Then he'd come face-to-face with the woman and damn it, she'd found a way to blast past his defenses, to put him off guard, to make him challenge everything he'd so fervently believed.

"Hell, what a mess!" He piled wood in the basket and headed back inside. As he entered, a rush of icy wind ruffled the curtains and caused flames to roar in the grate. Annie didn't say a word and he dumped the wood, then stormed outside, needing the exercise, having to find a way to expend some restless energy, wanting to grab hold of his equilibrium again.

Annie heated water for coffee and more formula and tried not to watch the door, waiting for O'Shaughnessy. Somehow she had to get away from him, to think clearly. From the moment he'd barged into her life, she'd been out of control, not knowing what to do. She was certain that as soon as the storm lifted, he'd be gone. With Carol. Her heart broke at the thought, for though she told herself she was being foolish and only asking for trouble, she'd begun to think of the baby as hers. Hadn't the card said as much? *For you, Annie.* What a joke. Nobody gave a baby away. Not even Nola.

But the baby was here.

If Carol were truly Nola's child and if Nola had left the baby on Annie's doorstep—presumably to raise, at least for a while—then didn't she have some rights? At least as an aunt, and at most as the guardian of choice. *But what if the baby is really O'Shaughnessy's? What then? What kind of rights do you think you'll have if he's truly Carol's biological father? Face it, Annie, right now Liam O'Shaughnessy holds all the cards.*

He shouldered open the door, shut it behind him, and dropped a final basket of wood near the hearth. "That should get you through 'til morning."

"*Me* through? What about you?"

"I won't be staying."

Dear God, he hadn't changed his mind. He was leaving and taking Carol with him. Panic gripped her heart. "You don't have to go—"

"Don't worry, Annie," he said, his lips barely moving, his eyes dark with the night. "I won't rip her away from you. At least not tonight."

"Noble of you."

He snorted. "Nobility? Nah. I'm just looking out for my best interests. It's sub-zero outside and I don't think I could move the Jeep even if I tried. The kid's better off here, where it's warm."

So he did have a heart, after all. She should have been surprised, but wasn't. His gaze held hers for a breath-stopping second and she read sweet seduction in his eyes. Her blood thundered and she looked away, but not before the message was passed and she knew that he, too, wondered what it would feel like to kiss. Aside from the baby, they were alone. Cut off from civilization by the storm. One man. One woman. She swallowed hard.

"Carol will be safe here."

"I know." He dusted his gloved hands and reached for the door.

"But I'll be right outside, so don't get any funny ideas about taking off."

"Outside?" She glanced at the windows and the icy glaze that covered the glass. "But it's freezing . . ."

"I don't think it would be a good idea if I slept in here, do you?"

The thought was horrifyingly seductive. "No—no—I, um . . . no, that wouldn't work," she admitted in a voice she didn't recognize. Sleeping in the same little house as O'Shaughnessy. Oh, God. She swallowed even though her mouth was dry as sandpaper.

"Yeah. I didn't think so." He crouched at the fire, tossing in another couple of logs before prodding them with the poker that had been leaning against the warm stones. Annie tried not to stare at the way his faded jeans stretched across his buttocks, or at the dip in his waistband where the denim pulled away from the hem of his jacket. However, her gaze seemed to have a mind of its own when it came to this man. Annie licked her lips and dragged her gaze back to the baby.

He dusted his hands together. "That should do it for a while. If it dies down—"

"I can handle it," she snapped.

His smile was downright sexy. "I know. Otherwise I wouldn't leave. I'll see ya in the morning." For the first time she noticed the lines around his eyes. "Think about everything I've said."

"I will." She didn't know whether she was relieved or disappointed. Relieved—she should definitely be relieved.

His smile wasn't filled with warmth. "I won't be far."

"But the storm—"

"Don't worry about me, Annie," he said, one side of his mouth lifting cynically. "I learned a long time ago how to take care of myself." He was out the door and Annie watched at the window where, despite the freezing temperatures and falling snow, he settled into his Jeep.

"Just go away. Take your incredible story and wild accusations and leave us alone," she muttered under her breath. But she couldn't help worrying about him just a little.

CHAPTER 5

"Come on, come on." Liam pressed the numbers from memory on his cellular phone, but the damned thing wouldn't work. He was too close to the hills or the signals were clogged because of the storm and the holidays. Whatever the reason, he couldn't reach Jake. "Hell." He clapped the cell shut and stared through the windshield as he tugged the edge of his sleeping bag more tightly around him. Nothing in this iced-over county was working.

And he needed to talk to Cranston, to report that he'd had a run-in with Nola's sister, found his kid, and suspected Peter Talbott of being the culprit in Bill Arness's murder. But he didn't want to use Annie's phone—not while she was in earshot.

Nola was involved. Up to her eyeballs. There was a reason she'd fingered him for a crime he didn't commit and it wasn't just vengeance because he'd broken up with her and unwittingly left her pregnant. Nope, it had something to do with Pete Talbott.

Liam glowered through the windshield. Ice and snow had begun to build over the glass, but he was able to see the windows of Annie's cabin, patches of golden light in an otherwise bleak and frigid night. Every once in a while a shadow would pass by the panes and he'd squint to catch another glimpse of Annie. His jaw clenched as he realized he was hoping to see her—waiting for her image to sweep past the window. Nola's sister. No good. Trouble. A woman to stay away from at all costs.

But he couldn't. Not just yet. His thoughts wandered into perilous territory again and he wondered what it would feel like to kiss her, to press his lips to hers, to run the tip of his tongue along that precocious seam of her lips, to reach beneath her sweater, let his fingers scale her ribs to touch her breasts and . . .

"Fool!" His jaw clenched and he pushed all kind thoughts of Annie out of his mind. So what if she was a package of warm innocence wrapped in a ribbon of fiery temper? Who cared if the stubborn angle of her chin emphasized the spark of determination of her green eyes? What did it matter that the sweep of her eyelashes brushed the tops of cheeks that dimpled in a sensual smile?

She was Nola's sister. Big-time trouble. The last woman in the world he should think about making love to. Besides, he had other things with which to occupy his mind, the first being to clear his name completely. Then he'd claim his daughter and then . . . then he'd deal with Annie. Just at the thought of her his blood heated and his cock started to swell.

"Down, boy," he muttered to the image glaring back at him in the rearview mirror. "That's one female who's off limits—way off. Remember it." But the eyes reflecting back at him didn't seem to be the least little bit convinced.

Jake Cranston wasn't a man who gave up easily, but this time he was more than ready to throw in the towel. Nola Prescott seemed to have vanished off the face of the earth. How could a woman disappear so quickly?

He'd checked with her friends and relatives, called people he knew who owed him favors on the police force and at the DMV, even spoken to the Social Security Administration, with no luck.

"Think, Cranston, think," he muttered under his breath as he walked from one end of his twelve-by-fifteen office to the other. It was a small cubicle crammed with files, a desk, and a computer that, tonight, was of no help whatsoever.

Not that it mattered. He'd done his part. Now it was up to

Liam. He didn't doubt that O'Shaughnessy would handle the Nola Prescott situation his own way. But still he was puzzled. Where the hell was she?

It wasn't often anyone eluded him, but then he hadn't given up yet. Not really. Deep in his gut he felt that Liam still needed his help and he owed the man his life. Years ago O'Shaughnessy had been the first man on the scene of the hit and run. It had been his grit and brute strength that had helped pull Jake from the mangled truck seconds before it exploded in a conflagration that had lit up the cold winter night and singed the branches of the surrounding trees. The driver of the other car had never been caught, but Jake had discovered a friend for life in O'Shaughnessy.

Now the tables were turned. It was time for Jake to pay back a very big favor and he wouldn't quit until he did. Getting Liam out of jail had been a start. The next step was hunting down Nola Prescott, no matter that she'd gone to ground. He grunted and reached into the bottom drawer for his shot glass and a half-full bottle of rye whiskey. His personal favorite. He poured himself three fingers, tossed them back, and felt the familiar warmth blaze its way down his throat to his stomach. Wiping the back of his hand across his mouth, he felt a little better. Finding Ms. Prescott was only a matter of time.

Liam awoke with a start, his heart pounding crazily, the dream as vivid as if he were still locked away. The sound of metal against metal, keys clicking in locks, chains rattling—all receded with the dawn. He was in the Jeep in the middle of a damned forest. Would it never end? Cramped and cold, he rotated his neck until he felt a release and heard a series of pops. Now all he needed was coffee and lots of it.

Sunlight penetrated the stands of birch and fir, splintering in brilliant shards that pierced his eyes and did nothing to warm the frozen landscape. He shoved open the door and, boots crunching through the drifting snow, made his way to the cabin to see the kid again. And Annie. That woman was playing with his mind, whether she knew it or not.

He lifted a fist to pound on the door when it flew open and she stood on the other side of the threshold. Before he could enter she stepped onto the porch, the dog at her heels, then closed the door softly behind her. "Carol's asleep."

"So?"

"I don't want her disturbed." Her gloved hands were planted firmly on her hips and she stood in the doorway as if she intended to stop him from entering. Her determination was almost funny— tiny thing that she was.

"She's my daughter."

Dark eyebrows elevated as the mutt romped through the drifts, clumps of snow clinging to his hair. "Your fatherhood has yet to be determined."

"You still want a paternity test?"

"For starters."

"Not a problem."

Her eyes, so fierce, were suddenly a darker shade of hazel, more green than gold and not quite so certain. "Good," she said with more bravado than he expected. "I'll arrange it. When the roads are clear."

"Fair enough." She was bluffing. And scared. Of what? Him? He didn't think so.

"But for right now, we're not going to wake her up—she had a bad night." Annie hitched her chin toward the barn. "I've got to feed the horses. You can help."

"Can I?" He couldn't help baiting her.

"Yep." She didn't waste a second, but stepped off the porch and started breaking a trail in the knee-deep powder. The dog galloped in senseless circles before bounding up the ramp that led to a wide door on rollers. With all of her strength, Annie pushed. The thing didn't budge. Liam placed his hands above hers on the edge of the door. His body covered her as he put his weight into moving a door that was frozen closed.

"Great," she muttered and was close enough that the coffee on her breath tickled his nose, the back of her jacket rubbed up against the buttons of his, and her rump pressed against his upper thighs. Through the denim of his jeans he felt her heat and his damned cock responded, stiffening beneath his fly.

"It'll give." He ignored the scent of her perfume and the way his body was reacting to the proximity of hers. Again he threw his weight into the task and the ice gave way, rusty rollers screaming in protest, ice shattering as the door sped on its track. Annie tumbled forward and Liam's arms surrounded her, catching her before she slipped on the icy ramp.

"Whoa, darlin'," he said, surprised that an endearment had leapt so naturally to his lips.

"I'm . . . I'm okay." She twisted in his arms and her face was only inches from his, so near that he could see the sunlight playing in her eyes. His gut tightened and his mind spun to a future that would never exist, a time when she would be lying naked in his arms, bedsheets twined through her legs, moonlight playing upon her bare breasts. At the thought, his mouth was suddenly dry as a desert wind and he cleared his throat. Slowly, making sure she had her footing, he released her. Her gaze shifted to his lips for a second before she stepped into the musty interior of the barn and he followed with an erection that pressed hard against his jeans. Silently he cursed himself. Hadn't he spent the night convincing himself that Annie McFarlane was off-limits?

A soft nicker floated on air that smelled of dry hay, leather, and horse dung.

"Think I forgot you?" she said as she popped off the lid of a barrel of oats and, using an old coffee can, scooped up the grain that she poured into the mangers of three horses. Liquid eyes appraised him and large nostrils blew into the air as the animals buried their muzzles into the feed.

Annie reached into the pocket of her coat and, walking to a stack of hay bales piled into the corner, pulled out a small jackknife, opened the blade, and sliced the twine holding the first bale together. She glanced over to Liam. "You can make yourself useful by tossing down a few more of these from the hayloft." She went to work on the second bale and he climbed up a metal ladder. Within minutes he'd dropped twelve bales and stacked them next to the dwindling pile near the stalls. Annie forked hay into the mangers and when he attempted to take the pitchfork from her hands to do the job, he was rewarded with a look that would melt steel. "I can handle this," she said.

"I just thought that—"

"That I was a female and since you were here you'd take over and give me a break. Thanks but no thanks. If you want to help out, grab a bucket and get them fresh water." She bit the edge of her lip. "You'll have to go back to the house, though, and use the faucets in the kitchen. I drained all the outside pipes just before the storm hit. Just be careful and don't wake—"

"—The baby. Yeah, I know." He grabbed a pail from a nail on the wall and trudged back to the cabin. He'd never met so prickly a woman and yet she was trusting him to be alone with his child.

He checked the makeshift bassinet as the bucket was filling and couldn't help but smile. The baby was indeed cutting a few z's. Barely moving, a blanket tucked all the way to her chin, Carol was lying there with such pure innocence that the little lump of flesh grabbed hold of Liam. How could something so perfect, so beautiful, have been conceived by an act of cold passion and grown in a womb devoid of love?

Despite Annie's warning, he pulled one of his gloves off with his teeth and touched a golden curl with the tip of his finger. The baby sighed quietly and in that barest meeting of callouses and perfect, baby-soft skin he felt a connection that wrapped around the darkest reaches of his heart and tied in a knot that could never be undone. Somehow, some way, no matter what, he would take care of this child.

With more effort than he would have imagined, he turned his thoughts to filling the pail over and over again until each animal had water enough for the day and the trail in the snow between the barn and the cabin was packed solidly.

Annie hung up the pitchfork and rubbed each velvet-soft nose as the animals ate, mashing their teeth together loudly and snorting.

"These belong to you?" he asked as she threw a winter blanket over the bay's back.

"No. I just care for them. They come with the house and grounds. This guy is Hoss, then there's Little Joe," she said, pointing to a dapple gray, "and Adam, there, the sorrel gelding." At the mention of his name, Adam's ears flattened. "All named after characters on 'Bonanza.'"

"I got the connection."

"Yeah, great guys, but they could use a little exercise." With a glance to the window, she frowned. "I usually walk them later in the day, but they'll have to wait for anything more substantial, at least for a few more days." Her eyes found Liam's. "Like we all have to."

"I might be able to get the Jeep out today."

She swallowed hard. "And what then?"

"I find Nola."

"Just like that?" she asked skeptically as she snapped her fingers.

"It might take a little time, but I'll catch up with her."

"You make it sound like she's running from you."

"She is. She just doesn't realize how futile it is." He said it with a determination that made her shudder, as if he were stating an obvious fact.

Nervously, Annie rubbed the blaze running down Little Joe's nose, then wiped her hands on the front of her jeans before leaving the stall. Liam shouldn't be here. He was too male, too intense, too close. Emotions, conflicting and worrisome, battled within her. She was attracted to him, there was no doubt about it, but he was here for one reason and one reason only—his child. "I—I'd better check on the baby."

"She's fine."

"I'll see for myself—"

He grabbed her arm so quickly she gasped. Even through the denim of her jacket and sweater beneath, she felt the iron grip of his fingers, the hard strength of the man. "Be careful," he said through lips that barely moved.

"Of what? You?"

"Of getting too attached to the baby."

"Too late." Tossing her hair over her shoulders, she glared up at him. "I'm already attached to that little girl and you may as well know that you can't bully her away from me."

"She's not yours—"

"Or yours." She tried to pull away, to keep her distance from him, but he drew her closer to his body, close enough that she noticed the pores of his skin and the red-blond glimmer that gilded a jaw set in silent fury. "She's mine, all right."

Oh, God, was that her heart beating so furiously? His gaze dropped to her throat and she sensed her pulse quicken. She licked her lips, tried to back away and was suddenly lost as his lips found hers. She was trapped, her breath caught somewhere in her lungs, her knees turning weak as his arms surrounded her. She tried to protest, to tell him to go to hell, to back away and slap him hard across the jaw but instead she opened her mouth willingly, invitingly.

It had been so long, so damned long since a man had held her, kissed her, caused her blood to race.

But this is wrong. And dangerous. This is O'Shaughnessy. He only wants you so he can get close to the baby.

She wouldn't listen to that awful, nagging voice. No, right now, she just wanted to be held. While the world was snowbound and frigid, she was warm here in Liam's arms. She felt his tongue touch the tip of hers. A hot shiver of desire, wanton and needy, skittered down her spine. With a moan she sagged against him and his kiss deepened, his tongue searching and exploring, causing the world to spin.

He's only doing this to get close to Carol, to find Nola, to further his own interests. Wake up, Annie. He doesn't care one iota about you. He's using you.

"No!" She dragged her head from his, ignoring the desire still singing through her veins. Breathing unevenly, she stepped back. "I mean, I can't . . . I won't . . . Oh, for the love of . . . just . . . just leave, would you?"

"That's what you want?" His lips tugged into a cynical, amused smile that sent her temper into the stratosphere.

"Yes. Just go!"

His teeth flashed white against his skin in a cynical I-don't-believe-you-for-a-second grin and it was all she could do not to slap him. "As I said, I—I'd better check on Carol." She tore out of the barn, gulped big lungfuls of crisp winter air, and hurried along the broken path to the cabin. Riley, barking madly at a startled winter bird, sprinted ahead of her.

She kicked off her boots on the porch and threw open the door. "How could you?" she muttered, berating herself as she saw her reflection in the iced-over windows. "I thought you were a smart woman." She pulled off her gloves, threw them on the back of her couch, ripped off her jacket, and closed her eyes. "Fool. Damned silly fool of a female!" What was she thinking, kissing O'Shaughnessy? No, *wanting* to kiss him, to touch him, to feel his body lying on top of hers . . . "Oh, for the love of Mike. Stop it!"

Thunk! The door banged open. A frozen blast of wind swept into the room, causing the fire to spark and the curtains to flutter as Liam stepped inside, his boots dripping on an old braided rug.

"You don't take a hint very well, do you?" she accused as he latched the door and they were again alone, away from the world, one man, one woman, and a sleeping infant. Her heart skipped a beat.

"You weren't serious." His eyes, blue as an August sky, held hers.

She cleared her throat and prayed her voice would remain steady. "About you leaving?" Why did she feel he could read her mind? "Believe me, O'Shaughnessy, I've never been more serious in my life." She turned toward a mirror mounted near the kitchen door and grabbed a rubber band from her pocket with one hand while scraping her hair away from her face with the other. With a flip of her wrist she snapped the ponytail into place. "I think it would be best for all of us if you just opened the door and took off."

"Liar." He was across the room in an instant, standing behind her, strong arms wrapping firmly around her torso, splayed fingers against the underside of her breasts. "You don't want me to leave."

"You arrogant, self-serving, son of a . . . oooh."

His lips brushed against her nape. Warm and seductive, his breath wafted across her skin.

A nest of butterflies, long dormant, exploded in her stomach as his tongue traced the curve of her neck. "Don't lie to me, Annie. You want me as much as I want you."

Oh, Lord, he knew. Her body trembled at his touch and she hated herself for the weakness. Slowly he turned her into his embrace and as she stared into his eyes, he kissed her, long and hard, and with a desperation that cried out for more. She shouldn't do this, shouldn't let her body rule her mind, and yet as he sighed into her open mouth, she wrapped her arms around his neck, closed her eyes, and didn't argue as his hands found the hem of her sweater and his fingers skimmed the skin of her abdomen with feather-light touches that caused her breasts to ache and her mind to play with images of making love all night long.

"I—I can't," she said as his fingers traced her nipple through the silky fabric of her bra.

"Can't what?" he said, kissing the side of her neck and bending farther down as his hands caressed her breast.

I can't love you! her mind screamed, but she swallowed back the ridiculous words. "Do—do this—oooh."

He unhooked her bra deftly and scooped both her breasts into his palms.

"Liam, please—" she whispered, but her protest went unheeded and she closed her eyes against the wave of desire that rippled through her. Without hurry he kissed the flat of her abdomen, then moved ever upward, his tongue and lips and teeth touching her so intimately she thought she might die. "Liam," she whispered as he found her breast and began to suckle. Wet and warm, his mouth seemed to envelop her and all thoughts of stopping him vanished. Together they fell upon the worn couch and he pulled her sweater over her head before tossing away her bra and kissing her again.

"Sweet, sweet Annie. God, you're beautiful." He stared at her breasts for a heartbeat, touched them lightly, watched in fascination as her nipples tightened, then resumed his ministrations.

Desire pulsed through her blood, throbbing deep in her center, creating a core of desire that played games with her mind. The fire crackled and cast the room in a golden glow that vied with the sunlight slanting through icy windows as Liam kissed her.

Annie trembled and held him close, her fingers running through the thick, coarse strands of his hair, her body aching for more of his touch. *This is wrong, Annie. So wrong. Remember, he's only using you.* That horrid voice—her reason—nagged at her. *And there's pregnancy—you can't risk it. Or disease. What do you know of this man? What, really?*

His fingers dipped below the waistband of her jeans and a series of pops followed as the snaps of her fly gave way easily. The lace of her panties was a thin barrier to the heat of his hands and as he traced the V of her legs with his fingers, she began to move to a gentle rhythm that controlled her body and mind.

He nudged her legs apart with deft fingers and pushed her panties to one side. Gently he touched her, slowly prodding and retracting, just grazing that sensitive bud that palpitated with need.

She cried out as he plunged ever deeper and her thoughts spun wildly in a whirlpool of desperate need that swirled ever faster . . .

She clung to him as he kissed her. Sweat broke out across her forehead and along her spine. She wanted more—all of him, to feel his body joined to hers. But she could only take what he was giving, that special touch that made her feel she was drowning in a pool of pleasure, gasping and panting and unable to breathe, yet still fighting him, knowing in her heart that this was wrong.

"Come on, Annie," he whispered against her ear. "Let go."

"I—I can't. Oh . . . oh, God."

"Sure you can, baby. Trust me."

With all of her heart she wanted to. Tears sprang to her eyes and yet desire reigned as he traced the tracks of her tears with his tongue while never letting up, his fingers continuing to work their own special magic.

He kissed her breast again and something deep inside of her gave way.

"That's it, girl."

Hotter and hotter, faster and faster she moved. A small moan escaped her. His lips found hers. His tongue delved deep into her mouth. He touched that perfect spot and she convulsed. With a soul-jarring jolt, her resistance shattered. Her body jerked. Once. Twice. Three times.

She heard a throaty, desperate cry and realized it was her own voice.

"For the love of God," she said, staring into his enigmatic eyes. Never had she felt so sated. Never had she been so pleasured. And never had she been so embarrassed.

Who was this man? Why had she let him touch her, kiss her, feel her most intimate regions?

As swift as a bolt of lightning, the reality of what she'd done shot through her. "Oh, no." She pushed him away, scrambled into her clothes, and with her face blushing a hot denial of her own wanton deeds, she climbed to her feet. "Look, this was wrong. All wrong."

"You don't believe that."

"Yes, yes, I do. And I just can't have sex with you. What about . . . about condoms and—"

"I've been tested," he said, climbing to his feet.

"But, I could get pregnant and . . . listen, the reason Nola left the baby with me is that I can't have children, can't seem to carry them to term and—"

He folded her into his arms and she let the tears run from her eyes. All this emotion. What could she do about him? For God's sake, she was falling in love with him. She let out a broken sob and the strength of his arms seeped into her bones. Sniffing, she pushed him away. "You . . . you have to leave."

"Annie, don't—"

"I mean it." She yanked the band from her hair and swiped at her eyes. Chin thrust forward defiantly, she added, "I don't know what I was thinking."

"You weren't." He was standing near the window, sunlight casting his body in relief. Good Lord, he was big. And strong. And powerful. *And dangerous. Don't forget dangerous, Annie. He just wants Carol and information about Nola.*

"Listen, O'Shaughnessy, you've got to go, to leave me alone—"

"So we're back to calling me O'Shaughnessy."

"Yes. No. Oh, I don't know." She shook her head, trying to clear the passion-induced cobwebs from her mind. "I just know that you've got to leave. Go do what it is you have to do. Find Nola, figure out this . . . break-in at the company—burglary, embezzlement, or what- ever it is and find out about Carol, if she really is yours."

"Is there any doubt?"

Annie glanced at the infant. Golden hair, crystal-blue eyes, arched eyebrows, cheeks as rosy as her father's. She swallowed hard. No, Liam was right. There wasn't a whole lot of question as to the baby's paternity.

"I'll take her in for a blood test as soon as I can get to the hospital. With DNA and all, it should be pretty easy to figure out."

"A snap." He reached for his jacket and shoved one arm down a sleeve. "I'll be back," he promised.

She didn't doubt it for a minute, but she had no idea what to do about it. She glanced at the phone. If she had any brains at all, she'd call the police. Biting her lower lip, she heard the sound of his Jeep's engine roar to life, then the crunch and slide of tires as the vehicle tried to find traction.

Carol let out a tiny whimper and Annie picked her up in an instant. Heart in her throat, she held the tiny body close and felt Carol's breath against her breast—a breast Liam had so recently kissed. Annie's stomach slowly rolled in anticipation at the thought of his touch. "This is such a mess," she admitted to the baby. "Oh, Carol, I'm so sorry." She pressed her lips gently to the baby's soft, blond curls. "I love you so much."

And Liam—do you love him, too?

She snorted at the ridiculous thought. She didn't even know the man. And yet she was ready to make love to him. She should never, *never* have let him kiss her.

What could she do? What if Liam truly was Annie's father? What if he made good his promise and took the baby away from her? Tears stung her eyes as she thought about how long she'd wanted a child, how desperately she'd hoped that she could have one of her own and now this . . . this little one was in her arms and oh, so precious.

"I won't give you up," she whispered, though she knew deep in the blackest regions of her heart that her words were only a silly, hopeless promise without any meaning.

Carrying the child, she reached for the phone and while propping the receiver between her ear and shoulder she bit her lip and dialed the number of the sheriff.

CHAPTER 6

Nola drew on her cigarette, waited for the nicotine to do its trick, then flicked the butt into the toilet of the Roadster Cafe. She studied her reflection in the cracked mirror in the tiny bathroom of the truck stop where she'd taken a job just two weeks earlier.

Her face was beginning to show signs of strain. With a frown, she sighed and brushed her bangs from her eyes. Dark roots were showing in the blond streaks she'd added to her hair. This wasn't the way it was supposed to have turned out. Not by a long shot.

She still looked good, or so she tried to tell herself as she applied a new layer of lipstick. Hardly any lines around her eyes and mouth—well, nothing permanent. Though she was younger than her sister by nearly two years, most people thought she was the eldest.

"Hard livin'," she muttered under her breath as she dabbed at the corner of her mouth with a finger to swipe away a little raspberry-colored gloss that had smeared. "But things'll be better." They had to be. She couldn't stand too much of this. Life on the run wasn't all it was cracked up to be. She was forever looking over her shoulder or spying someone she was certain she'd known in that other life. Was that only months ago? How had she gotten herself into this predicament?

"Love." She spat the word as if it tasted foul. And it did. Would she ever learn? Probably not.

Determined not to follow the dark path down which her thoughts invariably wandered, she tightened her apron around her waist and felt a glimmer of cold satisfaction that her figure was returning to its normal svelte proportions. Still a little thick around the middle, she was otherwise slim and her breasts were no longer swollen. Back to 36C. Nearly perfect despite the pregnancy. "Hang in there," she told the woman in the reflection, then felt close to tears yet again. God, when would this emotional roller coaster end?

Probably never.

Sniffing loudly, she wiped away any trace of tears from beneath her mascara-laden lashes. In the end it would be worth it and she consoled herself with the simple fact that everything she'd done— be it right or wrong— she'd done for love.

She ducked through swinging doors that opened to the kitchen, where the fry cook—a greasy-faced kid with bad skin and dishwater-blond hair—gave her the once-over. For some reason he thought he could come on to her.

Like he had a chance.

But then the kid didn't know who she was, or that she'd worked in much better jobs than this, making a decent salary in an office in a big city. For a second she longed for her old life back. Then she caught herself. She'd made her decision and there was no turning back. Not ever.

"I could use a little help up here," the other waitress yelled through the open window between the counter and the kitchen.

"On my way, Sherrie." Checking her watch as she passed through another set of swinging doors, Nola frowned. The call she'd been expecting was half an hour late. Worse yet, there was a customer using the pay phone—that same man she'd seen in here three days running—going on and on about the weather on the interstate. Great. Ignoring the nervous sweat that beaded between her shoulder blades and under her arms, she gathered up knives, forks, and spoons from the baskets at the busing station and began to wrap the utensils in wine-colored napkins.

Surely the guy couldn't talk all night.

"Hey, baby, how 'bout a refill?" At the counter, one of the customers, a trucker from the looks of him, was leaning over a nearly empty cup of coffee. The wedge of pecan pie she'd placed in front of him fifteen minutes earlier had disappeared, leaving only traces of nuts in a pool of melted ice cream. God, this place was a dive.

She plastered a smile on her face, the smile guaranteed to garner the best tips from these cheapskates, and reached for the glass pot of coffee warming on the hot plate. "Sure," she said. "On the house."

He chuckled and pulled at the ends of a scraggly red moustache. "Thanks, doll."

"Anytime," she lied as she glanced at the pay phone again. The guy had hung up and taken a table in the corner. Good.

Now, for the love of Jesus, call!

"Order up!" the cook shouted and rang a bell to catch her attention. She nearly jumped out of her skin and sloshed coffee onto her apron.

"Geez, Lorna, you're a bundle of nerves," Sherrie observed with a shake of her head. Her teased, over-sprayed black hair barely moved. "That's the trouble with you big-city girls. Jumpy. You got to learn to relax."

"I'll try." Wonderful. Now she was getting advice from a woman who raised chihuahuas according to the phases of the moon and believed that space aliens had visited her on the anniversary of her second husband's death. Good-hearted to a fault, Sherrie Beckett was a woman who could never hope to get out of this tiny town in the southeastern corner of Idaho.

Nola, or Lorna, as she called herself in these parts, grabbed the platter and carried the special—a hot turkey sandwich with mashed potatoes and canned cranberry sauce on the side—to the booth in the corner where the man who'd been monopolizing the telephone had settled with a copy of *USA Today* and a cigarette. He barely glanced at her as she slid the plate in front of him, but she had a cold impression that she'd seen him somewhere before—somewhere other than this podunk little town.

"Anything else?"

"This'll do just fine." He flashed her a disarming grin, jabbed out his smoke, then turned to his meal.

Man, if she were paranoid she would believe that she'd met him somewhere. But that was impossible. No one knew where she was, not even any member of her family. She'd chosen this wide spot in the road to hide for a few weeks, just until things had cooled down; then, after she heard from her accomplice, she'd split. For Canada. From there the plan was to head to the Bahamas.

And you'll never see your baby again.

Again the stupid tears threatened to rain. Shit, she was a wimp. A goddamned Pollyanna in the throes of postpartum trauma or whatever the hell it was. She had to quit thinking about the baby. The little girl was safe. With Annie. No one in the world would take better care of her. So why the tears? It wasn't as if Nola had ever really wanted a kid.

But she couldn't stop thinking about that little red-faced bundle of energy that had grown inside her for nine long, nervous months.

Oh, hell, the guy hadn't even taken a bite of his food and he was back on the phone, tying up the lines. She glanced out the window at the bleak, dark night. A single strand of colored bulbs connected the diner with the trailer park. Inside, a twirling aluminum tree was placed in a corner near the old jukebox. Familiar Christmas carols whispered through the diner, barely heard over the rattle of flatware, the clink of glasses, and the buzz of conversation in this truck stop.

I'm dreaming of a white Christmas . . .

Nola sighed and poured coffee in the half-filled cups sitting before patrons at the counter. *Yeah, well, I'm dreaming of a tropical island, hot sun, and enough rum to soak my mind so I forget about all the mistakes I made. For love.*

"Hey, could we get some service over here?" an angry male voice broke into her reverie.

"On my way," she said with a brightness she didn't feel.

"Well, make it snappy, will ya?"

And Merry Christmas to you, too, you stupid s.o.b. "Sure." She handed the three twenty-odd-year-old macho yahoos their plastic-coated menus and prayed that he would call—and soon. Before she lost what was left of her mind.

"Looks like you were right about Talbott. I'll be sure soon." Jake Cranston's voice crackled and faded on the cellular phone.

"You talked to him?" Liam's hand tightened over the steering wheel and he squinted against the coming darkness. Heavy snow-flakes fell from the slate-colored heavens so quickly that the Jeep's wipers were having trouble keeping the windshield clear.

"Not yet, but it won't be long."

"How long?"

"Well, I found our missing link."

"Nola?" Liam couldn't believe his ears.

"Bingo."

"Where?"

"Southeastern Idaho. A remote spot."

"But how?"

"Clever detective work." There was a chuckle, then his voice faded again. " . . . Got a break . . . speeding ticket . . . checked with the Idaho . . . police . . . "

"I can't hear you. Jake?" But it was useless. He couldn't hear a thing. "Call me at Annie's cabin. The phone there works." He rattled off the number that he'd memorized several days earlier. "Jake? Did you get that? Oh, hell!" The connection fizzled completely and he hung up. He'd spent the last three days doing some investigating on his own, if you could call it that. With his four-wheel drive rig and chains, he was able to travel around the hilly streets that had been sanded, plowed, and then snowed and iced over again and again. The entire northern Willamette Valley was caught in the grip of a series of storms that just kept rolling in off the coast and dropping nearly a foot of snow each time. Emergency crews were working around the clock and electrical service had been restored to some of the customers, only to be lost by others.

Liam had spent as much time as he could tracking down the people he'd worked with at the construction company and the rest of the time, he'd been at Annie's cabin, keeping his distance while trying to learn everything she knew about her bitch of a sister. The damned thing of it was he kept finding excuses to hang out there, to get closer to her. The baby was the primary reason, of course, and the most obvious, but, whether he wanted to admit it or not, his emotions ran deep for the woman who had decided to become the kid's new mom.

She'd been nervous around him although he hadn't touched her again and had resisted the compelling urge to crush her into his arms. He'd slept in the Jeep and dreamed about kissing her until dawn, making love to her until they couldn't breathe, holding her close until forever. He hadn't, because she was scared of him and the situation. Every time the phone had rung she'd jumped as if jolted by an electric shock. Twice he'd caught her looking out the window, staring down the drive as if she expected someone to appear.

Who?

Nola?

He'd begun to believe that she really didn't know if Nola was the mother of the baby, but something was keeping her worrying her lip and wringing her hands when she didn't think he was watching.

He turned into the drive and his headlights picked up fresh tracks in the snow. Someone had decided to visit Annie. Fear froze his heart. What if she'd decided to leave? To pack up the baby and take off? Had Nola sensed that Jake was on to her? He tromped on the gas past the main house and then, as he rounded the final corner to the cabin, he stood on the brakes. The Jeep shimmied and slid but stopped four feet from the back of a Sheriff's Department cruiser. Annie's Toyota truck was parked in front of the tiny garage, thirteen inches of snow undisturbed on the cab and bed.

What now? His hands, inside gloves, became clammy. For the first thirty-eight years of his life he'd respected the law and all officers thereof, but ever since his arrest and the days he'd spent in jail, detained on suspicion, his admiration had dwindled to be replaced by serious doubts. There were a dozen reasons the cops could be here—none of them good—but the worst would be if Annie or Carol were in some kind of trouble. Since there were no emergency vehicles screaming down the lane, Liam assumed that they were both all right.

No, this wasn't a medical emergency. The deputy was here because of him.

Bloody terrific.

He snapped off the engine, grabbed the two bags of groceries he'd bought in town, and stepped into the fresh snow. Whatever the problem was, he'd face it.

* * *

Annie heard the sound of the Jeep's engine and wished she could drop through the old floorboards. She'd called the Sheriff's Department three days earlier, explained about her predicament, and been told by a patient but overworked voice that they'd send someone out when they could. Other life-threatening emergencies were deemed more important than being visited by a man who claimed to be the father of a child who had been abandoned but was being cared for. Social Services would call back. The Sheriff's Department would phone when they were able, but she was told to be patient.

She'd regretted the call since she'd placed it and now, seated on the edge of the sofa, feeding Carol a bottle, she felt foolish.

" . . . It was a mistake," she said, not for the first time. "I shouldn't have bothered you."

"But the child's not yours." The deputy, fresh-faced and not more than in his mid-twenties, wasn't about to be put off. Determined to a fault, convinced that he was upholding every letter of the law, he scratched in his note pad and Annie gave herself a series of swift mental kicks for being so damned impulsive and calling the authorities.

Liam had returned and she'd never mentioned the call to him; instead she'd kept a distant and quiet peace with the man. He no longer frightened her and she nearly laughed when she remembered that she hadn't trusted him at first, that she feared for the baby's well-being. Since that first day she'd observed him with Carol and noticed the smile that tugged at his lips when he looked at his baby. His hands, so large and awkward while holding the infant, were kind and protective. No, as long as Liam O'Shaughnessy was around, the baby had nothing to fear.

"No, the baby isn't mine, but I have reason to believe that she is my sister's little girl. I've alerted the proper agencies and talked to Barbara Allen at C.S.D. She said they'd call when the storm passed."

"But this O'Shaughnessy was harassing you—"

"No."

"Trespassing?"

"No. He, um, just thinks the baby may be his. He's agreed to a paternity test and—"

Clunk! The door burst open and Liam filled the doorway. His eyes flashed blue fire as he set two full grocery bags on the table and kicked the door closed. "Is there a problem?"

"No." Annie was on her feet in an instant. Still carrying Carol, she stood next to Liam. "I was just explaining to Deputy Kemp how I found Carol—and about you."

"I'm her father."

The deputy scratched his chin. "So you came to claim her?"

"That's it."

"What about the mother?"

"Still looking for her. Annie's sister, Nola Prescott."

Deputy Kemp's eyebrows shot up to the brim of his hat and he started scratching out notes in his condemning little pad again. "The woman who accused you of breaking into the offices of the company where you worked, Belfry Construction, right? Where the night watchman ended up getting clobbered over the head and dying?"

"One and the same."

"You were hauled in for that one."

"Questioned and held. Charges were dropped." He saw Annie's eyes widen as she realized he'd spent time in jail.

"All because of Ms. Prescott's testimony—that she recanted."

Liam's nostrils flared slightly and he glared at Annie as if in so doing he could make her disappear. "Yep."

"Why would a woman you . . . well, you had a baby with want to send you to jail?"

"That's what I'd like to know." Every muscle in his body tensed and white lines around his lips indicated the extent of his ire. The stare he sent Annie would have melted nails. "When I locate Nola, believe me, I'll find out."

"The Seattle police don't seem to be very convinced that you weren't involved in the crime."

"They're wrong." Liam's lips were compressed into a razor-thin seam that barely moved when he spoke. "Was there anything else?"

"No." The deputy snapped his notebook closed and tipped his hat at Annie. "I'll be in touch."

"Thanks," she said weakly.

"And I'm sure C.S.D. will want to speak with you."

Liam followed him to the door and watched through the window as the cruiser skidded around his Jeep and slowly disappeared down the lane through the trees. Once satisfied that they were alone, he turned slowly, his irritation evident in the set of his jaw. "What was that all about?"

"I thought . . . I mean a few days ago when you came barging in here threatening to take Carol away and charging after Nola, I was scared and—"

"So you decided to turn me in?" he accused. "Damn it, woman, you're cut from the same cloth as that sister of yours!"

"No!"

"Both of you trying to set me up."

"Liam! No!"

Carol let out a whimper and Annie removed the nipple from her mouth and gently lifted her to her shoulder. Softly rubbing the baby's back, she sent Liam a look warning him not to raise his voice. He stalked to the window and stared outside while Annie, after burping and changing Carol, sat in the rocker and nudged the infant back to slumber.

Liam gave a soft whistle to the dog and stormed outside. Annie closed her eyes while rocking the baby. What a horrid predicament. With Carol smack-dab in the middle of it. As the rocker swayed she tried to sort out her life and came up with no answers. A few days ago, before the baby had been left on her doorstep, everything had been so clear, her days on a boring but regular track. Now she felt as if every aspect of her life was careening out of control. She loved Carol and was sure to lose her. She loved her sister, but was confused about Nola's intentions and she loved Liam . . . She stopped rocking. No way. She didn't love Liam O'Shaughnessy; she didn't even know the man, not really. What she felt for him was lust. Nothing more.

The baby let out a tiny puff of air and snuggled against her and Annie felt a tug on her heartstrings unlike any she'd ever felt before. *Precious, precious little girl, how am I ever going to bear to give you up?*

"I can't. I just can't," she whispered, her throat as thick as if she'd swallowed an orange. She thought to the future—first steps, learning to read, going off to school, soccer and T-ball, first kiss and high school prom. Oh, no, no, no! Annie couldn't not be a part of Carol's life. She blinked hard, realized she was close to tears, and finally, after Carol was asleep, placed the baby in her bassinet.

Sliding her arms through her jacket and wrapping a scarf around her neck, she walked outside where she donned her boots and gloves. She heard Liam before she saw him, the sound of an axe splitting wood cracking through the canyon. He was standing near the woodpile by the barn, the axe raised over his head. Gritting his teeth, he swung down and cleaved a thick length of fir into two parts, the split portions spinning to either side of the stump he used as a chopping block. Snowflakes clung to his blond hair and settled on the shoulders of his suede jacket. He reached down for another length of oak and set it in place.

"You want something?" he asked without turning. The axe was lifted skyward and came down with a thwack that split the wood easily as darkness fell.

"To explain."

"No need."

"But Liam—"

"So now it's 'Liam,' is it?" He slammed the axe down again, wedging the blade in the chopping block and turned to glare at her. "Just tell me one thing, Annie. What is it you expected to accomplish by drawing in the police?"

"I—I—just needed some peace of mind. You came in here like gangbusters, arguing and carrying on and threatening to take Carol away and I . . . I needed help."

He glanced at the sky and shook his head. "Did you get it? Peace of mind?"

"No." She shook her head.

"Me neither."

Swallowing back all of her pride, she lifted her head and stared him down. "Now it's your turn," she said. "You tell me just one thing."

"Shoot."

"What is it you want from me, Liam O'Shaughnessy?"

"Good question." His face softened slightly, the shadows of the night closing in. "I wish I knew."

She shivered, but not from the cold night air. No, her skin trembled from the intensity of his gaze and the way her body responded. She licked suddenly dry lips and willed her legs to move. "I . . . I'd better see about the horses."

"What is it you want from me?"

Like the icicles suspended from the eaves of the barn, his question seemed to hang in the air between them. *I want you to love me.* Oh, Lord, where did that wayward thought come from? She stopped short, her breath fogging in the frigid air. "I—I just want you to leave me alone."

His smile was as hard as the night. "I already told you what a lousy liar you are, so try again. What is it you want from me?"

"Nothing, Liam," she said and marched to the barn. She couldn't, wouldn't let him see how vulnerable he made her feel. Each day she'd snapped lead ropes to the horses' halters and walked them around the paddock for nearly an hour so that they trampled a path through the drifts, then returned them to their stalls with fresh water and feed and brushed the clumps of snow from their coats. They'd already been exercised for the day, but she walked into the barn and took in deep breaths of the musty air. From somewhere behind the oat bin, she heard the scurry of feet, a rat or mouse she'd startled.

She sensed rather than heard him enter. *Give me strength.*

"Annie."

Oh, God. She wrapped her arms around her middle, took a deep breath, and decided she had no choice but to meet him head-on. "Look, O'Shaughnessy—" Turning, she ran straight into him and his arms closed around her.

"No more lies," he said and she caught a glimpse of his eyes before his lips found hers in the darkness. She shouldn't do this, knew she was making an irrevocable mistake, but as his weight pulled her downward onto a mat of loose straw, she gave herself up to the silent cravings of her body. His lips were warm, his body strong, and she closed her mind to the doubts that nagged her, the worries that plagued her about this one enigmatic man.

She shivered as he opened her coat and slowly drew her scarf from around her neck, trembled in anticipation as he drew her sweater over her head and unhooked her bra, swallowed back any protest as he lowered his lips to her nipple and gently teased.

Warmth invaded that private space between her legs, and desire ran naked through her blood. Her fingers fumbled with the fastenings of his jacket and he shrugged out of the unwanted coat, tucking it beneath them, along with hers.

"I want you, Annie," he said as he threw off his sweater and her fingers traced the corded muscles of his chest and shoulders. His abdomen retracted as she kissed the mat of golden hair that covered his chest and he groaned in anticipation as she tickled his stomach with her breath.

"I want you, too," she admitted. "God forgive me, but I do."

His smile, crooked and jaded, slashed in the darkness. "It's not a sin, you know."

"I know," she agreed, but wasn't convinced. Only when his lips claimed hers again and his hands lovingly caressed her did she sigh and give up to the sorcery of his touch. His fingers tangled in her hair and he pressed urgent lips to her eyelids, the corner of her mouth, her throat, and lower still.

He skimmed her jeans over her hips and followed his hands with lips that breathed fire against her skin and through the sheer lace of her panties. She squirmed as he sculpted her buttocks, lifting her gently and kissing her with an intimacy that she felt in the back of her throat. Through the thin barrier he laved and teased until the barn with its smells of horses and grain disappeared into the shadows and she felt him pull away the final garment to reach deeper.

"Ooooh," she cried, wanting more, blind to anything but the lust that stoked deep in her soul. "Liam—"

"I'm here, love." In an instant he kicked off his jeans and was atop her, parting her knees with the firm muscles of his thighs, kissing her anxiously on the lips, breathing as if it would be his last.

She couldn't close her eyes, but watched in wonder as he made love to her, gasped and writhed, catching his tempo, following his lead, feeling as if her life would never be the same again.

"Annie," he cried as her mind grew foggy and she was swept on a current of sensations that brought heat to her loins and goose bumps to her flesh. "Oh, God, Annie." He threw back his head and squeezed his eyes shut. With a shudder, he poured himself into her and she convulsed, her body clamping around him, her mind lost somewhere in the clouds.

He collapsed against her and she willingly bore his weight. Dear God in heaven, how would she ever be able to give him up, to give this up? Her heart was pounding erratically, her breathing short and shallow.

You could get pregnant, Annie.

Would that be so bad? The thought of carrying Liam's child deep inside her was soothing rather than worrisome.

The doctor said you'd miscarry again, that you can't go to term.

But it was worth the risk.

Don't be a fool, Annie. Think!

Liam's arms tightened around her and he sighed into the curve of her neck, closing off all arguments with her rational mind. She knew he couldn't promise his undying love, realized that what she felt was not only one-sided but foolish as well, and yet she ached to hear the words that would bind him to her forever, inwardly cried to have him swear his undying love.

Slowly he lifted his head. Eyes still shining in afterglow, he pushed a stray strand of hair from her face. "There's something I want to tell you," he said, his voice still husky and deep.

Her heart did a silly little flip. "What's that, O'Shaughnessy?"

He winked at her and offered her that slightly off-center grin she found so endearing. "Merry Christmas, Annie McFarlane."

"To you, too, O'Shaughnessy."

"I think I've got a present for you," he added and his voice was rougher, more serious. She felt the first glimmer of despair.

"What's that?" she teased but saw that he was stonecold sober.

He cleared his throat and plucked a strand of straw from her hair. Gazing into her eyes as if searching for a reaction, he said, "Jake found your sister."

"What?"

"That's right." He kissed her on the temple. "He's bringing Nola here sometime after the first of the year, after the storms have passed, and she's done dealing with the police and Peter Talbott."

Annie was stunned. The thought of seeing Liam with Nola and their baby, Carol, *her* baby, was overwhelming. "Good," she said without a trace of enthusiamsm. It had to happen sooner or later.

"Once we talk to Nola, we'll figure everything out."

Annie's heart seemed to dissolve. She was going to lose them— both Liam and Carol. She knew it as well as she knew that tonight was Christmas Eve.

CHAPTER 7

"Will you marry me?"

Annie stopped dead in her tracks. They'd been walking from the main house back to the cabin, through the mud and slush still lingering in the forest. Liam was carrying a front pack with Carol sleeping cozily against him.

"Marry you?" Her voice seemed to echo through the forest.

Liam took her gloved hands in his and as rain drizzled through the fir and oak trees, he smiled down at her. "Carol needs a mother—someone who loves her."

Annie's heart plummeted. For a second she'd expected him to say that he loved her. In the past two weeks of being together, never once had he uttered those three wonderful words. "I—I—well, I told myself I'd never marry again." This was happening too fast—way too fast.

"I thought you wanted to be with Carol."

She bit her lip as she saw Carol's blond curls peeking up through the top of the front pack. "I do, more than anything, but—"

His smile faded and he rubbed his jaw. "Look, Annie, I never thought I'd ever marry. I liked being a bachelor, but then I didn't realize that I was going to be a father, either. I'm glad about that. Ecstatic—and I want what's best for my daughter." He brushed a moist strand of hair from her eyes. "Carol couldn't have a better mother than you."

Her throat became swollen and he pressed a kiss to her temple. "Would it be so bad, married to me?"

No, she didn't think so. Though she'd barely known him for two weeks, she loved him. Foolishly and reverently. Maybe in time he would learn to love her and, if the truth be known, she couldn't imagine living her life without him. He'd proven himself, exonerating himself of the crime in Washington, refusing to prosecute Nola for her false claims against him, sticking by Annie through the holidays and helping her care for the main house, cabin, and livestock as the frozen countryside thawed, creating floods and mud slides. Also, more importantly, it was obvious that he was completely taken with his daughter.

They'd laughed together, fought a little, spent hours upon hours at each other's side only to make love long into the night. He'd helped clean the gutters, thaw the pipes, and repair the roof when icy branches had fallen on the old shingles. He'd exercised and fed the horses, shoveled the driveway, fixed her pickup that refused to start after being packed in snow for ten days, done the grocery shopping, and kept the fire stoked until the old furnace kicked in. He'd been a gentle lover, a concerned father, and, it seemed, a man determined to clear his name. He'd watched Carol as Annie had reconnected with her clients and worked on her word processor, but the bottom line was that he didn't love her. At least not yet.

"But . . . how? Where would we live? Wait a minute, this is all so fast." She held up a hand and he captured it in his larger one.

"We'll live here. I'm moving out of Washington anyway. I'll sell my house and start my own company, either in Portland or Vancouver. If it's money you're worried about—"

"No, no." She shook her head. Money was the last thing on her mind. In fact, she hadn't told him but she was three days late in her monthly cycle. Not a lot, but, considering that her periods came and went like clockwork, something to think about. Something very pleasant to consider.

"You can keep your job, or become a full-time mother. We'll buy a place of our own eventually, when the time is right."

"Are you sure?" Good Lord, she shouldn't even be contemplating anything so ludicrous.

Smiling, he used the finger of one gloved hand to smooth the worried furrow from her brow. "As sure as anything I've done lately. Come on, wouldn't you love to be Carol's mother?"

"You know I would," she admitted, wondering if she was about to make the mistake of her life. She'd suffered through one divorce and she wasn't about to go through another. If and when she married again, it would be for life. "What about Nola?" she asked, concern gnawing away at her optimism. "She'd be your sister-in-law."

Liam glanced to the gray sky and frowned. "As long as she doesn't live with us and doesn't interfere with Carol, it'll be okay."

"She accused you of murder."

His smile was cold as ice. "Don't worry about Nola, Annie. I can take care of your sister."

"I don't think anyone can take care of her." They hadn't seen Nola nor heard from her, though, according to Liam's friend Jake, she'd turned in her boyfriend, Peter Talbott, who had embezzled funds and killed Bill Arness when he was startled while doctoring the company books. Talbott had coached Nola into lying about Liam's participation in the crime, then skipped town, leaving Nola, who had been in love with him, alone to hold the bag. She'd gone to meet him somewhere in Idaho, but he'd never shown up and Jake had confronted her and convinced her to turn state's evidence against Talbott, who was already long gone, probably hiding out in Canada.

All that trouble seemed far away from their private spot here in the forest. Carol gurgled in the pack between them, a fine Oregon mist moistened their faces, and somewhere not too far off Riley was barking his fool head off at a rabbit or squirrel or some other creature hiding in the ferns and bracken.

She could be happy here with Liam and Carol, she thought, warmth invading her heart.

Hand in hand they walked back to the cabin where, despite the rumble of the furnace, a fire was burning and near her desk stacked with correspondence, the small Christmas tree still stood, draped in garlands and shimmering with tinsel. From the oven, the smell of pot roast and potatoes filled the air.

Liam carried Carol into the bedroom and placed her tiny body in the crib he'd purchased just two days earlier. The baby found her thumb and snuggled her little head against a gingham bumper as Annie adjusted her covers. There was still so much to do. Social Services, upon learning that Liam was the father of the baby, had been lenient about Carol's situation. Marrying him would make the adoption all that much easier. And certainly Nola would comply. Though Annie hadn't spoken with her sister, she didn't doubt that Nola wanted her to care for the little girl. Liam had even gone through the formality of a paternity test, though the results wouldn't be confirmed for a few more days.

"Okay, Annie, what's it gonna be?" he asked and there was an edge to his voice she didn't recognize, a nervousness. He stood in the doorway of the bedroom, the firelight from the living room glowing behind him. "Will you marry me?"

"Yes." The word was out in an instant and Liam picked her up, twirling her in the small confines of the room. Startled, she gasped, then laughed. Carol let out a soft puff of a sigh. In the dim bedroom where only hours before they'd made love, she wrapped her arms around Liam's neck and kissed his cheek. "I'd love to marry you, Mr. O'Shaughnessy."

His smile was a slash of white as they tumbled onto the bed together. "We could fly to Reno tonight."

"Tonight?"

"Why wait?"

Yes, why? For years she'd wanted to become a mother. She thought of all the painful disappointments of her miscarriages, the guilt, the dull ache in her heart, the fear that she would never have a child. And now she had only to agree to marry the man she loved to become a mother. "All right," she finally agreed. "Tonight."

" . . . Mr. and Mrs. Liam O'Shaughnessy." The justice of the peace, a robust man of about sixty, rained a smile down on Liam, Annie, and Carol while his wife, dressed in polka dots, sat at the piano and played the wedding march.

"That's all there is to it?" Annie asked as she and Liam walked out of the small, neon-lit chapel and another couple took their places.

Outside, the traffic raced by and a wind cut through the dusty streets of Reno.

"It's legal and that's all that matters." Liam took her arm as she shielded Carol from the noise and cold night air. The city was ablaze in lights; the crowds, oblivious to the frigid temperatures, wandered in and out of the hotels and casinos lining the main drag.

Annie followed Liam back to the hotel where they'd booked a room for the night. She remembered her last wedding six years earlier—a church with stained-glass windows, a preacher in robes, three bridesmaids, Nola as the maid of honor, a flower girl, and a ringbearer. Ribbons and rose petals, David's sister singing a love song, candles and organ music, and all for what? Nothing. A marriage that had turned to ashes all too soon. This time there were no false promises, no stiff ceremony, nothing borrowed, blue, old, or new. *And no love?* her ever-nagging mind reminded her.

They took the elevator to the fifth floor where a roll-in crib was waiting for Carol and a bottle of chilled champagne waited in a stand packed in ice.

While Annie changed Carol and fed her a final bottle, Liam uncorked the champagne. Once the baby was fed, burped, and put to sleep, he poured them each a glass and touched the rim of his fluted goblet to hers.

"Here's to happiness," he said with a grin.

And love, she thought, but added, "And more children."

"More?" Blond eyebrows raised.

She nodded. "Maybe sooner than you thought."

"You're pregnant?"

"I'm not sure, but . . . well, I could be."

His smile grew from one side of his face to the other. He sipped from his glass, took her into his arms, and as champagne spilled between them, carried her to the bed. "I'd say congratulations are in order, Mrs. O'Shaughnessy."

"That they are, Mr. O."

He kissed her and Annie closed her eyes, refusing to listen to the doubts, to the worries, to the damned negative thoughts that had plagued her ever since she'd agreed to become Liam's bride. Tonight, on her wedding night, she would give herself to him. Nothing else mattered.

* * *

"This is a big mistake." Nola scratched both her arms with her fingernails and wished she was anywhere else but in this damned car with Jake Cranston. Some sappy country ballad was battling with static on the radio.

"You've made worse."

She rolled her eyes, but didn't argue. How could she? Without his help, the police in Seattle would have held her as an accomplice or material witness or whatever the hell else they could come up with in the Belfry break-in and murder of Bill Arness. She still felt cold inside when she thought about Bill. Guilt pressed a ten-ton weight on her chest. She had nothing to do with his death, but she had known that Peter was behind it. Even though Bill had surprised him at the computer and Peter had only meant to knock him out, the old man had died.

Peter Talbott.

Embezzler. Killer. Jerk. And so much more.

Tears burned behind Nola's eyelids. Jesus, she was an idiot. But she was going to see Annie again. And the baby. Her heart lightened at the thought.

Jake turned off the freeway and onto a two-lane road that wound through the hills surrounding Lake Oswego and West Linn. Metropolis one minute, cow country the next. He grabbed a pack of Marlboros from the dash and tossed it to her. "Light one for me, too."

"Thanks." She punched in the lighter, slipped a filter-tip into her mouth, and then, once the lighter popped out, lit up. "Here," she said in a cloud of nerve-calming smoke. She handed him the first cigarette, then shook a second from the pack.

Jake took the smoke and punched another button on the radio. Country music faded and an old Bob Seger tune met her ears.

Against the wind, I was runnin' against the wind . . .

Boy, and how, she thought, drawing hard on her cigarette and cracking the window. "He's gonna kill me."

"Who? Liam?" Jake snorted. "I doubt it. Not that he wouldn't have just cause."

"I know, I know. I was wrong, okay?"

"And lucky. Damned lucky that he's not got *you* up on charges."

"How could he? I'm his sister-in-law," she said, still hardly believing the news that Jake had given her only yesterday. According to Jake, Annie and Liam had gotten married over a week ago. "What a joke."

"It's no joke, believe me." Jake drove past a development, then turned onto a gravel road leading through a thicket of evergreens and scrub oak.

Nola's stomach clenched. What could she say to Annie? To Liam O'Shaughnessy? Oh, God. She took a long draw on her cigarette and noticed that her hands were cold as ice. This was no good—no damned good.

They passed a huge house with a peaked roof, turret, and dark windows, a gray Victorian that some people might think was quaint. Nola thought it looked like it had come right out of *Psycho.* "Annie lives here?" Nola asked, but Jake didn't stop and continued on the winding road to a much smaller house—a cottage of sorts— with a view of the lake and a barn nearby.

"She—well, they, I guess now, live here. Annie maintains the other house." He jabbed out his cigarette in the tray. "How close are you with your sister?"

"Sometimes closer than others," she said. "This hasn't been my best year."

"Amen." He cut the engine and reached across her to open her door. "Shall we?"

"If we must." She was already stepping out of the car and couldn't stop the drumming of her heart at the thought of seeing her baby again. How much had she grown? Did she smile? Would she recognize the woman in whose womb she'd grown for nine months? Heart in her throat, Nola took one last drag from her Marlboro, then cast the butt onto the lawn where it sizzled against wet leaves. "Okay. It's now or never." She walked up the two steps to the front porch and pushed on a bell.

In an instant Annie, flushed face, sparkling eyes, and easy smile, opened the door. In her arms was a blond baby with wide blue eyes—a baby Nola barely recognized as her own.

"Nola." Annie's voice broke.

"Oh, God, Annie, I—I—!" Tears sprang to her eyes and ran down her face. She threw her arms around her sister and smelled the scent of baby powder mingling with Annie's perfume. Happiness and worry collided in her heart. How had she ever given the baby away? But how could she possibly consider keeping her? Besides, she'd made a promise . . . Sniffing loudly, she hugged her sister and looked up to see Liam O'Shaughnessy in the small home, his presence seeming to loom in the interior. He was staring at her with harsh blue eyes that held no mercy, not a speck of forgiveness. Her blood congealed and she stepped away from her sister. "Liam."

"Nola." His voice was harsh.

"Look, I owe you a big apology."

"Save it." His jaw was set. Uncompromising.

"No, hear me out. I wish you and Annie the best."

He snorted. "Can it."

"Jake Cranston," the man with Nola said. He held out his hand and shook Annie's in a firm, sure-of-himself grasp.

"My wife, Annie," Liam said.

"I assumed."

Annie, her insides a knot, ushered Nola inside.

Jake grabbed a kitchen chair, twirled it around, and straddled it. "I think you should listen to what your sister-in-law has to say, O'Shaughnessy."

"Fair enough." Liam skewered Nola with his gaze. "Shoot."

"I know you hate me," Nola said and Liam didn't say a word, not a syllable of denial even when Annie shot him a pleading look, silently begging him to be forgiving. Nola had, after all, given them Carol. Nola cleared her throat and, cheeks burning, added, "But I did what I thought I had to because . . . well, because I loved Peter."

"Great guy," Liam muttered.

"I thought he was and"—she held up a hand when she saw the protest forming on Liam's lips—"I was wrong. I know that now. I'm sorry for all the trouble and pain I caused you. I am. But I can't undo what's already been done."

"She explained everything to the authorities," Jake said. "I've got copies of her statement to the police in my briefcase."

Nola blinked back tears. "I just hope in time, you'll forgive me."

"Of course he will," Annie answered, but Liam didn't respond. She didn't blame him. Nola had put him through a living hell, but it was painful to witness the hardening of his jaw again, the harsh intensity of his gaze. Ever since the wedding he'd been more relaxed and their lives here, with Carol, had been stress-free.

Until now.

Annie put a hand on Nola's shoulder and her sister turned. She spied the baby again and tears trickled from her eyes. "Can I hold her?"

"If you tell me what leaving her here was all about." Annie couldn't put off the inevitable talk another second. The baby was what her life was all about, the reason she got up in the morning, the impetus for Liam to have met her and married her. Even though there was probably another child growing within her, Carol would always be special. Carol yawned as Annie handed her to her natural mother and Nola bit her lower lip.

"She's beautiful."

"Yes." Annie's voice was low and hoarse with emotion. "But how did you leave her on the stoop?"

"That was Peter's idea," Nola admitted, avoiding her sister's gaze. "I knew I couldn't take care of a baby, couldn't raise her and give her the security and stability she needed. So Peter brought her here."

"And left her in the freezing temperatures on the porch," Liam said.

"Annie was home—"

"What if she hadn't heard the baby cry?"

"Peter heard the dog. He was careful to stay near the bushes and brush his tracks away with a branch from a fir tree. But he waited in the shadows until Annie answered the door."

"You didn't come with him?" Liam asked.

Nola shook her head and swallowed hard. "I—I couldn't. It was too hard."

"Did you ever think of calling me?" Liam asked.

"You?" Nola shook her head. "Why?"

"You know a father has some rights."

Nola's eyebrows slammed together. "That's why I went along with Peter's plan."

"What?"

"Since he didn't think it was time for us to settle down with a baby, I told him about Annie and we decided—"

"Wait a minute." Annie's head was spinning. She was missing something. Something important. "Why would Peter have any say about it?"

"Because he's, what did you name her—Carol? I like that. Well, because he's Carol's father."

"Father?" Liam asked, his voice low, like rolling thunder far in the distance.

"Yeah. He and I . . . " She let the words fade away. "Wait a minute. You didn't think that . . . oh, my God, Liam, did you really think the baby was yours?" She laughed for a second before she turned and looked at the horror shining in Annie's eyes. "The baby's Peter's."

"No!" Annie cried.

"Yes."

"You're certain?" Liam demanded.

"Of course. I would know—"

"But you would lie."

"Not about this and I know, Liam. You and I were over before I conceived this baby." She said it with such conviction Annie didn't doubt her for a minute.

"Oh, dear God . . . " Annie's stomach turned sour. Bile rose up her throat. How could they have made such a horrendous mistake? Why hadn't they waited for the paternity tests? She'd been so certain—so sure Carol was Liam's flesh and blood.

"Talbott's?" Liam's eyes flashed like blue lightning.

"Yes. But he didn't want her and—oh, sweet Jesus, you really thought you were her father, didn't you?"

"I am," Liam said, his jaw tight, the cords of his neck strident. "Make no mistake, Nola, I'm Carol's father. Now and forever."

"But—"

"That's the way it is." He looked past his sister-in-law and his eyes sought Annie's. "And you, Annie Prescott McFarlane O'Shaughnessy, are Carol's mother."

"As long as Peter or I don't interfere," Nola said, lifting her chin. "Now that Peter's gone and I have no one, I could . . . I mean, biologically and legally, Carol's my daughter."

Annie let out a little squeak of protest, but then bit her tongue.

What did she expect? That her sister would hand over the precious baby, that Nola wouldn't have second thoughts, that Peter Talbott, whoever he was, wouldn't exert his rights as the baby's father?

"I'll fight you," Liam said, his voice deadly as he advanced upon Nola. "If you try and take Carol away from Annie, I swear, I'll hunt you down and make your life a living hell. And I'll tell the court what a swell mother and role model you'd make. Don't forget I know you, Nola. Inside and out. Your fears and weaknesses and the fact that you abandoned your daughter, left her in freezing temperatures in a basket on a porch because it wasn't convenient for you to keep her. Then there's the lying to the court. I've been told I could press charges." He crossed the room in three swift strides to glare down at Nola who, despite her bravest efforts, cowered under the power of his gaze. "You've had quite a list of lovers, you've been involved in an embezzling scheme, you've never held a job for more than two years, and you disappear for months at a time. I don't know about you, but I think the court might find you unfit."

Nola swallowed hard. "You wouldn't dare—"

"Think about it," he warned.

"No, no, no!" Annie was fighting tears and shaking her head. "I—we can't do this. Carol is . . . " *Sweet, sweet baby, how can I give you up?* " . . . She belongs to Nola. And Peter." The floorboards seemed to shift beneath Annie's feet and somewhere deep inside there was a rending.

"Oh, God, not Pete." Nola waved her hands frantically on either side of her head. "He's useless. A criminal. A killer, for Christ's sake."

Annie's head was swimming; she held onto the back of the couch for support. Her blood pounded in her ears. She was losing the baby . . . no, no, no.

"And you were not only his lover, but his accomplice." Liam turned to Annie and his expression was unrelenting. "We are Carol's parents," he said.

"No." Her voice cracked and the absurdity of the situation struck her. He'd only married her so that she would be Carol's mother. Her marriage was nothing more than a sham. Hollow. Empty. A fool's paradise. "We aren't Carol's parents legally, not yet and apparently not ever." She fought tears, blinking rapidly as she removed the wedding band that she'd worn for so few days. "Liam, I'm sorry." An ache burned through her.

"So am I, Annie," he said without a trace of warmth. "So am I."

The first pang struck her dead center and she thought it was just stress. The second was more painful and she gasped.

"Annie?" Liam's voice was edged in concern. The world started to go black. "Annie?" Again the pain and this time she felt the first ooze of blood, the fledgling life starting to slide from her. "Annie, are you okay?" Liam was standing over her and as she let go of the couch and started to sway, he caught her.

"She's bleeding," Nola said from someplace far away.

"Annie?" Liam's voice was strident, filled with terror, but she couldn't see him. "Call an ambulance—" Her eyes fluttered closed and a beckoning blackness enveloped her. The last thing she heard was Liam calling her name and there was something wrong with his voice—it sounded muffled and cracked. "Annie, hang in there. Oh, sweet Jesus, Annie!"

"Mr. O'Shaughnessy, why don't you go down to the cafeteria and get a cup of coffee? There's nothing you can do for her."

In the blackness, Annie heard the woman's voice as if from a distance. She tried to open her eyes, failed, and licked her lips—so dry.

"I'm staying." Liam's voice was firm. "She's my wife."

"I know, but—"

"I said, I'm not leaving her side, woman, so you can quit harping at me."

"Fine, have it your way. Sheesh. Newlyweds." Footsteps retreated and Liam let out his breath. "Come on, Annie, you can do it," he said as if she were running a marathon instead of just sleeping. "Come on, girl, don't you know that I love you?"

Love? Liam loved her?

"Don't let me down now. Show me some of that fighting spirit. I need you. Carol needs you."

Carol? Oh, yes, the baby.

Annie struggled, her eyes moving behind closed lids. "She's waking up." Liam sounded surprised. "Annie, oh, thank God."

With an effort she forced her eyes to open, then winced at the light. "Where—?"

"You're in the hospital," Liam said as she focused on him and saw tears shining in his eyes. "And you're fine."

"Fine?"

"Everything's going to be all right, darling," he said, taking her hands and holding them in his as he sat near the hospital bed. "Nola's signed the papers, Peter's agreed that you and I are to be Carol's parents. Nothing's going to stop us now."

She smiled as a nurse entered the room. "Well, look who finally decided to wake up. How're you feeling, honey?" She rounded the bed, blood-pressure cuff ready.

Annie managed to hold up a hand and move it side to side.

"So-so? Don't worry about that—you'll be dancing a jig in no time." The nurse, a round little woman of about forty, slipped the cuff up Annie's arm. She took Annie's blood pressure, pulse, and temperature, admonished her to drink as much water as possible, and promised that food would arrive shortly.

"See, the red carpet treatment," Liam said, smiling down at her. "You had me worried for a while there, you know."

"What happened?"

"You fainted," he said, stroking the side of her cheek.

"Is that all?"

"No." Sighing, he held her gaze with his. "You were pregnant, Annie. And you lost the baby."

"No!" she cried and tears filled her eyes. Another child lost. Liam's baby.

"The doctor says we can try again. But that's up to you." Liam cupped her face in his big hands. "We still have Carol, Annie. And each other. That's more than most people have." He swallowed hard and pressed a kiss to her lips. She felt him tremble. "I love you, Annie O'Shaughnessy," he vowed, "and you just gave me the scare of my life. Don't ever do it again."

His words were like gentle rain, erasing some of the pain. "I won't, " she promised, "and I love you, Liam, more than you'll ever know."

Again he kissed her and for the first time she felt she really was his wife.

EPILOGUE

Nearly a year later

"*. . . I'm telling you why, Santa Claus is coming to town . . .*"

Annie sang off-key as she hung the stocking on the mantel of her new home, the old Victorian house that overlooked the little cottage where she'd first discovered Carol on her stoop. Outside, the Oregon rain peppered the mullioned windows and inside Carol was taking her first few steps, grinning widely and walking like a drunken sailor from the table to the chair and back again.

The rooms were decorated haphazardly. Some of her furniture, a little of Liam's, and the rest having come with the house, but a tree stood in the parlor, strung with popcorn, cranberries, and twinkling lights, which Carol found absolutely fascinating.

The front door burst open and Liam, smelling of pine and leather, wiped the dampness from his face. "All done," he said and flipped a switch. Through the window Annie spied thousands of lights ablaze in the surrounding forest.

"Oooh!" Carol said, toddling to the window and staring outside.

"Daddy did a good job, didn't he?" Annie asked and Liam laughed, crossing the room and snagging Carol from the floor. With a squeal she landed on his shoulders and Annie laughed, her life complete. She still had her secretarial business, but she was working less and less with the demands of being a wife and mother. Liam, on the other hand, was so busy with his consulting firm in Portland that he was thinking of taking on a partner.

"Where's Jake?" Liam asked as he bussed his wife's cheek. Carol, still atop his broad shoulders, giggled.

"Sleeping, as usual."

"Let's wake him up."

"Let's not," Annie said, shaking her head. "Liam O'Shaughnessy, if you so much as breathe on that baby, I'll—" But it was no use, Liam was already climbing the stairs to the nursery, a small room off the master bedroom. Annie followed him and watched as he stared down in wonder at his son.

As if the baby sensed he was the center of attention, he opened his eyes and cooed. "And your mother didn't want you to wake up," Liam said as Annie picked up her son and felt him snuggle against her breast. Jake Liam O'Shaughnessy had been born on December seventh and the only problem Annie had experienced during the nine months of her pregnancy was an incredible craving for cherry vanilla ice cream.

Nola was working in Detroit and was engaged to a lawyer, Joel and Polly had promised to visit after the new year, and Annie's mother and stepfather promised to fly to Oregon once they'd returned from a trip to Palm Springs.

Life had become routine and nearly perfect. Riley barked at the back door as the little family hurried down the stairs. The smell of cinnamon cookies and gingerbread hung heavy in the air.

In the kitchen, Annie opened the door and the dog bounded in. Liam placed Carol in her high chair and offered her a cookie.

"You spoil her," Annie admonished.

"And you don't?"

"No, I spoil her rotten."

Liam reached into the cupboard and withdrew a bottle of Pinot Noir. "I think it's time for a toast," he said, opening the bottle as Annie held her son and Jake blinked up at her.

"To?"

"Us." He poured two stemmed glasses, then handed her one. "To the family O'Shaughnessy. Long may it prosper."

"Hear, hear." She touched the rim of her glass to his.

"And to the most beautiful woman in the world. My wife."

Annie blushed. "Here's to you, Mr. O. The most unlikely husband in the world, and the best."

They drank, then kissed, then found a way to personally wish each other the merriest Christmas ever.